Sunset Over Chocolate Mountains

Born in 1968, Susan Elderkin is a graduate of Cambridge University and of the Creative Writing MA at the University of East Anglia. For the past five years she has worked as a freelance journalist.

D0813013

Sunset Over Chocolate Mountains

SUSAN ELDERKIN

FOURTH ESTATE • *London*

First published in Great Britain in 2000 by
Fourth Estate Limited
6 Salem Road
London W2 4BU
www.4thestate.co.uk

1 3 5 7 9 10 8 6 4 2

Extract from *Italian Folktales* (on p. vii) selected and retold by Italo Calvino,
translated by George Martin (Penguin Books 1982, first published as
Fiabe Italiane 1956, copyright © Giulio Einaudi Editore, SpA, 1956,
translation copyright © Harcourt Brace Jovanovich, Inc., 1980.

A catalogue record for this book is available
from the British Library.

ISBN 1-84115-199-8

Typeset in Fournier by MATS, Southend-on-Sea, Essex
Printed in Great Britain by Biddles Ltd, Guildford and King's Lynn

To my parents

and in memory of my grandmother, Ivy Dora Wyatt (1909–92)
who gave me my first typewriter

For two years I have lived in woodlands and enchanted castles, torn between contemplation and action: on the one hand hoping to catch a glimpse of the face of the beautiful creature of mystery who, each night, lies down beside her knight; on the other, having to choose between the cloak of invisibility or the magical foot, feather or claw that would metamorphose me into an animal. And during these two years the world about me gradually took on the attributes of fairy-land, where everything that happened was a spell or a metamorphosis, where individuals plucked from the chiaroscuro of a state of mind, were carried away by predestined loves, or were bewitched; where sudden disappearances, monstrous transformations occurred, where right had to be discerned from wrong, where paths bristling with obstacles led to a happiness held captive by dragons.

Italo Calvino, *Italian Folktales*,
translated by George Martin.

1

When he moved to Arizona and set up home amongst the giant saguaros of the Sonoran Desert, Theobald Moon developed the habit of getting up early in the morning, peeing in a glass, and knocking it back in a few quick gulps while it was still warm and fresh. He felt it running sharply over the back of his throat, spiralling the length of his oesophagus, and flushing out the ducts and cavities of his small intestine like a jet of scouring fluid. He emitted any gases with a small and perfectly rounded burp.

He had heard it said that people shrink when confined to small places and expand when let out in the wilds. Out in the vastness of the desert, with nothing between him and the horizon but the thin wands of ocotillo stranded in the motionless air like seaweed held up by the sea, there was certainly room to fill. Never one to ignore the slightest rumble or whine of his sizeable belly, Theobald indulged his every whim and fancy. He listened for the plaintive cries at night, scrambling out of bed at the slightest hint that somewhere, somehow, in the dark deep red caverns of his stomach, a hollow corner had not been adequately filled. He was a master of snack concoction, of putting together unlikely sandwiches at midnight. Sugary, salty, peppery, pickled. He matched and mismatched, let his imagination go. There was no one else to see, after all.

This is not to say that he was without vanity. Discarding the tanktops and t-shirts and corduroys he'd brought in a peeling leather suitcase from England, he took to dressing in voluminous white drawstring trousers and shirts that gave him the appearance, despite his size, of something that could be wafted by the breeze. Rolled along like a ball of tumbleweed. Twenty-two stone and counting, he glided up and down the wooden steps of his mobile home as if he were royalty, balancing a crown on his head.

The piece of land on which he settled was set back from the main road down a rutted dirt track bordered by mesquite trees and clumps of cholla cacti. Before him was the flat desert floor, the tall, stately stems of the saguaro cacti standing erect and motionless on its surface. At dawn the saguaros appeared to Theobald Moon to be facing east, patiently waiting for the first sharp blade of morning light to reach out from behind the house and slice their tops off like breakfast eggs, surprising them from their grey-green sleep and causing a band of thick golden yolk to slip extravagantly down their sides. But by early evening, without anyone noticing, they had swivelled round to face west, in order, perhaps, to watch the kaleidoscopic performance staged by the setting sun as it streaked the sky with yellows and oranges and fiery blood-reds from behind the uneven line of the mountains.

After the initial hypothesising about why he had come and whether or not he was mad or just typically English, the locals thought of him only when they drove past in their battered pickups and happened to catch a glimpse of what looked like a cloud or the sail of a yacht drifting behind the tall mast of a saguaro. He remained in their minds simply an oddity, an overly large Englishman whose pale, almost hairless skin gleamed like a buttered bird plucked and trussed for the oven and then turned a juicy pink as soon as he exposed himself to the sun.

He had brought with him a number of books. *A Manual for Living Comfortably in the Cosmos*, Culpeper's *Herbal Remedies*, *Awaken Healing Energy through the Tao*, *Yoga for Beginners* and *Meditation for*

Great Minds. He was still a little shy of their titles, and took off the jackets to use them as bookmarks – fearful, even here, of someone catching him reading them. He kept them on a shelf above his bed.

In a second-hand book warehouse on E. Speedway Blvd he picked up copies of *Discover the Sonoran Desert* and *Make the Desert Bloom!* and immediately set about digging his one-acre plot. Lured by a vision of himself surrounded by swathes of brightly coloured flowers, perhaps even with a Hawaiian-style necklace around his neck, he ordered seeds from an English garden catalogue which promised delivery anywhere in the world. Geraniums, rambling roses, hollyhocks. It would be a real cottage garden, a couple of beds each side of his front door so that the taller plants could climb up around the windows. Michaelmas daisies, red-hot pokers. Sunflowers.

Around the back of his house, he would leave the natural flora and fauna to its own devices – the sharp-edged clumps of sagebrush and lacy-leaved creosote which, after all, had been here longer than him. In the front, he'd develop a proper cactus garden, filled with different varieties. At Pleasant Desert on Tanque Verde he picked out the prickly pears with the most appealing names – Porcupine, Long-spined, Pancake – and sunk them into the ground wearing a pair of washing-up gloves to avoid getting into an unpleasant scrap with their spines. He bought a Strawberry Hedgehog and a Claret-cup Hedgehog, a Creeping Devil Chirinola and a Beavertail cactus. He bought two young desert willows in five-gallon containers to provide shade each side of the house, realising as he did so that he appeared to be planting with an eye to the future. *So what?* he retorted brusquely to himself. *Who says I won't stay here for ever?* And to prove to himself that he wasn't afraid of the thought he asked the attendant to uproot a sizeable century plant which, according to the label, would send up one magnificent long-stemmed flower in approximately forty-five years' time and then, majestically, expire. We'll see who goes first, he thought.

He asked Jersey to help him uproot a group of jumping cholla he had seen from Highway 10, the evening light ensnared on their spines like goldfish in a net, but Jersey would have none of it.

—I ain't taking on no cholla, no sir, not me. Get cut to shreds. And in any case they're the property of the Federal Government, and it would be cactus rustlin'.

—We'll do it at night. No one will see. Theo was impressed to find himself taking such a devil-may-care stance.

—I said I ain't taking on no cholla.

Rubbing his hand over the blond bristles on his chin, Jersey leant forward and told the Englishman about a local Tucson man who had dared to mess with a saguaro after an evening of propping up the bars. —Used it for rifle practice, he did, sir, three bullets in its trunk, and the saguaro keeled over and squashed the life clean out his lungs. Jersey let out a low, sobering whistle. —I tell you, Mr Moon, them cactus ain't as stupid as they look.

At least Theo was fortunate enough to have two saguaros on his lot already – beautiful, ancient specimens some thirty foot high, their hollow trunks laced with holes pecked out by gila woodpeckers, turning them into whistling flutes whenever the wind rushed down. It was an eerie sound – more like the music of the spheres, thought Theo, than anything you'd expect to hear on Earth. He liked to join in as he tended his garden, his off-key, meandering warbling blending with the natural accompaniment in a way that made him feel part of things.

Sooner or later, a maddened woodpecker would poke its head out of a hole and pierce the air with a sharp *hee-hee-hee* and a sudden red flash of its wings.

The hollyhocks, winter jasmine and red-hot pokers never made it beyond the seedling stage. But his cacti flourished. By the time his first spring came round, Theobald Moon walked out amidst a mass of brazen, squabbling pinks and purples and yellows, the petals thick and waxy as if they were made of plastic. He had to watch his ankles as he stepped between the low-growing spikes, and it took all his willpower to resist stroking the furry-looking down on the pin-cushion cacti. Within a month the husks of large, half-eaten fruits lay rotting on the ground, heady with the smell of fermenting nectar and crawling with alarmingly big, drunken black ants.

Only one part of his plot was left unplanted. A little area in the middle of the cactus garden, which he cleared of stones and tufts of prickly grass until there was enough space to stretch out his arms and spin without snagging the tips of his fingers. Taking off his shirt and hitching up his trousers, retying the drawstring above the swell of his stomach, Theobald Moon walked out here every morning before breakfast, spread out his sticky mat, and soaked up the night's coolness from the hard, dusty ground, solid as concrete beneath his back. Closing his eyes, he allowed the first milky rays of sun to play spiders on his face. He breathed in, breathed out, breathed in, breathed out. He was like a chuckwalla, heating itself up for the day.

In the space of a year he developed a considerable repertoire. He could do the Sun Salute, the Spinal Twist, the Crescent Moon and the Crow, the Foetus and the Forward Bend, the Alternate Nostril Breath and the Shining Head Breath. His favourite was the Lion: heels tucked under buttocks and hands on knees with fingers splayed out like claws, mouth stretched wide baring glistening bubbles around his teeth, tongue reaching for the dimple on his chin, eyes bulging and glowering at the sky. He braced himself, tensed arms and jaw and fingers, then shot the air from his lungs with a fearful *Ha!* that split the silence of the early morning, slammed up against the mountains to the west and somersaulted into the air like an acrobat.

Sometimes he snatched a quick look at the book to check he was doing it right, then dashed back into position.

2

Sometimes, in the middle of the night, I hear him calling me by his favourite names – *Sugar, Honey, Jelly-O, Cream Tea*. I open my eyes and there, blinking in the darkness, are the two tiny rounds of his eyes, the blue watered down until it is barely there at all. There's a shadowy dimple on his chin, like a finger poked in a wodge of dough. He is hovering by my bed, an eager-to-please smile on his face.

—Wake up, Jelly-O! Time to get up.

I am only four years old, but he wipes the sweat from his palms on the backs of his thighs and pulls me from my bed because the sky is clear and the stars, he says, have never seemed nearer to Earth.

—But I've *seen* the stars, I whine, toppling against him, too drowsy to support the weight of my own head.

—No you haven't, he says. Not like this.

I don't lift a finger to help. Propping me up against him, he does up the buttons at the neck of my nightie, pulls my moccasins on and scrabbles around under my bed for a jumper. When he gives up and goes to fetch one of his own, I keel over again. He comes back in with a large yellow cardigan, and I let him wrap it round me. He forgets to pull my hair out from underneath so I do it myself as soon he turns his back.

Outside, the cool shadows that lurk under rocks and beneath houses during the day have crept out for their night-time prowl.

Fingers of them climb up my legs beneath my nightie, chasing out the warmth of my bed. Cold beats hot, like stone beats scissors and paper beats stone.

My father is shining a torch ahead of him on to the path, as he has taught me to do, and we pick our way behind it, trying not to catch our clothes on the spikes of the prickly pears. Wide eyes appear in the beam of light for a second and then are gone. Ahead of us, something larger scuffles and snorts through the undergrowth, a flash of white flank, but my father doesn't notice: he is too intent on reaching the slab of granite that sleeps like an enormous guard dog at the bottom of our garden. He scrambles up, then pulls me up behind him, loose bits of grit digging into my palms and knees. Once on top we hold hands, my fingers swamped in the hot, clammy folds of his. It is not clear who is doing the holding and whose hand is being held.

The rock is our lookout tower, lifting us up off the desert floor and into the realms of the sky. From here we have an unbroken view over the valley floor and all the way to the mountains, hulking on the skyline like creeping thieves with bags of swag slung over their shoulders. A slice of white moon dangles above them, fine as a fingernail paring.

Tut-tut, says the moon at their hulking shapes, so precise and queenly herself. *You boys should neaten up.*

My father stands with his legs in an upside-down V, cleaving together at the top then splaying out to the sides, like a duck about to slip on a sheet of ice. Without a word, he tips his head right back. For a moment I think he's going to gargle the air. Then I tip my head back too, as far as it will go without pulling me over backwards, and suddenly I see them, thousands and thousands of pin-pricks of light, teeming and bickering in the deep blue velvet cushioning of the sky like tiny crabs crawling over the ocean floor.

They are proud creatures, the stars, and don't like to be pinned down. Stare at one of them too hard, and it dodges to one side.

—Can they see us?

I whisper, as if I might frighten them away.

—Oh yes. We're one of them too.

—What, you and me?

—No, the Earth.

Solemnly, as if we are in a holy place, a cathedral in England or Mount Sinai in the Bible, and receiving a list of dos and don'ts from God, my father begins to tell me the names of the stars, starting with the North Star and moving around the configurations. The Great Bear and the Big Dipper, Cassiopeia's Chair, Orion's Belt, Pollux and Castor, the twins of Gemini. Their whispered names are spells, enchantments, potions which pluck you from the normal world and make you believe that there really are mythical beings living up there, going about their daily business, Orion striding in his heavy, hobnailed boots and slinging down his sword after a hard day's battle, Cassiopeia whizzing past with a flutter of fingers, her long golden hair spilling out behind her like maple syrup from a jar.

In a quiet voice my father explains that the thousands of stars we can see here, above the desert, are only the start of it all. That beyond this universe lie frozen wastelands scattered with the debris of million-year-old explosions, with comets hurtling through at several thousand miles an hour and asteroids careering on wild, freewheeling orbits. And, further away still, beyond these wastelands, are other solar systems, calm and beautiful and in colours no man has ever seen before, complete with their own fiery suns and dying moons and spinning planets. These are other worlds, he says, and the words imprint themselves on my mind as if with a pen dipped in the deep inky blue of the night itself.

Other worlds!

We stand there for a long time, dizzy with imagining, until my eyes keep trying to shut and between them the points of the stars stretch like elastic down to the ground. I tug on my father's hand.

—Dad, can we go back now.

But my father doesn't move a whisker. He just stands there with his jaw hanging open, as if he has swallowed a hook and is dangling on the invisible line of a fisherman in the sky who will sooner or later be reeling him up for his tea.

Upsadaisy. Easy does it. Hey, look what I've caught, fellas! A large human being named Mr Moon!

I try to pull away but his grip is too tight. I begin to panic. What if we are stranded here all night, him stuck to the sky, me stuck to him?

—Dad, let's go back and make hot chocolate.

That does the trick. The fishing line snaps and he gives me a nod. We clamber down, me going first this time, me shining the flashlight on the path and making sure we don't tread on any creepy-crawlies. When we get back, it's me that puts a saucepan of milk on to boil. We wrap our hands around the hot mugs, dipping oatmeal cookies into the froth so that they're warm and mushy in our mouths, and that's when I notice that there are beads of sweat sliding down my father's face and a wild, empty look in his eyes. I chatter away to fill up the quiet between us, while my father pushes cookies into his trembling mouth, one after another, and thrashes around with his eyes.

—What are you thinking about, Dad?

I am only four years old but he swallows hard and tells me anyway.

—It's all that space, Jelly-O, going on and on for ever. An endless ribbon of time that goes back, way way back before we existed, and shall go on, way way after we cease to exist, not just you and me, Jelly Bean, but everyone who's alive now and everyone who's already lived and who will live in the future, and even the Earth itself, for ever and ever, Amen.

Sometimes I open my eyes and he isn't standing over me at all, but snoring very loudly in his bed across the hallway. I put my moccasins on and push his door open a crack. There he is, with the blankets thrown back, a hulking, navy blue whale with paisley teardrops shuddering gently in the whispery morning light.

It's cosier in his bed than mine. I creep in behind him and curl my body around the hugeness of his back, tracing the pattern of the teardrops with my finger. After a while the snores stop and a sleep-befuddled voice emerges from somewhere deep in the pillow.

—*Tickles.*

I carry on anyway.

—What time is it? *Timesit.*

—It's morning time!

—Too early is what it is. *Terlyswotiz.*

He yanks the covers up over his shoulder, bringing my game to an end. I roll over and busy myself with picking out the little pieces of cheddar cheese and cookie crumbs from the creases of the sheets instead.

—Shall I make you a cup of tea?

No answer. And then, a fluttering, loose-lipped snore.

I give up and go outside, jumping down the three wooden steps and out into the garden, because my father's no fun in the mornings and anyway it's special outside, in this hour before breakfast, with no one else to see. Everything is alive and shimmery as if it were expecting someone important to ride by, the Queen of England, or the Rajah of India, or the Emperor of Japan, and not just Josephine Moon in her nightie. A weak, lemony sun sweeps across the garden scooping up handfuls of dust, and the boastful saguaros throw their shadows from one side to the other as if competing to reach the fence. Up above, vapour trails play tick-tack-toe on the clean blue sheet of the sky.

I run to the end of the drive and lift the lid of the mailbox. Empty. It usually is, unless there's an order for ice-cream from Miss Gail's or an airmail from Aunty Drew. I let the lid drop down with a tinny clang. Then I pick it up and let it drop down again. The clang rings out all the way down the track to the main road and up into the sky, filling the space between me and the mountains like cymbals in an orchestra.

Clang! Clang! Clang! This here's Josephine Moon, telling all you sleepy-heads out there to wake up. Wake up, Tucson! Wake up, Phoenix!

Wake up Los Angeles, New York, Canada, Mexico City! Wake up desert, mountains, birds, saguaros, rocks—

There's a rustle in a bush and, suddenly nervous of what I might have disturbed, I run back down the track.

The garden is at its busiest now, before the heat is fully up. Grasshoppers with orange-tipped legs leap from the deergrass and battle for a few seconds inside the dark shell of my hands. Bees push their snouts into the trumpets of the flowers, wipe their butts on the pollen, then fly off weighed down with a new pair of yellow pants. I poke my finger down mysterious holes in the ground that could be home to poisonous spiders or scorpions or desert millipedes, and force myself to keep it there while I count up to ten. If I think I feel a tickle of tiny legs I leap away with a high-pitched screech like the whistle of the Santa Fe railroad train and run round the garden till the fright is all let out.

When I get too hot, I do handstands against the fence and let my nightie fall over my head so that the breeze can brush itself against my skin like a cat. Through the veil of pink cotton I can see a dark shadow moving about in the kitchen, filling up a saucepan of water, turning the tap off so hard it makes a banging sound all the way down the pipes. I drop down and run inside.

—Go on, Dad, just a quicky.

—But it's not bed-time, Sugar.

—A breakfast-time one, then.

—Not now. Go and get dressed.

On the table are two bowls of steamy porridge. My father levers open a tin of maple syrup, winds a golden rope around his spoon, then dangles it on to his porridge. Three circles around the outside and a *T* for Theobald in the middle, like he always does.

In the middle of the day, when everything is stony and silent and just trying to stay alive while the air gets boiled around it, the desert offers up its treasures to me. These are mostly dead things – an upside-down beetle baked to a crisp, a mummified wren that has impaled itself on a cactus spike and which crumbles into a ball of dusty feathers and splintering bones in the clutch of my hands. Others are treasures which have been lost by someone careless – soda cans that glint and gleam like the beads from a broken necklace, hub caps and fenders that have rolled all the way from the highway, headscarfs and handkerchiefs snagged on a twiggy bush and left to flap prettily in the breeze.

I carry these treasures home and set them down on the kitchen table, my face smeared with grime and my hair falling out of its tight morning plaits.

—Go on, Dad.

—Well, all right then, Sugar Pie. Just the one.

He always sits down first. He does a little cough, *ahem*, ever so polite and dainty, shrugs his shoulders, smooths the creases in the tops of his trousers. Sometimes when he does that he notices a bit of dried porridge on his lap, and starts picking it off.

—Da-*ad*.

—All right, Sugar Pie. All right.

And so he begins. He gets out his musical up-and-down voice that he keeps for stories, and the words spill out of him, soft and dreamy, like soap bubbles blown from a ring.

Sometimes he takes too long getting to the point, and I have to bring him roundly back.

—Wooah! Hold it right there, mister! What about the sock?

—Be patient, Sugar Pie. I was just getting to it.

—But *who* does the sock belong to?

—It must be the giant, says my father.

—What giant is that? I ask, although I already know.

—Why, the giant of Sonora! says my father. Looking for a little girl who's wandered too far from home.

—And what will he do when he finds her?

—He'll string her up by the legs and salt her like a ham, and he'll cut delicate slices from her flanks for his breakfast every morning for a week.

—For a week?

I haven't heard that bit before.

—Little girls don't go very far.

Sometimes it sounds like there's a bunch of wild animals running around on the roof, stampeding as if we are in Africa, and I open the blinds to find that it's raining outside. The rain is so loud it drowns out my father's snoring.

From the kitchen I watch the pattern of miniature streams running over the hard ground, carrying all the loose stones and twigs away. I worry about the desert millipedes being slooshed out of their holes and the bees being too wet to fly. If they've got any sense, they'll have run for cover beneath the steps of our house or climbed inside a hole in one of the saguaros. I want to be like the animals, so I climb into the cupboard in the hallway where we hang our coats and find a ledge at the back to sit on and wait to be discovered. It's dark and airless in the cupboard and my father's rubbery anoraks glide like snakeskins against my face. I stick my hand into all the pockets to see what's been left behind – a stick of liquorice with little bits of Kleenex stuck to it, a chipped chocolate chip covered in Jimmies, a Coca-Cola chew with the top bitten off. All of a sudden there's a caving-in beneath me. The ledge is not a ledge after all but a stack of boxes – smooth, oblong boxes. I scramble off the pile, find a lid and pull it off.

Inside is something wrapped in tissue paper. I pick it up, a hard shape between my hands. Pulling the tissue away I find straps, a little buckle that gleams in the crack of light from the door, a high heel. I bring it up to my face and breathe in the smell of leather.

It's a gold sandal. A woman's gold sandal.

I unwrap the other one and bring them both out to the hallway. They're delicate and flimsy, toppling to one side when I try to stand them on the carpet. The straps are curled at the ends and carry the indent of the buckle. Somebody has worn them before.

I go back into the cupboard and pick up another box and find a pair of flat pink sandals inside. I go back for more, tipping the contents out into a pile, until there is every kind of shoe you can imagine – walking boots, multi-coloured sandals with a thick wedged heel, heavy, wooden clogs rimmed with a line of studs, boots with tassels around the top. On the inside sole of each is written something I don't understand: *Baťa. Kožený zvršok, kožená podrážka.* There are sheepskin slippers a bit like my own moccasins and a pretty pair of green shoes with pointy toes. In amongst the pile I catch sight of a shoe about the right size for me – a little shiny black shoe with a buckle – and then I lose it again. There's a pair of tall red boots with a zip up one side and a flash of lightning up the other, stuffed with tissue paper. I gaze at them in wonder, and stand them upright on their box.

No, madam, we don't have that one in your size, I am so dreadfully sorry. If you'd care to come back tomorrow—

I pull off my moccasins and find the gold sandals. Carefully, I do up the tiny, flimsy buckle around each ankle. I stand up, shakily. My toes slide down to the ends. I have to drag them along the carpet so as not to leave them behind.

—Dad!

The face that's squashed into the pillow gives a jolt, then a hand comes out and swipes blindly at the air, as if to fend off a fly.

—Dad, it's only me. Look what I've found!

—Hmmm?

Still he doesn't open his eyes.

—Tell me the story of the shoes!

The eyes open with a start. For a moment, he looks blank. Then his gaze follows mine to the floor and I wriggle my toes where they poke out at the front of the sandals.

—Aren't they beautiful?

He's fully awake now, staring at the shoes with a startled expression on his face.

—Do they belong to a princess?

—No, Sugar Pie, he says quietly. They do not.

His face is flushed. For a moment the only sound is his breath coming hard and fast through his open mouth.

—Then who?

—Take them off.

He swings his legs down to the floor and something about the movement makes me do as I'm told. Quickly, without a fuss. My heart is beating fast and I don't know why. In one large movement he scoops up the gold sandals with his hand and marches into the hall. He picks up the assorted shoes and the pieces of tissue paper and stuffs them back into their boxes, not bothering to match the pairs together, just packing them roughly away. I think of all the beautiful straps being crushed, the heels scraping against one another. He tosses the boxes back into the cupboard, and shuts the doors behind him before they have a chance to tumble out.

No story? I ask him with my eyes, because by now I don't dare to speak.

Not that one, he replies with his. Not yet.

He turns a key in the lock of the cupboard door and slips it into his pyjama pocket.

During the daytime, the stories my father tells are for me. But at night, he tells them to himself.

I pad across the hallway and push nervously at his door. There he is, hunched over his desk, the thin cotton of his shirt pulled tight across the wide stretch of his shoulders. I think he hears me, but I can't be sure, because he carries on scribbling until I'm standing right beside him, tugging at the sleeves of my nightie to stop the cold creeping up.

The anglepoise lamp casts a circle of light on the desktop. It's a magic circle, lighting up his head and shoulders and the pencil in his hand and the large, hardback book with smooth pages. Just outside it, in the shadows, is a box of Crackerjack, and every now and then his hand strays out of the circle, gropes around in the dimness until it hits the top of the box, and plunges in.

More than anything else I want to step inside that circle and become a part of it. I watch as he moves his index finger down the ladder of the lines. The crackle of the paper as he turns a page. I'm so close I can smell the sugar on his breath. But I wait because he isn't my father any more; he's someone from one of those Other Worlds.

At last, when I'm about to give up and go back to bed, he puts down his pencil, draws me in with the crook of his arm and gives me a sideways smile. There are little bits of Crackerjack stuck in the gaps between his teeth.

—Where did we get to?

—The forest.

—Black and spooky?

—So thick he has to leave his horse behind and *go it alone.*

—I remember, he says, and flicks back through the book.

These stories are complicated. They have plots, subplots and sub-subplots. He hushes his voice for the scary bits (when the little girl is lost in a forest full of twisted trees and yellow eyes) and for the soppy bits (when the prince kisses the dead princess and she wakes up and demands eggs for breakfast), and he raises it for the chases and the fights, the slayings of dragons and the roaring of giants, and whenever a king gets angry, he thumps his fist down hard on the desk making the Crackerjack jump out of its box and spill on to the table.

Sometimes there are quests, things to find and bring back. *Follow me!* he'll go, and grab me by the hand as we run to escape the North Wind that's chasing us down the road. *Over here!* he cries as we leap on the backs of wild-eyed horses that canter across the desert. *Look above you!* he goes, and we grab the ankles of enormous birds with taloned claws and golden beaks and swing beneath them over the crests of the waves. *Now!* he cries, and we tumble down on to a deserted beach where he throws me over his shoulder and strides with me through thick pine forests and rows me over sparkling lakes, and crashes with me through thorny thickets and over wooden drawbridges, up spiral stone staircases and into castles. We duck beneath a low doorway before drawing ourselves up tall to get a good view from the battlements, out over the green rolling fields and lakes and snow-capped mountains. *Sssh! Can you hear that?* he asks, and we press our ears against the clammy stone wall of the turret to hear the *tap-tap-tap* coming from the other side.

I look at my father and see the stories race behind his shining eyes.

—Hold it right there, mister! Is this *another* princess? What about the one you left locked in a dungeon three pages back with only a packet of Gummi Bears and a can of Seven Up to live off?

—Patience! Patience! he replies, wagging his finger at me, and making it look like everything in his stories happens on purpose.

Sometimes I stop listening to the words and all I can hear is the rise and fall of his story-telling voice, lifting me up and dropping me back like waves in the sea. On and on he goes, deeper into his world of golden peacocks and magic carpets and ugly frogs and handsome princes until I see that he no longer knows where he is, or what he's doing, or who I am, and most of all he does not know that I am only four years old and should be tucked up in bed asleep.

—*Dad*, I hiss. Da-*ad*.

But on nights like this it's best just to take myself quietly off to bed.

3

You are thirty-four years old, Theobald Moon had declared to his naked reflection in the mirror as he stood on the bath mat, dripping. *It is time to leave home.*

He had watched himself closely for a reaction, but the weak blue eyes merely blinked back at him through the steam.

He tried another tactic. *It is not just time to leave home, but to leave Clapham. To leave London. Holy Moses, you might even leave the country!*

Flickering somewhere at the back of his eyes, he thought he detected a note of alarm.

He gave himself a brusque little nod. That seemed to have worked. And he began to dry himself.

Some weeks later he had come across an advert in the travel pages of *The Sunday Times*:

TAKE A TRIP OUT WEST TO A LAND OF POTENTIAL
Here in Arizona we get 4,000 hours of sunshine per year – free of charge! Old folks will find the dry air a great curative for arthritis and rheumatism.

His father had been American – a GI stationed in England during the war who now lay buried somewhere in Northern France with his name on a small white cross – and he was duly permitted to travel and settle in America at any time, if he so wished. It had never appealed before. Or, to be precise, while his mother was alive it had never occurred to him to leave home.

The advert was accompanied by a picture of a man in a cowboy hat sitting down to a slab of steak two inches thick. A chunk of meat pushed out the skin of his cheek. As he stared at it, Theo found himself substituting the face of the man in the picture for his own – seeing his small, meek eyes peering out from beneath that greasy leather brim, his own padded fists wrapped around the wooden-handled knife and fork – and to his surprise, he did not look so out of place.

In fact, he looked rather good.

After that, events had taken a momentum of their own. Within a month, Chaz D'Sousa, 'Dealers in real estate since the landing of the *Mayflower*', South Central LA, had confirmed his purchase of a one-acre plot fifteen miles outside Tucson. They were thoughtful enough to enclose a photograph: running across the bottom of the picture was a strip of grit half an inch high flecked with tufts of grass. The rest was blue. Theobald Moon put it on the mantelpiece alongside his mother's collection of toby jugs and eyed it suspiciously from his armchair while watching the nine o'clock news. He wondered if he'd bought a chunk of the sky.

Over the next few weeks he sold the house, his mother's car, closed his own and his mother's Post Office savings accounts, and pooled the proceeds into one bank account that could be easily transferred to America. Three months to the day after his mother's body was wheeled out on the kitchen trolley and shafted feet first into the back of the St John's ambulance, he pulled the red velvet curtains around the bay window of the front room, took one last look at the way the carpet was pressed into stripes by the Push 'n' Pull, pulled the toggles tight round the hood of his orange cagoule, picked up his two leather suitcases and trudged through the rain to the tube.

He had expected sand dunes. Oases, at least. If pressed, he may even have admitted to imagining caravans of wandering nomads draped in long white robes and headcloths, riding on camels and pitching their tents at night.

He pulled down the window blind and leant his temple against it. He had no idea why he had come, or what he was going to do when he got there. He closed his eyes and willed himself back to sleep.

He slept through the Mojave Desert, missed the view to Hackberry Mountain, the Colorado river, the 'Welcome to Arizona' sign. Only when the driver shouted *Kingman!* did something in his subconscious give a jolt and propel his body, stumbling, out into the searing light, his heart thudding in his chest as it struggled to keep up. He immediately found himself wrapped in a hot grey fug of diesel, the Greyhound's farewell kiss.

As the fumes dispersed, Theobald Moon watched the landscape piece itself together around him. Pale, gritty earth, a scattering of unimpressive, scrubby bushes, the tarmac road cutting a quivering black slice through the middle of it like an oil slick at sea.

So this is it, he thought. What all the fuss was about. Clapham Common had more going for it than this.

Something gave him a hearty slap across the back of his neck. He turned round to face a bristling, beaming sun. One thing it is, is hot, he admitted, and blinked miserably as blisters of sweat began to collect on his forehead and dribble, stinging, into his eyes.

If anyone else had got off the Greyhound with him, they'd evaporated in the heat already. Looking round, he could see no sign of life at all. He clung to his suitcases as if they were ballast, the only thing fixing him to the ground. To the right, the road ran uninterrupted to a wavering vanishing point on the horizon. To the left its verges were sprinkled with a clutch of untidy neon signs: Motel 6, Phil and Diane's Diner, Whataburger, Ron's Kar Kare. A promise of civilisation – of sorts.

He started walking towards the signs, the coarse lining of his corduroys rubbing at his inner thighs. His stomach felt as if it were home to a swarm of bees. Something settled on the back of his neck and he put down his suitcases to swat it. But it was only a dribble of sweat. Holy Moses, what was he doing here?

It was noon, mid-July, and the daytime temperature had not dipped below ninety degrees in that part of Arizona for ninety days in a row.

He was about to pick up his suitcases again when he heard a vehicle behind him. Staggering round, he lifted his arms above his head and waved in slow motion, as if he were the last man on a sinking ship. The truck skidded to a halt on the tarmac beside him, belching dust and overheated metal. It was a battered Ford pickup which might once have been navy blue but was now covered in a solid coat of grey dirt.

Theobald Moon dipped his head to peer through the wound-down window and found himself looking into the frankest pair of eyes he had ever seen: wide and round and the same blue as the sky, staring at him without blinking. They sat in a large, uneven face divided up into sections like a cauliflower, together with a bulbous nose, a flat-lipped mouth.

As Theo stood there, those clear blue eyes travelled unashamedly down his own body, over his faded orange t-shirt hoisted around square breasts, the brown cardigan knitted for him by his mother with her over-sized needles, his thick corduroy trousers, the runnels worn smooth where his thighs rubbed together at the top, the brand new pair of Oxfords on his feet. Such scrutiny! A wave of grief and pity charged through Theobald Moon – grief for the world he had just left, for the habits of his thirty-four years, for the mother who had taught him to dress like this, and whose taste and judgement he was now subjecting to the gaze of this stranger from Arizona.

—I know who you are, mister, said the man in a high-pitched voice, his mouth stretching into a sudden grin, narrow in the middle and wide at the sides like a cartoon dog's bone. I bin sent.

Theobald stared. He didn't know what to say.

—Name's Jersey, said the man, offering a hand through the window. Work for the rancher who sold you your plot. Said you had no transportation of your own, and there ain't much to be had around here in the way of double-decker buses.

Pleased with his pre-rehearsed line, the man grinned again, and Theo gave a faltering smile back.

—I had no idea Arizona was so small.

—Oh, it ain't small. It's jus' that we don't get many folks like you.

The clear blue eyes flickered down momentarily to the buttons on Theo's cardigan, and up again. Theo shook Jersey's hand, his fingers compressing like damp sponge cake inside the man's strong clasp.

—We'll get straight on to Tucson, sir, if that's OK with you.

Theo replied that it was, slung his suitcases into the back and got inside.

Jersey was the sort of man for whom silence was the natural state of being and words an unwelcome interruption. When Theo began to comment on the heat, Jersey shot him a look of such wide-eyed surprise that he didn't dare open his mouth again for several hours. Relieved to be absolved of a social convention he wasn't much good at anyway, he looked out the window instead, at the looping cables of the electricity pylons that seemed to race the truck like playful dolphins, the dusky pink of the mountains in the distance that formed themselves into shapes – a camel's back, a roof with chimneys – only to shed them for something else as soon as they drew near. One minute he thought he had a grasp of the landscape around him, the next it was strange and unfamiliar again. He turned away, disconcerted. This place is teasing me, he thought, and decided to keep his eyes on the road ahead, or what was visible of it through the layer of squashed insects and hard-baked bird shit on the windscreen. He would have liked to ask the ranch-hand if they could stop for something to eat, but he didn't dare.

Theo had always been a tentative man. Brought up to believe that other people were not to be bothered, he had learnt to see himself as a nuisance. He frequently failed to say what he meant for fear of overstepping the mark. *Would you like milk?* the white-haired women would ask him in the café where he ate his lunch every day. *Just a little*, he'd reply, motioning with a pincer shape of his finger and thumb, even though he actually liked a lot. *Awful shame about your mother. Of course you're not over it yet, dearie, these things take years. A happy release, in the end, was it?* They tipped their heads to one side, in sympathy. *Oh, yes, I suppose so, in a way.* Sometimes he spoke so imprecisely he wasn't sure what he meant himself. Pussy-footing around the issue, his Aunty Drew would have declared. That's how it seemed to others – as if he were unwilling to make a stand, always leaving himself the option of retracting, of swapping sides. *It's what we don't do as well as what we do that we answer for on Judgement Day*, said Aunty Drew once, nailing him with an accusing eye. She'd left it at that, leaving him to make of it what he would.

But it wasn't that he didn't know what he wanted to say, or do, or feel; it was more of a case of not *daring* to know it. It was the same with his physical presence. Wherever he was, he was never sure he had the right to be there. Even after his mother was gone, he hadn't dared take up the whole of the bed; he had slept only on a slice of it, half sliding off the edge.

By early evening, the rumbles of Theo's stomach were becoming increasingly audible. He watched mournfully as a succession of promising-looking roadside eateries receded in the side mirror. At last, as the light was fading, Jersey turned off at a sign for Dateland and pulled up outside a low, flat-roofed building advertising 'Date Shakes, Date Pie and Great Dates!' Jumping out the truck, Jersey proceeded to take off his t-shirt, grabbing a handful of cotton from the scruff of his neck and pulling it over his head.

Theo couldn't help admiring the ranch-hand's torso – wide as his own, but divided up into muscles instead of one big smooth acreage and sporting a perfect bib of curly blond hair. He watched as Jersey used his t-shirt as a towel, rubbing under his armpits and round his neck, over the florets of his face, making it into a strap to dry his back. He threw the soiled t-shirt into the back of the truck, plunged his arm into a canvas bag for a fresh one, punched a head and two thick arms through it, rotated his jaw in its socket. He wiggled his finger in his ear, found something there, and flicked it out. When at last he was finished he looked up, and there was a moment of startled eye contact between them. Theo blushed and turned away, whipping his eyes from side to side around the car park. For a moment he was paralysed. But by the time he regained his composure, Jersey had kicked his door to with the heel of his boot and was leading the way inside, relaxed and whistling, as if nothing had happened at all.

The only person in the diner was a ten-year-old girl leaning over an exercise book at one of the tables.

—Mom.

A small woman appeared through a beaded curtain. Without acknowledging them she put on a pair of washing-up gloves, set to at the sink, and began humming loudly, as if it were her job to provide the background music and create the illusion that the place was busy. Above her was a blackboard with 'No. of Date Shakes Sold This Year' written across the top and a series of tally marks chalked underneath.

—*Mom.*

—What is it?

—What's a decimal point?

—Like a period but with numbers either side. Go tell your Uncle Mikey to start the fries on.

—I'm busy.

—Go on.

The girl slipped off her chair and pushed the beaded curtain noisily to one side as she went through. The woman twisted her neck to watch the beads spray out, her eyes tired and bored. Her short, bleached-blond hair was pushed up into tufts by the collar of her shirt. Sensing that she would turn to them next, Theo dipped his own gaze to a row of cakes on small white plates under cellophane wrapping. Beside him, Jersey opened his mouth to speak.

—Menus on tables, the woman said abruptly, and turned back to the sink.

They sat face to face tucked up on orange plastic chairs fixed to an orange plastic table, two men too big for the furniture, their square knees hammering underneath as if in some ritualistic tribal greeting. Jersey ripped open plastic sachets of red sauce, yellow sauce, brown sauce and made little dollops of them, like oil paint, around the rim of his plate. He closed his fingers around six or seven fries, dragged them through the sauces, swirling the colours together, and pushed them in a wad into his mouth. Without swallowing, he reached for his bottle of beer, held it up and grinned his dog's-bone grin.

—Want some?

Theo looked at the beer, then down at his Navajo taco piled high with red chilli beans and grated cheese and shredded lettuce, the large doughnut on the bottom looking like an undercooked Yorkshire pudding, and for a fleeting moment wondered if he was going to be sick. He ached to be in the kitchen in Clapham having half-past-four tea with his mother, a jar of thick-shredded Chivers for his toast, a man's cheery voice reading out the questions for the news quiz on Radio 4.

A hot jam tart if he was lucky.

Marzipan cake.

A few days later, Theobald Moon found himself walking along the verge of Valencia Road, to the south-east of Tucson, clutching a map drawn for him by the man at the reception desk of his motel. The road wound past a vintage aircraft museum where the skeletons of once proud World War II bombers stood unshrouded and bare. Although the paint was peeling off and the engines no longer turned, the aircraft still retained an air of dignity and importance, of having flown on dangerous night-time missions, landed in unchartered territories, and carried in their cockpits handsome men in flying jackets and goggles who laughed and winked at the girls in the face of death.

The road then took a turn to the left, dipped into a valley, and rose to reveal what at first appeared to be a hundred sets of false teeth grinning in a dentist's display cabinet: the spanking white mobile homes on sale to Tucson's retirees.

Theobald headed for a sign saying 'Happy Families – Experts in Mobile Home Living – Ask for Myrna!' and wiped the sweat from his eyes. When he looked up, a woman even larger than himself was coming at him from out of the office. She thrust a large, padded hand in his direction and stared at him through spectacles that magnified her eyes, giving her a look of permanent amazement.

—Welcome to Happy Families, sir. I'm Myrna. Are you a double-wide or a single-wide?

She drew back her lips in a well-practised smile. Lavish slices of gum showed above and beneath her teeth.

Confused, Theo glanced down at his belly.

—I suggest, said Myrna slowly, looking even more amazed than before, that we begin at the very beginning.

She took him around their show-home, a perfectly sealed white box with turquoise and pink-papered walls, a carpet that sprang back in the wake of his feet, curtains with ruched lace along the top and heart-shaped clips to hold them back. Knitted lampshades in the shape of a woman's ball gown, like the toilet-roll covers at home. A high queen-sized bed, spotlights directed on to it from the ceiling.

—We don't do panelling any more, we do tape and texture, said Myrna. She spoke slowly, as if for a child. She opened kitchen drawers and bedroom cupboards and closed them again before he'd had a chance to look inside. —And popcorned ceilings. Lace curtains and drapes in the bedrooms, carpeted throughout. This one's plum, but you can have mocha or cotton candy. You have two types of wallpaper on each wall, striped on the bottom half, floral above. 'Course they all come with washer and drier and you've got either swamp cooling or air conditioning, which is extra. The problem with swamp coolers is your cheese crackers tend to get soft.

The magnified eyes gazed at him dramatically through their thick glass ponds.

Theo stumbled over his words. —Do you have anything a little less – fancy?

The sun blasted furiously through the open door.

—Excuse me?

—I mean, well, these are all so lovely, but they're rather *feminine*. I'm not, really. If you see—

He wiped the sweat from his upper lip with the side of his hand.

She sniffed and turned without a word down the steps, teetering on heels too tiny for the weight of her. Theo followed obediently, keeping his eyes on the full calf muscles that bloomed beneath her skirt. Out in the sunlight she pointed to a building half hidden behind her office, tight up against the chicken-wire fence. It was smaller than the others, and the only one painted blue.

—Then you'll have to take something like that, sir. Used. Built in '62. Her voice lowered, as if finding the words distasteful. Two bedrooms, two swamp coolers, only $2,990. You've got seven years to pay, at 17.5 per cent interest. On top of that we suggest you invest in a nice little set of wooden steps that turn the corner, just $250 wholesale. And for this month only there's free delivery within a fifty mile radius. Her voice brightened up again. You'll be living at the Carefree Village Mobile Home Park on North Romero, I presume? I hear they have shuffleboard and bingo there.

Theo didn't reply. He could picture it already, standing on his one-acre plot, the faded blue paint flaking at the bottom. It would look as if it had been there for ever. He produced his new Well's Fargo credit card and the following day they brought it out on the back of a trailer, complete with wooden steps that turned the corner, and set it down on four cement blocks, leaving him instructions to fit wooden skirting in the gap between the ground and the bottom to stop snakes curling up in its shade.

Theo flicked the locks on the first leather suitcase. He took out a couple of pairs of heavy corduroys, another of lighter polyester, an assortment of brightly coloured t-shirts. One pale blue shirt with a stiff collar and a clip-on bowtie. He could hear her now: *Because you never know, Theobald, who you might meet out there.* Somehow, he still had a need to please her. A couple of cardigans, *because it gets nippy in the evenings*, a striped pullover, several knitted tank-tops – *a lot of work went into those.* Socks and pants by the dozen, two string vests, a pair of checked swimming trunks with a draw-string waist, still in their Woolworth's bag. Tucked into the corner of the case was a tin of Coleman's mustard powder and a carton of strawberry Nesquik.

The mobile home had come with the minimum of furniture – a narrow bed in the main bedroom, a pull-out table in the kitchen with four matching chairs, and not much else. Theo wandered round looking for somewhere to hang his clothes, and ended up hooking them all on the back of the bedroom door. When he flung the door open and they tumbled off, he pretended he hadn't noticed.

He flicked the locks on the second suitcase. From this he took three packets each of chocolate digestives, full butter shortbread, fig rolls, Jaffa Cakes and what his mother had liked to call squashed fly biscuits. A tin of Quality Street, three tubes of squeezy whipped cream and two empty ice-cream tubs filled with one-pound bags of loose sweets, weighed out from screw-top jars at Sweet Things, the corners of each bag twisted over into ears. The girls behind the counter had raised their eyebrows at one another when he'd produced a shopping list. On the street outside he'd heard the held-in laughter gushing out like water from a blocked pipe.

He'd have to ration himself to make them last. Then, when he was nearly out, he'd get Jersey to take him down to the Pick 'n' Mix counter at the supermarket and he'd have a transition week, some of the English, and some of the American, to help him get used to the new ones. He hoped he'd develop a liking for the American ones in the end.

He began sorting the sweets into small piles. To each pile he allotted one lemon bonbon, one stick of liquorice and one tube of sherbet powder, two cola chews, two shrimps, an aniseed wheel, an eyeball gobstopper, three or four pear drops and a couple of sweet cigarettes. He broke the peanut brittle into squares, scattered in a few marshmallows and added a Curly-Wurly to every seventh pile. That would be Sunday's treat.

When he was finished he sat back and surveyed them, stroking the soft channel than ran between his nose and his lips with his middle finger. Then, sweeping today's ration into his trouser pocket, he put on his Oxfords and stepped outside.

Dusk was short-lived here. No sooner had the sun been speared by the top of a mountain than it turned a violent, bloated red, and within a few minutes had dropped out of the sky completely, like a drunk passing out behind a bar. As soon as it was gone, a purple-grey haze flooded the valley like a cooling ointment, swamping everything in its path, and he could almost hear the landscape breathe out a sigh of relief. The outlines of the saguaros furred and dissolved until they merged with the mountains behind; the mountains themselves slumped, gratefully, into the desert floor, as if they had been forced to sit upright all day, nagged like he used to be – *Do sit up straight, Theo* – jerking her own shoulders back a few seconds before she said it so that he could not accuse her of failing to sit up straight herself.

With the land submerged in monotones, the sky took the opportunity to steal the show. Pink, threadbare clouds streaked the horizon to the west, while turquoise ribbons interlaced to the east. The whole effect was soft and furry, like the markings on the underbelly of a dog.

Theobald Moon stood at the bottom of his garden, his hands clutching the posts of the fence, taking it all in. Somewhere, in the distance, he heard a woman shout 'Jack!', just once, the sound travelling to him clear and unmuffled, with nothing to absorb it on the way. He calculated that his nearest neighbours lived about three miles away, and he wondered if he would ever meet them. Eisenhower houses, some of them. Made of wood, with five acres of land and a water tank, the fan of the cooler system sticking up above the trees like an identity flag. He had seen the tracks leading off the main road, the tin mailboxes sticking out of brown Bermudagrass verges, the names painted by hand on wooden signs or on to the surface of a rock: Valley Vista, Welcome Home, Luck's Roost. Names chosen by people who had come here to make a fresh start, like him. Sentimental names, full of optimism and hope.

As he stood there, reaching into his pocket every now and again for a Dolly Mixture or a Jelly Bean, Theo felt a wave of awe wash over him. How wrong his first impressions of the desert had been. This was a landscape the like of which he had never encountered before. The sheer scale of it – the majesty of it – was enough to take your breath away. It was a landscape that commanded attention. That insisted on being admired. It was a long, long way from anything in England – he saw that now. A long, long way from Clapham Common. There was something timeless about it, something humbling and strange.

Looking out, that first night, over the softly purpling valley, the tall silhouettes of dead agave flowers lined up like limbless shadow puppets against the vast sky, Theobald Moon felt the first tuggings on his heartstrings, a slight stretching of what he presumed was his soul. And he knew that in this great, still landscape, in this place of determined, insistent life, he would find what he was looking for.

4

Four a.m. and a horn blasted through the darkness. Moments later they began to collect beneath the street lamps, the moisture in their breath settling on one another's faces like the touch of damp sheets on a line. Fresh snow had fallen in the night and their boots sank through this new soft layer with a dull crunch, compressing it into the ice beneath. They were unwieldy, sexless, their hands thrust deep in pockets, their legs hidden beneath the heavy fleece coats, their hair covered by hoods and hats, the shapes of their bodies forgotten.

As they met, the men singled themselves out from the women by bending towards one another, as if to bow in greeting, cupping their hands around flames that spluttered and were snuffed out quickly by damp fingers and thumbs of air. The first cigarette thumped home with a welcome familiarity, easing them back to life. As they smoked, their jaws loosened up for talk.

They talked of the weekend's skiing in the Tatras. Someone had taken their children down the slopes for the first time. Another's brother had shot a bear.

—What's he done with it? My mother-in-law's always on at me for a pair of bear-skin slippers.

—You know Miro. Straight up on the wall.

—Showy bastard.

From down below came a deep rumble: the factory coming to life. It was like the reluctant stirrings of a monstrous, sleepy animal, the huge presses stretching stiff, leaden jaws, creaking their oily joints. Somewhere deep inside the internal workings, conveyor belts gave a complicated jolt before begrudgingly starting to roll.

This was the signal that it was time to move, and the workers began to make their way downhill, the ends of their cigarettes darting up and down like fireflies as they gesticulated with their hands. From other parts of the town more groups appeared, shadowy shapes emerging out of the blackness. At each junction, the groups merged and became one.

The men's jobs were in the heavy rooms, curing and tanning the new hides. They plunged their arms up to the elbows in vats of coarse salt and lime which attempted to turn their own skin to leather. They sliced the hair from the flesh with razors, stealing from the hides the last evidence of having once encompassed a living, pounding heart. The hides were then dipped in a series of tubs – tannic acid, bleach, oil – before being stretched over frames to dry, stiff and dead.

In these rooms juices, squeezed from the freshly razed flanks of cowhide, dripped from the presses and covered the floor with a pale red film, making the men's boots squelch and creating a mess of bloody footprints that trailed off down the corridor towards the toilets and the coffee machine. The air was so dense with the smell of raw flesh that it caught at the back of their throats and made their muscles convulse. Most of them had worked here all their lives and didn't notice the stench any more, nor the scraps of flesh that got stuck under their fingernails, nor the blood that splashed around their mouths. It was all in a day's work.

Other men worked with the powdered dyes which rose in great clouds of fine particles – red and green and yellow – that swirled in the light from the strip of windows high up near the ceiling like a slow-motion, airy firework display, before drifting down to settle in the nooks and crannies of their hands and faces, where sweat mingled with the dye and released it as liquid pigments into their skin. Several of the older men of the town had become veined with colour in this way, rainbows on the knuckle joints of their fingers, around the cuticles of their nails, along the crow's feet at the corners of their eyes. Children would point them out as if they were an exotic, fancy breed. Chameleons to everyone else's grey lizards.

The younger men, more conscious of their appearance and not wanting to be so obviously labelled by their role at the factory, wore a sort of Muslim yashmak, an upside-down shuttlecock which caught the particles of colour in their webbing before they had a chance to stain the skin. This produced a division between the generations: the older, colourful generation considering their younger colleagues to be overly precious – *dievčatká*, the little girls, they called them – and in their shuttlecock veils it could seem to an outsider that these young men had indeed taken the part of the females in an otherwise all-male environment. To defend themselves, the younger men became cocky and loud and bragged about their plans for their lives after the factory – the places they would travel to, the jobs they would do. The famous men and women they would meet. No one believed them, but no one ever tried to shut them up, either. There wasn't a single man there who hadn't entertained such fanciful notions himself at one time, and though the old men shook their heads in apparent scorn, what they really felt was a secret wave of tenderness for these young lads who so reminded them of their younger selves.

On the other side of the factory were the light rooms where the machining, the hand-stitching and the decorating took place. This was where the women worked, lined up one behind another as if in a classroom, the clattering of their machines drowning most attempts at conversation. Here mothers worked behind daughters, grandmothers behind granddaughters, aunts behind nieces. There wasn't so much a feeling that age didn't matter as an implicit understanding that, within these four walls, they were all nineteen years old. On their right hands, which played around the bouncing of the needles, they wore gloves made of a pliable metallic weave, like the fabric that hangs from visors to protect the neck. Every so often these chainmail-clad hands rose up to a lever which controlled the lifting and dropping of the needle – seventy hands responding at random to the inaudible questions of an invisible teacher. On either side of each woman's table was a box, the left one filled with pieces of leather in different sizes, the right with the completed, stitched uppers, soft and malleable and without soles.

It was still dark when the workers arrived at the heavy iron gates. They bunched up behind the turnstile like the individual segments of a caterpillar, and passed through one at a time, a metallic *clunk* chopping the caterpillar into pieces again. On the other side of the turnstile a glass panel divided the gangway down the middle, and the men channelled off to the right, the women to the left.

Some days, a pair of fingertips met either side of this glass panel, and ran down the length of it in tandem before the corridors turned off at right-angles, forcing the fingertips apart. One of these sets of fingers belonged to Eva Ligocká. Like most of the women who worked at the factory, she wore her dark hair in a frizz of tightly permed curls that clung to her head in the shape of an outsized motorbike helmet. As with most things in the country at the time, there was not a great deal of choice when it came to hairstyles. The town had only the one hairdressing salon, Lilia's, and Lilia had only the one size of roller. You could smell her little dish of perming solution all down General Svoboda on Saturday afternoons.

The other set of fingertips belonged to Pavel Dugat. Occasionally, during the course of the morning, Pavel found a reason to cross the factory courtyard and visit the room where Eva worked on the pretence of checking on the quantity of stitched uppers stacked in the box to the right of each worker's table. Pavel wasn't senior enough to be checking anything, let alone the output of seventy female stitchers, but everyone knew he was soft on Eva Ligocká, and everyone indulged a man in love. Factory romances being, after all, free entertainment for all.

When Pavel appeared at the front of the room that housed the sewing machines, throwing little glances in Eva's direction, but somehow always managing to catch the steely, narrowed eye of her sister-in-law to her left, all seventy women became girlish. They generally responded to the attentions of one man as if he were making a play for them all. Adept at conversations without words, they communicated with a repertoire of raised eyebrows, manipulations of the mouth and winks of the eye, and in this way messages were passed around the entire room within seconds, the silent chatter moving fluently up and down the rows, flung over the shoulders of grandmothers and granddaughters alike. Sometimes laughter rolled back around the room in a wave, causing each woman's chest to rise and fall in turn.

Today, only the chest of Eva Ligocká remained unmoved. Instead, she gave her frizzy helmet an irritated toss, or tried to, for it wasn't the sort of hair that moved very much. She had only flirted with Pavel for lack of anybody else to flirt with, and now look what he was doing. Practically pulling his pants down in public.

At eleven thirty the horn sounded again, and work at the factory came to an abrupt halt. Skins about to be dipped in bleach were left draped over the side of bubbling vats, abandoned to an uncertain fate; soft leather uppers were left staked flat to the machine under the merciless clamp of the needle; the secretary in Mr Baťa's office broke off halfway through a letter to her boss's new lady friend, carelessly leaving it in the typewriter for anyone to see. *En masse*, the entire factory workforce surged through the narrow corridors, searched for faces, distinctive-coloured clothes, fingertips, and forgot about work for an hour.

Most took their lunch break inside during winter, rushing to get a seat in the canteen as much for the comfort and warmth as for the food, which was hot but had a tendency to be oversalted and watery. The windows steamed up and the conversation was generally on the steamy side too.

But today a few filed outside to get some air. There had been a shift in the weather since the morning. The sun was out, the sky was blue, and if it hadn't been several degrees below freezing, the day might have passed itself off as spring. The caterpillar reformed, this time facing in the other direction, and one by one they had their passes punched beneath the závodny 29. augusta sign before wandering off in little groups of twos and threes. Husbands and wives met up to have complicated discussions about the evening meal and whose turn it was to collect the children at half past two. Others broke free of the groups to grab a moment of peace and quiet by themselves.

It sounded very faintly at first – a dissonant jangling in the air, perhaps just a tinnitus in the ears. One or two shook their heads, fearing their ears were at last wreaking revenge after years of assault from seventy sewing machines. But then it came again: a cluster of tinny, metallic notes filtering down through the trees above the town.

Several of them had stopped to listen now, tilting their heads to one side, some putting up a hand to bring the conversation to a halt around them. They did not know what it was, but it was as familiar to them as the chimes of the carriage clock in their front rooms at home. It was an enchanted sound, like a call from far away. It brought to mind images from their childhoods, of sultry summer evenings spent by the lake out towards Prievidza, lying on the rocky shore and waving to someone on the opposite side with long, slow sweeps of their arms.

And then, suddenly, they knew. Of course! It was the jingle of the ice-cream van. But now? In the middle of January? They laughed. The ice-cream man must be off his rocker.

Romany blood, they muttered. Curdles like milk the minute the sun comes out.

*

When Eva Ligocká saw him, she felt as if she were watching the performance of a magician. He spread his eloquent fingers into a star and slotted the cones neatly in between. Then, unwittingly mimicking the movement made by the women at their sewing machines, and triggering an affectionate note of recognition on several of their faces, he pulled the lever down with his left hand and the cones became spokes in the hub of a wheel as he held them, one by one, under the individual nozzles, coiling the ice-cream on top. One pink, one white, one brown. He bounced them slightly to bring each coil to a point.

—You're not seriously expecting us to eat ice-cream on a day like this, grumbled one of the older men.

The ice-cream man shrugged, unconcerned.

—January is exactly the right time of year to eat ice-cream, he said.

—What's he talking about? someone mumbled, as if he wasn't there.

—What do they eat in India? Chillies. Gets the body's cooling mechanism working. What do you eat when it's cold? Something that gets the body to heat itself up. It's common sense.

The older man jerked his hat down over his ears.

—Never heard such rubbish in my life.

—Got to admire him for trying, though, said one of the younger women, reaching into her handbag for a coin.

—Got to admire him full-stop, murmured a woman standing next to her.

Nobody knew quite what to do. They weren't used to their ice-cream men engaging them in conversation like this, and they were a little put out. Who did he think he was, being so bold? But that of course made him all the more intriguing. Several of the older women stepped forward to take a closer look.

He was dark-skinned, like the others. A crop of oily curls fell across his forehead. He had wide, arched nostrils flaring to a point, darting eyes that were very black indeed, almost the colour of peat.

Some of them noticed a redness around the rims and concluded he was a drinker. All concluded he was a Romany.

They all were, the ice-cream men. They made good ice-cream men – when they didn't try and rip you off. The business suited their nomadic lifestyles. They could cover most corners of Eastern Europe within the course of the year, picking up supplies in the cities and distributing them throughout the villages until they reached the next big town. The good thing was they never hung around in one place too long. You never could be sure of what they'd get up to. All sorts of petty crime, and some not so petty either. Much as everyone likes an ice-cream man, you liked seeing the back of them even more. Or at least, that was the official line.

A group of older women, daring to be the first, took their ice-creams and sat down on a bench, their untapered legs fixed squarely to the ground. The lacy edgings of their frocks showed beneath the hems of their coats.

—He may be a Romany, but he's quite a looker, said one.

—Twenty years ago I wouldn't have said no.

—I wouldn't say no now.

Eva stood with her arms crossed over her trench coat and stared at the ice-cream man unashamedly. She was transfixed by the way he moved, how he worked those agile fingers, managing to exert the right amount of pressure to hold the cone but not to crush it. How his stocky, compact frame manoeuvred neatly within the small confines of the van, reaching up to a shelf behind him for a cone, pushing what looked like a stick of chocolate into each ice-cream, leaning out to meet a customer's stretching hand. In between transactions, he bounced up and down to keep warm. He wasn't wearing a coat – just a thin green jumper, with no shirt or vest beneath.

The chocolate sticks he was giving away with the ice-creams were causing considerable excitement. Some people were coming back to demand an extra one, but he refused to hand them out on their own.

—If you want another one, you have to buy another ice-cream, he said.

Did he make them himself? they asked.

The ice-cream man tapped a finger on his nose.

Well, where did he get them from, then?

But he just laughed and, to everyone's annoyance, refused to give anything away.

Then, amidst all the commotion, he looked up. Either her immobility or the intensity of her stare must have caught his attention. Their gazes locked. At once, they knew as much about one another as they would ever need to know. Eva panicked, gave him an enormous smile, and instantly felt stupid. The ice-cream man offered a disarmingly beautiful smile of his own. Eva looked round, wildly, expecting everyone else on the forecourt to have noticed and to be laughing and pointing at her.

An exchange of smiles, that was all. Such apparently mundane gestures, and yet the little scene which they had just enacted was like a tableau from something much larger which, they both knew, would now inevitably follow. What they didn't know was that at odd, quiet moments throughout the rest of their lives, they would both be momentarily enchanted by the memory of this, their first sighting of one other, outside the shoe factory, závodny 29. augusta, and that they would each embellish the scene with extra details that they would come to believe were true. In Eva's version, the ice-cream man threw her a free stick of chocolate and everyone around her watched in envy. In the ice-cream man's version, the woman with the large green eyes came over and put her tongue in his mouth.

In the kitchen of the flat where Eva Ligocká lived with her mother, her father, her maternal grandmother, her father's brother Michael, her own three elder brothers, Rudy, Marek and Julo, her sister-in-law Sylvia, and her nephew Gregory, condensation fugged up the windows and the lids on two bubbling pans clamoured on the stove.

There was a strong smell of burnt cabbage which her mother was trying to camouflage by talking very loudly and ushering everyone quickly to their seats.

This evening, as every evening, her three brothers, her father and her uncle made the mistake of trying to sit down around the circular table at the same time. As usual, after their first failed attempt, the two older men stepped back to let the younger men go first, and then slotted themselves into whatever spaces remained.

As she entered the tiny kitchen, ducking to avoid a plate of sliced dumpling, cutlets and the venomous cabbage that was being passed from hand to hand above her head, Eva was struck by the notion that she was seeing her family through somebody else's eyes.

She looked at her father, happiest in this small moment between sitting down to supper and taking his first bite. As he saw his plate coming, he joined his palms together, then bounced them over his slicked-back hair, careful not to spoil the perfect grooves ploughed by his comb. She looked at the few soft, silvery strands that were starting to curl in indiscriminate directions at his temples, as if considering themselves too old or too dignified to be swept back with the rest, and felt a wave of sadness pass through her, as if she had lost him already. She saw him glance around the table to ensure that each member of the family had their plate before them, pausing while his mother-in-law slowly manoeuvred her large bottom to the edge of her chair. He caught Eva's eye, winked and held up his glass.

—*Dobrú chut'!*

At the beginning, eating took precedence over talking. Hungry from the working day, they reached across one another's plates for thickly cut slices of hard, yellowy bread, bobbed their chins over the table to catch the drips of thin gravy, and tilted their plates to scrape up the runniest bits with their spoons. As a family they were unafraid of touch. Under the table was a tangle of legs, of bumping knees and even little piles of feet and crossed ankles that mounted up without anyone finding it necessary to acknowledge whose was whose. Above the table elbows propped themselves up against arms, shoulders knocked shoulders, and sometimes one of the women swiped her neighbour's cheek with a handful of tossed hair.

It was only Eva who, this evening, tucked her feet beneath her own chair.

It occurred to Eva that her grandmother also maintained a certain distance from the rest of the family. She too was watching the proceedings, though with a face so placid an outside observer might have concluded she was fantastically bored by it all. Unsmiling, one arm resting on her thigh so that her body was on a tilt, she looked like a heavyweight boxer in her corner of the ring, psyching herself up for the fight. She always wore one of three embroidered smocks that buttoned down the front and pulled tight with coloured stitching across her bosom, causing her breasts to be widened and flattened and squared off at the ends, as if the idea was to make them fit into a loaf tin. Her grandmother had lived most of her life in a farming village in the High Tatras, and went bare-armed even in winter. Eva's father had once announced loudly to a roomful of friends that his mother-in-law was so hardy you could leave her outside all winter and she'd still be alive when you dug her out in the spring.

As the process of eating slowed down, it was gradually replaced by conversation. Driving a square of bread around the edge of his plate, Mr Ligocký embarked on a detailed account of a conversation he'd overheard between two of his colleagues at the factory. He worked in the cutting rooms, sorting hides into sizes and weights and punching soles and uppers from sheets of leather like jam tart bases from dough.

—I tell you, that's what he said. He said he'd got a flat on the Šimonovany estate within two months of applying. It was Boris's son, the one who got married in December. Married a girl from Brno. Nice little thing, although Boris thinks she's a vegetarian.

—Well, Boris Tamchov sits on the factory board, said Julo.

—It doesn't make any difference, said their mother. You must've heard it wrong, Anton. Julo and Sylvia have been waiting two years.

As if on cue, a small boy suddenly careered around the corner, arms outspread into an aeroplane, and pulled up just short of the table. It was becoming a hackneyed entrance – he'd done it hundreds of times before – but merely walking into a room, like adults did, was out of the question, and he had yet to come up with an original alternative.

It was his grandmother's knees he scrambled on to, curling himself into the familiar curve of her lap as expertly as a dog. Under-estimating his knowledge of her dresses, of which ones were slippery and which ones weren't, Mrs Ligocká pressed him un-necessarily firmly into her bosom. Gregory made no objection, and opened his mouth wide to receive the little flakes of dumpling on the end of her fork which she had taken from her own plate, whispering into his ear with her wide, soft mouth. Julo reached over to ruffle his son's hair, then crossed his arms and leant back in his chair.

Eva's grandmother, her food rearranged but largely uneaten, nudged her plate away and gave a slack, uncontrolled cough.

—May I, Gran? asked Rudy cheerfully, and without waiting for an answer, scraped her food on to his empty plate, and started all over again.

Eva looked from Rudy to Marek to Julo to Gregory to her mother, eyeing them all with the curiosity of an outsider. This was her home, and the people she saw every day. They were her world. And yet, for some reason, she felt as if she now belonged somewhere else.

Between Lilia's salon and the bakery was squeezed an uncomfort-able, flat-roofed building painted a brilliant shade of lime green in an attempt, presumably, to appeal to the youth of the town. In fact, the colour simply made the building look as if it was not meant to be there, and that it actually belonged in another town, or even another country altogether.

This feeling of confusion was compounded once inside, where the upturned red glass lampshades lining the walls turned the room the same colour as the blood-spattered heavy rooms at the factory. Indeed, some of the men stopped short at the door, shoulders squaring as they braced themselves for the expected onslaught of stench and noise.

These two disorientating factors might nevertheless have proved to be the cause of Babička's success. Most people who came through the door found it necessary to head straight for the bar and drink something quickly in order to regain their composure. The healthy takings had allowed for a recent lavish refurbishment with red, crescent-shaped sofas that were easily the most exotic sofas anyone in the town had ever seen.

For Eva and Rudy, the brother closest to her in age, it was a welcome change after the claustrophobia of the flat. Rudy immediately spotted some men he worked with and, without thinking to consult his sister, strode over to join them. His colleagues were more interested in who was following behind him, and several of them inched to one side to make room for her.

—Excellent, smirked Miro, as Eva bent to kiss him on the cheek, drawing back quickly at the prickles of his beard. How could Katka stand that against her face every day?

—Where's Katka?

Miro paused. —There's entertainment, you know.

Eva scowled at her brother. —Rudy forgot to tell me about that. Who have we the pleasure of tonight?

—A new one. Daughter of the Topol'čany butcher.

Someone handed her a Budvar and almost immediately the red lights dimmed and a white spotlight planted a circle in the centre of the makeshift stage. A girl of about Eva's age stepped out from behind a curtain, wearing a brown suede mini and short-cropped jacket, both edged with tassels, cowgirl style. Her fishnets bunched up above the tight heels of her stilettos.

There was a squeak of a microphone, and a disembodied male voice introduced her as Vita. Twenty years old, said the God-like voice, and with them for the first time. Watch out for the beauty spot, he added, but he wasn't going to tell them where it was. Well, just a hint. Keep your eyes below the waist.

43

Eva looked at Miro out of the corner of her eye. His moustache was tangled in a confused grin. He shot her an apologetic smile and shrugged his shoulders.

Meanwhile Vita had stepped into the spotlight and was smiling broadly, as if she were standing behind the counter in her father's butcher's shop in a blue-and-white-striped apron. There was silence in the room. Then, with a concertina-type lurch, the music started, several bars into the song, as if someone had just found the switch connecting the speakers. Vita leapt eagerly into her routine, stepping each leg out to the side and lowering herself down, running her hands down her thighs, the suede tassels falling either side. She closed her eyes to create a more sultry mood, or perhaps to show off the glitter on her eyelids which ran in isosceles triangles all the way to her temples, and began to bounce slowly up and down.

Miro nuzzled himself into the sofa, crossing his short arms across his chest. He was grinning properly now.

—I met Katka on a night like this, he said, his voice dropping to a gravelly whisper. We watched a girl and then we took to the dance floor and carried on where she left off.

He giggled and gyrated his body from the waist.

—You must have been irresistible, whispered Eva.

A slow clap had started up. Vita had her back to the audience and was letting her jacket slip off her shoulders. She caught it by the collar and began to twirl it like a lasso, the *pièce de résistance* of her cowgirl theme. With a little jolt of surprise, Eva noticed that Vita was wearing the same style of bra that she had on. It was one of three styles available at Jednota in Topol'čany. Like hers, it had gone a little grey in the wash.

—I must have been, I tell you. Six weeks later we got engaged.

She was twirling it faster now, standing sideways on, ready to let go.

—Don't fling me the jacket, jump on me yourself! shouted Miro suddenly, and the words were received with approving jeers and laughter around the room.

—Was it love at first sight?

Miro looked at her in surprise. —What, with Vita?

—No, you idiot. Katka.

Miro hadn't had time to wipe the look of surprise off his face before the jacket hit him square between the eyes. He pawed it off, trying to retrieve his dignity and win back the men's approval by making a big show of shrugging his shoulders, looking round.

—Well?

He looked at her blankly. —What?

—You and Katka, getting engaged so quickly.

—Oh. Same reason as everyone else around here. He patted his hand against his stomach.

Eva looked back at Vita and saw that the girl was watching them, herself and Miro. She had lost her poise: her shoulders were slumped and her tummy was sticking out. Miro's remark – or her own response to it – had evidently made her lose her concentration. Catching Eva's eye, she snapped herself out of it, pulled her stomach in, and promptly realised she didn't have a clue what came next. Was it time for the stockings yet? Or did the skirt come first? She began to fiddle uncertainly with the zip on the side of the skirt, but then changed her mind and went back to the spread-legged movement she had started with, only this time with her back to the audience, running her hands right up over her naked buttocks, giving herself time to think. The audience soon got back into the rhythm, and began to whistle their approval as she walked her fingers, spiderlike, up to the clasp of her bra, unhooking the plastic hooks, lifting the straps off one shoulder and then the other in what was, in the end, simply a slow-motion version of the perfunctory way she had no doubt been taking off her bra every night since she was thirteen, the way that Eva did it herself, and when she turned round there was a hush in the room at the sight of her breasts, large and pale and soft with the nipples compressed as if she were in her own room at home and getting ready for bed.

*

45

Tanya stretched out a long, woollen-ribbed leg and shoved the back of Eva's stool with her foot.

—Don't play coy with me, Ligocká.

Eva tilted her head to one side, so that Tanya could see she was listening. Tanya just laughed and started up the noisy clack-clack-clack of her machine, pressing her foot down flat on the pedal and leaning into it as if it were the accelerator on a car.

Eva turned round.

—Go on then. I admit. I want to know.

—What's it worth? shouted Tanya above the racket.

Eva eyed the pile of unfinished uppers in the box to the left of Tanya's worktop.

—Halves on that box.

—God, you're easy.

A little irritated at herself, Eva grabbed one of the soft leather pieces from Tanya's box and curled the two ends round to make a circle, joining them with a line of stitching so that the leather began to take the sloping form of a foot. Tanya laughed at her enthusiasm and took her foot off the pedal, leaning across the table on her arms. When she spoke it was loudly but in a low, steady voice, so that the other women wouldn't be able to hear.

—He parks his van in the forest on the outskirts of the town at night. You have to go up that trail, the steep one, just after the petrol station on the way to Bošany. My aunt followed him as far as the turn-off yesterday afternoon.

—Your old aunt Eleonóra?

—I know. She has a somewhat distorted self-image.

—How far up?

—I don't know. Somewhere up there among the trees.

—How long has he been there?

Tanya shrugged.

—What's he doing up there?

—Not selling ice-cream, that's for sure. I should think he's beating his chest and pulling out his hair and refusing to eat his dinner — the things you do when you're in love with a girl you glimpsed one cold January morning outside závodny 29. augusta . . .

Eva wrenched the half-finished upper from under her needle and chucked it at Tanya, skimming the top of her head.

And they went back to their work, smirking, their needles bouncing up and down a little faster than before.

5

For the first two weeks, Theo's internal clock was in a state of disarray. He woke at five in the morning and by mid-afternoon he was snoring deeply, succumbing to the seductive enchantments of jet lag as cleanly as if he had been dealt a soft blow on the back of his head. In the meantime, he saw the desert around him through uncertain, unfocused eyes. Which, for the purposes of acclimatisation, was probably just as well.

One morning, as soon as the sun was up, he stepped out on to his top step to sniff the day. It was going to be a scorcher. Already the heat was shimmering on the horizon, so that the mountains seemed to melt and bubble at their base. You could almost be forgiven for thinking that, any moment now, the haze would materialise into a stampede of Red Indians on horseback tumbling with their high-pitched war-cries over the plain.

As he turned to go inside, Theo glimpsed something long and sinewy slide beneath his house. For a moment, he was too shocked to move. And then, as the ghastly truth sank in, he began to edge slowly back towards the door. It was just as the men from Happy Families had warned. Snakes.

Safely inside, he slammed the door shut and leant against it. In the seconds that followed, the thin tail he had seen blossomed in his imagination into a sleek black cobra as thick as his arm with a darting forked tongue and evil yellow eyes. With trembling hands, Theo made himself a cup of tea and sat down with it at the kitchen table. His eyes came to rest on an advert in the *Tucson Weekly*, spread open before him. 'Practical Handgun Courses at Lemans West, Speedway Boulevard,' he read. 'We do Shooting Stances (including Kneeling and Prone), Drawing the Handgun from the Holster and Multiple Targets.' He tried to picture himself with a holster slung round his hips, but the image wouldn't come.

Half an hour later he heard the rumble of an engine and looked up to see what appeared to be a vast mechanical digger approaching down the track. What a dramatic way to be rescued! he thought. He tapped frenetically on the window as Jersey jumped out, but the ranch-hand didn't hear him. Instead he proceeded to walk all around the edge of the property, calling Theobald's name. Eventually Theo saw him climb up on to the flat-topped slab of granite at the bottom of his garden and scan the horizon. He put his hands on his hips and shook his head.

He thinks I'm dead, Theo murmured to himself, rather touched.

When Jersey jumped down and headed back towards the digger, Theo realised it was his last chance.

—Help! he wailed, in a high, thin voice. He scrabbled with the latch of the window and jerked it open. Help!

Jersey turned, a frown buckling up the florets of his face. He strode over to the house, put his hands in his pockets and tipped back on his heavy heels.

—Don't tell me. Locked in. Butane heater blown your legs off.

Theo shook his head violently.

—Snakes! Under the house! Don't come any closer.

Jersey sent a high-pitched chuckle into the air, bending backwards.

—Oh! Are they friendly?

—*Friendly?*

Jersey grinned. He got down on his hands and knees a few feet away from the house and peered underneath. The wooden skirting still stood stacked against the wall.

—Ah, I see the fella. Well, Mr Moon, looks like you've got your-self a killer rattler there, a big daddy-o diamond-back, yes siree, and wherever he is, there's likely to be at least half a dozen others rovin' around. Looks like you'll have to stay inside on a permanent basis, Mr Moon, or at least 'til we gets your skirting up.

To Theo's horror, Jersey disappeared beneath the house. I should go and save him, he thought. But he couldn't bring himself to move. The next thing he saw sent an uncontrollable shudder down his spine. Jersey's face popped up, right outside the window, with the snake draped around his shoulders, cosy as a scarf.

—Seems real friendly to me, Mr Moon, said Jersey, stroking the snake down its length.

Perhaps realising that there would be a hell of a thump if Theobald passed out, Jersey relented.

—What you got here is an old bicycle tyre, Mr Moon. They's nice, bicycle tyres, if you handle them right.

Theo wiped the sweat off his face with a piece of kitchen roll and went out on to the step. He didn't know what to say.

—Rancher told me to keep an eye on you, said Jersey. Make sure he doesn't go crazy, he said to me. Or at least doesn't die, anyways.

Theo smiled, embarrassed. He didn't really mind. He liked the frank-eyed ranch-hand. He seemed to accept Theo with all his oddities, and not really mind about them – the sort of person who didn't see it as his place to criticise. Theo hadn't met many people like that before.

—Will you come in for a cup of tea?

—Tea? Jersey let out a little chuckle. Ah, no thank you very much sir Mr Moon. I'm tea-total. Don't touch the stuff.

There had been a well on Theo's plot for many years, but the owner of the ranch had let it fill over, unwilling to travel out to tend to its upkeep. A huddle of mesquite trees still grew around the spot, bending their heads together and rustling their fragile grey-green leaves as if they had gathered round to see where the water had gone.

They worked the digger together, Jersey at the controls and Theo directing him like a traffic controller on an airport strip – *a little to the right, down now, back off.* When the first bubbles of water oozed to the surface, Jersey jumped down and threw his hat in the air and let out a high-pitched *Woooo-oaa!* The next thing Theo knew, he was in the other man's arms and staring at the open pores on the end of his bulbous nose.

—*Shit* man, I feel like I'm in Texas and we just struck oil!

Startled by the unexpected intimacy, Theo extricated his limbs clumsily and agreed that it called for a toast. Using a bucket on a rope they dredged out the first crop of water and filled a couple of glasses. It was pink and full of grit. Jersey looked at it with a crooked mouth, then shrugged and pulled out two beers from under the seat of the digger and knocked the caps off against the cement surround of the well. He handed one to Theo.

—Think we'll just stick to the brown stuff, Mr Moon.

But by the end of the day they had reconnected the old wind-powered pump and started filling the two-hundred-gallon tank that sat on a platform at the level of Theo's roof. Jersey showed him how to work the gear box to slow the propellers down, and advised him not to produce anything that needed flushing until the tank had had a chance to fill up.

Stepping into his house, it cupped him in grey, cool hands and seemed to blow on the back of his neck, drying the sweat on his skin.

It was a relief to be by himself again. He took off the sodden shirt and sat bare-chested on a cushion in his living room, the late afternoon light planting soft squares on the floor. Looking down, he inspected the folds of his stomach, cleaning out his belly button with his finger until he was nauseous from too much poking and prodding. He farted out loud, making a sound like ripped fabric in the silence, and smiled in delight. He could never have done that if his mother had been around.

He found he didn't miss her as much as he thought he would. She had never been part of his life out here, after all. In general, she tended to occur to him only at night, when, once his eyes were closed, he might have been anywhere.

Sometimes he saw her as she was when she was well – big-boned and blue-eyed like him, her pale blond hair piled up high and curling over at the top like the pinnacle on a meringue. The easy laugh that made her neck quiver. But mostly he saw her as she was at the end, the deflated hair turned not exactly grey but colourless – almost translucent – and her once robust face drained of all expression.

—A mockery, he'd catch her muttering under her breath, her broad shoulders caving in as if she'd been winded. Wretched soldiers.

He had nursed her, talking to her constantly in a way that he hoped would soothe her, banal utterances on the subject of porridge, or the neighbours, or the shrub roses in the garden, half hoping that she would look up at him one day with an expression of irritation on her face. *What a load of nonsense you talk. You should hear yourself.* He would listen out for her at night, waiting open-eyed in the darkness for the inevitable sounds of her nocturnal wanderings. Once he found her struggling to put her coat on over her nightie at the front door, mumbling something about 'going to look for your father'; another time he had woken to the smell of gas and found her trying to make herself an omelette in the dark. Each time he had led her gently back to bed, stroking her hair and shoulders in a way he had never done before, feeling an ache of tenderness for the pliant body that moved whichever way he turned it, the soft red pouches of delicate skin beneath her vapid eyes that seemed to sag a little more each day. More than once she mistook him for the American GI she had met in a Piccadilly tea house, who had taken her to the theatre and later to the altar on Lavender Hill, only to wash up dead on a Normandy beach three months afterwards. As he tucked her in, pulling the sheets up to her chin, and turned to head back to his own room, she admonished him sharply: *And where do you think you're going?*, the look of shock and betrayal etched so painfully on her face

52

it was as if she had been slapped. He had been unable to bear it. He had climbed into bed with her, whispering that he wasn't going anywhere, nowhere at all, and lain stiffly beside her, inhaling Nivea and Johnson's baby powder, the hot milk on her breath, terrified that she might try to touch him where she shouldn't. When, in the night, he found a dry palm resting on his stomach, he took it quickly between his own and rubbed the slippery skin on the back of her hand, the lacy cuff of her nylon nightie grazing his wrist. Later he woke to find himself curled up behind her, his knees wedged into the backs of hers, and a single colourless hair, brittle as a strand of Brillo pad, poking out of her hairnet and up his nose.

The problem with putting a house where no house has been before, Jersey told him, is that you never knew what creatures were already living there. —If it were a scorpion, for example, said Jersey, becoming more loquacious after a couple of mid-afternoon beers – and I'm not saying it necessarily was, but just for example – then you're going to have to accommodate it. They's creatures of habit, scorpions, yes siree, and a patch is a patch, even if it suddenly sprouts rooms and a fridge. And scorpions know their patches.

Just in case, Theo decided to stand his bed in four plastic cups of water, topping up the water each night, as if he were trying to make the bed legs grow. In *Discover the Sonoran Desert* he read: 'If, in the night, you feel something in your bed, lie very still and try to locate its exact position. Then, quick as a flash, and all in one movement, swipe it to the floor.' Every night, religiously, he flung back the sheets and blankets and shook them, then made the bed again. He didn't mind the bother. It felt good to establish habits. They made him feel that his life out here was taking shape, becoming as real as the one before.

He had been there no more than a week when he was first woken by the coyotes. Their ghostly howls were distant at first, but came closer and closer, until they sounded as if they were right outside his window, a full discordant choir, sent on behalf of a malevolent desert to serenade him. He gripped the top of his sheet and started concocting an unfeasibly acrobatic escape route in the event of their getting into the house – swinging himself out the window and on to the roof, agile as a monkey. But before long their barks were trailing off again, and he pictured them running as a pack with their noses and necks held low to the ground, bellies brushing the undergrowth and bushy tails sticking up in the air like flags for their young to follow. Later, he was to spot solitary coyotes at close range quite often – scavenging in the bins in the back yard, or frozen in the beam of his torch on the side of the track, their grey hair matted with dirt.

He came to dread the sound that they made. The way the thin howls echoed in the darkness, lonely and bereft, first here in the valley, and then, he imagined, rising up into the unhearing void above, rippling outwards in ever widening circles, through the Earth's atmosphere and beyond, to haunt darker and darker recesses of space. For ever and ever, Amen.

Jersey helped him equip his house by taking him to second-hand stores and garage sales. Theo filled his kitchen cupboards with chipped china bowls and imitation cut glass – things that had probably belonged to people who were now dead, he realised. Jersey even persuaded him to buy a large mattress for the spare room, just in case his Aunty Drew ever came to stay. Theo tried not to think what had happened on that.

On Wednesday afternoons Jersey collected him for a regular expedition to the Tucson mall. He seemed to like taking Theo along – perhaps because he found the prospect of choosing what to put in his fridge somewhat daunting by himself.

Not that Theo was any better at it. He spent most of the morning making a list, crossing out each item with a blunt pencil at least once before scribbling it in again. Traipsing from his bedroom to the bathroom to the kitchen and back to his bedroom again, he stared inside cupboards and into drawers in an effort to jog his memory. He even found himself standing at the door of the empty second bedroom as if he might find the answers in there. The truth was, it had always been his mother who did the shopping. There were the obvious staples, of course – bread and cheese; milk for his porridge, which he bought by the gallon and kept in the freezer, remembering to take it out the night before to defrost; frozen chips, frozen peas and toilet paper. But after that it got more difficult. The pork pies wrapped in paper that he was used to having for his lunch with a dollop of English mustard on the side didn't seem to be available over here. Nor was the Ambrosia tinned rice pudding that he and his mother had liked to eat with a teaspoonful of raspberry jam on top. Little by little he discovered some alternatives – pecan and treacle and blueberry tarts, and the pot chicken that was made for two, and therefore just the right size to allow for a second helping.

What he found hardest to get to grips with were the non-food items – soap, washing-up cloths, that sort of thing. All the brands were unfamiliar and he had no idea which ones to choose. The question of household cleaners stymied him every time. What sort of cleaner did he need for what? Could you use the same cleaner for the bath as the bathroom floor? Did you have to use a different cleaner in the kitchen from the one you used in the bathroom? He usually ended up buying a bottle of bleach to cover the lot and for the first year his mobile home smelled like a newly disinfected hospital ward.

Usually he slipped the shopping list into his pocket and, once they'd arrived, forgot it was there. The mall was full of distractions – huge and white and endless, filled with every type of shop you could imagine, and with an electric piano version of *The Planets* blaring out over the speakers, sharp and crackly at the edges like the 78s they used to play at home. He hurried after Jersey's purposeful stride, wishing he dared ask to stop and look.

The supermarket itself was both familiar and unfamiliar. He wandered up and down the aisles feeling comforted one minute, disorientated the next.

He bumped into Jersey in the frozen foods aisle.

—Best place to head for in this heat, I reckon, yes siree.

—Oh, yes. Absolutely.

—Anything special you seen this afternoon? Jersey's expression was a little sheepish. He was curious to see what was in Theo's trolley, but seemed reluctant to let Theo scrutinise his own. There wasn't much to hide: a big-value pack of pork sausages, another of white soft buns, a couple of tubes of mustard. Several six-packs of beer.

—I'm trying to find a shoulder of lamb. I thought I might have a go at roasting it on Sunday.

—That a fact, said Jersey, nodding slowly, running a large hand over his uneven face. Well, I'll meet you at the check-out in fifteen, if that suits.

—Yes. Fine. See you then.

Coming home from these expeditions, Theo took his time to unpack his purchases and find a home for them in his cupboards. He liked to linger over the sense of security he got from knowing he had a plentiful supply of biscuits in his tins. He took so long arranging and rearranging the packets in his freezer that his fingers grew numb and afterwards he had to thaw them out around a cup of tea. From his pocket he fished out the little squares of coloured paper that he had been handed as he walked through the mall:

Earn $$$
while losing weight
NO SELF-DISCIPLINE REQUIRED!
5 more people needed for our free trial
WE pay YOU to lose 10-100lbs
• Dr Recommended
• No cravings
• No appetite
800-970-8643

said one. Another,

WE NEED
100 people to try our new all-natural
botanical herbal skin-care
routine. 100% biodegradable. Absolutely No
Animal Testing. No Children.
405-843-9349

They were like messages from the real world. Tucson, the city, where people lived normal lives, went out to work in the morning and came back at half past five. Suddenly his mind was alive with fanciful notions of what might happen if he were to respond – the people he would meet, the weekly monitoring sessions. It might lead to a full-time job. But then he stopped himself. He'd come out here to do exactly what he wanted, not what somebody else told him to do.

—Can try your hand at ranchin', if you like, Jersey had offered, trying to be helpful. Right now it's just me and a few hundred head, and I'm used to a couple thousand, so I don't need no help with them. But the boss sure could use some help on the financial side of things, if you're any good at math. Each year he sells off a few sections to people like yourself – if he's got a bit of capital he builds a house, if he ain't he just sells the land as is – and his wife Elise puts the profit in her purse and trots off with it downtown. She's a lovely lady, Elise, but damn it if he's got a handle on her. She don't dress western when she goes out. She dresses *fancy*. She told me once he's like a bull in bed, goes at her at a charge, and the violence has wearied her out. That's why she needs a break from time to time. Says why don't he put a stamp on her rump same as the steer, might as well, she won't be mistaken for anybody else's after that, and he can stop his jealous bleating. Can you imagine, R.d.S. big and black and steaming across her sweet wet ass? Just think of it, the shock a man would have pulling her panties off. If you'll excuse my imagination, Mr Moon.

It was the longest speech Theo had ever heard him make. He

stared at Jersey, wondering at the unexpected passion behind those frank blue eyes. He coughed and brought the subject roundly back to himself.

—Well, it's very nice of you to ask, but I'm not actually very good with figures. I was thinking of something a little more, you know, *creative*.

Jersey wiped the moisture from his mouth, struggling to compose himself.

—You wanna be creative?

Theo nodded.

—Well, I'll be damned, Jersey chuckled, scratching at the bristles on his cheek.

He did the heavy digging in the evenings, when it was cooler, often finding himself surprised by nightfall, suddenly unable to see the bottom of his hole. Jersey had lent him a pickaxe to get through the three-foot layer of caliche that lay hidden beneath the soil, like the cement foundations of phantom houses that had never been built. When the hole was big enough, he lowered himself into it, and had to use a chisel and a crowbar instead, there not being room to get a swing on the axe.

For the desert willows he dug holes five foot square, emptied in a sackful of steer manure, followed by precisely measured amounts of ammonium phosphate and soil sulphur, as directed in *Make the Desert Bloom!*

'Don't criticise your plants when they fail to perform as expected,' he read. 'The desert is a difficult place to live, as you know from your own experience. It may be that your plant was pot-bound when you bought it from the nursery. It may be that the site you have chosen is too exposed to the wind, the heat or even the cold. Each plant is different, and has its own genetic tendencies, just like people. Criticism will only make things worse.'

The passage had touched something in Theo. As he trawled back and forth with his watering can he made a mental note to appreciate his plants however badly they fared. He would love them all, the big ones and the small ones, the natives and the exotics, and they would love him back.

But his fantasy was cut short when he opened the book again in bed that night. 'Don't expect your plants to love you,' he read. 'Remember that plants don't think. They simply do what they have to do. You can't change their behaviour. All you can do is to provide them with the best conditions to enable their personalities to thrive. Then they will give their best performance – for themselves, and not for you.'

Suitably chastised, Theo slipped the cover in to act as a bookmark and settled down to sleep with the smell of manure still trapped between the hairs of his nose.

At first, he lay with his eyes and ears straining in the darkness, not daring to move in case he missed a rustle or a squeak. The slightest noise gave him the jitters – the whimpering of an owl or even the little thud of a hawk moth flying into his window pane. He grew so tired of trying to decipher each noise that he found himself yearning for the mind-numbing revving of cars, the exhaust farts of the buses, even the *beep-beep-beep* of the pedestrian crossing outside the house on Bellissima Street. The sound of a human scream could go unnoticed amidst all that.

But one day in late October, just over three months since he'd arrived, he realised quite suddenly that he was sleeping more deeply than he ever had in his life. He woke feeling extraordinarily alert, scraped clean like a new potato. He got up the minute he opened his eyes, and when his spirits were really high, he gargled his morning urine instead of knocking it back in one go, even adding a tune – 'The Hills are Alive with the Sound of Music', or 'Somewhere Over the Rainbow'. As he wiped the dribbles from his chin, he beamed at his magnified reflection in the shaving mirror.

He soon developed a routine, finding it helpful to apportion different tasks to different hours of the day. Yoga first thing, as early as possible, followed by a hearty breakfast of porridge and a couple of pieces of French toast, sometimes with bacon and marmalade – a combination he'd always liked and which, at last, there was nobody to tease him about. A couple of chocolate biscuits to round it off. After that he tended his garden.

He stopped for lunch at 12.30 on the dot, dropping his hoe or his trowel abruptly, as if someone had called to him from the house. The midday meal usually consisted of a double open sandwich – two separate slices of bread on top of which he spread and piled as much as he could without anything toppling off. That was the challenge, at least. Afterwards, he liked to take a nap to allow his internal organs to devote their full attention to the job of digestion. He slung up a hammock between two posts cemented into the ground by Jersey, and hoisted a white sheet overhead to protect himself from the sun.

He did not fall deeply asleep in his hammock; it was more a case of skimming the surface, lolling in that layer of semi-consciousness where dreams can be controlled. He liked it better that way. He chose which dream to have, allowed it to take him somewhere, then rolled over to shake it off if he didn't like the direction it was going. Between dreams he came up for air, his vision mingling with the red undersides of his eyelids, which deepened and paled with the play of sunlight through the sheet.

Often his dreams took him back to his school days. It was as if, having removed himself from his former life, he was now in a position to review it. As he tucked himself up to his old wooden desk, his bare thighs squeezed painfully between the chair and the desk frame, his head filled with the smell of pencil shavings and the stale blue ink that stained the grooves gouged out with a compass. *Mr Nibbs wanks under his desk. I screwed Dawn. Theobald Moon stinks.* Before him, he saw the blue-squared maths book in which he used to doodle, using the squares as a template. There, in the margins, were tiny, intricate castles, tall and slender with a profusion of needle-sharp spires and slit windows, often surrounded by forests. Sometimes a face peered sadly from behind a barred window, or a cloaked figure on horseback galloped over the drawbridge, or someone would be scaling a rope down the sheer wall of a turret. In the distance the mountains were pointed and capped with snow. *You and your little games*, his mother would say dismissively, whenever she found any of his drawings at home. She never really approved of anything that didn't involve her. *Come and help me in the kitchen, if you're so bored.*

Sometimes, his wandering mind went back further still, and a sudden blast of sound assaulted his ears – thirty descant recorders shrieking out the scale of C major, each note teetering like a seagull on a cliff. He was sitting cross-legged on the music-room floor, spittle dripping on to his bare knees. A sharp voice almost like a recorder itself — *C, D, E, F. No, someone's playing F sharp. Who is it? Who's the culprit?* His uncoordinated fingers wavering in panic above the holes, little round circles like fairy rings pressed into the soft pads of his fingertips.

At three or four in the afternoon, he would rouse himself from these mental excursions and take himself on a physical one. The aim was to walk a little further every day. The click of the garden fence reverberated behind him and he felt a tickle of anxiety as he looked out at the vast open plain before him. 'Never go anywhere without your snake-bite kit,' he had read in *Discover the Sonoran Desert*. 'This should consist of a razor blade, a suction cup and a tourniquet. Always carry plenty of water – and drink it! It does you no good in your canteen. Wear heavy, loose-fitting boots and thick socks. If you are very nervous, wear thick gloves as well. And don't hike alone. If you must, tell someone of your trip plans.'

Feeling slightly sorry for himself that he not only had no one to hike with, but no one to tell his plans to, he took extra care to kit himself out properly. He slung a flask of water round his neck and shoved a supply of sweets into his pocket. Despite the fact that he had no telephone, he had diligently copied out the Poisonous Animals Helpline number and stuck it to the door of his fridge. 'And always keep an ear out for the buzz of a rattler. You'll know it when you hear it.' In the first few months he heard it everywhere – in the wind disturbing the branches of a mesquite tree, in a pebble dislodging beneath his foot, in the rustle of a cicada. But gradually he learnt to identify the noises for what they were, and to keep himself calm.

At first he never wandered out of sight of his house. It was as if he were held on reins, and he turned back as soon as he felt a tugging on his ribcage. It would be easy enough for him to lose his bearings out here. But as the weeks and the months went by he got to know a few trails and even created new ones of his own. No longer preoccupied solely with finding his way back, he became more aware of his surroundings. He headed for high places so that he could stand on top and cast his eyes round in a 360° sweep. He became familiar with the pattern of the plants growing on the valley floor – how the larger species, such as the saguaros, were spaced at regular intervals, each one guarding the minimum radius it needed to survive with fistfuls of spines; and how the smaller cacti grew in their shelter, benefiting from the cool of their shadows and the occasional drop of stalled moisture. He learnt to identify the little hoof marks of javelinas, the wild, bristle-backed pigs that he hadn't yet seen, but whose grunts he had heard in the night. He stepped over the lacy skeletons of dead cholla branches, resisting the urge to pick them up in case something nasty was hiding inside. Once he found the narrow-jawed skull and ribcage of an animal with horns – presumably a desert bighorn that had wandered down off the mountains. It was picked clean by vultures and ants to the polish of ivory.

On these occasions he rarely saw another human being, although there were plenty of tell-tale tracks – charred remains of barbecue fires, empty drink cans and cigarette packets, little squares of toilet paper neatly folded and poked between the twiggy branches of a creosote bush. When he asked himself which he'd rather meet – a wild animal or a human being – he found himself opting for the former. He had come to believe he could trust his instincts in a confrontation with an animal – just as the animal itself would do. With a human being, instincts were not enough. Their behaviour was too complicated, too unpredictable for that.

At five o'clock every day the light became magical: low and soft and sweeping in golden swathes over the valley floor. For the next hour, the desert was infused with a warmth and softness that was quite at odds with its usual character. Lit from behind, each saguaro and stem of cholla cacti became outlined with a brilliant, effervescent halo, as if strung with white neon. The sight was so beautiful, it took Theo's breath away.

But the lowering sun was also a signal that it was time to head for home. He didn't want to get caught out by darkness and besides, his mother had always insisted on half past six tea, and he wasn't ready to override her on that one just yet.

Sometimes, Theobald would sit down to eat at the kitchen table, his knife and fork and spoon marking out a little square, a glass of water at the ready, and realise with a shock that he was completely alone. That there was no one over the other side of the table. Nor would there be tomorrow, or the next day. It was just him and the four thin walls of his mobile home.

While he ate, he found himself giving the objects around him much more attention than they warranted. The ladles he'd hung on the wall and which he never used; the strip of chillies that the rancher's wife, Elise, had sent over to him as a house-warming present; the little pocket radio that emitted more fuzz than music.

He turned the radio on.

'Next! Learn why life is worth living, even when you're not! Heaven Help Us, coming up next on Channel 13.'

He turned it off and wondered instead, for the hundredth time, what he could do about the smell of butane that stuck at the back of his nose and seemed to flavour each mouthful of dinner with a little dash of chemical sauce every time he swallowed. He stared at his napkin. It was dirty – a smear of ketchup from another meal in one corner. For a whole minute he continued to stare at it, wondering if it was dirty enough to change, or whether he should make it last the week.

A rattle of a breeze at the front door made him look up. For a moment, he tried to picture his mother letting herself in, stopping to pat her hand to her mountainous hair in front of an invisible mirror, and then shuffle off towards the spare bedroom with her handbag. *It's on the table!* he wanted to shout, as if the sound of his voice might induce her to materialise. *Your favourite – steak and chips!* He was tempted to have a conversation with her anyway, filling in her lines himself, but he thought he might frighten himself.

One evening, without thinking too much about it, he suddenly gathered up his dinner and took it outside. He stood a chair in the middle of the garden, spread a napkin on his lap and arched his feet on tiptoe so that his thighs formed a flat surface for the plate. As he chewed he looked out towards the purple mountains that rose up so abruptly from the plain, his eye muscles enjoying the stretch to the horizon. He attention was drawn by a pair of white-winged doves hopping silently along the posts of his fence. The squeak of his knife sawing against the enamel prompted one of them to fly off, and the other followed, but a few seconds later they were back. He listened to the friendly witterings of the cactus wrens playing in the branches of the mesquite trees, over by the well. A sudden playful breeze spun the blades of the water pump, and then reached him, fluffing up his crest of tawny hair. Theo tipped his head to one side in acknowledgement. When a few chips fell off the edge of his plate he left them on the ground for the ants to carry away on their shoulders – his gift to the inhabitants of his garden. He would never feel lonely out here.

He prepared flower beds either side of his front door. He made them three feet wide and twelve inches deep and filled them with Super Compost from Pleasant Desert. The soft black soil felt so good between his fingers that, for a moment, with his hands plunged in deep, he felt a wave of nostalgia for the squelchy earth of the garden in Clapham and even for the tight square of lawn covered in little mud mountains excreted by the worms. With a little stab of regret, he recalled the straggly rose bushes which tried to grab at you with their thorns when you walked by. Even the damp pile of bricks and roof tiles which had for as long as he could remember been stacked in the corner by the fence, waiting for that far-off day when they might be needed for repairs to the house, and in the meantime growing moss and white lichen and running with earwigs and wood lice as soon as you lifted them up. All of a sudden the smell of drizzly, woody, sodden-earthed England flooded his nose and he was filled with an almost unbearable surge of grief.

When the seeds arrived he pressed each one into a foam container full of compost, and lined them up on every window sill in the house. Within a fortnight the spindly green shoots were ready to plant out. Theo marvelled at the sight of them, so dramatic in colour and yet so fragile against the big black clods of soil. He gave them several good sprinklings with his watering can, fingered them gently as if to reassure them that he was there, then whispered goodnight and went to bed.

They didn't even make it through the night. Somehow aware of what had happened, he woke with a sense of foreboding in his stomach, and rushed out to find his worst fears realised.

It was a scene of devastation. The flower beds were a churned-up mess of pointed hoof-marks, and the skirting boards of his house were muddied with the smears of greedy snouts. On the far side of the garden one of the gate posts was broken. Theo felt as if he himself had been attacked, set upon by a crowd of bullies in the school playground, and a lump formed in his throat like a mouthful of Cheddar cheese that wouldn't go down.

He didn't often give in to the urge to cry. Generally he recognised the signs in time and blinked back the tears that prickled in his eyes, swallowed hard and made himself think about something else. *Think about going on holiday!* his mother used to say, despite the fact that the only place they ever went to was Aunty Drew's in Bookham, and that was hardly an antidote to tears.

But today, for the first time since he had arrived in Arizona, he succumbed. Just a little splurge, he told himself, except that once he had given himself the green light, so to speak, it came in an overwhelming, caterwauling barrage. *Holy Moses*, he thought, part of him stepping back from the great, heaving, sobbing mass of himself that sat down heavily on the step and buried its face in its hands, and looking on. *I never knew you had* that *inside*.

Struggling for breath between sobs, he went into the bathroom and tugged off a few sheets of toilet paper. He blew his nose so hard that the tissue tore in two and he was left with yellowish threads of snot weaving between his fingers. It wasn't so much that his seedlings were gone – he could cope with not having roses and geraniums – but that he had been *rebuffed*. After all the feelings of warmth he'd bestowed on it, the desert had responded with a two-fingered sign. He flushed the tissue down the toilet, used his sleeve for the last bit, and went back outside. He paused for a while on the doorstep, looking for consolation, then walked over to the slab of granite at the bottom near the fence. Already, he had developed a special fondness for this solid mound of rock that sat there and didn't move, that didn't change from day to day. It was something he could rely on. He climbed on top, letting his legs dangle heavily down one side, and took a few yogic breaths – *in, out, in, out, close left nostril with left finger, in, release nostril, out*.

What he had to do was learn not to take it so personally. It wasn't as if the desert had anything *against* him. His seedlings had simply provided a delightful midnight feast to a pack of hungry javelinas, who no doubt could hardly believe their luck at finding such a tender green harvest at this time of year. They had probably thanked him profusely with gleeful honks and snorts as they snuffled and munched their way round his beds. What he had to understand was that it was a free-for-all out here. They were just wild creatures helping themselves to an unexpected meal – and who could blame them for that?

Survival of the fittest: that was the crux of it. To thrive in this place, he had to hold his own. And if he wanted to keep out the javelinas, he would simply have to reconsider his fortifications.

It was only when he remembered that he hadn't yet emptied his bladder that he knew what he would do. The emotional outburst had exhausted him, and he perched on the edge of his bed to fill the glass. He carried it, still steaming, into the kitchen and decanted it into a Tupperware basin. From their hook on the wall, he lifted down Elise's string of red chillies and, taking a sharp knife, carefully made a slit down the centre of one and prized it open, like a jacket. Its tang filled the air and made his eyes smart. He scraped the contents into the basin, working carefully so as not to waste a single seed, and chopped the flesh itself into strips. One by one he worked his way through the entire bunch and threw the discarded stalk into the bin. Without thinking, he wiped the sheen of sweat from the top of his lip with his finger and gave himself a burning moustache.

Theo surveyed the little white seeds and cusps of red floating prettily in the pool of yellow. A smile tugged at the edges of his stinging mouth. He felt like a wizard, concocting a new potion. He opened the door of his condiment cupboard and scanned it for possible ingredients. Tabasco sauce, curry powder, powdered Coleman's mustard, a plastic squeezy lemon, white wine vinegar. He poured and spooned in generous amounts of anything tangy and gave the whole mixture a quick whizz in the food processor. He lifted a frothy spoonful to his nose. Involuntarily, his face twisted to one side, and his nostrils flared to a point. It had a definite kick.

When he sauntered down the steps, the dangerous mixture swilling between his hands, Theobald Moon felt a sense of imminent power. He could have sworn the garden was watching him – the saguaros and even the mesquite trees, over by the well, eyeing him suspiciously. And they had reason to. He tipped the mixture into his watering can and, fixing the cauliflower head attachment so that it would spray evenly, walked around the perimeter of his land dousing the top of the fence. It dribbled down the sides and soaked into the ground.

When he had run out, he went back inside and drank three glasses of water in quick succession, in preparation for another batch. As he stood at the kitchen sink, a movement caught his eye. He looked up to see a ginger tom-cat with a torn ear that belonged to one of his neighbours leap on to the fence, freeze in stiff-haired terror as it was hit with the odour of the creature whose territory it had inadvertently invaded, and hurl itself back the way it had come.

He was not bothered by javelinas after that.

In the night, Theo woke abruptly with a bladder fit to burst. Not surprising, really, given the number of cups of tea and glasses of water he'd consumed that day. In his semi-conscious state, it didn't occur to him to use the toilet in his house; somehow he thought only of depositing his urine on his land. Pushing his bare feet into his Oxfords, he stumbled down the little wooden steps and out into the night.

There was a full moon, and the landscape was lit with an eerie, greenish tinge. The saguaros stood sentry as black silhouettes against the sky. Theo lurched down the wooden steps and struck out towards the garden fence. Halfway there he couldn't wait any longer and yanked at the drawstring of his pyjama bottoms, letting them fall around his ankles, and unveiling the pale ovals of his buttocks to the night. He wriggled his penis, shrivelled and tiny in the cold air, and aimed it at the ground, a little distance from his feet.

For an agonising few seconds nothing happened. He had kept it in for so long it didn't want to come out. There was a slight dribble and then – *ah!* the delicious warm gush rushing through and splashing against the ground, pummelling the dry grit. It spread in a puddle on the hard-baked ground, trickling back perilously close to his feet. But he didn't care. His bladder thumped with relief, the pain reaching its climax a few seconds after he started, then gradually easing off.

From behind him, the cool air slapped its wide, flat tongue against his buttocks, squeezed its way into the crack, and curled around his perineum towards his balls. Theo began to feel aroused. He looked up at the sky, laid out like a black robe studded with diamonds. How beautiful it looked! All of a sudden, he felt quite overwhelmed. Not with fear, but with a sensation of wonder – and of what he could only describe as *oneness*. Oneness with the sky, the stars, the night itself. All day he had been marking his territory with his scent and now he felt as if he *belonged*. He was part and parcel of the beauty around him. He was no different to any of the other creatures – the bighorns, the diamond-back rattlers, the coyotes, even the lions and bears that were supposed to be up there roaming the forested peaks of the mountains.

He looked up at the moon, round and perfect above him. Before his eyes, the yellowish hollows and mounds on its surface rearranged themselves into eyes, nose and mouth, the features of the man in the moon, his namesake. How he loved that moon! It had followed him all the way from Clapham Common, London, and now at last he felt united with it; brothers in the same universe. He gave it a con- spiratorial wink.

Elation reached into Theobald's throat and before he knew what he was doing, he found himself filling his lungs with the cold night air – filling them so that his chest rose up – and letting it out as a howl. It was not the howl of a wolf, or a coyote, but his own peculiar howl, a sound that took shape instinctively in his throat.

—*Yaaooooh. Yaooooooooooooh.*

The sound billowed out, clear and perfect and strong. It travelled over the flat plain and all the way to the mountains, and then it curled back, the softer echo flooding the desert floor like a liquid, seeping into the rocks and the ground, into the desert's memory, becoming a part of the eternal catalogue of sound and shape and colour, taking its place in the line of what had come before, what would come after. He waited for it to die away, enthralled, and then he howled again, louder this time, sending out the instinctive animal nature from the very bottom of his stomach, his heaving breast, his ever-yearning soul, calling out to the universe around him, making his presence felt.

Suddenly, from somewhere behind him, perhaps as close as the rubbish bins behind the house, there came an answering call, the frightened yapping of a young coyote, like a finger rubbed on a pane of glass.

Theo jumped, suddenly aware that he had his trousers down. Shaking the last drops from his shrunken penis, he hurriedly pulled his pyjama bottoms up and scrabbled around for the drawstring. For some reason he could only find one end of it. In his panic, he yanked too hard and the lost end promptly disappeared inside the waist band. Damn and blast! It was such a fiddly job to get it back out. Vaguely he remembered his mother teaching him some trick involving a safety pin, but that wasn't much use to him now.

And then, quite suddenly, he stopped himself. He stood still, attempting to regain control of his frantic breathing. He remembered the lessons he'd learnt in yoga: letting the ribcage expand, the abdomen relax. It occurred to him that he didn't necessarily need to be afraid; that he didn't have to run away. Why should he be afraid of that creature yapping behind the house if – and it was a tentative *if* at first – that creature was more afraid of him?

As the idea took hold, a smile began to play around Theobald's soft red mouth.

Because it was true: he had scared the coyote. And why shouldn't he? He had his place in the pecking order, too. There were the wrens, the woodpeckers, the snakes, the spiders, the scorpions, the javelinas, the bighorns, and there was Theobald Moon. The Englishman. All twenty-two stone of him. One of the more magnificent creatures to be found in the Sonoran Desert, by all accounts.

Rolling his shoulders back, much as he had seen Jersey do, Theobald bunched the excess pyjama fabric in his fist, bowed solemnly to the moon, and walked with great dignity back to his house.

6

In the evenings when it's cold we light the butane heater and surround ourselves with cushions and blankets, put on the toadstool nightlight from my bedroom and huddle in its reddy glow. My father wears his Afghan jumper and dishes out two big dollops of steamed suet pudding with lemon inside, and he tells me everything he knows.

—First, says my father, there was nothing. And then there was an almighty BANG called the Big Bang when a cluster of stars exploded in space and each little fragment was an atom of hydrogen or carbon or oxygen and the fragments rained down and some of them collided and stuck together and became the Sun and the Moon and the Earth. And the Sun shone on the Earth and heated it up until the atoms began to bubble and squirt like bolognese sauce in a pan and this went on for several millennia until one day one of the bubbles was cooked and became an amoeba.

—What's an amoeba?

—Don't worry about that right now. What's important are the implications of what I've just described.

—The *implications*?

—Yes! Don't you see what it means?

I shake my head.

—It means we're made of star dust, Sugar Pie! Isn't that a thought?

I consider this for a while.

—But what happened to the amoeba?

My father looks at me, disappointed.

—Well, after several more millennia had passed, the amoebas grew into fish and birds and snakes and tigers and monkeys and the monkeys grew into men and women and you and me. And when your children have children and their children have children and all of us have lived and died and been written about in the history books, and a long time still after that, the universe will find that it has expanded to capacity and cannot expand any more. And so the elastic snaps, gravity sucks in on itself, and there is an almighty CRUNCH called the Big Crunch, where everything is gulped back down and disappears like dirty washing-up water down the kitchen sink.

He stops, a little breathless. Everything swims giddily in the glow of the nightlight.

—Then what?

—Then nothing. That's the end. *Finito*. Curtains. End of story.

—Well, if it's back to nothing again, maybe there'll be another Big Bang?

—Well, yes, Sugar Pie, you're not the first person to suggest that. That there have been a hundred million Big Bangs already and there are a hundred million still to come.

—Big Bangs banging on for ever and ever—

—Yes, that's right, he says softly. Bang bang.

When it gets really cold he lets me inside his Afghan jumper too, our heads poking out together at the top. We each have second helpings of suet pudding and wipe out the bowl with our fingers.

—Your grandmother used to make this. For Sunday lunch.

—Was she a cook too?

—In a manner of speaking, yes. She made a lot of things. The best shortbread you ever tasted. Blackberry and apple crumble. Lemon meringue pie. And treacle tart. Her tarts won first prize at the Horticultural Society's Autumn Show.

—Why don't you make treacle tart?

My father pulls my hair away where it's stuck to a smear on my cheek.

—To tell the truth, Sugar Pie, I quite like the ones in the supermarket.

—Well, why don't you make treacle tart ice-cream, then?

—That's a very good idea. But at the moment I'm a bit stuck on the butterscotch. Can't seem to get it to gel.

I study my father's frowning face for a while before deciding to speak. The whorl of his ear is shiny like plastic on the inside.

—I don't like it.

—What? The butterscotch ice-cream?

I shake my head.

—Not even the new batch?

I shake my head again.

—What's wrong with it?

—It's runny.

—Well, that's just a technical point, Sugar. Easily ironed out. Just a matter of time. It's the taste that matters.

—I don't think it tastes very nice either.

—Really? Is that what you think?

Without ceremony, he pushes my head back down inside his jumper, suffocating me for a moment before I come out the other end. He gets off our cushion and I hear the soft crunch of the freezer lid opening, the little blast of arctic air. A few minutes later he presents me with a dish of half-melted ice-cream, a leaning fork staked in the middle, like the flag on the summit of a mountain.

—Try that.

I look at him plaintively.

—I'm full up.

—Nonsense. There's always room for ice-cream. It doesn't exactly take up much space.

The fork comes to my rescue. It topples in slow motion, flicking a large prongful of ice-cream on to the floor as it goes. My father looks at the spilled dollop for a moment, then scoops it up with his finger and puts it in his mouth. He chews, thoughtfully.

—I agree, he says at last. It's not very nice.

He shoves the plate away, as if he can't bear to be sitting too close to it.

—It doesn't matter, I say, tentatively. You can always try again.

He looks at me, and starts to nod.

—You're right, Sugar. That's what my mother used to say. If at first you don't succeed—

He tails off, looking lost. I take hold of his soft hand, still sticky from the ice-cream, interlace the fingers with my own and give it a squeeze.

Every day my father and I go on our rounds. When he picks up his watering can, I pick up mine and we water alternate plants along the bed. When he stoops to finger the waxy, yellow petals of the barrel cacti blossom, or peers through a hole in the hollowed stalk of the giant saguaro to see what it looks like inside, or adjusts a stone with his foot, or wipes the sweat from his forehead with the sleeve of his shirt or scratches at his groin with his fingers, I do those things too. I follow him into the bathroom and perch on the edge of the bath and talk to him while he does his business there, and when he's finished and climbs into the hammock for a nap, I climb in with him and lie with my head on the great heaving mound of his belly so that my head rises and falls like a boat at sea, and listen to the groans and splutterings going on inside.

Blabble blabble boom boom whine splutter erk.

I imagine the interior of my father's stomach to be fitted with shelves and cupboards like a kitchen, the food dropping down and re-arranging itself back into place – the candies plopping back into their jars, the cookies going back to the cookie tins.

—The desert, booms my father's voice, surprising me through the microphone of his belly, is a very dangerous place, Josephine. You must never forget that.

He says this in his serious, monotone voice.

—It is populated with deceitful and dangerous presences, all competing for survival.

He takes a bite of a ketchup sandwich, avoiding the crust round the edge.

—You've got to keep your wits about you.

I pat the front pocket of my smock.

—I've got some.

—Some what?

—Some wits.

—The fact is, he continues, chucking the uneaten crust of his sandwich on to the gravel, your biggest danger is yourself. I bet you didn't know that!

—Me?

—Oh yes. Did I ever read you the paragraph about the main cause of death in the desert?

A loud whinnying noise travels all the way down from his throat to his belly button. I stare at the surface of his skin. A few minutes later, a little fart comes out the other end.

—I think so.

—Well, let me read it to you again. You can't hear it too many times.

He holds the book up above his head.

—'Each year the desert claims lives. The main cause of death is not snake bites, as scaremongers would have us believe. It is their own stupidity.' Are you listening, Josephine?

I nod, my cheek on his belly.

—'Dehydration creeps up swiftly and silently in the dry desert air. Desert walkers have been known to drop suddenly, without feeling particularly thirsty, unaware of the desperate state their body is in. The single message here is: DRINK. Carry water at all times and take regular drinks from it. Every twenty minutes is a good guide.' Are you listening to this?

When he doesn't get a reply, he places his hand gently on my head and strokes my hair.

—Sugar Pie Mountain, he murmurs.

He thinks that I'm asleep.

—My little Shining Star. Have you any idea how precious you are?

My father might tell me things, about what to be scared of and what not to be, but he doesn't necessarily believe what he says himself. I know this because I saw him go pale with fright when Jersey told us he found a tarantula in the back of his truck and caught it in a yoghurt container, and then gave it a concussion when he hurled it on to the road. Sometimes, in the night, he wakes me up by shouting out to me, across the hallway – *Sugar! Jelly-O! Are you all right?* – and I know that the coyotes have been running past with their little scaredy-cat yelps. I shout back that I'm OK, and just as I'm drifting back off again he calls out, *Just checking!* and jolts me awake again. And sometimes, even during the day, I catch him at the kitchen table, not moving, just sitting stock still like he's seen something out there he wishes he hadn't.

Sometimes when my father is busy writing in his room, or stirring a batch of semi-frozen ice-cream in the kitchen, I sing myself to sleep. I only know six songs and I sing them all, one after the other, as if they were all one song.

—*There were ten in the bed and the little one said, roll over, roll over . . . Ging gang goolie goolie goolie goolie watcha, ging gang goo . . . But sometimes in the spring time and sometimes in the fall, I jump into my little bed with nothing on at all. That's the time you oughta see me . . . Dai-sy, Dai-sy, give me your answer do.*

I want my father to hear me, but at the same time I don't. When I know he's outside, in the garden, I sing as loudly as I can, hollering out the high notes, and sliding down the scales. But when I know he's in the kitchen, and I hear him taking down a mug for his hot chocolate and putting the water on to boil and letting the cupboards jump back on themselves with the magnets, my voice goes thin and wavery like the whine of a mosquito.

He never comes into my bedroom when I'm singing, or mentions it in the morning, but sometimes, very quietly, and in a meandering sort of way, like he hasn't decided whether to or not, except that he already is, I hear him joining in.

There are days in the summer when it's so hot you wish you could crawl down one of the holes in the ground and stay there for ever. Your legs stick to the chairs and you can't walk into the damp clothes hanging on the line because the clothes are bone dry already, and you can't receive a rush of air from the windmill, because the windmill isn't budging an inch.

—Pretend it's snowing, or howling a terrible gale, says my father, hovering longer than necessary over the open mouth of the freezer, and guiltily closing the lid when he sees me watching.

Outside, the air and everything in it refuses to stay still. The mountains jump and dodge all over the place. The flies climb over your face because they know you won't bother to brush them away. If you look at the sun directly, it climbs inside you, and suddenly there are two suns, stamped like gold coins on the backs of your eyes.

Now, looky here, hot day, don't you think you're being kinda demanding? Why d'you always have to be the centre of attention? Can't you go and be hot quietly in a corner by yourself?

It's especially bad when the swamp cooling breaks down and my father starts pouring chocolate chips into the tubs of Peppermint Toothpaste Refresher by mistake and then we have to spend an hour picking them out and there's still ten more tubs to go before the half-past-three pickup. At three o'clock my father takes to his bed and lies there naked and panting, saying it's a terrible thing to be an ice-cream man in Arizona and he's convinced he's going to die. When the old man from Miss Gail's comes by in his ice-cream van and says it's going like hot cakes in this heat and Peppermint Toothpaste Refresher is the runaway favourite and he hopes we've got our twenty tubs ready and can he pick up the same again tomorrow?, I take him around to the back of the house and show him my father through the bedroom window. The delivery man gives a low whistle between his teeth, and the next day another van comes down the drive with 'The Merry Mechanic' on the side. My father comes out with a sheet wrapped round him right up to his armpits like he's a man from Ancient Greece. He asks the Merry Mechanic in a grumpy voice if the rotten thing's malfunctioned again and the Merry Mechanic takes off his cap and wipes it round his neck and puts it back on and says in an even grumpier voice than my father's that it hasn't mal anything much at all, as far as he can see, because it didn't look like it functioned in the first place, and why don't we try opening the windows. He scribbles the price down on a piece of paper and tears it off and gives it to my father, and then he looks at his watch and says that he'll see us again in three weeks, maybe four, because of the great demand.

Even worse than the hot days are the sick days. My mouth fills up with spit and I have to keep swallowing it down. Then my stomach heaves and I stop it coming and that's when I'm sick into the orange washing-up bowl on the floor beside my bed.

My father, hovering in the hallway, only comes in when he's sure I've finished. He holds a piece of toilet roll around my nose and tells me to blow.

—Here you are, Fruit Cake. This will make you better.

He holds out a spoon, alive and quivering with something thick and white. He has poured it from a bottle that's as blue as the blue jays. You'd think from the colour that it has something nice inside, but the blue is all a lie: what's inside is Milk of Magnesia, and I'm not letting it in.

I shake my head at him fiercely.

—Now now, Sugar Pie. I'll have none of that. The thing to do is to pretend it's a spoonful of ice-cream.

—I don't like ice-cream, I say, quickly closing my mouth again.

—Don't be ridiculous. You've liked ice-cream since the day you were born.

I try to be sick again. I lean over and inhale the smell of the plastic washing-up bowl.

—Come on, Jelly-O, I can't wait around all day. I'm going to spill it on the floor in a minute.

We stare at each other, each competing to be the most fearsome, and the next thing is the spoon has disappeared inside my father's mouth. I watch, wide-eyed, as his lips purse tightly around the metal to get the thickness off. He swallows, then quickly swallows again, although he doesn't mean to this time, as if he's just doing it to keep from retching, and I can tell from the look in his eyes that he wishes straight away he hadn't done it at all. He puts the bottle down quickly, and thinks about what to do next.

—Well, I'll just leave it there, Sugar Pie.

He tries to clear his throat, the coating of white on it sludgy as paint.

—And you can help yourself if you feel any worse, he says, and beats a quick retreat.

Alone in my bed I play the alphabet game.

—Apple. Banana. Cherry. Damson. Elderberry. Fig. Grape. Hairy chestnut.

(That's cheatin', Josephine Moon.)

—Imaginary fruit. Josie's fruit. K-Mart fruit.

You cheat! You little cheat!

—Lovely fruit! Magnificent fruit!

I'm warnin' you, Josephine—

—Nectarine. Orange. Pear.

The advantage of being an only child is that you can make up the rules yourself. My father knows this, too, as he was one himself.

—What you must never forget, Cream Tea, is that I'm your ma and your pa and your sister and your brother, all rolled into one, he says.

When I'm feeling better we make a batch of chocolate crispies in crinkly paper cases. My father stands me on a stool at the kitchen worktop and I stir in cocoa and sugar with a spoon. We eat most of the mixture before it gets to the paper cases and by the time we've finished we haven't got any appetite left for tea.

Sometimes I wonder if I am the only real person and everyone else is pretend. Perhaps it's all an elaborate game laid on for my benefit, to make me feel as if I'm not alone after all. Perhaps my father, Jersey, the desert and the mountains are all scenery and actors and props and I, Josephine Moon, am the only real thing that exists.

I am standing on the top of the steps, one foot in the air, getting ready to land. But it does not land, or at least not yet, because the hugeness of this thought has brought everything else in my brain to a standstill, little stop signs springing up everywhere.

Woah there, mister, no instructions to moving feet beyond this point, we have a bigger thought coming down the tracks, and everything else has to make way to let it pass.

I decide the only thing for it is to come clean with my father and Jersey first thing in the morning.

Now looky here, I'll say. *You don't have to pretend any more. The secret's out, you blew it, go back to doing whatever it is you do.*

They'd act like they were astonished at first; look at me as if I was mad. But they'd soon realise that it was no use. I'd caught on; the game was up. They'd cough, embarrassed, and eye one another nervously, and then after a while they'd breathe a sigh of relief. Five years they'd been pretending – and what a thankless task! They'd get up, brush the waffle crumbs off their laps and take off their disguises, my father stepping out of his white shirt and trousers, leaving them in a crumpled heap on the floor, Jersey tossing his Lucky Strikes behind him, saying he never liked smoking them blasted things anyway. And they'd go right on back to wherever it was they came from, to whatever it was they were doing before I came along, not even bothering to say goodbye, nice knowing you, or being your father, or anything like that.

*

When Jersey comes, he tosses me over his shoulder and dangles me upside down until I scream. It's not because I'm frightened but because it's a surprise to find myself the wrong way up. The sweep of his arms is strong and I can feel all the muscles in his body connecting one to the other right down to his legs.

The cigarette between his dry lips wobbles as he speaks.

—Well, howdy Miss Moon, what are you doin' floating around with your feet in the air?

Sometimes he takes me out to the café on the reservation and we have two pieces of fried chicken and biscuit for a dollar. The old man who brings it to us says, Aren't you the lucky one with a pretty little thing like that? and Jersey holds up his beer and says, Oh she's a beauty, yes siree, and he gives me a wink and when the waiter's not looking he lets me have a swig. When we get home my father is waiting at the end of the drive looking red-faced and anxious and we jump out the truck and Jersey and my father hold one hand each and swing me down the drive, so high that I'm lifted clear off the ground, until my father complains that his shoulder is about to come out of its socket and he and Jersey have to swap sides.

One Saturday there's someone sitting beside him in the truck. My father and I watch in silence as she climbs out and sways on her long, thin legs as if she were made of pipe cleaners. Her hair is blond and bouncy and catches in the light like a web.

Jersey says, This here's Cindy, and looks at his feet, shuffling them together on the ground. My father mumbles something about Jersey having told him all about her after the party at Bill and Elise's, but then he looks at Jersey and stops halfway through. Cindy smiles, and says she's heard all about us too, especially me, and she shakes our hands as if we were very important and as soon as she does there's a sense of something special in the air, as if it's somebody's birthday, though it's not.

—Let me come and help you, she says to my father, who's already

81

on his way to get some refreshments from the house, but he calls back that he's quite all right and hurries on up the steps.

Cindy's teeth are big, like a horse's teeth. Jersey says you have to go to Texas to get teeth like that these days. From out of her bag Cindy pulls a pair of mufflers attached by a black band over the top and tells me that when she doesn't want to hear what Jersey says she puts these on. She fixes the band on me instead and all of a sudden there's a singing man inside my head.

—*I walk the line*, sings the man, *because you're mine*.

Cindy smiles and tucks my hair behind my ears with her fingers.

My father comes out with four little dishes of ice-cream with umbrellas in the top.

—It's got champagne in it, he says, and after he's handed one to Cindy he looks down at his feet, just like Jersey did.

When we've finished we all pile in the pickup together, Cindy and Jersey at the edges, my father and me in the middle. Cindy makes her own cigarettes, picking out pinchfuls of tobacco from an envelope. My father and I watch in silence. We've never seen anyone make their own cigarettes before. The top of my father's head brushes against the ceiling of the truck, and whenever Jersey can see a bump coming he shouts *Duck!* and my father has to stick his neck forward and then Jersey shouts, Did you see that? and we ask What? and he says, Why, that duck that keeps jumping out from behind a bush and scaring your father so much.

There is an excitable gleam in Jersey's eyes. He won't tell us where we're going. Perhaps we're going to see the prairie dogs that stand up on their hind legs when they see you coming and then fall over backwards, because Jersey told me once that after a while they remember that the world is round and that makes them lose their balance. *Maaay*be, says Jersey, rolling his cigarette from one end of his mouth to the other. Cindy smiles at him with her long Texan teeth and then her eyes drop down to where his hands are on the wheel, big and rough hands lined with dirt in the creases, and the smile changes shape, as if she can read the backs of those hands like some people read the palms, and I wonder what it is she sees in them.

Jersey swigs from green bottles when he's driving and Cindy doesn't like it when he throws an empty bottle out the window. She makes him pull over and she jumps out and picks it up where it's fallen on the shoulder and throws it in the back and sometimes it clanks against other bottles, as if this has happened lots of times before, and there are always bottles rolling around in the back. While we're waiting for her Jersey says she's got a mind of her own, this woman of his, and I wonder who hasn't got a mind of their own, and why he makes it sound like an awkward thing to have, when surely it would be far more trouble if she had to share a mind with somebody else.

Cindy says when she was my age she'd go and stay with her pa over in Death Valley and at night when the heat was real bad they'd throw a mattress into the back of a truck and drive into the mountains, five thousand feet above the valley floor where the air was cool and lovely, and there they'd sleep, out in the open and under the moon and the twinkling stars, listening to the whosh of the elf owls as they swooped down to land on some little creature to eat. In the morning they were woken by rabbits coming out to play. Her voice when she talks is thick as maple syrup. It tilts and rolls from one word to the next, like all the words have melted and joined together at the edges. Sometimes she gets stuck on one word and doesn't want to leave it behind, so that she keeps on making a sound, and sometimes it's a word, and sometimes it's just a sound, and sometimes it could even be a tune.

I fall asleep listening to Cindy, tucked inside the crook of my father's armpit, and we drive and drive and when we stop someone clutches me around the ribs and lets me down to the ground. I open my eyes and find myself in one of my father's fairytales. I turn round and round to see if I'm awake and Jersey nods and smiles and pushes me before him down a wooden path edged with jagged triangles of broken glass sticking out of the ground. All around me are bottles of every imaginable colour. They hang from the branches of the juniper trees – purple bottles, yellow bottles, red bottles, brown bottles – all sparkling and swaying in the sun. They are piled up into mountains and castles, they spill out of old bath tubs and they're stacked up against the house. There are turquoise bottles, green bottles, clear bottles. Some of them are strewn on the ground, with clumps of dry grass sprouting up in between. Some have dead insects inside, preserved as if in beautiful glass coffins. Chains of bottle necks that have been cracked clean off at the top swing in coloured loops along the fence. Topping a line of wooden stakes bleached white by the sun are upturned bottles the colour of blue jays, like a row of tall blue hats.

—I know what *those* had in them, I whisper to my father.

There's a shout and a man comes out of the house. He has a big strong face like Jersey's but his arms are gangly and long. He opens them wide, and runs towards us with a bend in his knees as if he is going to scoop us all up and shovel us into his mouth.

—My boy, my boy, he says to us all. There's a catch in his voice, like he's going to cry. He takes Jersey's face in his hands and kisses him on each cheek.

The man is Mr Kozinski. He unravels a yellow garden hose from its berth on the wall and turns on the tap. He gives me a wink, not just with his eye but with one whole side of his face.

—My boy, he liked doing this when he was a little critter like you.

He puts his thumb over the end of the hose, so that the water spurts out fast and furious and then he lets it shower down from on high, all over his glass garden, and the water runs down the sides of the bottles, washing the dust of the desert away, and the bottles swing and dance and light up like jewels in the sun, all running with water and glinting with light and beautiful with colour and the whole garden tinkling and swaying with the gentle clinking laughter of glass against glass.

Everybody says Ah! and claps, as if we are watching fireworks.

Mr Kozinski explains that every bottle in his garden used to have something in it. There are soda bottles, beer bottles, salad dressing bottles, medicine bottles. You can play the story game a hundred times over. I run around the garden in delight, picking out the bottles that I like the most and bringing them back to Mr Kozinski. He lifts me on to his lap.

—Sylmar Brand Olive Oil, he says loudly, as if he is making a public announcement. From the city of the angels, before they planted all the orange trees. And that? That is a glass conductor from the electricity pylons they took down in '49. There's Dr Coldwell's elixir was once in that. This pint jar here, you can read it, it says: Federal Law Forbids Sale or Reuse of this Bottle. See? Pure American whiskey, that was. 1950. Enjoyed every feckin' drop.

He lets me go so that I can fetch some more. Jersey and Cindy and my father stand around and watch. Jersey has his arm around Cindy's waist.

—An original Michelob from St Louis, Missouri. Hard to come by now. That? You don't know that? Original Heinz Ketchup bottle from Pennsylvania, 1916, is what it is. And that is Mrs Butterworth's Pancake Syrup bottle in the shape of delicious Mrs Butterworth herself.

Cindy turns and goes back to the truck and gets out some of Jersey's bottles and gives them to Mr Kozinski. She is taller than Mr Kozinski, and he looks up at her shyly and wonderingly, and his eyes glitter as if they too were stuck with little bits of glass.

—Coors, 1983. What a lucky son of a bitch is my boy, he says, looking her up and down as if she was the best bottle of the lot, and Cindy looks pleased and says she'll send their boy here if ever he needs reminding of that fact.

Jersey helps Mr Kozinski bring out his dining-room table and his dining-room chairs and we sit down amongst the dancing bottles. There's a cake shaped like a loaf of bread, which is hard and yellow inside. As Mr Kozinski saws it with a knife he asks Jersey how his cattle are, and Jersey says they're dumb 'n' ugly bitches, same as ever, and then Mr Kozinski asks Cindy if he's more respectful with her, he hopes he is, and Cindy says she's used to it because she works at the Wild Wild West on West Ina Road but that she's giving it up real soon because she's going to Vegas to work on the blackjack tables at the casino where her friend Mona works. Mr Kozinski says there ain't many cows in Vegas and what will his boy do there? Jersey frowns at him and Cindy says that cows ain't the only livelihood a man can get and she believes he'd make more money in a month out there than he makes now in a year and she looks at Jersey and he looks back at her and my father chokes on his glass of beer and everybody jumps up and runs round to slap him on the back.

—Who's going to Las Vegas?

—No one's going anywhere, Miss Josephine! cries Jersey, ruffling my hair with his hand. Don't you worry your sweet head 'bout that.

But Mr Kozinski leans over from the other side of the table and takes my face in his hands just like he did to Jersey and his thumbs are rough on my skin.

—When you grow up, he says, and become tall and shapely like this fine lady, one day you'll meet a boy and make his heart leap up into his throat like a jackrabbit and he will go all doolally, jus' like my boy here, and then that boy will follow you to the ends of the feckin' earth, oh yes he will, and he won't care about no feckin' cows no more, nor anything else but you.

Mr Kozinski looks at me hard with his dark, glittering eyes.

—And that's the way it should be. Because I believe that a man needs a woman and a woman needs a man, and when they find each other and the feeling is right, then nothing should stand in their way.

And at the end of this there's a silence and Jersey looks over his shoulder and shakes his head and my father stares down at his plate and Cindy smiles at Mr Kozinski so wide that I wonder if her Texan teeth will fall into her lap.

By the time we leave the bottle garden it's too late to drive all the way home so we stop for the night at El Vado's Motel. There are a row of adobe family cottages and we have one to ourselves. The motel keeper gives us a key with a large plastic tag and we open the door in the darkness. The others go in but I stay outside, where the breeze is up and I run round trying to cling on to everything that has happened, not wanting the day to end.

—Honey-chil', calls Cindy in her low, lilty voice, will you stop prancin' around out there and come to bed, and I'll read you somethin' or other from one of these goddamn books to send you to sleep.

So I go in and get undressed down to my knickers and vest and the sheets are tight across the bed. I squeeze in one half and Cindy gets in the other with her jeans still on. I put my head on her lap and her thighs are hard and the studs press into my scalp. When she reads, she reads the words but she's not listening to the story, and when she yawns she carries on reading, the words having to make their way around the yawn like they're making room for a balloon.

—Cindy, will you be my mother? I interrupt.

She snaps the book shut and tosses it on to the end of the bed.

—Well that's about the most ridiculous thing I've ever heard in my whole life. No one can replace your mother, honey-chil'.

—Why not?

—Well, for starters because your ma was to me what an orchid is to a dandelion, from what Jersey says. And besides, I ain't got plans to be anybody's mother for a while.

Outside the cars swish past on the road.

—What else does Jersey say about my mother?

She looks at me for a while, and strokes the side of my face.

—I don't know anything more about her, honey-chil'. Except that you must have got your dark hair and your prettiness from her, because it certainly ain't your father's. Have you ever seen a picture of her?

I shake my head in silence.

—Do you know what she was called?

I shake my head again.

—Well, I'll be darned.

From somewhere outside comes the faint sound of Jersey whistling. There are little pauses in the tune, where he takes a drag of his cigarette.

—Dad says I don't need a mother when I've got him.

—Well, maybe he's right. Lots of people only have either a ma or a pa. I didn't have much of a pa myself. My old man loved Death Valley more than he loved us kids, or so it seemed, if the amount of time he spent up there was anything to go by. He was Park Warden for twelve and a half years, used to travel up from Wichita Falls where we lived and not come back for months at a time. There were six of us, though it beats me how my mother ever managed to keep a-hold of him for long enough to get pregnant so many times. We was kind of noisy, an' he couldn't stand bein' around us all the time. He was a solitary man, loved his dog and the peace of the open spaces. A bit like Jersey, I guess.

—Is that why you like Jersey?

—You think I like Jersey, huh?

I wriggle round so that I'm looking up into her face. She's trying not to smile.

—He's an all right kind of guy as guys go, I suppose.

—I think he wants to marry you.

—Oh you do, do you, missy? And what makes you think he'd want to do a thing like that?

—Because he likes you more than his cows.

She laughs out loud then. —Well I guess I should be flattered by that, but only just. Now you shut your trap before I stick my boot in it. It's time to sleep.

She gives me a quick, firm kiss on the cheek and swings her long legs off the bed.

When you go somewhere with people, you don't talk to the place because you're too busy talking to the people. But when you go to a place by yourself, you can lie on the ground and feel the Earth beneath you and look at the bowl of the sky overhead and you're safe between the ground and the sky, as safe as if you were the yolk in the shell of an egg.

A place is like a person, it has a mood and a way of looking, and sometimes it's quiet, and sometimes it has a talk with you, like Mr Kozinski's bottle garden, all chattering and laughing, but even when it's quiet you can tell that it's there and that it's alive because when you lie down and put your ear against the ground and listen very hard, you can hear the beat of its heart.

Te dum. Te dum. Te dum.

It's not just the beat of its heart that you hear but other things too, the pitter-patter of tiny ants' feet, running up and down their tunnels, and the sleepy wrigglings of the snakes trying to get comfortable in their holes, and the shovel-shovel-shovel of the prairie dogs, whispering breathlessly to each other that eventually they'll reach the other side, because the Earth is round, they've heard – what a giddying thought! – and beneath all the noises of the busy creatures there's the silence of the rock, which is cold and stern and goes a long way down. And in the very middle, in the centre of the Earth, are huge churning rocks and fire and molten lava, like the insides of a volcano, and this is the heart of our star, which is the same as all the other stars in the universe, and it's here that the beat comes from. *Te dum. Te dum. Te dum.*

And what I think is that if we are made of star dust, as my father says we are, then we all have a bit of the heat of the stars in us, and the *te dum* which you hear in the ground is also your own *te dum*, because the one inside your head is an echo of the bigger *te dum* in the ground, and that is how we all stay alive, and how the moon and the stars and the planets and all the constellations in the universe stay alive, because we all share a bit of the same heart, taking our beat from the same source, all of us beating the same *te dum*.

7

There was no pattern to the way the blocks of flats were grouped together in the Kúpel'ný ostrov estate. The bald, white buildings, each eighteen windows up by eighteen across, stood at higgledy-piggledy angles to one another, like awkward guests at a party. They shared a central open space that was white in winter and green in summer. The morning sun caught the first block full on, and then brushed the corners of the others behind it, catching fewer and fewer of the windows until it missed the last block completely, leaving it permanently in the shade.

On days like today, when the white sky was thinning in places to reveal a layer of blue underneath, like a petticoat, the buildings were daubed with colour as washing was hung out to dry from plastic clothes-horses clamped within the window frames or protruding from the sills. Sometimes a vest or a pair of underpants fell, damp and heavy as a dead thing, landing with a muffled thud in the snow, and was not discovered until after the spring melt.

Buttoned up in her long coat, and with a red scarf wrapped round her head, Eva strode out to the middle of the communal area, put two fingers in her mouth and cut the freezing air with a wolf-whistle, the warm mist of her breath shooting out in two plumes like a visible manifestation of the whistle itself. Several hopeful heads bobbed out, eager to see the inspiration for such a sound, then bobbed back, unimpressed. A few seconds later, a second figure emerged from one of the blocks.

—I've told my mother I'm at your place.

—So have I.

They marched quickly through the town, heads down, as if they were simply on an errand to fetch the washing from the launderette. They passed the red-and-white-striped chimney, belching soot, the wrought-iron factory gates and the park with its giant shoe made of living flowers – turned into an icy white slipper at this time of year – and struck out along the lower Topol'čany road, towards Bošany. It was half past two, and they had less than an hour before dark.

They found the turn-off without any difficulty. It took them up gently at first, meandering through the trees, the surface rutted with hard-frozen tyre tracks, and then became steeper and narrower, zig-zagging back and forth. When they saw a light flickering and filtering through the spindly trunks, they left the path and headed straight towards it, grabbing at the trunks of the trees to haul themselves up. It was spruce forest up here, but the winter freeze was holding it in suspension, and the trees rose up like limbless bean poles in an attempt to claim their own small scrap of sky.

Suddenly they were confronted by the pale outline of the ice-cream van parked square ahead of them on the track. *'Zmrzlina!'* it announced in bright red lettering. The rear doors of the van were open, and they crept a little closer until they could see inside.

The ice-cream man, dressed in the same thin green jumper as before, was standing at a narrow worktop attempting, rather unsuccessfully, to slice a loaf of bread with the blade of a penknife, his oily hair swinging to and fro with the motion of his arm. In the orangey, flickering light, the interior of the van looked warm and cave-like. On the floor, around the ice-cream man's feet, was an untidy pile of blankets, strewn with the odd trouser leg and shirt sleeve, a few socks and pieces of underwear. Several books lay around the place with their pages splayed out face-down. On the worktop beside him was a single plate, a cup and a bottle of red wine with a cork in the top. Emanating from the whole vehicle was a sticky, sweet cloud, which settled on Eva's tongue when she breathed in through her mouth like a fine dusting of icing sugar.

But it was at the ice-cream man's feet that both of them found themselves staring – the choice of footwear being, inevitably, the first thing either of them noticed in a man. To their surprise, his feet were laced up in a brand new pair of climbing boots, the leather polished and hard. They were a Baťa design, from the latest menswear line, made for export only.

Tanya looked at Eva with something like reproach.

—*What?* hissed Eva, pretending not to know what she was thinking. She shifted from one foot to the other, uneasily.

—Look, perhaps we should go, she suggested. He's going to think we're after him.

—You *are* after him.

—I suppose we could say we were just passing.

—Oh, sure, like this is really on the way to somewhere.

—I wouldn't stand out there too long. There was a bear around earlier.

They stepped back, embarrassed. His black eyes darted out to them, flashing with amusement.

—I asked the bear to leave, but he hadn't had any visitors for a while either, so—

He shrugged and carried on battling with his crumbling loaf of bread. —*Shit.* You didn't happen to bring a knife with you, did you?

—No, but I brought you this.

Eva reached beneath her coat and unstrapped a jumper from around her waist. It was an old one of Julo's that she'd found at the back of his wardrobe. She stepped into the glow of the lamp and held it out. For a moment, looking at one another, they were confused, as if neither was able to take in anything else but the impact of the other's face. Then, wiping his palms on his trousers with the motion of someone used to wearing an apron, the ice-cream man took the jumper and put it on. The sleeves barely covered his elbows.

—That must be why Julo doesn't wear it any more.

—Oh, but it looks . . . it's really you, said Tanya, nodding.

Suddenly self-conscious to find himself the object of two such scrutinising pairs of eyes, the ice-cream man turned back inside his van.

—D'you want some wine? He tapped the cup upside down on the worktop. I'm afraid there's only one of everything. We'll have to share.

Eva parted the curtain of her curly fringe with one finger and took the cup with her other hand.

—*Nazdravie!*

—How the hell d'you keep warm up here? asked Tanya suddenly, flapping her arms across her chest.

—I build – *shit!*

He threw down the knife, jumped out the van and disappeared round the back. They heard him muttering to himself, the sound of flapping arms and stamping feet. He came back dangling a blackened piece of meat between two fingers and flung it on to the plate.

—I'd offer you some, but—

—What is it?

He laughed, and it came out as an undisciplined giggle, a little off-kilter. Eva smiled.

—It's steak. Sort of.

—I think I'll give it a miss.

—Me too.

—That's probably wise.

Taking two uneven wedges of bread, he made it into a sandwich, and twisted off a large mouthful, smiling down at them as he chewed. For a moment he looked a picture of perfect happiness. Then, as if remembering his social duties, he jerked his head to one side, jumped down and led them round the back.

The stamped-on remains of a small fire marked the centre of an area cleared of snow. The ice-cream man spread out a tarpaulin and motioned for them to sit down. Eva passed the cup of red wine to Tanya.

—You're my first guests. It's very nice of you to come.

—How long have you been here? asked Tanya.

—Not long.

—Don't you get cold? she asked again, evidently considering the fire to be too paltry to make a difference.

—I don't feel it too much.

—Where are you from?

He shrugged and took a bite of his sandwich, tearing at the meat. Tanya repeated her question.

He waved his hand unhelpfully in the air behind his head.

—Oh, I see. Over there.

—Give her some more wine, will you? he said to Eva.

An uneasiness dropped on the little group. The ice-cream man stared into the forest as he chewed. Eva opened her mouth, searching for a way to lighten the atmosphere.

—So. An ice-cream man, Tanya said loudly, clearly thinking that it was up to her to make the effort. Isn't it a bit unusual, selling ice-cream in winter?

—You're big on questions, aren't you? I'm an ice-cream man. It's what ice-cream men do. I haven't got anything else to sell. What am I supposed to do in winter? Hibernate?

Eva, renouncing any hopes she may have had for a pleasant afternoon, let out a sigh. It was her turn to stare helplessly into the forest.

—Well you must be doing all right if you managed to get a pair of those boots.

The ice-cream man shot a sharp look at Tanya, and then moved his gaze to Eva. In that moment something passed between them once again – an acknowledgement, then an acceptance, then a pact of complicity.

—They did release some to the shops in Prague, said Eva, a little too quickly. As a trial.

The ice-cream man was embarrassed. He wanted to look away, but he couldn't let go of her eyes.

Tanya looked from one to the other. —Ah, yes. He must have got them there, she said, laying on the sarcasm. Excuse me for a moment, will you?

She got up and wandered to the edge of the clearing. A thin line of spruce marked the crest of the hill before the ground fell steeply away towards the town, too steeply for any but the smallest, most tenacious trees. The daylight was fading fast now and electric lights were coming on in some of the flats, isolated squares punching a random pattern into the gloom. There were one or two cars and motorbikes about, and the sound of their accelerating engines reached up to her like the droning of bees. Beyond the town you could just make out the eel-like contours of the Nitra, and beyond the Nitra the softly undulating waves of the hills, the nearest ones darkest, then paling in sequence until they became the same grey as the sky, and then they became the sky itself. For the first time, Tanya noticed how jarringly incompatible the concrete blocks of the housing estates were with the curvaceous landscape around it, as if a portion of a large, congested city had been sliced off and dumped in the middle of open countryside.

She hugged her arms. It was freezing up here. She'd go back and tell Eva they were leaving, and once they had left she would tell her that she didn't think much of her ice-cream man. She stepped on plenty of twigs to give warning of her approach. But when she came through the trees, the clearing was empty. She stared at the fire irritably, as if it were to blame for not keeping them there, then made her way over to the van. The rear doors were shut, and the little curtains inside had been pulled across.

She hesitated, her hand held up to knock. Suddenly there came a high-pitched shriek, which collapsed into a fit of giggles.

The little tart!

For a moment Tanya felt angry. Did they even care whether she was there or not? For all they knew she might have been bumped off by the lonely bear. She stood in front of the van, feeling stupid. Just as she was on the point of raising her knuckles to knock again, the door swung open and the ice-cream man appeared before her, stark naked.

—Hang on. You'll need this.

He turned his buttocks on her. She couldn't help looking at them, the tawny-coloured skin, the fist-shaped dents in the cheeks. He came back with the lamp. Startled, she raised her eyes.

—Don't you need it?

—Not for what we're doing.

He grinned at her, clearly enjoying her embarrassment. Anyone would have thought that she were the one who was naked instead of him. He pushed the lamp towards her.

She scowled, grabbed it, and left without a word, the image of his buttocks still imprinted on her mind.

When Eva Ligocká passed through the turnstiles of závodny 26. augusta the following morning the smell of the factory leapt down her throat and made her gulp in surprise. She closed her mouth, swallowed hard, and ran down the corridor that divided the men from the women.

—Had a lie-in, did we?

She looked up through the glass divider, guiltily.

—Yes. She paused. We did.

Pavel's eyes opened wide. —We?

—That's what you said.

—I meant—

—Well, I meant it too.

Pavel ran his hand over his cheeks, his dark eyes bruised.

—I'm sorry, said Eva, giving a shrug, and trying to look it.

—Who is he? he said quietly.

—He's not from here.

—What's his name?

She stared at him, blankly, her mind scrambling through the

events of the previous evening. Pavel started to laugh.

—Oh, I see. It was one of *those*.

—No it wasn't.

But Pavel had cheered up now.

—It's OK, don't be embarrassed. A one-night stand. I can take that.

—Can you?

He laughed. —Of course!

—Oh.

She turned, disappointed, and walked down the corridor towards the room where she worked.

—A well-made shoe, Eva's father liked to proclaim when it was getting late and he was surrounded by friends and empty bottles of *slivovica*, is like a good husband. As long as you keep it clean, tie its laces every morning, and give it a regular *polish*, it should give you good service for many years to come.

At lunch she slipped away from the canteen and made her way through the maze of corridors at the back of the factory that serviced the storerooms. She passed the double doors leading out to the delivery vans, and a draft of cold air fell into step behind her. There was no one around – everything had stopped for lunch – and her footsteps sounded loud and hollow on the white plastic flooring. She counted off the numbers of the doors: 201, 202, 203. When she reached 209 she slipped inside, turned the large key in the lock and pressed her back against the door. The long strip bulbs flickered on, flickered off, steeled themselves for a final effort, and sprang on again.

Rows and rows of white boxes, stacked one on top of the other, surrounded her in twenty-foot walls. It was hushed and silent, like a library, and to Eva that's more or less what it was – each box encapsulating a little world beneath its lid. She wandered up and down the aisles, checking the pictures on the labels, until she found the ones she wanted.

—A well-*worn* shoe, her father would continue, his voice even louder now that he knew he had an audience, even though that audience had mostly fallen asleep, is like a good wife. After a while, it moulds to your shape, and you can slip in without the need of a shoe-horn.

Shoes were one thing to her father, another to her. To the people of this town they were many things. To none of them were they simply something you wore on your feet.

Moving the ladder around, she collected three boxes, balancing them on her head and steadying them with one hand in a posture that was ancient and feminine, as if she were carrying water from a well. Keeping her head very upright, she sat down in the narrow aisle and arranged the boxes around her like a child lining up her birthday presents.

Each of the lids came off first, and were laid carefully to one side. Then she lifted out the three bundles of tissue paper. She paused, savouring the moment, wanting to do it at precisely the right pace. And then, one by one, she unwrapped each bundle from its parcel.

In the first was a tiny pair of black patent child's shoes, no more than three or four inches long. She stood them on the palm of one hand. Punched into the leather of the round-ended toes was the outline of a spread-winged butterfly. Without creasing the leather, she carefully threaded the straps through the intricate gold buckles and pushed the prong through one of the tiny holes. Then she held them up to the lobes of her ears and swung her head from side to side as if they were earrings.

They were expensive enough to be. These little shoes would one day be bought by a wealthy mother in Western Europe or America, perhaps for her daughter's fourth or fifth birthday. She'd wipe the child's face with a flannel, dress her in a stiff party frock and white knee-length socks, tie her hair with a ribbon and then help her put them on. Left shoe on the left foot, right shoe on the right. It was hard to imagine a human foot, complete with toes and toenails, fitting inside such a small space.

In the second bundle was what could be considered the adult version – a pair of gold sandals with a delicate ankle strap and a pencil-thin heel. When she tapped the heels together they made a satisfying click, and a little shower of excess glitter fell off. She ran her fingernail over the delicate cross-stitching along the edges of the straps and smiled to herself. To the workers at the factory, these shoes represented the height of glamour. A girl in a pair of these would be a big hit at Babička's on a Friday night. Desirous of associating himself with such a lifestyle – and such a girl – the factory manager kept a pair of them on his desk, one perched coquettishly over the other.

The final bundle was big and heavy. Inside were a pair of women's walking boots. They were made of brown suede, with heavy, square heels and strong woven laces that tied up around the ankle. She pushed her hands down into the darkness of the toes, a soft, secret place like the inside of a mouth, and scratched the suede with her fingers to stimulate the smell. Then she put the opening of the shoe to her face and inhaled.

There, in that dark, rich, animal smell was contained everything Eva knew. It was the smell of the factory, the smell of the town, even the smell of her family. A single breath could conjure up a flurry of memories: getting up in the dark winter mornings, the monosyllabic breakfasts with her family, the bread and smoked cheese that lay heavily on her stomach all morning. That feeling of surrendering to the rattle of the sewing machines with her head still wrapped in sleep. Tanya's bad-tempered post-lunch scowl. Counting the hours till two o'clock, coming home to the overheated kitchen, the din of the TV set, a block of doughy poppy-seed cake, the clamour of cutlery as someone laid the table for supper.

And yet she would never own a pair of boots like these. Nor would any local girl ever dance in gold sandals at Babička's. All three designs were for export only. They did not belong here, but in Western Europe, America, Russia. The lives she imagined them leading were grand, aristocratic, full of idle hours. She saw the gold sandals sinking into the soft green lawn of a large country house, or clip-clopping on the marble surround of a swimming pool. She saw the child marching down the streets of Amsterdam or Paris, watching her shiny reflection in the windows of expensive boutiques. She saw the heavy heels of the walking boots caked in the mud of the vast, strange fields of the American prairies or the South African veld.

They might be her past, these shoes, but they were somebody else's future.

And yet——. She thought again of the ice-cream man in his stolen boots. It was as if, by putting them on, they were going to take him with them. As if he could make their future his own. She wondered if she could do the same.

Back at her desk Eva stared at the soft suede on the underside of a tongue. With a fingernail she made two parallel lines down the centre, like tyre tracks in the snow. Then she threw it irritably to one side, and got back to her work. A few moments later she slipped the soft working slipper off her foot and touched the cold steel of the paraffin lamp with her bare toe. She wondered how many times she could go through the events of the previous night in her mind, scene by scene, before she began to bore even herself.

—He didn't give a straight answer to any of my questions. Not one of them, said Tanya, guessing what was going on in that distracted head, and in the mood for a squabble.

—It was the way you asked them. Like an interrogation.

—And he didn't ask us any questions at all. I can't stand men who do that, just talk about themselves.

—But he didn't say anything about himself either. You just admitted that.

Tanya pulled the lever of her machine down hard without checking that the needle was up. It wasn't and it snapped.

—*Shit*. Third needle today. So what did he say after I'd gone?

Eva thought for a moment, holding her head to one side.

—He didn't say anything. Nor did I.

—Oh, great.

—Yeah. She smiled, slowly. It was.

That evening she walked up the forest track alone, the paraffin lamp banging against her calf. It seemed an easier journey now that she knew how far it was. She could smell smoke from a long way off, and when she rounded the corner into the clearing she laughed out loud at the size of the fire he'd built. For a moment, looking up, she thought that he was on fire himself – she could see the outline of his body amongst the flames. But then she realised that he was standing behind the fire, leaning against the side of his van, his arms folded. He was waiting for her.

She walked up to him until she was so close she could see through the weave of the too-small jumper she had given him. The hairs on his chest formed the shape of a *T*.

—Are you trying to burn down the entire forest?

—I didn't want you taking the wrong path. You might have stumbled into the arms of the wrong ice-cream man.

—You'd better tell me your name, then, for future reference.

—I'm Tibor.

He looked her up and down. —Were you as short as this last night?

—You think I might be the wrong girl?

Abruptly, he disappeared through the back door of the van, reappearing moments later with a wooden crate.

—Try standing on that.

Now she was on a level with his mouth. The lips were dry and strong with hardly a dip in the centre and at each end were little curved creases, as if the entire mouth had been placed in parentheses. An afterthought, which you could take or leave. She stared at the brackets for a moment, watching them deepen with the beginnings of a smile. She was about to lean forward when he placed an arm around her waist and lifted her feet off the ground. She let out a little yelp of surprise. —No, you're definitely the right girl, he said, and carried her inside the van, kicking the door shut behind him with his foot.

After that she climbed up every afternoon when her shift at the factory was finished. Sometimes she arrived before Tibor and got a fire going, hauling logs from a pile he had covered with the plastic tarpaulin. When she couldn't get it started with twigs, she tore a page from the front of one of his books which he'd shoved under the tarpaulin, among the logs. She wasn't much interested in what they were – stories by men with foreign-sounding names. Most of them were written in English, so she wouldn't have understood them anyway. They were all splayed open, face down, and she reasoned that he had read up to the point where each was open and wouldn't miss the early pages.

When her family were out, she rifled through the coats hanging by the door, found a couple of old jackets that nobody would miss and packed them on to a sled together with jars of pickled gherkins and green tomatoes, sweet bread with strawberry jam, tins of goat's cheese in brine, squares of boiled bacon, bottles of her father's home-made plum brandy. Tibor found the *slivovica* so sweet that he spat it out on to the fire, causing the flames to sizzle and streak up high. After that Eva always shook a few drops of it on to the pages she tore from Tibor's books.

In the night, undressing shyly in the orange light of the paraffin lamp, Eva wrapped her scarf around his eyes as a blindfold.

—You'll have to imagine it. Tell me what I'm taking off.

—Your trousers, one leg at a time.

—And now?

—Your long-sleeved vest.

—What makes you think—?

—An educated guess. Ah, and matching knickers.

—Give me that scarf.

They tussled for it, until he grabbed her round the thighs and she fell backwards with a yell, sitting down heavily on a large cardboard box.

The box split its seams and she compressed the contents to the floor.

—You've ruined me! he shouted cheerfully above the splintering noises, climbing on top of her. He took hold of her shoulders, grinning delightedly. She laughed up at him, not understanding.

—Better than feathers, wouldn't you say?

He clung to her and rolled them both over so that she was on top and could see what she had done. Beneath them lay the remains of Tibor's entire supply of ice-cream cones.

They only ever saw each other up here, in their circle melted into the forest floor, away from the town and everybody in it. They sat listening to the noises of the forest, the flap of pigeon wings in the tops of the branches, the snap of a twig under the foot of some small creature, drawn by the smell of roasting chestnuts or baking potatoes. When the fire was good and strong, they spread the tarpaulin out and made love on it with the flecked light weaving through the tree trunks, straining to reach their nakedness. They were voracious, finding a charge and an energy in the touch of one another's skin that lit their eyes and made their mouths bold and hungry. Insects hovered uncertainly over them, lured by the heat and the unfamiliar smells. Afterwards Tibor propped himself up on his elbow, lit a cigarette and retreated into himself as he watched her through circles of smoke, his eyes wandering over the rounded contours of her small, plump body, the sweep of the waist to the hip, the breasts with their nipples that nosed slightly upwards. Her body had been a surprise to him – the childishness of the rounded tummy, the sloping shoulders, the paleness of her skin. He had not been able to imagine how it would be through all the layers. Her eyebrows, beneath the fringe, were plucked to a delicate arch that trailed off with a tiny upward twist towards the temple. Each one seemed to balance just above the muscle that worked it. They captured, for Tibor, what he found most compelling about her: both her innocence and her impatience with it. And the fact that she had not yet grown into her beauty.

She eyed him suspiciously as he thought these things, looking out from beneath the curtain of her fringe. For her, it was more important to attempt to read his thoughts in this moment after making love than to involve herself in her own. She would do that later, when she was alone.

But Tibor rolled on to his back, not letting her in, and smoked his cigarette.

Since that first night, his name was about the only piece of information he had parted with. As the weeks went by, unasked and unanswered questions began to accumulate between them like furniture covered in dust sheets, ghostly presences that joined them around their fire.

To keep things equal, she told him very little about herself. She enjoyed this to begin with, the chance it gave her to escape the defining context of her life, to be someone new. But after a time it began to worry her. The less they knew about one another's lives, the less claim they had on one another. The process of swapping information was like the putting down of roots. Without it, they could slip too easily away.

And so one evening, unprompted, she simply began to talk about herself. It made her uncomfortable at first, afraid she was forcing herself on a disinterested audience, and she skipped over the details, hurried through the sequence of events. But gradually she realised that although he gave her no encouragement, and never asked any questions, he did not miss a single word that she said. His attention was careful, poised. He was like a diligent student on the eve of an important exam. Her confidence bolstered, she began to go back and elaborate, to fill in the gaps with anecdotes that made him smile.

During these one-sided conversations he became very slow – slow to look away, slow to move. He took his time peeling a potato before tossing it into the pan they had boiling over the fire. His mouth became firm and serious, the brackets deepening so that, for a moment, lit harshly from the side by the flames, she thought she saw what he would look like when he was an old man. She wanted to take that old face in her hands and shake it, force those lips to crack open. Your turn! she wanted to say. But something always stopped her, an invisible hand holding her back.

By the following morning he would have returned to his usual exuberant self, the Tibor that didn't take anything seriously at all. She had never met anyone who was so utterly unable to stay still. He woke abruptly, and got up straight away. Outside he would fling himself into a handstand and walk around on his hands, stark naked, letting his feet topple over backwards and, if she came near, falling on to her, bringing them both to the ground in a noisy heap. Or he would hoist himself into a tree and walk along the length of a branch with his hands outstretched for balance, before jumping to the ground. He always had faith that his knees would hold him. When he jumped between one branch and another, he knew that he would be able to make it. He had an unequivocal trust in the capabilities of his body, as if he and his body had long ago made an agreement that they would never let each other down. She loved this in him – an almost professional knowledge of himself, of what he could do within that compact, firmly built frame.

If there were a sureness like that between us, she thought. If we had an agreement like that.

When she wasn't with him, it wasn't the look of him so much as his smell that she found herself missing. It was a dark and boyish smell, of needles from the spruce trees, of earth beneath the fingernails, of thick fibrous hair – all this strangely overlaid with the powdery sweetness of the ice-cream mix that he emptied from large sacks into the mixing vats, showering himself with a fine coating from head to foot. He tried to shake it off with wild flings of his head, like a dog shakes off water, but she tasted it on his skin. She fantasised that there were some way of extracting this smell, of boiling it down into a hard sweet that she could keep in her mouth all day. She didn't know why she was so caught up in his smell. Perhaps it was because he was the only man she knew who did not smell of leather.

Sometimes, while he slept, she lit the paraffin lamp, turning it down very low so that it gave off no more than a weak pool of yellow, and set it down on the floor far enough away to illuminate his body but not his face. And then she drew the covers back and observed him – not desiring him, but as if she were a vet inspecting a horse for sale.

She had never had the opportunity to study a naked man in detail before. Now, prone and vulnerable before her, the tension gone out of the muscles in his face and his legs, the damp curls of his underarm hair splayed open like one of his books for her to see, she could gaze at any part of him for as long as she wanted to. At first her gaze was coy, avoiding the areas she was least familiar with, but after a while she grew more bold. Each time he shifted position in his sleep, she moved with him, lifting her limbs then placing them down again as if they were both engaged in a slow, synchronised dance.

Whatever position he lay in – on his back, front, or on his side with his arms curled around his chest – she took advantage of it, and scoured the terrain of skin, hair and muscle available to her. She studied the soles of his feet, the skin of his elbows, the front and backs of his knees, the hairs around his nipples. It wasn't long before she found clues to the story that he hadn't told: tiny white scars on his fingers, burn marks on the insides of his wrists. A mouth full of even, white teeth, fillings in several of the back ones. She never handled him, never touched any part of him that she might not have brushed against in her sleep.

One night he opened his eyes and found her straddling him, the muscles of her thighs held taut.

—Are you about to rape me?

She jumped in alarm.

—No. I'm a member of the secret police. I have suspicions that you are involved with a subversive underground movement. I will hand you in eventually, but not until I've checked you out thoroughly myself.

—Well, take your time.

—I intend to.

—Because once you get to the bottom of me, you'll leave.

—Your bottom is far from being a reason to leave.

She lifted the paraffin lamp so that it took in his face. Her voice was quiet now, not the urgent theatrical whisper it had been before.

—Do you think I'm only interested in you because I don't know who you are?

She slid down beside him, allowing their bodies to touch, bringing her face close to his.

He shrugged. —Everyone loves a mystery.

—Is that all there is to you?

He didn't answer.

—That's why I don't read books, she said. I don't see the point in reading something just to find out what happens in the end. That sort of curiosity – it's facile.

—But that's not why I read them, either. I read them because they take me places. The books that I have with me now – *Huckleberry Finn, Tom Sawyer* – I've read them all several times. They're beautiful. They spirit you away to the places where they're set. Haven't you ever wondered what it's like in the West? In America? I can't get enough of it. As soon as I've finished one, I start from the beginning all over again.

—You do? She looked at the books open on the floor, remembering the pages she'd burnt. Shit.

He was not a Romany, for a start. He had no holes pierced in his ears and, although the skin on the soles of his feet was hard in places, the feet themselves were narrow and well formed. They were not the feet of someone who was given an older brother's cast-offs, or who was left to run around barefoot in summer.

He spoke Czech, but she guessed he wasn't pure Czech. There

was an arrogance and strength about his features that suggested a haughty ancestry, a darker blood – perhaps Hungarian. It would account for the heaviness of his eyelids, the reddish rims, the thickness of his hair. It might even account for his nomadic occupation, minorities of any sort being made to feel unwelcome in small Slovak communities like hers.

She guessed he had once worked as a chef. The burns on his wrists were consistent with those made from accidentally touching the top metal rack in a hot oven. Her grandmother had similar burn scars from her bread-making days. And the little white lines on his fingers, those were the careless snips of a vegetable knife.

At night he clasped her tightly – so tightly that she had to disengage herself from his arms whenever she wanted to shift position. But by morning she always found him curled on his side, his arms wrapped across his chest and his hands tucked under his armpits. It was the position of someone who was used to sleeping alone. Alone, and in a cold place.

She herself was so much a part of the world she knew that she found it difficult even to begin to piece together a possible history for the ice-cream man, or to guess at the reason he chose not to talk about himself. Because of his strangeness, she found that her sense of reality became suspended when she was with him. She felt cut adrift from the day-to-day life that she knew, left to float in a place where nothing was known, and anything possible. The longer she spent with him, the more this sensation deepened. First she lost her sense of time. Below them, the lights of the town flickered on and off, brief lives that came and went. A day, or a hundred years, might have passed down there. Sometimes in the early morning they woke to find the entire town buried beneath a layer of low cloud, as if it had been submerged by the dust of a volcano in the night. A ruined Pompeii, with only the factory chimney rising above the ruins.

Then she began to lose her sense of herself. When she went into work, ate lunch in the canteen, when she went home and ate supper with her family, her responses were no longer automatic. She relied on the roles she had to play – the friend, the colleague, the daughter, the sister, the granddaughter – and her actions became based on what she knew was expected of her. Her family had heard mention of a certain Pavel Dugat, and knew him as an admirer of Eva's at the factory, and she didn't disillusion them when they assumed it was him she was spending so much time with. Pavel himself was initially bemused and a little hurt by the winks and nudges he was treated to by the Ligocki brothers from time to time – and certainly by the unexpected pinch on the cheek he received from Eva's mother in the queue at the butcher's one morning – but after a while he accepted such offerings as a show of heartfelt consolation and regret that he was unlikely, after all, to become their brother and son-in-law. As for the nights when she didn't return at all, her parents accepted her explanation that she'd stayed with Tanya, as Tanya lived only with her mother and there was more space for her there. But they weren't stupid, and when she stopped making excuses, they stopped asking her for them. She became a little separate from the rest of the family, not expected to be present or to join in family events, but welcomed when she did. A similar distance had occurred when her older brother Julo was courting Sylvia, and no one expected anything other than that the antisocial behaviour would sooner or later culminate in a shy declaration that she had become engaged to be married.

In the van she and Tibor slept on the floor under a heap of old coats and blankets, most of which had been purloined from her family's flat. At four o'clock in the morning, when the horn honked three times, calling the workers to the factory gates, the sound reached her as a distant echo, a memory of some far-off country where she no longer lived. She tasted the synthetic sweetness of the ice-cream mix on Tibor's skin and forgot that the sound of the horn had once been so loud it had shaken her out of bed.

One Sunday morning in late spring she climbed up through the forest and found that the thaw that had begun two weeks ago down in the town was now happening up here too. A freshness had taken root, a coming alive after the winter freeze. There were movements in the branches – the sounds of squirrels and birds venturing out and looking for food. It had rained during the night, and the pine needles were smelling strongly underfoot, and in the background, just faintly, was the honey-like smell of resin that was starting to ooze from the cracked trunks of the trees. The air hung damp and close, keeping its lovely new perfumes close to its chest.

She too clutched something to her chest – a little bundle of greased paper containing breaded meatballs and strips of smoked curd cheese for their lunch.

As she neared the place where the van was usually parked, she found herself slowing down. A coldness had lodged itself in the pit of her stomach. She knew that her body did not normally lie on such occasions. And when she stepped into the empty clearing she found that she had been expecting this for some time.

She walked around the clearing slowly, as if to make sure. The debris from the fires was gone, swept in amongst the trees. The pile of wood had been dismantled and scattered. She realised now that he had been letting the pile dwindle, not cutting any more for the last ten days or so. She realised too that the last time they had sat here was the morning he had handed her his penknife with the tiny scissors pulled out.

—I want it short.

—I don't. I like it as it is.

—My hair. My decision.

Reluctantly, she had gripped a curl between her fingers and pulled it up. It was strong, fibrous. It would be like cutting leather.

—Are you sure?

—Really short.

So she had done as he asked, beginning at the top, taking off one curl at a time. The stark whiteness of his scalp, with its uneven surface of hollows and humps, had surprised her. It was new territory – a part of him she had never explored before – and she had warmed slightly to her task.

Afterwards, she had barely recognised him.

—My god, you look naked. Like a pig.

—Thanks.

And then she had wiped her hands on her thighs and said she had to go. She remembered feeling a sense of irritation, perhaps because she had got the little hairs stuck to her hands, and now she'd wiped them on her clothes, or perhaps because she would have liked him to come with her, and she knew that if she asked him, he would say no.

—I told you. It's little Gregory's birthday.

—You didn't tell me.

—Well, I am now.

—Will you come back afterwards? Stay the night?

—There's no point. It'll be dark. I'll come tomorrow.

—You don't like me with my hair short, is that it?

—That's it, yes.

And so she had left. He was right, she hadn't told him. Perhaps she had been punishing him for always refusing her invitations to meet her family. Now, she wondered if she had also sensed what she knew now, that the cutting of his hair had been a prelude to his departure.

She sat down heavily on the damp ground, breathing in the smell of the forest as if it could anaesthetise her dismay. She closed her eyes and, just for a moment, allowed herself to imagine the thud as he jumped down from an overhanging branch, a gleam of laughter in his black eyes.

Hah! You really thought I'd gone, didn't you? Vanished into thin air!

No, of course not. You wouldn't just leave like that, without telling me.

But of course he would. Why else had he been keeping himself back, all this time, not letting her get too close? If you don't know somebody's past, you will not know their future. Had he said that, or had she?

—I am in love with your hair, she had said to him, that first night, when she'd returned with the lamp.

—Only my hair?

—So far, yes, only your hair.

Hair that he had made her cut. That he had scattered in the forest amongst the pine needles. She sat there for a while longer, and then she got up, distractedly leaving the bundle of food on the ground. She walked back down the mountain slowly, feeling hollow inside, as if she had been cored like an apple.

'When the hognose snake is trying to avoid a predator,' Theo read, balancing a mug of hot chocolate on the summit of his knee cap as he sat propped up on two pillows in bed, 'it flops on its back, writhes violently, and covers itself with dust, vomit, excrement, musk or blood.'

Theo sighed and let the book slide to the floor. He was bored with reading about the desert. He was bored with trying to teach himself the names of everything. Who cared whether it was a white-throated woodrat or a kangaroo rat. A rat was a rat and he didn't want to meet either kind, thank you very much, and he'd rather not be reminded that he might.

He came to bed early these days, before he was really ready to go to sleep. It got dark so suddenly, and once it did he was surrounded by a black void where a moment ago there had been the line of his white-washed fence and his granite mound and his two saguaros, keeping an eye on him. It was as if he'd been cast adrift on a raft at sea. Having the lights on made him feel vulnerable; he might as well have lit a shining beacon announcing himself as an easy target to all the wild creatures out there. But turning them off was no answer either, as then he worried that there was something waiting to pounce on him behind every door in the house. Bed, it seemed, was the safest place to be.

He wished he had someone to read to him, like his mother used to do. *Listen, Theo. Look at the lovely pictures.* Those bedtime stories had taken him into another world – an enchanted world where all the women were princesses and all the men were princes and animals could speak and mysterious old witches in black cloaks gave you magical talismans to help you on your way. The more the young Theo had become transported by these stories, the more his mother had lost interest, her voice trailing off as she started to make mental notes about who she had to ring or what she was going to watch on television as soon as she'd got him off to sleep. He had started reading those books again the night she died. At first he had lain there beside her in the dark bedroom, listening out to the terrible silence emanating from her motionless body. She lay with her back to him, facing the wall. He didn't dare look to see whether her eyes were open or shut. How strange, he remembered thinking, that you only notice the sound of someone's heart once it has stopped. He had read the fairytales to distract himself. How could it be that her body, that long night, had seemed heavier, more indestructible, than it ever had in life?

Out here, in the desert, was a bit like losing yourself in a fairytale. You could forget that reality existed, or that it lay so far beyond the mountains that it didn't relate to you any more. Out here there was a blank canvas, more or less. It was a separate, protected world, like living inside one of those snow-storms that you shook for a thirty-second blizzard. Except that inside his bubble there was dust and desert instead of snow.

He had known that he needed space. It wasn't his physical body that demanded it – although Lord knows, it took up more space than most – but his soul. Ah! – that word again. The fact was, imaginations like his needed a lot of room to breathe. And out here there was nobody to tick him off. No one to laugh at him, tell him what to do, or – worst of all – tell him to grow up. Out here he could be exactly what he wanted to be. He, Theobald Moon, could now discover what Theobald Moon did when left in a world of his own.

He burped. 'Scuse me, he mumbled quietly into a curled-fingered fist. There were so many things that he'd done, in his old humdrum life, that he hadn't actually needed to do. Which he'd done for the sake of other people – because of what they might think of him. And which, actually, he didn't have to do any more. Don't 'scuse me, he corrected, to his empty room.

Draining the last of his hot chocolate, the thick, brown sludge at the end leaving a trail on his top lip, Theo twisted round to see if there was anything else on his bookshelf that looked interesting. Without their jackets on, all the books looked terribly serious, like academic texts. He pulled down *A Manual for Living Comfortably in the Cosmos*, simply because it was the only one he hadn't looked at yet, and let it fall open at random on his lap.

'Everything in the Universe', he read, 'derives its life force from the Universal Energy – every man, woman, plant, bird, fish, mammal, and even inanimate objects, such as roads and rivers and mountains. Not only is each and every one of us linked to this divine source of Life, but we are also interconnected, one to another. With every breath that he takes, every movement he makes, a man taps into the Divine Interconnectedness of Being.'

Theo leant back on his pillows. He liked this idea very much. It seemed to confirm what he had come to believe – that he was in some way a part of the desert he had made his home and whose rhythms of day and night, hot and cold, light and dark, so affected his own. He turned the book over to mark the place and climbed out of bed, the seed of excitement sown by the book making him feel like a snack. Without turning on the kitchen light he lifted a jar of peanut butter from a shelf and spread it thickly on a couple of digestive biscuits – thoughtfully sent over by Aunty Drew – then cut a thick chunk of cheese from the block in the fridge. As an afterthought, he picked up the entire packet of biscuits and took them with him back to bed.

Again, he opened the book at random.

'Choose your dreams with great care,' he read. 'The Universal

Energy will give you what you ask for. Some psychologists refer to this as the Perception Principle. Whichever way you choose to see it, the Divine Truth remains the same: what you look for will find its way to you. Thus, a sad man will always find reason to grieve, a hypochondriac will always find illness, an optimist will always find cause for celebration and laughter. Decide today what it is you are looking for in your life!'

Theo swallowed hard to help down a sticky lump of peanut butter. There it was, in black and white. You get what you want; what you think you deserve. Quite incredible! Lord knows, he had no shortage of wants. His belly was full of those. Sometimes he felt as if his soul was stretched to capacity with wants, and would shatter into a million pieces if it took on a single one more. *His* problem was one of definition. The yearnings were vague and nameless. He couldn't tell them apart. It was as if he had a nestful of chicks inside him, all clamouring with wide open beaks, and he didn't know which one to feed, or what to feed them with.

He broke off a corner of cheese and balanced it on top of a biscuit. Perhaps he should meditate, he thought. Maybe that way it would become clear what he should ask the Universe for. He shook the crumbs out of the spine of the *Manual*, ignoring the fact that this served only to transfer them to his sheets, and got out of bed again, taking his little cheese and biscuit concoction with him into the living room.

He didn't need a book to do this. He could almost get into the Lotus Position, but not quite – a few more months of yoga would do it. As he pulled up one knee his dressing gown gaped, exposing his genitals. For a moment he considered going back to his room to put his pyjamas on, but he didn't. It would be good for him to learn to be naked. He knew he rather liked it, really – he just didn't usually allow himself to admit it. So now he would. In fact, while he was about it, he'd admit to himself that he liked all those little jobs that having a body involved from time to time – rubbing the grime from between his toes, scraping out the crusty bits in his ears, softening his nails with Johnson's baby oil and pushing the cuticles down. Splashing talcum powder under his armpits and over his chest and into his belly button (but stopping there, because he was never quite sure whether it was hygienic to go any further down). Even picking out the spines of the teddybear cholla – the worst of all the chollas to get embedded in your skin – with a pair of tweezers and a magnifying glass. Such little tasks gave him a sense that he was in touch with his body – communing with it, so to speak.

The yoga helped with that too, of course. He ran through his mental checklist. Cheeks of the buttocks pulled back. Weight even on each side. Sternum up. Side ribs up. Thighs turned out. Knee caps soft. Inner ears opened up, muscles at the sides of the eyes and around the mouth relaxed. Jaw unclenched. He became aware of the clog of well-masticated digestive stacked up against the backs of his front teeth and packed in little parcels into the hollows where his wisdom teeth had once been. He went round with his tongue, dislodging it all and swallowing it down.

Resting his upturned hands on his knees, Theobald closed his eyes and arranged his mouth into what he hoped was an expression of serenity, showing his contentment with the world. Theobald Moon at peace. He began to breathe deeply, monitoring the intake, feeling the little hairs in his nose twist upwards, his diaphragm rise and fall, and the hairs twist downwards again. A little bubble of snot popped in his right nostril. Without opening his eyes he felt in his dressing gown pocket with one hand for a hanky. He couldn't find one, and sniffed hard instead.

When he was little, he had meditated instinctively, in his own way, reaching a trance-like state in which he became oblivious to everything around him. He did it in bed, and sometimes he did it at school. Once he did it lying beneath the piano at the nursing home where his mother had worked, and where, eventually, he had worked too, helping out in the garden and doing odd domestic tasks. His mother had played the piano every year at the Christmas party and sometimes on people's birthdays as well. She played it very loudly and vigorously, not worrying too much about the wrong notes, and never varying the volume. She liked the rousing things best – the patriotic hymns, the old songs like *Daisy, Daisy* that the elderly people knew. They were mostly old ladies and they made a warbling choir, the occasional male voice providing an uncertain, disaffected bass beneath them, like the uneasy prowlings of a male lion around a den of females. Lying beneath the piano, its hefty body forming a heavy arch over him on its three pin-thin legs, he had been mesmerised by the way the pegs lifted and dropped and the thick bass strings vibrated. As the chords resounded in his head, he had thrilled himself with the possibility that the huge black instrument might, at any moment, and with a thunderous *clerroomph* of hammers and strings and splintered planks and a waterfall of white notes and black notes, come crashing down on him in a fantastic, fatal avalanche.

His mind was wandering. Theo acknowledged it, forgave himself, and brought his attention back to his breathing. He started to count the in-breaths. He'd see if he could make it to ten without thinking of anything else.

Sometimes, on the rare occasions when his mother was invited out in the evenings, the granddaughter of one of the ladies in the nursing home had come to babysit. Her name was Gwyneth. She had russet-red, curly hair which sat very tightly on her head, like a sponge. Over her shoulder she wore a hessian bag on a long strap and she proudly got out a large record, slipping the lovely black shiny disk from its sleeve and holding it between the palms of her hands as if it were the most precious thing in the world.

—Don't touch, she snapped at Theo, who wanted a look.

Carefully she lowered the stylus. There was a scratching sound like his mother frying bacon and livers on a Sunday morning. Then there was silence. And then there was a blast of noise, loud and furious, which wasn't anything like the quavering, wavering ladies around the grand piano. *Well it's one for the money, two for the show, three to get ready now go, cat go . . .*

Gwyneth started to dance. She brought one foot up on to the toe and began to twist it, gyrating from the waist. *Waa waa waa* she went, as soon as she ran out of words, tipping her head back and creasing up her eyes. The twelve-year-old Theo backed away and sat timidly on the edge of the sofa. He watched in stunned silence. But after a while he plucked up the confidence to slip off the sofa and join in. Gwyneth didn't seem to object. He jumped up and down with both feet, thud thud thud.

The stylus jumped, and the middle of another song sprang up.

Blue Moon, you saw me standing—

—*Theo!*

She fell to her knees, whipped the stylus away and lifted the record between her palms, so tenderly.

—You little twerp! It's scratched right across!

He took one look at the expression on Gwynie's face, and ran from the room. In bed he hid himself fully dressed beneath the blankets. Gwynie hadn't come up to see him, not even to make sure he'd brushed his teeth.

Theo yawned. Oh dear. So much for the meditation. But it was time for bed now and anyway his knees were starting to complain. He straightened them out and got off the floor, stiffly, remembering to brush his teeth on the way back to his room.

By the time the anniversary of his first year in the desert approached, Theo's afternoon hikes were taking him further and further from the house. He had learnt to cope with the heat, simply putting the fact of it to one side and occupying his mind with something else. He did his best to cover his skin. His ears suffered most, sticking out just beyond the brim of the little white golfer's hat he had bought, so that the rims were more or less continuously red. He diligently applied camomile lotion to them every night.

Although he was happier in the winter, when most of the nastier creatures were safely hibernating a few feet underground, he didn't let them deter him during the summer months. Once he had a close encounter with a javelina, rounding a corner to find himself a few feet from its backside, near enough to get a waft of its unpleasantly sharp, musky smell. The bristles on its back stood perfectly upright, as if they were fixed with hairspray. Theo coughed, politely, not wanting to take it by surprise. The creature sprang round, all four feet off the ground. For a full minute they stared at each other, the tip of its black snout glistening. Very slowly, Theo bent his knees and curled his fingers round a stone on the ground, planning to throw it and run. The whole drama unravelled so slowly that he had time to be impressed by his own composure. As he rose to his full height the pig grunted, and began to back away. Theo did the same, narrowly avoiding being tripped by a clump of deergrass behind him.

In late March, to his surprise, the plain was transformed into a carpet of yellow and pink as the creosote bushes, the prickly pears and the brittlebush came into bloom, along with a scattering of unexpectedly delicate-looking wildflowers. Theo cut handfuls of them with a pair of scissors and arranged them in jam jars around his house. The splash of colour made a big difference to his otherwise rather clinical surroundings – the only other decoration being the postcards Aunty Drew sent from Bognor Regis or the Isle of Wight, which he stuck to the door of the fridge. He didn't like reading them more than once. Their initial chattiness slid quickly into reminiscences about the past, and lurking behind them was always a suggestion that he was at fault.

'Am sitting on the esplanade where your dear mother and I used to come when we were young and full of life. They don't have tea dances any more, it's all crazy golf and discos now. But the men still remember your mother on the dance floor. Too pushy by half, she was, for most of them. Mind, she needed that strength, with what the God Lord threw her way. Don't get me wrong, Theo, you were always a good boy, but you were a big child and took a lot of looking after. You meant the world to her, I'm sure you realise that. I say a prayer for her every night, that she's getting some peace and quiet at last. Barbara is taking me out in her car this afternoon for a cream tea. Hope you've made some nice friends in America, dear.'

Sometimes his walks took him north, past the Rancho del Suerte. The house itself, home to Bill and his alcoholic wife – who, since hearing Jersey's voracious description, he rather hoped he'd never meet – was down the end of a long drive marked with two upright posts and a crossbar, as if it were some sort of modern-day castle. In the fields around it were a few dozen horses that were hired out for pony trekking in the holiday season. The cattle roamed in a large expanse of desert, watering themselves out of a trough fed by the large open-air tank. Jersey told Theo he could use the tank to cool off whenever he liked. Sometimes there was no more than a foot of brackish water in the bottom, as turgid and thick as a cup of luke-warm tea. He climbed down the little iron ladder with his trousers rolled up to his knees and waded through it as if it were a paddling pool, relishing the feel of the water wrapping in circles around his hot ankles. Beneath his feet was a soft silky slime, and sometimes he thought he could feel the tickle of tiny fish nibbling at his toes.

By the time the heat of the summer returned, Theobald Moon felt almost invincible. His routines were rarely interrupted. His cactus garden was thriving. After the crazy colours of the spring, the plants had slipped into their summer dormancy. The leaves of the desert willows turned brown, and though he panicked at first, a quick consultation with his book assured him this was normal and that there was no cause for concern. Sometimes there were fleeting summer showers that affected half the garden, and not the other, and he walked through a sunlit curtain of rain, like the beads that hung in the doorway of Aunty Drew's kitchen. He could stand in the middle of it and hold up his palms, and his left would be dry, his right wet.

—Darn gully-washer, Jersey would say. Don't know why it bothers.

The plants responded quickly to these bright, brief showers, taking the opportunity to come out of their dormancy and invest in a short spurt of growth. His two saguaros swelled up like a couple of fat medieval kings after a feast. Within twenty-four hours, the ocotillos became fleshy and tipped with red – rather disturbingly, Theo thought, although he didn't feel able to tell himself why. A week later the leaves had dropped off again, and their wavering arms were dry and sterile once more. While the sap was down in his trees, he did some gentle pruning using a little hand-saw from Pleasant Desert and holding his book open at the pruning diagrams with his free hand.

He never lost his respect for the sun, for the way it ruled the landscape. Over the course of the day, the light seemed to leap in great, broad sheets, striding from one rock face to another all the way to the mountains, sloshing them with bucketfuls of colour – pink, then lilac, then blue. It was when the sun was directly overhead that Theo felt most at its mercy. Noon could be a terrifying hour. The sun became remorseless – picking out each stone, each blade of tufty grass with a shocking clarity. The jagged edge of a granite outcrop, the gravel at the bottom of a dry creek, the twisted frame of an immobile creosote bush: each was produced as a terrible fact, with no room for ambiguities or discussion. Everything he looked at glared back with the sun's reflected severity, and Theobald developed a squint, two parallel crevices in between his eyebrows, like a pair of antennae. Sometimes he felt drunk on the heat, staggering like a rudderless boat in the shadowless midday, the dry air stealing the moisture from his eyes, his armpits, even from the inside of his mouth. Often he passed the fleshless ribs of a long-dead saguaro, or the skeleton of a rodent on the ground and thought, that'll be me, one of these days, my skin torn off by vultures and my bones gnawed clean by coyotes. Large black ants would carry away any last soft morsels. His teeth and the plastic sweet wrappers in his pocket would be all that was left of him.

On days like this, to walk under the cool lip of a rock was as sweet a relief as any he had known. If he followed the dried-up arroyo away from the tank and towards the low foothills to the south, he reached an area where corners of naked rock stuck out like the exposed bones of the Earth. There was an overhang that he could shelter beneath, and its stony cold breath always came as a surprise – welcome yet chilling, too, like entering the mouth of a dead man. He'd been there several times before he saw the little pictures scratched into the granite around him – the suns and animals and prancing men. They were Indian petroglyphs. He traced them with his finger, marvelling that they should be here, unsignposted, awaiting accidental discovery by walkers like him. He was almost tempted to carve his own initials into the rock beside them.

Here in the shadows, his mouth dry as he rationed the water in his flask, he would close his eyes and tease himself with fantasies about Icicle Pops and ice-creams. It was a test of his growing mental strength. He pictured a fat, creamy Mr Whippy with a flake stuck in the side, the melting vanilla dribbling down his hand. An Orange Maid, releasing a gush of icy cold fruitiness into his mouth. An ice-cream man had regularly come down Bellissima Street. His mother, in her last year, would call out, *Theobald! It's the Stop-me-and-buy-one man on his tricycle!* That's what they'd had before the war. A brickette, she'd ask for – two thick slabs of chewy vanilla in a wafer sandwich. But they didn't make those any more. He usually got her a tub – Tub Tahiti, Tub Italiano – or some such thing, and she didn't notice the difference. Personally, he had a soft spot for the Lyons Maid lollies, the Lolly Gobble Choc Bombs, the Haunted Houses, Mr Mens and Zooms. For 15p he could get a Mini Milk or a Cider Barrel and still have change for a few 1p chews from Sweet Things down the road.

In the early evenings, coming back from his expeditions, he soaked his weary body in a long, cool bath, watching the water turn pink from the layer of dust on his skin. He soaped himself all over, working his way up religiously from his feet and using a separate flannel for his genitals – a habit he'd had ever since he was small. Even out here, where there was no one else to check on him, he stuck two little plastic hooks on to the tiles and made sure to hang the right flannel on the right hook, so that he didn't end up using the wrong flannel on his face. It had happened to Aunty Drew once, when she came to stay, and he still recoiled from the memory. He'd spied on her from the hallway, her hair tucked up in a net with a large pink roller at the front and a blue one at each side, a quilted dressing gown buttoned up to the neck. She'd spread cream all over her face, rubbing it into the corners of her nose where the powder collected, and wiped it off with a piece of cotton wool. Her hand had hesitated for a crucial moment in front of the little row of flannels, and instead of going for the guest flannel, nearest to her, she went for the furthest one, perhaps thinking that it would be the least used. Hardly daring to breathe, he had watched her wipe his special flannel all over her soft, pouchy face, drawing it firmly across her mouth. He hadn't been able to look her in the eye after that.

When he emerged from his bath, he angled the shaving mirror so that he could inspect his naked bulk, at least in sections. His skin smarted pinkly from where he'd scrubbed it too hard with the loofah, and his body looked raw, like the joints of an uncooked ham. The half-moons of his breasts hung down heavily. As his image emerged through the steam, he made out the freckled scalp of his head. Somehow his skull seemed smaller, more rotund, than it used to be – particularly in relation to his face. His cheeks seemed to have become chubbier, and the excess flesh had stolen the shape of his jaw. For the first time, he realised that his face defied pinning down to a particular age. He could be anything between thirty and fifty, he estimated, to someone who didn't know.

He unscrewed a family-size pot of Nivea and slapped generous dollops of it on to the bits of him that had caught the sun that day – his neck, his ankles, his ears – and then on any other areas that looked as if they could do with it. It took a while to rub in, but it was cooling and the smell reminded him of England. When he perched his buttocks on the edge of the bath and bent down to reach his ankles, his suspicion that he was putting on weight was confirmed. His belly no longer folded itself into three, as it used to. Now it struggled to fold itself into two. In fact, now he came to think about it, Jersey had made some reference to his weight recently. He'd been giving Theo a lecture about going out walking on his own.

—They drop like flies, every year, he'd said. Two or three last summer alone. People like you who don't know the signs.

—I always take my water bottle with me, Theo had said defensively.

—You ain't no judge of when to drink. When you gets too hot, you get real pissed. You're pissed at everything there is. The insects, the way your pants hitch up around your waist, the way the sweat gets in your eyes. You're pissed at the sun and you're pissed at the desert. You're pissed at your water bottle and you throw it away and then you're pissed at everyone you know for not appearin' out of nowhere with another water bottle in their hand. And then you're pissed at yourself for being so darn stupid to be out there in the first place. You think about everything you ever saw and did and laughed about, and you can't see what in the hell was funny about anything anyway. And then when you gets so darn worked up that your head starts to hurt and your vision goes blurred and you want to shout and scream about it, you start to go a little bazooky in the head and there ain't much can save you after that.

Jersey had looked at him in that way he did sometimes, holding on to his eyes for a second longer than was strictly necessary, the beginnings of a question he never asked forming beneath the skin on his otherwise clear forehead.

—You don't strike me as being in peak physical condition, is all it is, he ended up with, quietly, and his eyes had come to rest on the mound of stomach that sat on Theo's lap like an extra bag of shopping.

Perhaps, he thought, as he pulled his pyjamas over his still sticky body, it was time to cut down on the night-time snacks.

That night, instead of a packet of biscuits, he took to bed a large, hardbacked book with blank pages that he had bought in the mall, closed his eyes and allowed his mind to fill up with images. It began as a more or less random association – one minute he saw a packet of Jelly Beans, the next he saw an old crone in a black cape hovering over a cauldron. He had the old crone slice the heads off the Jelly Beans and fling them into her bubbling pot. Slowly at first, but soon picking up speed as his confidence grew, Theo gripped his tongue between his teeth and began to write.

9

In the middle of the desert is a water tank with walls of corrugated iron and a little rusted ladder up the side. The water is dark and filled with the reflection of the eucalyptus trees and the sky. Nothing moves except for the clouds rolling slowly across and the whirligig beetles and the flat, long-legged striders that dart over the surface on the tips of their toes, making little dimples in the water but somehow managing not to sink in. No one, not even my father, knows how they do it, and the striders aren't going to tell. Sometimes a bird swoops down from an overhead branch and skims one of them off in its beak, as if in the hope that it might disclose its secret on pain of death. The ripples spread out in circles, warning all the other striders to watch out because one of them's just been swiped and they all go still for a moment, riding the waves, while they take the bad news in.

Well I'll be darned! Another one of us bites the dust. That leaves just twenty-six, by my count. Twenty-six of us left to keep the secret safe!

The cattle watch us from a wary distance as we approach, marching down the arroyo with our towels wrapped around our waists and our fishing nets over our shoulders. We haven't got anything on except our swimsuits and our sneakers and socks, and as soon as they realise this, their wariness turns to disdain, as if we are turning up in the middle of a private party, inappropriately dressed.

Not that they look much better. Folds of scraggy skin sway beneath their chins and balls of jumping cholla stick like badly shaven beards around their lips. Every time they swipe their backsides with an irritated flick of their tails, the flies rise up in a swarming cloud, then drift back down again.

When my father jumps into the water, he makes a splash that stops everything in its tracks for at least a mile around. Tidal waves surge outwards, drowning several striders more *(twenty-one and going down – glug-glug!)* but when the waves die down, the mound of my father's belly rises up out of the water, calm and lovely. It's sunburnt in red and white stripes like a deckchair from the way it folds up when he sits. Sitting on the edge with my eyes half closed, I can see a palm tree sprouting out the top, sandy beaches running round the edge. Suddenly my father slaps at it with his hand, because a dragonfly has mistaken him for an island too, and with all the slapping he loses his balance, and the island tips up and capsizes into the sea.

—Teach me to dive, I whine, dipping my feet in the water one at a time. I stick my thumbs up the elasticated legholes of my swimsuit, which is white with a yellow bumble-bee on the front. My father and I chose it together at K-Mart. I let the legholes ping back.

—OK, Fruitcake. Watch me first, and then you can have a go.

He hauls himself up on to the rim and the water runs down him in brownish streaks. He blows his nose between his finger and thumb and wipes it on his leg. Then, raising his arms above his head, he touches his fingers together as if he were going to pray, tucks his head in, and begins to count.

—*One, two, three.*

He holds it very still for a moment.

—*Four, five, six.*

He holds it still for a moment more, breathing hard through his nose.

I wind the end of my ponytail round my finger.

—*Seven. Eight.*

Then, without looking at me, he gives a little sigh, clambers back down, and slips into the water feet first.

He doesn't say a word and neither do I.

On the morning of my seventh birthday, Jersey fixes me up a swing tennis game in the garden. This consists of an iron pole stuck into the ground with a tennis ball attached by a string from the top. I hit it one way, and Jersey hits it back, while my father dodges and ducks on the sidelines, afraid that the ball might break loose and hit him on the side of the head. Jersey says I have to restrain myself, because if I give him a hernia from all the running around, Mr Kozinski will come knocking on my door.

When he's had enough, I run in circles around him as he stands with his shoulders hunched over at the top, lighting a cigarette in the protective cup of his hand.

—For Chrissake, take it easy, he says, and he gives me the meanest look out of the corner of his eye.

—Ooo, Jersey, I croon in my sweetest voice, taking slow, lolling steps back towards him and peering up from beneath his chin. Am I making you feel old?

He's got no choice after that but to do something silly, like scoop me up and plonk me on his shoulders where I grab at his ears and scream and try to tuck my flapping legs under his arms while he races me round the garden and into the house and dumps me head first on my bed.

In the afternoon Cindy arrives. She's got a present for me too. She sits down on the side of my bed and gets out a tiny red bottle. For a moment, I wonder if it's something from Mr Kozinski's garden. But then she unscrews the top and pulls out a brush on a stick.

—Put your hand on my knee, she says, low and sing-songy and full of the treat that's in store, and she starts to paint my nails, careful not to go over the edges. A smell of chemicals fills the air and makes me want to sneeze.

—Don't you go and move on me! she shrieks, so I hold the sneeze in. Once she's done one hand she moves on to the other, and then she does my toes. I have to stick my hands up in the air and wave them around to dry. The weight of the paint presses down.

Jersey comes in looking for his pack of cigarettes. His face breaks into a wide smile when he sees us sitting there.

—Well, what a sight is that. Now I've got me two beautiful women, he says, sitting down on the other side of me. Cindy puts her hand on my head and strokes my hair and the three of us sit there admiring my hands and my feet until my father taps gently on the bedroom door, pokes his head in, and tells us it's time for tea. He doesn't say anything about my fingers and toes, although he takes it all in, and after he's gone Jersey winks at Cindy and me.

My father has laid out the best cups and saucers. He looks at us hopefully, expecting a comment, but Jersey is too busy telling us something important. He says that when his father came here from Poland in 1938 – and Cindy asks how'd he get in and he says as part of the quota system, and the Captain of his boat made sure they were first in line on New Year's Day, and Cindy asks has he ever been to Poland himself, and Jersey says no but maybe he will one day. *But*, he says, getting heated with all the interruptions, when his father arrived here from Poland, no one much lived in the desert except the ranch-men and their cattle. Little by little, he says, the folks have come wanting their water supply and their electricity supply and their schools and their hospitals and their golf courses, and if this goes on for much longer the desert won't be a desert any more.

—That's what the cities does, he says. Look at Los Angeles and San Diego. Ate up the desert in no time at all, and now all the folks living there want to come and be in the wilderness here, but it beats me what they think will become of the wilderness if they do.

—We're all of us guilty of that, says Cindy. It ain't like you don't use the hospitals too. Guilty just by bein' here.

—I ain't never been in a hospital, says Jersey.

—You know what I mean.

—Well, I believe there's a difference living *in* it to living *off* it, that's what I believe, and if you're working with cattle you're using the land in a way that don't disturb it.

—Unlike working in the Wild Wild West, I suppose, says Cindy drily.

—Well, that ain't no place for a woman, to my mind, that's all. He says it quietly, avoiding anyone's eye.

My father rests his finger on the lid of the teapot as he pours. Jersey studies his cup, as if he's working out how his finger will fit through the tiny handle.

—Why, ain't that just dainty, cries Cindy, suddenly, bringing her hands together over the little tea service. And what's this, with the little pink and yellow squares?

—That, says my father, proudly, pleased that his efforts are at last being noticed, is Battenberg cake. Josie found it in the mailbox this morning, from Aunty Drew.

—It's your birthday cake? she asks.

—One of them, says my father, with a secret smile, and he disappears into the kitchen and a few minutes later reappears carrying a three-tiered chocolate cake covered with icing and with a circle of seven pink sugar mice on top, their tails dangling over the sides. We all let out a gasp. The mice have candles stuck in their backs. Jersey says this surely calls for something stronger than tea, and puts down his cup and goes outside to his truck.

They all sing Happy Birthday, Cindy and Jersey and my father, and I blow out the candles. We eat the sugar mice, dangling them by their tails, and laughing as we bite off their heads. And then my father hands me a parcel and watches Cindy and Jersey's faces as I tear off the wrapping paper. Through the cellophane window I can see a fairy's outfit, complete with net tutu and wings and a magic wand.

—Put it on, put it on! says my father, who's even more excited than me.

I start pulling my smock over my head, but Cindy takes my hand

and says why don't we do it in the bedroom and she comes with me and helps me with the fastenings on the back and adjusts the wings until they're straight, and when we come back my father has his camera at the ready.

—Let's have you up on the rock, he says. Against the sky.

We go out into the garden and Jersey lifts me up. There's the sourness of beer on his breath.

—Hold on! Hold on! I've forgotten something!

My father runs back inside the house. We wait in silence, Cindy with her hands on her hips, Jersey taking swigs from his bottle of beer. When he comes back he's carrying a small oblong box beneath his arm. He puts it on the ground, takes off the lid, and unwraps the tissue paper.

—One pair at a time, Sugar Pie. Every year on your birthday, until there are no more left.

He says it quietly, so that only I can hear.

—I would have started giving them to you earlier, but I lost the key, he adds.

Cindy watches as he hands me the little black shoes. I can hardly believe my eyes. They are even prettier than I remember them to be, with a pattern of holes in the top.

—They're gonna be way too small, says Cindy. She's got bigger feet than that.

I don't have to try them to see that she's right. My father and I look at them in disappointment.

—One minute, he says, and disappears with them back into the house. When he comes back, he's carrying a larger box. He takes out the gold sandals and stands them up on the rock. Just like the first time, my feet slide down to the ends. This time my red toenails peep out.

—A little on the large side, this time, mutters Cindy.

—There we have it! Perfect! says my father.

He stands beneath me, one finger curled over the button on the camera.

—Smile, Sugar Pie! Smile!

—When you were born, says my father, there was thunder and lightning and it rained every day for a week.

He stops brushing my hair and looks into space for a moment, and then he changes his mind.

—Actually, that's not entirely true. The thunder and lightning came earlier, and by the time you were born, the rain had stopped.

From outside we can hear the rise and fall of Cindy's voice. She and Jersey are sitting on the steps. Every time her voice gets loud, my father speaks over the top.

—Mind you, you were earlier than we expected. About four weeks, I think it was.

—Does that mean my life will be four weeks longer at the other end too?

My father finishes on the left side and shuffles around on his knees to do the right. Cindy is shouting now.

—Well, that's a good point, Sugar Pie. Maybe it does. There you have it, a four-week bonus! What will you do with those four weeks, I wonder?

—I don't know.

—Well, you should think about it.

My father kisses me on the nose and strands of my hair reach up like tentacles and attach themselves to his face.

—Look at that! You're generating your own personal electricity. You want to watch that, Sugar Pie. You might electrocute someone.

—Will Cindy come and say goodnight?

—I'll ask her, Jelly-O. See you in the morning. Pancakes and cream for breakfast.

He pulls the covers up to my chin and turns out the nightlight.

—Dad? I ask the darkness.

—What?

—What are they arguing about?

We both listen out, but now there's nothing coming from the steps.

133

—I can't hear anybody arguing, comes my father's voice. I can just make out the white oval of his face, hovering in the doorway, the dimple in his chin.

—Is it about the shoes?

—The shoes? Why would she be cross about the shoes?

We listen out again, but there's an uneasy silence outside.

—You go to sleep, Jelly-O, my father says softly. Don't think about Cindy. She's nothing to do with us, is she? With you and me. It really doesn't matter what she thinks. You promise you'll go to sleep?

—OK.

—That's a good girl. Sleep tight.

He shuts the door. I keep my eyes open as long as I can, waiting for her to come. And then, in the night, she does, except that part of me knows it's not really her. She comes into the room and leans over me, and her hair is not blond, but dark and the ends of it brush against my face. I can hear her talking, and I can feel her stroking my hair back from my forehead, as if she doesn't want me to go back to sleep just yet. She has a voice as clear as mountain air, and when she laughs her mouth reaches out, as wide as the sky. She calls me by a name that I don't recognise, and the unfamiliar word resounds like a bell in my head, over and over again. She presses her lips on my cheeks and lifts up my nightie and blows raspberries on my tummy, all the time whispering my secret name, and though I say the name over and over to myself for the rest of the night, in the morning I can't remember what it is.

Sometimes, over the next few weeks, I think I see them coming, and I run to the bottom of the garden, and climb up on to the fence. Sometimes it's a ball of dust from another car on the high road into town. Mostly it's just a mirage at the end of the track. And then, one day, when we're least expecting it, his truck pulls up outside. I rush outside and open his door and he sits there with a sheen of sweat on his face. His breath is so strong when he bends down to ruffle my hair that I have to take a step back. My father looks into the back of his truck, raising his eyebrows at all the bottles, and Jersey says that he's just on his way to his father's, and did we have any of our own that we wanted to add? I run inside to get a ketchup bottle I'd saved and cleaned out, and we wave him off, watching him clank his way back up the drive. Only afterwards do we realise he didn't even get out of his truck and I forgot to ask if Cindy's coming next time.

After that, he drops in to see us as often as he used to, but he always comes alone and he always has beer on his breath.

The following summer a stranger walks down the drive. My father and I are curled up together in the hammock, and I open my eyes to see him there, standing at the foot of the steps. He must have parked at the top of the drive and walked down without us hearing. He's dressed smartly, in a pale jacket and trousers to match. As I watch he knocks on the door. My father stirs at the sound, and the man turns round when he hears the *creek-creek* of the straining rope, like a tree about to fall down. I stay as still as I can, hardly daring even to breathe. It takes him a while to work out what he's looking at, the bizarre contraption hanging between two posts covered with a white sheet like the curtains of a four-poster bed. He crouches down with his hands on his knees and his bottom sticking out, and peers beneath the sheet. Eventually he makes out the scoop of a large human backside. Then his eyes follow it round until they meet mine. He makes a clicking noise with his tongue, and bares his teeth in a triumphant smile.

I give my father a dig in the ribs. —Dad. There's someone here.

My father rolls over too quickly, thinking he's in bed, and the stranger watches in startled bemusement as my father and I tumble sideways on to the ground, a tangle of limbs and rope and white cotton. We disengage ourselves from one another and get up unsteadily. My father rubs the sleep from his eyes.

—Sorry to disturb you, folks, says the man, striding forward and giving the air a jaunty stab with his shoulders. Underneath the jacket, he is thin and wiry. Name's Dalway, Tucson and Pima County Public School Board. Pleased to make your acquaintance.

He offers a hand to the air and pins us with his narrow eyes.

My father, his head still in a sleepy whirr, tries to make sense of the announcement. Not noticing the floating hand, he rubs the flat of his own against his nose.

—Name's Moon, he says, dumbly, and lets his hand drop to his side.

The stranger whips out a clipboard from under one arm and clicks the top of his pen up and down.

—Moon, he says, ruminatively, flicking loose sheets of paper over the top. Certainly don't have no Moon child on my list.

Something in my father wakes up, then, and he instinctively reaches behind him to where I stand and puts his clammy palm on the crown of my head. In a quiet voice, he asks what particular list Mr Dalway has in his hand.

—Local county register, says Mr Dalway grandly, and flaps the board in the air as if to suggest that within those flimsy pages are written all the biggest secrets in the world.

My father invites Mr Dalway indoors and gives him a cup of tea. I skulk in the background as they talk, Mr Dalway peppering the air with questions, my father answering softly. He writes down what my father says on a pink form, repeating each word out loud.

—Name, Josephine Moon. Date of birth, August sixth, 1979. Father, Mr Theobald Moon, aged forty-two. Mother—

—None.

—Do you mean deceased? He looks up.

—If you'd prefer to put it that way, says my father, yes.

—Brothers and sisters—

—None.

Mr Dalway looks up sharply again. —They passed away too?

—There were never any in the first place, says my father quickly.

—Education to date, I take it, none.

My father turns sideways to look at me, where I'm fidgeting in the doorway. We know what the other is thinking: that Mr Dalway is the Sandman, come to take me away in a big, black sack tied at the top with a knot. He'll throw me in the trunk of his car along with other black sacks and nothing will ever be the same again. My father blinks, watery eyed and helpless, and turns back to the pink form.

—Mr Moon?

My father looks up blankly.

—What was the question?

Mr Dalway collapses back in his chair and clicks the top of his pen for a few seconds. Then he opens one side of his jacket to reveal a hidden pocket and tucks the pen inside.

—Your daughter is nearly eight years old, Mr Moon. She's already three years behind most other kids. Do you want her to be educationally handicapped?

He pauses, dramatically, savouring the moment.

—Of course not, mumbles my father, avoiding Mr Dalway's eye.

—I am assuming that you have taught her the basics yourself?

My father coughs, and says something into his fist.

—Excuse me?

—I said yes.

—Josephine is going to need all the help you can give her at home, Mr Moon, before she begins.

My father looks up, forcing his lips into a brave smile.

—She'll start this coming semester at Santa Catalina. It's a fifty-minute drive by car.

—By car? The smile collapses.

Mr Dalway peers over towards me and I step succinctly behind the frame of the door. I don't want those sharp little eyes on me.

—I suggest, Mr Moon, he says, clipping the words irritably, that you equip your child with some clothes that are suitable for wearing outside of the house, a handkerchief for her nose, and that you teach her to wash her hands.

The next time Jersey comes I tell him about the Sandman. He slides his fingers into the tops of his pockets and tips back his head and laughs.

—Thought it was about time the world caught up with you, missy. It ain't nothin' to be scared of. I'll see what I can do about a car.

A few days later we're having breakfast and there's an unfamiliar rattling coming up the drive. We go out to see what it is.

—This, says Jersey, jumping out of his truck and sweeping his arm in the direction of a small white car, tied to his own with a tow-rope, is your new pride and joy. Got her off a bunch of hippies up in Pima Canyon country. You'll have to excuse the 'Make Love, Not War' signs. She don't have no wipers, either, and the gauge for the gas don't work. But we can soon fix her up. They insisted she answers to the name of Mabeline, but I guess we can fix that too.

The car is small and white, rusted around the rim, as if it has been dipped in a pool of orange. There are so many stickers on the windscreen there's hardly any room to see out.

—I can't drive, says my father.

Jersey looks at my father as if he's just announced he can't use a knife and fork.

—Every son of a bitch can drive, says Jersey quietly.

My father shrugs his shoulders.

—Shit, man, that's somethin' else.

We get in Jersey's truck and take the white Bug to the dusty paddock on the ranch where they break the horses in. A couple of ranch-hands are sitting on the fence, their knees spread out to the sides, making triangles of their legs. They brush their fingers to the brims of their hats when we go by, and carry on watching us after we've passed.

—They're here for the rodeo show, says Jersey, with a chuckle. That's us.

My father squeezes himself into the front seat of the Bug and I get in beside him. There are necklaces hanging from the mirror and little squares of white paper on the dashboard.

—I'll stay out here and give directions, shouts Jersey. Remember what I told you – right foot on the right two pedals, left foot on the left. No swapping. And remember to let the handbrake go.

—That's your job, Sugar Pie, whispers my father, urgently. We've already agreed that he'll do the steering and the pedals and I'll do the gears and the handbrake and help keep a lookout for any obstacles in our way.

My father turns the key in the ignition and brings his left foot up. I release the handbrake. The car jerks forward and bucks with its nose to the ground.

—I think you forgot something.

My father says nothing, just wipes his hands on his trousers and starts again. Once more the car jerks forward, but this time it keeps on moving, jumpy at first, but getting gradually faster and smoother, and as it does the engine revs higher, until it's making a high-pitched squeal like a jazz clarinet on the radio. I twist the rear mirror towards me until I can see Jersey's reflection in it. His arms are flapping up and down.

—*Now, Sugar Pie, now!* says my father, shouting above the scream of the engine, and using both hands and coming right up out of my seat, I jerk the gear stick down.

My father gives me a big, sweaty smile.

—Well done, Sugar! Well done!

Triumphantly we move from second to third gear, and then to fourth, and then, without warning, my father slams his foot on the brake. The front wheels lock and we spin round in a circle like an ice-skater executing a final flourish on the rink.

—Well, you folks, says Jersey, running over as we bail out. You didn't go through any fences, anyways. How long did you say we got?

—A little under three weeks, says my father.

Jersey says nothing, but rubs at the side of his mouth with his hand. The men on the fence have started to clap.

*

My father props an open book against the salt and pepper pots. I sit before it, gripping a purple felt-tip in my fist.

—Other hand, Jelly-O.

—No, I want to do it in this one.

—Well, OK, if you really think so. See this line here? *The giant lived in a cave . . .*

My father wraps his soft damp fingers around mine, guiding my hand across the page. We've only done a couple of letters when he stops.

—Are you sure?

—What?

—That it feels all right in the left? Because it doesn't for me.

—I'm sure.

—All right then. *And every morning bright and early . . .*

I watch, transfixed, looking at the line in the book and then at the purple shapes that we're making on the page. They don't look the least bit alike.

—*he tore the clucking heads off two chickens and thrust their bodies whole down his neck.*

We lift the pen together, his fingers mixed up with mine. The side of my hand, dragging across the page, is covered in a purple smudge.

—Josephine Moon, what in the name of holy Jesus do you think you're doing?

I look up to see Jersey standing on the edge of the garden with his hands on the gate posts, his head tilted stiffly on his neck, as if he has just been threatened with a bunched-up fist.

I tuck my wand behind my back. —Spells, I murmur quietly, so quietly I hope he can't hear.

—*What?* He puts his hand to his ear, creases up his face.

—Spells.

Jersey casts his eyes away and rakes them over the landscape, as if trawling the plain and the mountains for something that's been lost.

—I just never seen a fairy before in Arizona, is all it is, he says.

I cast a quick glance behind me, just in case I succeeded in turning one of the cacti into something else.

—Dad says—

—Yeah, well he would.

Jersey jumps the fence using a hand to propel him, and comes up close. He doesn't bend down to me, but makes me look up to him.

—How old are you, Josephine?

—Eight.

—Well let me tell you somethin'. Did you know that there aren't any fairies older than eight, anywhere in the world?

I shake my head.

—Well that's the way it is, missy. Fairies only go up to seven. And what with starting school an' all, I thought you oughta know.

I nod my head. Jersey shakes his, and carries on into the house.

The night before, my father sits at the kitchen table reading to himself. He holds his book very upright, like the preacher at Saint Xavier, his eyes peeping out at me over the top. There's no sound, except for the steady hum of the freezer. I've got my felt-tip pens out on the floor.

—Sugar, do you believe in me? he says quietly.

—I believe in you.

—And I believe in you, too.

In the silence that follows, he turns over a page.

Ten minutes later he's looking at me again.

—Sugar Pie, he says. You know that no one will ever love you like I do.

I look up from my drawing.

—Promise me you'll never go away!

His voice is husky and barely there at all.

I put the lid on my felt-tip and go over to where he's sitting. Uncertainly, I stroke the back of his hand.

—All right, Sugar Pie, it's all right.

He sniffs. I can see his mouth beginning to go.

—Shall I get the toilet roll?

He nods, his mouth pulled suddenly wide, like it's made of elastic. I go and fetch a few sheets and hold them out to him.

—It's all right, really it is, he says, but he blows it anyway.

The next morning my father hovers outside the bathroom door.

—Are you sure you've done everything you need to? Both kinds?

I pull my panties up and let him in. There's an anxious crease on his forehead in the shape of an *M*.

—Yes.

—Are you quite, quite sure? Because they won't let you go just whenever, you know.

His eyes water a little as he says it, as if he cannot quite bear to hear his own words. A bubble forms between his lips.

—You have to go when they want you to go, he explains. His tongue comes out and licks the bubble away. When they ring a bell, that means you can go. And when they ring it again, that means you can't.

He stops and stares at me, a little out of breath.

—That's stupid, I say.

—I know. I quite agree.

He blinks and shrugs his shoulders.

That's the outside world for you, he says with his eyes. *What else did you expect?*

It is beginning to dawn on me that the outside world is not like the world we inhabit, my father and I. So far I know our house and our garden and Jersey and what we can see of the desert from our garden fence. The outside world is a whole new place entirely.

—OK then, Sugar. If you're sure.

I'm suddenly not at all sure about anything any more, but I pick up my new schoolbag and we go out together, hand in hand.

I know the names of the Santa Catalinas, the Rincons, the Santa Ritas, the Tucsons and the Tortolitas. I know that in winter Mount

Lemmon is covered with snow, that there are Douglas firs and ponderosa pines up there, and mountain lions and white-tailed deer and golden eagles and even black bears. I know the Santa Cruz, the Rillito and the Pantano Wash, which are dry all year round except after a rain, when they are liable to bring down flash floods. I know how the world was created and what will happen at the end of time. I know the recipes for twelve different flavours of ice-cream, and which sell the best at different times of the year. And I know my times tables up to five and how to write my name.

—Who's the President of the United States? shouts my father, above the squeal of the engine.

—President Reagan. And he's married to Nancy.

—And who's the Queen of England?

—Elizabeth I. And she's married to Albert.

—No she's not.

—William the Conqueror?

—Nope. Third!

—*Who* the Third?

—Third gear! Quick! *Quick!*

When we get out of the car the air is thick with the sound of children's voices – bleats and shouts and wails. Before us, divided up into little hexagons by the chickenwire fence, hundreds of little girls and boys about the same height as me are running round and round in circles. Sometimes they collide, and one of them falls over, and another one falls on top, and then there are frantic screams until a teacher comes over and pulls them apart, dangling them by the scruff of their necks, like rabbits.

I look up at my father, to see if he's as frightened as I am, but his attention has been caught by a group of women standing in a ring on the side of the road. They are dressed very prettily – in brightly coloured dresses with full skirts – and, despite the heat, they each have a short cardigan buttoned up over the top. They stand with their heads bowed together and every now and then one of them tips her head backwards and laughs, her arms still wrapped across her waist, and the others follow suit. The shape they make when they laugh is like a flower with its petals opening up.

I turn back to look at my father.

—I'll go in there, if you go and talk to them.

He looks from me to the women, his red lips heavy and wet. The women bend their heads together to hear the next part of the story, the petals closing up again.

—Oh, I don't know about that, Sugar Pie, he says, the corner of his eye catching the light.

—Go on, Dad.

I let go of his hand.

—Don't go just yet, Fruitcake.

—Will you be all right driving back on your own?

—I think so, yes.

He doesn't say good luck or even goodbye; he's too preoccupied for that. I begin to walk the length of the chickenwire fence, holding my schoolbag tightly by its handle. The gate creaks as I open it, and springs back behind me. When I get halfway across the playground a bell rings, and all the children start running towards me.

I look around wildly for my father. He's still where I left him on the side of the road, but he's not looking my way. He's staring wide-eyed at the group of women, his clenched fist raised to his mouth. I try to catch his attention, but soon the running children are all around me. If I don't run with them I'll be knocked down. I raise my hand in a last wave which he does not see, then I turn round and let the surge of feet sweep me up among them, up the short flight of steps and into the adobe building, with its rounded orange walls and little windows sunk in deep.

10

—Russian. He was definitely Russian.

—I heard he was Vietnamese. Janko said he saw him being turned away at the swimming pool. The Vietnamese are only allowed in the day before it's cleaned.

—Either way, he was obviously married.

Wise heads nodding in sympathy travelled round the room in a wave. Only the head of Eva Ligocká remained unmoved.

All week it was as if a circle had been chalked around her chair, separating her from the other women. Anxious glances had been offered her along with slugs of whisky in her coffee, invitations to supper, suggestions that she go to Lilia's and have another perm, perhaps even put in a little colour. The name Pavel had been dropped into conversations with the frequency of stitched uppers dropping into boxes. Pavel himself had appeared at least once a day too, angling for an after-work drink.

—Perhaps tomorrow, Pavel.

—That's what you said yesterday.

—That's why I said perhaps.

—So it's yes for tomorrow?

—Perhaps.

—Perhaps it's yes, or yes, perhaps?

Somehow she heard it from within the heavy walls of the factory, and above the rattle of seventy sewing machines. Her first reaction was that the sound was in her head; that the tinny music had etched itself into her brain to taunt her. She got up from her desk and started walking along the corridor. By the time she was outside, she knew it was for real, and she broke into a run. It was getting louder. She leapfrogged the turnstile, ignoring the shouts of the man at the pass-punching machine, and propelled herself across the forecourt and towards the moving van as it drove past so quickly that when she slammed into the window with her fists Tibor thought for a terrible moment that he'd knocked her down.

He jammed on the brakes and stared at her in amazement.

—Meet me round the back! she instructed, then turned and ran back inside.

A little shaken, Tibor did as he was told. The man at the goods entrance waved him in without any questions. Tibor smiled to himself; an ice-cream van could get him entry to anywhere. On one side of the tarmac a line of men had formed a human conveyor belt, passing shoe boxes to one another and into the back of a lorry. They looked up when they heard him, ten surprised faces in a row. Those who didn't have a box in their hands automatically patted their pockets.

They called out for change, one to another, down the line.

—Hugo, it's that crazy ice-cream vendor again. Go and get us all something, will you?

One of the men left the line and started to move towards the van. Tibor watched from the driving seat, unsure of what to do. He had no intention of opening up and selling ice-creams today. He wanted to drive on, out of here. He glanced in his side mirror, hoping for a sign of Eva, but she wasn't there. For a while he and the man named Hugo eyed each other like two figures approaching each other for a dual. Registering the firmly shut window, Hugo slowed in his tracks and raised a bewildered hand to his mouth. At the same moment, a movement in the side mirror caught Tibor's eye. Two stacks of white shoe boxes were coming towards him, a thin pair of legs kicking out underneath. The boxes swayed, about to topple. The anticipation of disaster was terrible – like watching a clown attempt the tightrope at the circus. He leapt out, ran round to the back of the van and opened the doors just in time for Eva to let the twin towers spill on to the van floor.

The men in the conveyor belt stood still, apparently mesmerised. By the time any of them had roused themselves, Tibor and Eva had run round to the front of the van, jumped in, and were accelerating out of the open gates, loose gravel spitting in their wake.

The men turned to look at one another sheepishly.

—What on God's earth were you waiting for? one of them shouted at Hugo in rebuke, and then the others joined in.

With his spare hand, Tibor reached into a box beneath his seat, pulled out something in a plastic yellow wrapper and untwisted the wrapper with his teeth.

—Here.

—What is it?

—It's a Flake. They come from the West.

He watched her take a tentative bite.

—Eva, you should have asked me to do it.

She turned away from him irritably.

—I could have done it without anyone noticing, he went on. I'd have done it between half past eleven and twelve, when the delivery men—

—Had gone inside for their lunch.

—Exactly. If you knew that, why didn't you—

—Well, you didn't leave me much choice, turning up out of the blue like that.

They sat in silence. Eva ate her way through the Flake.

—Anyway, I wanted to be noticed. That was the whole point. I'm on the run now, too.

He gave her a derisory look.

——An outlaw, eh?

—We've all got to start somewhere.

There was an uneasy silence. Eva screwed up the Flake wrapper and flung it behind her. Attempting to put a brightness in her voice, she asked —Where are we going, anyway?

Tibor hesitated for a second, his eyes not leaving the road.

—Well I don't know about you, but I'm going to the Land of the Free. To the land of Huckleberry Finn! I'm going to make my fortune.

Eva swallowed her last mouthful of chocolate. She had no idea if he was being serious or not.

—You don't believe me, do you? He whistled through his teeth. That's a shame, because it's one of the few times I've told you the truth.

One thing was certain: they weren't going anywhere fast. The highest speed the van could muster was fifty kilometres per hour and, lacking any suspension to speak of, it spun them out of their seats every time it hit a hole in the road, which was often and with a surprising regularity, as if the holes were an integral part of the road design. The cheery and defiantly atonal jingle accompanied them all the way, singing out, over and over, to anyone who cared to listen, going fast when they went fast, slow when they went slow.

—Can't you turn that damned thing off?

—You've got to try and pretend it's Beethoven. Only way to handle it.

To begin with the towns they passed through were much like her own, with their concrete high-rises, formal flower beds covering the roundabouts like doilies, the line of Škodas parked nose to tail on the side of the roads. Between towns, the fields fanned out in alternating squares of pale and dark brown, depending on where they had ploughed. At junctions in the road, eight-foot stone women stood sentry, clasping bales of wheat in their strong, labourer's forearms, scythes resting on shoulders wide enough to strap a harness to. Between the trees they glimpsed grand country houses that had been abandoned during the move to the cities, their estates given over to farmland, their roofs and walls to the spread of ivy. They had a dishevelled beauty, like women half undressed. Sometimes they spotted a lonely pig nosing amongst rubble and nettles in the yard.

Several people tried to hail them – a man selling ropes of pink sausages on the side of the road, and then, as they drove through a village, a group of children playing football who parted to let them pass, and then gave chase, shouting and waving their arms excitedly. Eva could see them in the side mirror, a tumult of small, expectant faces.

—Tibor, you've got to stop. They only want to get an ice-cream.

—I haven't got any made up.

—You've got lollies in the freezer.

—Eva, we're on the run. You said so yourself.

It was like he was the Pied Piper and the jingle his pipe. The children followed instinctively, not stopping to question whether or not they really wanted an ice-cream; they just did what children were expected to do. Eva felt that she and Tibor were breaking an unspoken rule. She looked out the window and watched the excitement draining away from their faces as they realised, with confusion, that the van was not going to stop; it was not going to give them what it promised in large red lettering on the side. One by one they fell away, unable to keep pace, the largest boys the last to give up, until they were left standing on the road clutching their one-crown pieces, disappointment falling across their faces like clouds across the sun.

—Isn't America a bit drastic? she asked him, later. I mean, it's not as if we're murderers or anything.

—You're not.

—Oh, and I suppose you are.

There was a short silence. She stared at him in mounting horror.

—Don't look at me like that.

—How do you expect me to look at you?

—I'm not a bad man, Eva.

—Oh, so you're a good murderer.

149

They held each other's eyes for a moment. Eva felt as if she had died and woken up somewhere else completely.

—Look in the pocket in front of you.

She released the little door and felt around with her hand. Inside were a sheaf of papers, and a blue passport.

—Open it.

Inside was a picture of Tibor with his hair cut short, as he had it now. Underneath were the words: *Didier Jacob, né 1954, La Rochelle*.

—So your name is Didier?

—At the moment, yes.

—And how is your French, Monsieur Jacob?

—*Ça s'améliore.*

—And Tibor? Who's he?

He looked at her apologetically and shrugged. —You liked him, didn't you? he said with a sudden grin.

—And what about the man who killed someone. Who was he?

—That was a boy. A fifteen-year-old boy.

—What was his name?

—That doesn't matter any more.

—And the man who left without telling me he was going?

The ice-cream man was silent.

—I suppose that was Tibor, she said drily, and he doesn't exist any more, so he doesn't have to explain himself.

—I went to Bratislava to get supplies for the van.

—And did you intend to come back for me?

Silence.

—No, of course not, she said.

—But now that you're—

—It's all right, she interrupted. You don't have to say that.

They drove on in silence again.

She rang home from a call box.

—He has an aunt in Prague. We're going there. Don't be cross with me. I'll be back in a week, I promise. Tell work I'm sick, and I'll return the shoes. I'll explain everything.

Tibor listened from where he stood on the side of the road, having a cigarette.

—Married? Yes, we're getting married.

He raised an eyebrow at her as she turned to face him through the glass. She shrugged in silent reply.

—Yes, but he's a nice gypsy, she said. She gave him a wink. You'll like him. No, he's not a vegetarian.

They spoke little that first afternoon. Neither seemed ready to consider what might be happening. As the daylight faded and the countryside became submerged in a blanketing darkness, Eva kept track of the time by remembering what she'd be doing if she hadn't left. Sitting down to supper, helping her grandmother with her bath, perhaps getting ready to go out. As if triggered by this internal clock, she took out a little zipped make-up bag, opened her compact and tipped up her chin to put on lipstick, smudging it with pieces of tissue paper which she tossed out the window. She pulled her knees up to her chest, kicked off her shoes, and wedged her bare feet on the dashboard.

—Seeing someone special tonight? asked Tibor.

She turned to look out the side window. The hardness in his voice filled her with confusion. She felt that she was seeing a new side of him now, a side he had not revealed to her in their unreal world in the forest. This was the reality; the past few months little more than a dream. Sensing her distress, he suddenly slipped his spare hand between her thighs. She turned and looked at him, grateful for this first touch.

—Why did you leave, really? she asked.

—I was only passing through, you must have known that. Waiting for the weather to get better. For the last week I've been in Bratislava, like I said. I had to pick up supplies, say some good-byes. I've got enough ice-cream mix and cones to keep us for two months.

—We're going to live off ice-cream?

—No, Miss Ligocká, we're going to live off the proceeds.

She squeezed her thighs around his hand, but still she looked away.

As the evening wore on the red of her lips retreated to the edges, dissolved by the vinegar from the gherkins that they picked out of a jar to keep them going. When it was late, Eva's head fell against the window, and when a pothole jolted her awake, it was to register the jingle again, sounding out across the empty landscape like a ghostly lullaby.

The next time she woke the van had stopped. They were on a track off the road, parked tight against some trees so that they could not be seen from the road. Tibor was spreading out a roll of bedding between the fridge and the shoe boxes in the back of the van.

—Where are we?

—Český Šternberk. If there was a moon we'd be able to see the outline of the castle up there on the hill.

She heard him turn the temperature dial on the freezer chest. It shuddered and lit up like a small space craft, its strange, alien light catching the whites of his eyes. He tucked an upholstered cushion from the front seats beneath her head as a pillow, the musty odour of car journeys greeting her nose. He ran a finger across her face, then rolled away.

—I couldn't have asked you to come. You know that, he said into the darkness.

—Then it's lucky I invited myself.

He said nothing. He had offered her an apology; she realised she should have accepted it.

—Who did you kill, Tibor?

—A vendor in a food market in Prague. I was attempting to steal a cabbage.

—You killed him for a *cabbage*? She scanned what she could see of his face. The glow of the fridge made his skin ghostly and pale.

—Actually, I killed him *with* the cabbage. I was trying to stop him

152

chasing me. It struck him on the side of his head and he fell backwards on to a steel spike. It went through his neck. There was a lot of blood.

—Why were you stealing the cabbage in the first place?

—You want the whole story?

—I don't want a story.

—It's a true story.

—OK.

He rolled over to face her. The story was different to anything she had imagined. He had grown up in Prague, he said. His mother was the daughter of a wealthy landowner; his father worked as a copyeditor for *Pravda*. One day, when Tibor was fifteen, his father had substituted a column written by a leading Communist playwright with a poem by a dissident writer living in America. He was immediately demoted to typesetter – a show of leniency allowed him only on account of the editor's friendship with his wife's father. A week later he tried the scam a second time and was caught in the act, fired outright, and forced to take a job as a stucco decorator. He came home each night with stone dust in his hair, looking as if he had turned prematurely white. *This country will not allow you to find happiness with your head*, he told his son, *so you must find it with your hands.* He wanted Tibor to become his apprentice, but Tibor scorned him and registered at the university. He started stealing food to make up for the fact that he wasn't bringing any money home. He noticed that the stallholders in the market set up during the early hours of the morning, then left to go to breakfast for half an hour. For a while, the market was left unmanned – until they realised that someone was taking their vegetables.

—Were you arrested?

—They traced the bicycle I'd been riding back to my father. He denied all knowledge, of course, but he only had to look at me to know what had happened. He was furious, and ashamed. He packed me off to an old girlfriend of his who ran a chalet in the High Tatras. Irene Jacob, a French-Russian who'd lived in Slovakia since the war.

She learnt to cook in Paris in the twenties and thirties. I was expecting to meet someone like my mother; but Irene was an old lady when I turned up. To think – my father with an older woman! But she became like a mother to me. Every morning she'd put her long grey hair up in a bun and it would fall out gradually during the course of the day and there were always grips on the kitchen floor. You'd come across them when you swept up.

—She taught you to cook?

—Yes. I worked there as a chef.

—That's where you got the scars on your hands and wrists.

He looked at her, surprised. —Yes.

The night was divided by the hum of the fridge and the eerie quiet in its wake when it cut out, juddering to a halt, the occasional swish of a car going past on the main road. It was so cold that they kept their clothes on, thick socks on their feet, scarfs around their heads. At some point she heard the sound of him blinking, the click of the watery membrane breaking over his eye, and, knowing that he was awake, moved in and found his mouth with her own. For a moment they breathed from one another's lungs. And then a pair of hands reached downwards, looking for a way in.

—Don't you dare.

—What?

—It's too cold. Don't you dare.

He laughed at her childish language and pulled at the buttons on her trousers, a pair of his that she had borrowed, plunging a cold hand into her knickers. She kicked and screamed and tried to retaliate by slipping a hand up his jumper, but he caught her wrists and clamped her to the floor and moved on top of her. The instant she felt the weight of him, a charge surged through her, and she was hungry for him, tearing at his trousers and inhaling the smell of his skin, his hair, crying out almost immediately at the shudders he drew from her body.

Afterwards they rolled into a cocoon of blankets as far from the fridge as possible. She lay behind him as he fell asleep, looking at the pale neck exposed by his newly short hair.

In the morning she was woken by branches tapping against the roof of the van. She leant over him and saw that he was locked in sleep, his arms crossed tightly over his chest, hands tucked neatly into opposite armpits.

—Tibor. Didier. Whatever your name is. Wake up.

She had only been to Prague once before. She had forgotten how big it was – the sprawl of high-rises that began when they were still a long way from the centre. Many of the estates in these suburbs were still under construction, with cranes towering over rubble-filled streets.

—What about money? she asked him, as they jingled their way over the criss-crossing tramlines. It was an enormous relief to be asking questions now, after all this time.

—Irene died six months ago. She had a load of French currency in a safe. The gardener and I shared it between us.

—Didn't she have any family?

Tibor shrugged. —Probably. I don't know.

—And the passport?

—That was hers too. I took it to some people here in Prague who personalised it for me.

—How long have you been planning this?

—It was Irene's idea. Before she died, she showed me her old French Citroën in a disused shed. I've got the number plates in the back.

In Prague Eva left him by the Koruna Palace in Wenceslas Square while she posted a letter to Tanya. By the time she came back he had gone. She looked around the square, seized by a mixture of panic and anger. She saw a gaggle of schoolgirls grouped around their teacher, their brown leather satchels strapped across their chests, two nuns apparently squabbling over a loaf of bread, several men in dark suits marching diagonally across the square. The teacher with the school-girls turned to her and waved. A dozen envious fourteen-year-olds watched him make his way towards her.

Eva spun around and walked in the opposite direction, swinging her hips emphatically.

—Is that supposed to be me? he asked, catching up with her.

—You recognise yourself, then.

—I do not swagger like that.

—You do.

—I do not.

—Well obviously you're not aware of it, because if you were you'd die of embarrassment.

—Well if you're so ashamed to be seen with me, why don't you die of embarrassment yourself?

—I think I will.

Demurely, she handed him her bag, held her arms out to the sides and dropped backwards, all in one movement, hitting the cobble-stones in the shape of a star. Even though it had happened in silence, everyone in the square turned to look – the nuns forgetting their argument with the loaf, the schoolgirls raising their hands to their mouths in horror, even the businessmen wondering what act of domestic violence they had just witnessed. Tibor looked around him, anxiously. Eva's eyes were closed.

—Eva?

There was no answer. He crouched down, close to her face.

—Eva? For God's sake. Say something. Shit, Eva. Answer me.

She opened her eyes.

—My God. I thought you'd knocked yourself out. Are you hurt? How did you do that? They all think I hit you.

—I'll tell you if you make love to me.

—Right here?

—Yes.

—I can't do that.

—Then I won't tell.

156

He shrugged. —Fine.

She bit her lip.

—Make love to me anyway.

—No.

—Why?

—Because I'm late for an appointment.

—What appointment?

—We're getting married.

She sat upright. —I don't remember hearing you ask.

—I didn't. You don't have an option. See that church?

She followed the direction of his finger.

—The dark, Gothic one?

—Go and wait for me in there.

—But I can't get married. I'm wearing trousers. Your trousers.

—It doesn't matter. I haven't invited any guests. See you in a couple of hours.

—Two hours?

—You shouldn't rush into these things. We both need some time to think.

He kissed her on the forehead, then zipped his jacket up to his chin and headed off across the square, his head hunkered down and his hands in his pockets.

She was left to get up from the cobblestones by herself.

In the church she sat down on a pew at the front, a vault of air reaching high and chill above her. A succession of elderly women moved forward to light candles on the altar stand, each mouthing their own small words as they touched their unlit wicks to a flame, the sudden flaring as the flame moved from one to the other lighting up their faces as if in response to their murmured prayers. Under their dark fur hats, they wore thin chiffon scarfs in pale lilacs and pinks.

You've got to admit, he's more fun than Pavel. God, I can't believe I ever kissed that grease-block. Oh. I didn't tell you. It was last Tuesday night. I went for a drink with him after all.

She pictured Tanya reading the letter under the table at the factory.

If we really do go somewhere to make our fortune, you can come and join us. I'll send you the money. I promise!

She curled up on the hard, upright pew and closed her eyes. She was exhausted after the uncomfortable night in the van, and drifted off quickly. She dreamt that she saw Tibor as a boy of sixteen walking across a field of snow. He was wearing an apron and carrying a pair of skates in one hand.

He reached the shores of a lake. It was completely frozen over. The sixteen-year-old Tibor kicked with his heel to see if it was thick enough yet. The skates were old and basic – a rusted metal strip on a flat stand, like an upside-down iron. In his hand was a tangle of red laces that would tie over the top of his boots.

He stepped out on to the ice, the first, tentative steps. And then in one sweep he found his confidence. And there they were, a boy and a grey-haired woman, mock waltzing. *May I have this dance?* Her skin was fragile and thin in the biting air. As they spun, her hair came down on one side in an untidy clump. She didn't notice it falling, and wouldn't have cared if she had. *Why have you got your apron on?* Her voice was high and querulous, like a little girl's, rising up and filling the echoey space between the mountains. She undid his apron, flung it away with a flourish, the beginning of an elaborate striptease.

—I can't believe you just slept through it.

She prized her cheek from the hard pew.

—Tibor?

—Look.

He was holding something in front of her. She wiped her eyes with her hand and hauled herself into a vertical position. It was the open passport. *Monsieur Didier Jacob*, she read. And in new letters, underneath, *& Madame Ernestína Jacob.*

—*Ernestína?* What sort of a name is *that?*

Tibor hung his head. —My mother's, he murmured.

—You're joking.

158

He looked at her, wincing.

She leaned back and folded her arms. —Remind me never to trust you with names. Was I an expensive wife?

—You were, rather.

He stood up and offered her his arm, a shy smile on his face.

—Will you let me walk you down the aisle?

—Seeing as I missed the rest of my marriage ceremony, I think that's the least you can do.

Half an hour from Cheb they pulled into a lay-by. Tibor slid himself under the chassis of the van and swapped the Czech number plate for the French one.

—I am not getting in the fridge, said Eva, adamantly. I don't see why I should. What was the point of becoming Madame Jacob if I can't *be* her?

Silence from Tibor.

—Don't you think I make a good Madame Jacob?

Tibor scrambled to his feet, rubbing snow between his palms to get rid of the oil.

—OK, then, Madame Jacob. Or may I call you *Ernestína*.

—You certainly may not.

She glowered at him from beneath her fringe.

—OK, Madame. Give me your worst Czech in your best French accent. Not Slovak, Czech. And tell me why you look like a Slovak girl? The way your hair is done, your make-up. And why are you wearing a pair of men's trousers? Where are the clothes you brought with you from Paris?

—Give me ten minutes and I'll take these trousers in, she said. Her voice was quiet, hurt. I've done it enough times before. I can make them look like mine.

—Oh, and then you'll look like a real Parisian woman, will you? In taken-in men's trousers?

She turned away from him, offended. He had a way of making her out to be more parochial than she felt. Tibor scratched the back of his neck, a little ashamed of himself, and when he spoke again his voice was softer.

—Come here. This'll make you laugh.

Reaching in through the passenger door, he took a parcel wrapped in brown paper from under the seat and tore it open. Inside, neatly folded, was a white shirt with large orange flowers embroidered in two rows either side of the buttons. He held it up and Eva let out a delighted squeal.

—Where on earth did you get this?

—D'you like it? Look at these. These are even better.

He shook out a roll of fabric to reveal a pair of worn denim jeans, flaring out to the sides in wide bell bottoms. He held them up against his legs.

—I never saw anything so ridiculous in my life.

He stripped down to his underpants and put on the whole outfit, complete with a pair of round, gold-rimmed glasses with pink-tinted lenses.

—You cannot be serious.

Tibor held his arms out to the sides. —How do I look?

—You really want to know?

He nodded.

—You look like a Czech-Hungarian dressed in some crazy get-up sold to you by a fraudulent rogue in Prague for too many American dollars by convincing you that's what they're wearing on the streets of Paris these days.

He looked down at himself. —You really think they could've been taking the piss?

She took a sideways glance at him and then started putting on his discarded jumpers over her own.

—I think I'll ride in the fridge.

As soon as it began to get dark they set off again. Tibor had put the temperature of the fridge up as high as he dared. A few kilometres from the border crossing, he pulled over. They spread the tarpaulin down first, and she climbed in, covering herself with a blanket. Tibor ran the back of his finger across her cheek.

—Think about a day in midsummer, he said. Ninety degrees in the shade.

He lowered the tray of choc-ices and ice lollies in on top, let the lid of the freezer drop with a thud and she was left in darkness, her mouth close to the ventilation hole, which was also her only source of light. Beneath her head was a canvas pillow stuffed with fifty-dollar bills. No mere chicken's feathers for her, he had said. She felt the vibration of the engine as he started the van again. It ran through her body like a drill. This wasn't going to be a pleasant experience.

The van swung out into the road and immediately swung back again, sending her crashing against the back of the fridge. The horn of a passing car blared out.

—For God's sake, Tibor, she muttered.

The roads here were just as bad as those nearer home. Every time they hit a hole in the tarmac, Eva was jolted from one side of the fridge to the other. Good job I'm turning numb, she thought. It wasn't taking long for the chill to start eating through her jumpers. Partially melted ice lollies began to drip through the rack overhead and dribble on to her face.

Ten minutes later the van slowed to a halt. She heard the window being wound down. A loud laugh, then muffled voices. A voice she barely recognised, artificially high-pitched, the accent thick. *Didier Jacob. That's right, Monsieur . . . Bratislava. Best ice-cream in the world! Much cheaper too. Duties? Bien sûr.* The muffled voices conferring, two thwacks of a palm on the side of the van. The engine started up. That was it, they were through. Thank God. Not so bad, after all. But instead of moving forwards, the van was reversing, turning to the left, parking again. She heard the slam of Tibor's door, footsteps walking away. Silence.

She waited. Different scenarios began to unravel in her mind – the possibility that they would detain Tibor for the night, and she would be trapped in the fridge for eight hours. That they might confiscate the van themselves, and force him to leave without it. She had no idea whether it was possible to open the fridge from the inside. Even if it were, would she be able to lift the tray of ices above her?

When she moved her head, she could feel the tug of her hair where it was beginning to freeze to the wall of the fridge, stuck as if with glue. The airlessness was making her nauseous. She wished she could at least turn over, lie on her other side, give her right ear a chance to thaw out. Just knowing that there wasn't room to turn round made her desperate for it. She fought a growing urge to kick.

The minutes passed. Fifteen, perhaps thirty. It was difficult to tell. Then there were footsteps, more than one pair. The rear doors of the van were flung open.

Anything you like. Didier's voice. *Help yourselves.* The lid of the fridge was wrenched open and the internal light came on. She held her breath and closed her eyes like a child believing that if you can't see them, they can't see you. The van shook as someone else jumped in. Hands rummaged in the choc-ices on the tray above her. An ice lolly fell through a hole in the lattice tray and landed on her face. She dared not shake it off. The nausea rose once again in her stomach and she fought with it, swallowing the saliva that gathered quickly in her mouth. The ice lolly was burning her cheek like an iron. She heard the doors at the front open, the sound of the front seats being wrenched up. They were searching the van.

—Have you got one of those ones with nuts on? Chocolate and nuts on the outside?

—Yuri, what are you going to have?

She lost count of the number of people who had jumped up into the van.

—Viktor, look underneath, will you? Hang on, Mr Beatles, we have another customer here. Ahoj! You're just in time. We've landed ourselves a nice little treasure chest here.

More hands scrabbled amongst the ices. Under the ice lolly, she had lost all feeling in her cheek. A hammer banged against the underside of the van, right beneath her left temple. She lifted her neck in an effort to protect her head.

Gentlemen . . .

—Oh don't you worry, Mr Beatles, we're just making sure you're not over the limit. You wouldn't want to be over the limit, take it from me.

The hammer banged beneath her again, then moved on down her body, against her shoulder, her elbow, her hip. It was like some sort of Chinese torture. Count, she thought. I'll count to a hundred. I can make that.

She got to twenty. When I get to a hundred, I'll scream, she thought. I'll scream and all that'll happen is I'll get sent back home and it'll be fine. Tibor can disown me, pretend he's never seen me before in his life. If they find the dollars they'll probably just keep them for themselves. She counted to thirty, forty. The fridge door slammed down and she was in darkness again. Dribbles of melted ice lolly ran, tickling, into her ear and down her neck. Fifty, sixty.

—What's this, Mr Beatles? Like to doll yourself up, do you?

She stopped counting. Her make-up bag. She remembered now, leaving it in the compartment in front of the passenger seat.

There was a silence. Think, Tibor, think. She heard him give a nervous laugh.

—These Czech girls, they seem to like a Frenchman.

She heard muffled laughter. —I'll bet they do. Lucky bugger. Better lay than the Frenchies are they?

—Not bad, but you can keep them. I've got one at home.

—So you have, you dirty bugger, so you have. The engine started. Cries of *Au revoir, Mr Beatles* in the air. The van picked up what little speed it had.

—*Tibor!* She slammed her feet and fists against the walls of the fridge. Tibor! For God's sake, let me out!

She could hear the maddened caterwauling of the jingle drowning her out.

—*Tibor!*

She was sobbing when at last he was far enough from the border to retrieve her, gasping for breath between the hysterical contractions of her throat, flailing at the ice lolly stuck to her face. —It's OK, he whispered, lifting her out of the freezer and clutching her against him as he pulled off her clothes and rubbed her vigorously with a towel, prising the lolly carefully from her face, and trying not to laugh. He cocooned her in the towel, then rummaged around in a bag for dry clothes, smelling the socks and grimacing before he put them on her. He was jubilant, high on the thrill of escape. —We made it. Jesus! I can't fucking believe it. My poor *zlatko*! Look at you! You'll never have to be that cold again, I promise. We'll go somewhere where it's always hot. Half laughing, he rubbed at her arms, her ribcage, blew on to her face, pressed his lips on to hers, then carried her over his shoulder to the passenger seat. He had the engine running and warm air blowing through the extractor fan.

—Here. He brought a cup of apple brandy to her lips, gently tilting it in. He held her jaw in his hands until her teeth stopped chattering.

—The desert, she said, firmly.

—What?

—You said you'd take me somewhere hot. We'll go to the desert. You and me. Do they have one of those in America?

—I'm sure they do. They have everything there.

He knocked back the last of the *slivovica* himself and warmed her mouth with his own.

They drove through northern Bavaria – the Land of the Thousand Hills – and down towards Munich. At night they slept in the van; by day they stopped off to sell ice-creams so that they had German currency to buy food. Each morning she got out her boxes and put on a different pair of shoes, watching the way they changed her mood, the way she walked. She squeezed her feet into a pair of black plimsolls, a size too small, the elastic puckering a section of her skin, and became lithe and girlish. She wore a pair of flat pink sandals with two large buckles across the bridge of each foot – comfortable shoes that were good for the heat. Another day she wore a pair of tassled ankle boots and stood with one leg out to the side, tipped up on to the heel. Tibor's favourite were a pair of red knee-high boots, and in these she swung her hips, took strides, felt capable of anything. One night after a particularly good day's takings they went to a bar to celebrate and she wore a pair of delicate mock-crocodile evening shoes, pale green and sharply pointed, teetering on a heel the size of a pea, and she became a wisp of a creature, breezy, flirtatious, hooking one foot round the ankle of the other, her arm through Tibor's for balance.

When it was her turn to drive, she often went barefoot. She liked to feel the rough pedals beneath her soles.

—Where did you learn to take corners like that? asked Tibor, clinging to the dashboard.

—Nowhere, said Eva. I've never had a lesson in my life.

Tibor laughed. —Adding to your list of petty crimes, then.

—I've got some catching up to do.

They drove in circles around Munich for a week while they waited for their visas to come through. By now they were completely out of ice lollies and relying only on the churning vats of ice-cream mix. Eva became adept at curling the thick mixture on to the cones, using Tibor's technique of slotting the cones between her fingers.

One morning, as they were driving between one village and the next, she brought her hand down hard on the dashboard. —Pull over! she commanded.

She scrambled out and immediately doubled over to vomit, bending at the waist like a snapped stalk, pressing her hair to the sides of her face to keep it out the way. The cars zoomed past on the road behind them. Afterwards she hung there for a moment, turning her face to the side to gulp the air, wiping back the damp strands of hair that stuck to her temples. When she breathed in, the air was cold and clean against the rims of her nostrils and the skin stung at the back of her throat.

Tibor laid a hand on her back. She stood upright, wiping her lips, and when she drew her hand away it was attached to her mouth by a clear thread. They both stared at it, uncertainly. Then Tibor pulled the sleeve of his jumper over his hand and wiped it away.

—I was meaning to tell you, she said.

Tibor turned abruptly and went back to the van. When he appeared again, she searched his face for some sort of response.

—Open your mouth.

She did as she was told and he put a spoonful of something cold on her tongue. It teased the back of her teeth and made her eyes smart. When she pressed her tongue to the roof of her mouth, she felt it begin to melt, spread out its sweetness to the tastebuds on the edge of her tongue. Holding it there, it seemed to sparkle in her mouth.

—What is it?

—It's how we're going to make our fortune, said Tibor. It's my first batch. It's called Lemonade Fizz.

11

From the windows of Santa Catalina Elementary School you look out on to the foothills of the Santa Catalina mountains. Sometimes, higher up where the sides of the mountains are sheer and bald, you can see climbers pinned to the surface, little figures in black or white or red. From this far away they don't appear to be moving, just sunning themselves like butterflies with open wings.

I wish I was out there, instead of here.

—You talk funny, says Loretta, the big girl sitting opposite. She has very small eyes packed tightly to the sides of her nose and her voice is scratchy like a violin. Where were you born?

—In Arizona.

—You don't sound like it, the way you speak. She looks at Martha, to her left, and raises her eyebrows in a way she's copied from people much older than her.

—Can you read and write? asks Martha. Martha has tight black curls and a faceful of large, uneven freckles.

—Yes.

—D'you hear that? 'Oh, yes!' She's stuck up.

Jane, the girl sitting next to me, gives me a weak smile. She has dark blond hair with a greenish tinge that sticks together in clumps. Blue veins show through the delicate skin beneath her eyes. From the way she's looking at me I can tell that she's normally the one who gets teased, and she thinks this will make us friends.

I decide I'll make friends with Loretta and Martha, not Jane. They're brawny and loud, and it's safer to be on their side. At recess, Martha gives blood-curdling screams on request. Loretta runs up behind the boys, grabs them round the waist and lifts their feet clear off the ground. The boys shuffle nervously around her, half fascinated, half afraid. She tells us her father is a boxer and is going to be in the Olympics.

Everyone brings their lunch in small plastic boxes with handles. Sometimes they bring strawberry jelly sandwiches, sometimes it's peanut butter and jello. The sweeter the better, as a rule.

—I can make those, says my father. Just leave it to me.

I learn the rules very quickly, and I pass them on to my father. The strawberry jelly must not have seeds in it, and the peanut butter has got to be smooth, not crunchy. The bread must be white and pre-sliced and you must never have anything resembling the sort of food adults eat, like a chicken leg or a piece of cheese, or anything wrapped in aluminum foil. My father nods and takes it all in. Once, I tell him, a boy named Simon Bartholomew brought in a banana and they teased him about it for a week.

—So mashed banana sandwiches are out? My father looks disappointed.

—I don't know, I tell him. I'll check.

—If anybody's ever nasty to you, my father says that night as he brushes my hair with long, downward sweeps, the thing to do is to shut your eyes and imagine you're somewhere else.

—Fifty, fifty-one, fifty-two.

—You're always safe in your own head. You can make anything happen. You can imagine that you're a tree, for instance. Or a— or a—

—Or a lion? I suggest.

—Yes! he shouts, delighted how quick I'm catching on.

—How about a seven-foot bruiser with a Smith & Wesson?

He stops brushing and I hear a pause in his breathing.

—Well, I suppose so, Sugar Pie, if you really think it's necessary.
He starts brushing again, more slowly.
—Or an Uzi with full-metal jackets. That would be even better.
—I don't know, Sugar Pie. Where did you learn all this?
—Loretta's father has guns. He keeps them in the cupboard by his bed.
—Oh.
—It's all right. He's never had to use them. Yet.
I look at my father and start to giggle.
—You know they're really not a laughing matter, guns.
—I wasn't laughing about the guns. You've got a fly on your nose.
He twitches his nose up and down like a rabbit until it goes away.
—Where did we get to?
—Fifty-eight, fifty-nine, sixty.

Miss Carroll comes from Laurel, Mississippi. She teaches us to spell it forwards and then we learn to spell it backwards.

—Anyone here seen the Mississippi? asks Miss Carroll. Her voice is so full of wonder it's as if she were talking about Elvis Presley. We like her because she doesn't sit on the chair behind her desk, like some teachers do, but on the desktop itself, crossing her legs and leaning back on her hands. Her legs are strong and brown and bulge at the top. She has thick orangey bangs which cover her forehead, and the rest she tucks behind her ears. If you look at her straight on, you can't tell that she has any hair at the back at all, just that bowl cut on top. One day, Loretta says, Miss Carroll will get married and she won't need to wear above-the-knee skirts and white blouses with puffed sleeves and the buttons undone at the top any more. We've seen her standing behind the classroom at recess smoking a cigarette and sliding one fingernail under all the others to get the dirt out and looking like she's a million miles away. Loretta says she's mooning about her boyfriend, but it seems to me she could just as easily be mooning about Laurel, Mississippi.

There are eighteen of us in second grade and none of us has

ever seen the Mississippi. We shake our heads in silence.

—*You haven't?* Oh, lordy-me, you haven't *lived*. Her eyes roll up and disappear into her bangs so that all that's left is the whites, and her voice goes thick and creamy. It is so darn *wide*, she sighs, that you can't see the other side. She closes her eyes and her narrow lips curl upwards at the ends, like a cat's. And it never, ever runs dry.

Miss Carroll's voice is almost as nice as Cindy's, so I'm annoyed when somebody taps me on the knee. Loretta slips a scrap of paper into my hand. *i bet she goes all gooey like that wen shes with her boyfrend*, I read. I curl my hand around the paper, trying to think of something to answer back that suggests I was thinking the exact same thing, but really I just want to hear what Miss Carroll has to say about her river. As far as I was concerned, rivers and creeks were something that got full of water after it rained and when the water had run down and out to the sea, they were dry again. I'd like to put my hand up to ask whether it rains all the time in Laurel, Mississippi, but Loretta is waiting for an answer. It suddenly occurs to me that I like Miss Carroll more than I like Loretta, and that what I'd really like is for me and Miss Carroll to be alone together, her talking about rivers, and me sitting on her knee. But you can't make friends with the teacher. *i can C her Panteez from hir* I scribble back to Loretta, fold it over and shove it under the desk, wondering if I'll ever find out how it is that the water in the Mississippi stays still.

—We don't have a television set, or a record player or a microwave, I point out to my father, as he and Jersey battle with a broken windmill blade at the weekend. We don't have a waffle iron, or a calculator, or a telephone. We don't have Thanksgiving parties or fourth of July parties. Other people do.

—We can have a party if you want, says my father.

—Who would come? We don't know anyone.

—We know Jersey and the rancher, and you can invite your friends from school.

—I already did.

My father wipes the sweat from his forehead with a handkerchief.

—And what did they say?

—Loretta says her mother won't let her go to a house where there isn't a woman around.

—I'm your ma and your pa rolled into one, reminds my father. You tell her that.

—I already did. And I told Miss Carroll, too, and Miss Carroll says everyone has a mother. She says it's a rule of thumb.

My father turns back to the windmill, holding a screwdriver out to Jersey.

—There's always an exception to a rule. And anyway, we do have a camera.

—Jersey agrees with Miss Carroll, don't you Jersey? You said so. You said there are no exceptions to the rule on mothers. You said every son of a bitch got one tucked away somewhere. I asked you.

Jersey stands up straight and turns round. It's late afternoon and the individual bristles on his unshaven chin have turned gold, like cactus spikes. He avoids my eye, groping in his breast pocket for his soft-pack of Lucky Strikes.

—You should ask these questions to your father, missy, not me.

I look at my father. He's staring off into the distance.

—He'd just say I was a heaven-sent thing, like out of a fairytale, wouldn't you, Dad?

Jersey raises his eyebrows and scratches at the back of his head, then looks at me and we both look at my father, who's still staring off into the distance. Jersey lights his cigarette and blows a little cloud of smoke into the air between us all.

—Well, I'd say he's got that just about right.

—Miss Carroll says fairytales are a load of old garbage and aren't I too old for all that.

Jersey's mouth hitches up at one side as if it's been pinched with a peg.

—Well, and she might just have a point there. What's your father say to that?

My father's face emerges momentarily from behind the veil of smoke. He tries to hide the panic in his eyes.

—I say you're never too old for all that, he says shortly. He says it as much to Jersey as to me. Then he presses the screwdriver irritably into Jersey's hand and walks away.

—Well, Missy Josie, says Jersey, reaching out to give me a pat on the shoulder. I reckon your father knows best. Now you hold that blade steady while I get done on this blasted screw.

—What's *that*, asks Martha, in horror. Out of all the kids in my class, Martha is the one to watch. She sticks her big face in close and watches every little thing I do. Loretta is too slow and dumb to notice.

Everyone sitting around the table stops eating and stares at me. I blink at the gaggle of round-eyed faces. She'd caught me just after I'd taken a bite, and now I don't know whether to carry on chewing or try to swallow it whole. I decide to speak with my mouth full, then swallow or spit depending on the response.

—Chocolate spread and potato chips.

—You're kidding.

I shake my head, keeping my jaw very still.

—Give it here. Martha thrusts her hand out so that I have no option but to hand the partially eaten sandwich over. All ten faces around the cafeteria table turn to watch as she curls the top piece of bread back. Underneath is a thick layer of chocolate with little bits of potato chips sprinkled over the top.

Martha passes the open sandwich around the table as if it were an archaeological exhibit. Her audience is captivated, caught up in the thrill of my torture. I am suddenly aware of a desperate urge to pee.

—Cool.

It's almost a sigh, the way she says it. She draws it out soft and low, and when she looks at me there's an unmistakable glint of admiration in her eyes.

—Josephine, that's so cool. Your mom lets you have chocolate and chip sandwiches for lunch.

I am so relieved I almost pee on the spot. I swallow my mouthful at last.

—It's my dad, I blurt. He makes me lunch every day.

—Your *dad*?

—She doesn't have a mom. I knew that, chips in Loretta.

I quickly try and bring the subject back to food.

—Yeah. He'll make me whatever I want. I'll probably bring in ice-cream sandwiches tomorrow.

They're all watching me now, and there is envy in their eyes.

—Ice-cream? breathes Simon Bartholomew.

—Oh yes. We eat ice-cream all the time at home, I say, breezily, warming to my theme. Never in my entire life have I had so many people listening to me at once. Breakfast, lunch and dinner. You see, my father is an ice-cream man. He makes thousands of cartons a year. At the moment we do nineteen flavours, but he's inventing more all the time. My father and I are both addicted, naturally.

—What's addicted? When Loretta's confused she squints and her eyes look even closer together.

—You know, like you want to eat it all the time. My father says I've been addicted from birth.

—What kind of flavours? asks Martha, sharply.

I roll my eyes, extravagantly, as if this were the most stupid question in the world.

—Oh, anything you can imagine, he makes it. When we have it for breakfast, it's Shredded Wheat flavour. For lunch we have hamburger flavour.

—*Ham*burger flavour?

—Yeah, and French fry flavour, although that's not so good.

I'm running out of ideas now, so I take another bite of the by now much-fingered sandwich, hoping that they'll all go back to eating theirs. But Martha hasn't finished with me yet.

—Your dad's English, isn't he?

I shrug, which I consider should let me off the hook one way or another. The other children around the table look between me and Martha, uncertainly, but she seems happy enough with my response and so they all get on with their lunch.

I put my sandwich down on the table, my appetite gone.

Loretta passes me a piece of paper, folded in four.

do u think she puts her tung in his mouth?
whos mouth?
her boyfrends u moron.
wat for?
to practiss having sex.

I don't want to think of Miss Carroll having sex, with her tongue or with any other part of her body. I want Miss Carroll to marry my father and become my stepmother.

At recess we make Jane wander aimlessly around the school grounds so that we can stalk her, pressing ourselves flat against the walls of buildings and making a dash from one corner to the next. We squeal with giggles every time we try to cram ourselves behind a single fence post. In theory, if she turns around and spots one of us, that person has to take her place, but we make up impromptu rules every time that happens. *It doesn't count if we turn our backs. It doesn't count if you see more than one of us. It only counts if we say so.*

After three days of this, Jane makes an attempt at revolt. She sits on the steps of the music block and refuses to move.

—I'm not stopping you playing your game, she says, but she doesn't move for so long we get bored and tell her she's no fun to hang out with any more. Back in class, she cries silently, little sobs jolting her thin body. I consider holding her hand under the table, but if I did she'd probably start wailing out loud, and then Miss Carroll would want to know what it was all about, and then she'd be angry with me, and she wouldn't want to marry my father.

When I've been at Santa Catalina for two semesters, Mr Dalway brings a new boy to our class. This means I'm not the new girl any more, and that's good news.

—Apparently he's mixed race, declares Martha, leading the pre-arrival speculation.

—He probably talks funny, I say hopefully. I have no idea what someone of mixed race looks like, and from the blank faces around me, none of the others does either. I vaguely imagine someone who is black down one side of their body and white down the other.

When the new boy arrives, the class is so quiet it might have been plunged under ten feet of water. There's not even the scrape of a chair leg against the floor. It is a giddying silence. The new boy feels it too and takes hold of the edge of Miss Carroll's desk for balance. I look in his eyes to see how frightened he is, but he's looking straight ahead, his dark eyes resting steadily on some distant object beyond the classroom altogether. He is very tall – much taller than any of the other boys – and he stands with his shoulders so far back that his little barrel chest sticks out. His skinny legs dangle from a pair of baggy gingham shorts. There's a tremble in one of his knees.

—Everyone, this is Walter. I hope you will all be very nice to him.

Walter doesn't move; he just holds his head up high, as if his eyes and nose and mouth were jewels on a cushion. His large brown lips are full of tiny creases, as if they are usually stretched taut into a wide, ecstatic smile and only wrinkle up when they're slack.

Miss Carroll gives him a little push, and he goes to take his seat. The boys at his table edge away, but Walter doesn't alter the upward tilt of his chin. He does allow himself a quick glance up at Miss Carroll to check he's not doing anything out of line. Miss Carroll claps her hands and announces it's time for math, and Walter simply rests his palms on the table before him and waits for the eyes to leave him alone.

I wonder if his mother will let him come to my house so he can play with me.

One by one we go up to the front of the class and pick out a sum card from the appropriate pocket in the shoe organiser hanging on the back of the door. The sum cards are written out by Miss Carroll with a thick black oily pen and sealed in sticky-backed plastic. You can't smell the pen through the plastic though we all give it a try. I've been stuck on card 4 since the end of the first semester, and today the blank boxes are still as unfathomable and mysterious to me as ever.

$$16 - \square = 8$$
$$9 - \square = 2$$

I put my hand up for Miss Carroll. I like it when she comes and leans over me, the bolt of orangey hair falling out from behind her ear and brushing against my cheek. While I'm waiting, I notice that Walter's been given a pink card too. He looks up and catches my eye. I give him my friendliest smile, as wide as it will go, and for a second I see a slight tug on those pleated lips. But then he stops himself, glances warily at Miss Carroll, and his huge proud eyes drop down.

I put my hand on my heart, wondering if it's about to jump into my throat, like Mr Kozinski said.

When the bell goes for lunch, I hold back from the others. If I miss my place at the table with Loretta and Martha I can sit next to Walter instead.

—Josie, can I have a word?

My heart sinks. Why today, of all days? I go and stand by Miss Carroll's desk. Loretta throws me a half-anxious, half-relieved look, grateful it's not her, but aware that she's probably implicated in whatever it is I've done and wondering if I'll cover for her. Miss Carroll perches on the side of the desk and gives me her curly-ended smile.

—Josephine, do you like school?

In my head I run through all the things I could possibly have done wrong. I shift from one foot to the other. I nod my head.

—That's good. I'm glad about that. And do you like the sort of things you're learning about?

I nod again.

—What's been your favourite lesson so far?

Flustered, I cast my mind back through the day's classes, and yesterday's classes, trying to think of something I've learned. My mind goes blank.

—The Mississippi, I blurt out, immensely relieved to have thought of anything at all.

She gives a low laugh and a little shake of her bangs.

—OK. That's OK. I'm glad you liked the Mississippi, although that was really some time ago. Now, go eat your lunch.

By the time I reach the cafeteria I'm too shaken to think about Walter. Martha's voice cuts through the babble like a chainsaw.

—Hey, Jo-Jo! We wanna see your ice-cream sandwiches! Get your ass over here!

—*How* big? I ask my father.

—Very big.

—But what's *very*.

—Well, bigger than yours.

—I know *that*. I'm not an *id*iot.

My father looks up in surprise, a forkful of thick-shredded coleslaw halfway to his mouth.

—No, Sugar Pie, I didn't say you were. Why do you want to know, anyway?

—I dunno. Just wondering.

It's my tenth birthday, and we've come to The Moose's Last Laugh. I wanted Sonics or Denny's but he said it had to be here because the food was better. In front of my father sits an enormous slab of steak, at least an inch thick, flopping over the edge of his plate. I've got catfish in batter, hushpuppies, curly fries, two slices of Texas toast and a peach punch. In between us are mountains of more fries and coleslaw and a big jug of Cowboy Jake's Hot Pepper Sauce.

Beneath the table I press my left toes against the heel of my right foot to get my sneaker off.

There are already a few couples on the dance floor, sliding over the sawdust in time to the squeaky bluegrass fiddlers in the corner. The one on the violin is going so fast the tip of his bow is all a blur. Watching in silence from around the walls are twenty moose heads with pupil-less, glassy eyes, their brown, rubbery lips curling up to reveal large, yellow Texan teeth. Above the bar is a sign that reads 'Good Home Cooking, just like Grandma makes'.

But we're stuck in our booth because my father wants to eat. He's slicing away energetically at his steak with a serrated, wooden-handled knife. As he cuts down, the steak splits open with a little pop and a burst of oozy juice, and there, sandwiched between two pale layers of brown, is a layer of bright, startling red.

—How big will mine get, eventually? Big as yours?

—I think that's highly unlikely, Sugar Pie. Especially if you don't eat up.

He jabs his fork into the square of meat he's just sliced off, as if to catch it before it makes a dash for the edge of his plate, and bends his head down to meet it. Chewing is a long, difficult job. His jaw rotates in circles, like the jaws of Jersey's cows, and he has to concentrate so hard he hasn't got time to blink. He prods towards my plate with his knife.

—At least eat some fries, he says with his mouth full.

—How're you doing here, folks?

The waiter is almost as skinny as me. His jeans are flat at the back where most people's asses stick out. Holding them up is a conchoid belt set with a heavy turquoise stone that looks like it's going to do the exact opposite of what it's supposed to do and pull his pants right down. He wears a badge that says Derek.

—Fine, thank you very much, says my father, attempting to catch a browny-red dribble with his fork. He misses and it collects in his dimple, like a little rock pool. I give the waiter a big grin with fries inside.

—Derek, will *you* dance with me?

The waiter flashes me a nervy smile. One of his front teeth sticks out at an angle over the other.

—Your pa would get mighty jealous, don't you think? He darts a quick glance at my father, and backs off.

Under the table, I let one sneaker drop to the floor and get to work on the other.

—Please, Sugar Pie, don't just play with it. Put some ketchup on your plate and dip your chips in that. Or some mayonnaise.

—Just give me a *vague* idea how big my feet will get.

He looks at me blankly, chewing hard, as if he's thinking about it, but then he sticks his finger and thumb inside his mouth. For a moment nothing happens, just little movements of his tongue, until suddenly, with a look of triumph, he pulls out a lump of whitish gristle and inspects it, rolling it around as if it were a semi-precious stone. By the time he tucks it tidily underneath the rim of his plate, he has completely forgotten the question.

My bare feet brush against sawdust as I push my sneakers out of the way and tip the lid off the shoe box. My toes find their way inside, pushing themselves down to the ends. I scrunch them up tight to bring the heels up, and lift them clear. The boots are uncomfortable without any socks on.

—Shall we?

My father swallows too quickly and has to reach for his glass of water to help the mouthful down. I hold out my limp wrist to him as he splutters and coughs.

—Beg pardon? Shall we what?

—Dance.

He wipes his mouth with his napkin, still managing to miss the resilient little rock pool on his chin, and stares at me over the top.

—Well I don't know, Sugar Pie. Do you really want to?

—Yes.

—The thing is I haven't quite finished—

—We'll just tell Derek not to clear it away. You can finish it when we get back.

—I suppose I can.

I shuffle out of the booth, not daring to lift my feet from the ground.

179

—But *dancing*, Sugar Pie. I mean, are you sure?

Step, step, one back, slide slide, around the back. Step, step, one back, slide slide . . . We've got it pretty good now, or at least I have and my father's doing his best, watching two steps ahead and then doing everything in double time to catch up.

—Don't jiggle your shoulders around so much. You're not supposed to move anything above the waist.

Around us each couple stands face to face, some in waltz position, some with their hands on their hips. The women are wearing short denim skirts and tasseled boots that come halfway up their calves. Mine are not as high as theirs, but they still have a tasselled fringe. The men are all in Levis with potbellies and little coloured ties pinned at their necks. The guy on the mandolin notices the trouble I'm having with my boots and gives me an encouraging nod. His hair is combed back from his forehead and fixed with hairspray so that it bounces up and down in one big clump.

After two dances, my father's face has turned the colour of the inside of his steak. Little blobs of sweat are flying off him in all directions. It's only when he slumps down on a chair at the edge of the dance floor that his eyes drop to floor level, and he sees what I've got on my feet.

—Sugar. He speaks very slowly, using a voice I've never heard before. I told you very clearly. Not outside the house.

He glares at me and for a moment I don't recognise him. His face seems to swell before my eyes.

—Put your trainers on. We're going home.

—What trainers?

I say it more out of habit than a desire to fuel the argument.

—Don't be difficult, Sugar. Your *sneakers*, then.

—But we haven't finished our meal.

—I said we're going home.

My father has always been big, but he has never looked as big as he looks now, his face and chest puffed up like a snake. It's the first time he's given the impression that he *knows* he's big. All at once I feel a terrible doubt of him, the beginnings of a fear although not the fear itself.

—I have to pee.

—Quick, then.

I sit on the toilet for a long time even though I don't need to go. My legs dangle down in their cotton-panty shackles and I let the ankle boots fall heavily to the floor. I stare at the way the linoleum is cut around the trunk of the basin, how it doesn't meet the trunk but leaves a gap you can see the concrete through.

He's waiting for me outside the restroom door. He takes the boots without a word, then watches me tie my sneakers up. Behind us, the band has switched to a gospel song.

Sister, you gotta get down on your knees and pray. Oh yes. I said, sister—

Outside, the air is thick with the hiss of cicadas. A couple of cars pull into the parking lot as we pull out. I wonder if he has remembered to pay the bill.

We drive in silence and when we get home, we make our own separate ways to bed.

Charlie Dee, the most popular girl in fourth grade, is telling us a story. All of us are riveted, even Martha and Loretta, who are not normally friends with her. The changing rooms smell of stale pee and gym clothes that haven't been taken home to be washed. Some girls are sitting on the lockers, others dangle from the wire dividers where we hang our clothes, some sit cross-legged on the floor. With a lovely, curling motion of her hand which reminds me of Miss Carroll, Charlie Dee scoops up the hair from one shoulder, and drapes it over the other.

—So then he comes up behind her and grabs the back of her apron strings and pulls them real tight around her waist so she screams, and he says, You *whore*, Marina, you little *whore*. And then he spins her around and hits her full smack in the face like that – she pretends to smack the girl next to her but stops just short of her cheek – and my mom's face goes all twisted and ugly—

—Your *mom's*?

—Yeah. It was my mom and dad. This morning.

Charlie picks up her hair again and twists it into a rope. She has a scar on her forehead – a dent just above her eyebrow, as if someone once took a screwdriver to her head and gave it one clean blow with a hammer. All the girls in fourth grade would like to have a scar like that.

—And then the next thing is she's taken hold of one of his bottles by the neck and goes to smash it over his head and he turns all pale and says, 'Marina, now you know that's the last drop I have in the house, why don't you use a rolling pin instead?' But she's shaking by now, and she can't stop herself, even though she kind of seems like she wants to, and she brings the bottle down hard on the edge of the counter and bits of glass go flying everywhere and the sound of it breaking surprises her so much that she just stands there covering her mouth with her hand, and my dad looks at his liquor all over the floor and his hands are trembling too but otherwise he doesn't move – he's real still, still as a statue – and he says, all quiet and gentle, What am I going to have for breakfast now, Marina? Huh? Answer me that.

Charlie Dee stares at the floor, perhaps pretending to be her father, perhaps because that's all that she can think of to do.

It's Loretta who speaks first.

—Breakfast? she says, incredulous. He drinks whisky for breakfast?

Charlie Dee looks Loretta straight in the eye.

—Oh yeah. Every day, first thing that passes his lips.

A shocked silence fills the room.

—That's nothing. My father drinks his own pee.

It came out before I could stop it.

Martha looks at me aghast. —Eerugh! That is *too* disgusting! You mean he puts his face in the toilet bowl and laps it up like a dog?

—No, he drinks it from a glass—

There are squeals of delighted, horrified laughter. Someone shouts, —So does he make pee-flavoured ice-cream then, too, your dad? After that they're all laughing so hard they can hardly breathe. One of the girls drops down from the wire dividers and sits on the bench beside Charlie.

—I heard things about your dad. My mom says he's not all there in the head.

They stop laughing, then. Nobody wants to miss this.

—Mine says that too. And that he looks like a Thanksgiving turkey.

—He's so fat he can't wear normal clothes.

Their eyes are shining with the thrill of what's being said.

—He could be a psycho.

—Retarded people sometimes are.

—No wonder your mother left him.

—There probably wasn't any room for her in the bed.

More shrieks of laughter. All their eyes are fixed on me, waiting to see how I will respond.

—My dad says he's queer.

I don't wait to hear any more. I grab my gym bag and run out of the room and down the corridor and out into the bright daylight.

He's my father, I say to myself, to calm my racing heart. *And I'm his daughter.*

I slow down to a walk, struggling to catch my breath. I don't know where I'm heading, I just keep walking away from the gym.

I believe in him, and he believes in me.

I cross the school yard and go around to the back of the cafeteria. I sit down on a concrete step, among the garbage cans, and stare down at my feet and tell myself, over and over: *We belong to one another. Him to me and me to him. For ever and ever, Amen.*

—No hands, remember, says my father.

I roll my eyes at the sky.

—I *know*.

We are lined up, Jersey, my father and I, around the plastic yellow kiddie pool. Nine potatoes bob around in it. They're supposed to look like ducks.

—*Go!*

My father and Jersey squat down on the ground with their hands behind their backs and stick their asses in the air. I get down too, because part of me wants to join in, though the other part of me doesn't want anything to do with it. They've been trying to entertain me all through the summer vacation. It's their fault for not letting me go to summer camp where everyone else has gone.

Almost immediately Jersey gets a potato between his teeth. He sits upright, his eyes almost popping out of his head with excitement. He looks like someone who's been gagged. Then he bites down and the potato falls to the ground and he carries on munching the bit that's left in his mouth.

He's trying to make me laugh, but I'm not playing along.

—It's not fair. Your gobs are bigger than mine.

—It's not a *gob*, Josie. It's a *mouth*.

—Well, mine's a gob.

—Stop being a drizzle-pot. And that's not true, anyway, Sugar Pie. No one's got a bigger mouth than you.

—Well you've got longer teeth, then.

—Jeezus peezus, Josephine, cries Jersey. If you were to quit the talking and get down to it, you might have more of a chance.

I stare at Jersey, shocked. He's never been sharp with me before.

—Who wants to play a stupid kids' game anyway? I'm too old for all this. My face is hot. I stand up, and then as an afterthought give the kiddie pool a little kick. The water sloshes over and into Jersey's lap. I'm as surprised by it as he is.

—Well, thanks. Thank you kindly, ma'am. That's exactly what I needed. How'd you guess.

—Stop being stupid.

I look at my father for support. He takes off his white hat and rubs

184

the top of his head, then puts it back on again. He looks at me blankly, his hands on his hips.

—And you're stupid too!

My father gives a little shrug.

—Both of you! You're just as bad as each other.

Jersey stands up slowly, the damp patch on his thighs spreading out towards his knees. He scratches at the back of his neck. I wait for a while to give them a chance to say something. I want them to argue back. I want them to tell me something to make it all right. I want them to put their hands on my shoulders and look me in the eye and tell me that it's all right.

But they just stand there, awkward as hell, neither of them saying a word.

I stalk off to my room and slam the door as loudly as I can.

12

'Only in solitude', Theo read in *A Manual for Living Comfortably in the Cosmos*, sitting on his granite mound as near to the Lotus Position as he could comfortably get, 'does one encounter one's True Self, one's Innermost Nature, the Essence of what is generally referred to these days as the Soul.'

It occurred to Theobald Moon that he could be on the verge of some sort of discovery. It was mid-July, the first anniversary of his arrival in the desert, and over the last few days he had had a growing sense of anticipation, of expectancy – a sense that something significant was about to happen. Perhaps, he thought with a little chuckle, his True Self was about to emerge, and he'd discard the old Theo like a snake casting off its old skin.

It was true that the experience of solitude had a profound effect on a man. It was certainly a state in which you got to know yourself. But there was more to it than that. It had a quality of greatness to it, and if it wasn't such a big, cumbersome, *difficult* thing to manage, he'd say he'd like to be solitary for the rest of his life.

As for encountering his True Self, he wasn't entirely sure he really wanted to. What it would be like was anybody's guess. He didn't even know if he'd recognise it when it came. He had a fleeting vision of this True Self arriving unannounced one day – a new, improved Theo knocking at the door, and telling the old Theo to move on.

He looked up from his book and let his eyes wander out towards the mountains. What he saw was a huddle of indistinct mauve shapes beneath an unusually pale sky, the colour of ashes after a fire. Only thirty minutes ago, he reflected, those same mountains had been the washed-out grey of dirty paintbrush water in a jar. And yesterday, glancing back at them as he retreated inside to escape the suffocating heat, they had been bleached almost transparent, the brutal strike of the sun catching them square in the chest and winding them of their substance completely. Clearly, neither sky nor mountains could decide what colour to be at the moment.

A year ago he would have taken such inconsistencies personally. It would have seemed to him that the desert was trying to deny him a sense of familiarity with itself – the chance to form a bond. He'd have felt tricked into a false sense of security by all that friendly glinting and gleaming in the morning, when all the time it was planning to pull the rug out from under his feet with a blood-red evening sky so severe and calamitous that he'd end up wondering what if there had been an atomic explosion in LA.

These days, however, he had no such illusions about his own importance. The desert, of course, did not care tuppence whether he existed or not. It certainly wasn't going to bother to *play* with him. How the desert chose to behave, he now knew, bore no relation whatsoever to the fact that he lived within it. These days, it was not so much a question of Theobald Moon versus the desert, as one of equals. To survive in the desert, you had to believe you could match it, and these days he felt that he could.

The secret was adaptability. Change, transformation, metamorphosis – whatever you wanted to call it. They'd all been through it – the trees and plants, the animals, his own beloved cacti, even the rocks, everything that had seemed so static, so *old*, in the beginning – they were only there because they'd found a way of defying the desert, of surviving in the face of it. It was just a matter of confidence, of drawing on the strength inside.

He looked back down at his book. His True Self – whenever, *if* ever, it appeared – would thrive in the desert. That he was sure about. It would be all-powerful and strong. Perhaps his burgeoning size was proof that the metamorphosis was already starting to take place – a physical manifestation of what was happening inside. Perhaps he needed to grow in order to contain the hefty proportions of his Soul.

Shifting his left leg from beneath his right on the granite mound, Theobald chided himself for entertaining such fanciful thoughts. He was putting on weight because of his increasingly indulgent diet, and because he had allowed his daily ration of sweets to creep up a bit. That was all. And if he allowed it to carry on at the same rate, he really would drop down in the desert one day, just as Jersey had warned.

A sudden, warm breeze flicked over a page of his book as if it were trying to read over Theo's shoulder and had become irritated by his slow progress. Theo looked up. Behind him he could hear the clank-clank-clank of the windmill, spinning at top speed. The mountains were now completely black, as if covered with a layer of soot. He looked about him, suddenly sensing a strangeness in the air. There were no birds singing, he realised. In fact, apart from the noise of the pump, a deathly quiet had descended over the entire plain, as if it had been covered with a muffling blanket. Theo had the unnerving feeling that he was the only living creature left outside, that everything else had run for cover. Nervously, he swivelled round to see if there were any clues behind him – a troupe of hyenas about to descend on the valley, or a flock of spiralling vultures, perhaps, in the sky. But there was nothing – just a numbness, a muteness, an eerie sense of doom.

Disconcerted, Theo cast his mind back to the last few days. The heat had been building steadily, come to think of it. According to the thermometer in his house it had been well over the hundred mark today. He sniffed the air and yes, he could smell what he had subconsciously been smelling since the morning – a fragile, tinder-dryness that gave the air an unfamiliar edge.

He looked at his watch. It was five o'clock. Normally at this time of day the light would be hazy and soft, and there would be movement in the grasses. What did the rest of the desert know that he didn't? Where had everything gone?

Suddenly the breeze whipped through all the pages of his book at once. Theo took the hint, snapped the book shut, and retreated inside his house.

First there was an almighty crack, like the sound of a sheet being ripped in two. For a second the entire house was lit stark white. It caught Theo on his way out of the bathroom, and he let out an involuntary yelp and froze to the spot. Had he been struck? Electrocuted? He wiggled his fingers tentatively and, finding himself in one piece, ran to the kitchen window to take a look.

Forks of lightning were rupturing the sky in sharp white lines, crackling down in a shape like the diagram of a plant's root system. As he watched, the entire landscape was lit up for a fleeting moment – the grey rock, the greenish saguaros, the white lines of his fence – caught in a breathless second of ghastly white light, as if suffering from acute shock.

He steeled himself for thunder – thunder being the thing that had frightened him most as a child – but no thunder came. Just the splintering electrical strikes, one after another, so that after a while Theo began to wonder if there was some sort of competition going on – a bolt of lightning in one direction being answered by an even mightier one from somewhere else.

Theo had never been a Catholic. Nevertheless, he made the sign of the cross on his chest. He'd always coveted this visible plea for protection, and didn't see any reason why he shouldn't be able to borrow it from time to time. Just in case he were now guilty of blasphemy, or some such sin, he crossed his fingers as well. And, just to cover all options, he peered out the window at his two tall, feathery desert willows that were trembling at their tips, and mumbled a quick prayer to the Universal Life Force to please ensure that neither he, nor they, got struck, and that peace and harmony would return to his little kingdom soon – or something along those lines.

He had read about electrical storms. He had seen the blackened ribcages of unlucky saguaros. He knew that they meant business. Sitting at the window as if it were a television screen, he emptied a packet of caramel-coated peanuts into a bowl and fed himself handfuls of them as he watched the pyrotechnic display. Each time a fresh current ripped through the tense air, he coiled his toes and lifted them off the ground – an involuntary reflex action that somehow seemed to prepare his body for receiving a direct hit, should it occur.

Theo's mother had once told him that she could never sleep when there was a full moon. Something to do with her cycle, she had said, and his face had gone crimson – menstruation and any of its euphemisms being a fail-safe trigger for a top-to-toe blush.

Her words had stuck in his mind. Not because of the embarrassment, but because, even then, he had felt vaguely envious. Did all women, he wondered, live in sync with the planets? Wasn't he made up of the same amount of water as women – if not more, considering the size of him – and therefore just as liable to be lured to and fro by the cycles of the moon every month?

Now, however, he had found a much more powerful connection. Being up against such a strong adversary as the desert had made him into a stronger person – no doubt about it. Take this storm, for instance. He was not at its mercy. He was not separate to it at all. He was part of the ecological make-up from which the storm had been generated. The air that was warmed within his lungs, the wind currents that he deflected as he moved around the landscape. He was all part and parcel – albeit a very tiny part of a very much larger parcel – of the natural world, and as such he was in part responsible for the storm he was witnessing this evening. In fact, he *was* the storm. Just as Jersey's cows were the storm, farting copious quantities of methane gas into the atmosphere which no doubt went some way to tipping the balance of things up there.

It seemed so obvious now, and yet he had had to come all this way to discover it. Who controlled the wind and the force of the sun? He and the rest of the world. Who, whilst he was about it, controlled how many rattlesnakes were to slither into his garden today? He and the rest of the world; although seeing as he was the only one likely to be concentrating on the matter, that one would really come down to him.

Consciousness was all, he reckoned. With awareness came unlimited power.

With a flash the room lit up. Theo's feet came off the ground and in the second of pure brightness, he saw how the hairs on his arms were standing bolt upright, too, hundreds of them, like the tensile spikes on a prickly pear. Feeling suddenly afraid, Theo decided to take himself off to bed.

Three days later Theo woke to find the world had gone quiet. He opened his eyes in surprise.

He took his morning cup of tea and a pocketful of Jujubes outside. There was a stillness, a tentativeness, about the landscape, as if it were still in shock to find itself alive after its extraordinary beating – and, more unusually still, to find itself wet.

Theo made his way down the little gravel path, put his mug of tea down on the ground and did a few Sun Salutes. It was too damp to lie down and do the whole workout. And anyway, he wasn't in the mood. The storm had broken his routine, and it would take him a few days to get back into it again.

Instead of coming up at the end of the last Sun Salute, he went back into a Dog pose. With his hands on the ground and his buttocks sticking up in the air, he peered through the arch of his legs. There was quite a good view of the garden from this position, albeit an upside-down one. He noted a number of casualties – several oval-shaped stems of prickly pear had snapped off, and a couple of the smaller cacti appeared to have been washed away completely. Quite a lot of debris – rocks and twigs and what looked like the contents of his dustbins – had piled up behind one of the saguaros and around the posts of his fence. It would take him most of the morning to get everything shipshape again.

Bored with the Dog pose, he hauled himself upright, a little inelegantly, picked up his tea, and went to take a closer look.

Theobald didn't feel so grief stricken at the plundering of his garden as he might have expected; for the truth was that it was looking extraordinarily beautiful. A hazy sun was already at work evaporating the little puddles of water. *Puddles.* It was a long time since he'd had a need to use that word. He mouthed it softly, liking the shape it made of his lips, the way the moisture stuck around the *p*, the skin having to pull apart again. And then he remembered why it rang bells for him: it was the name of the dog his mother had had when she was a child. Puddles the dog. A spaniel or a terrier, or some such thing. He smiled to himself at the memory.

Little quivering drops clung like pearl earrings to the tips of the aloe vera leaves. Theo marvelled at how they added a freshness, a sparkle to the usually rather dusty grey-green plant. He peered down the neck of the yucca and saw that there was a well of water inside from which a tiny horned lizard was taking dainty sips with its darting tongue. Each time the tongue touched the surface, the pool shuddered. It must seem a miracle to the lizard, finding a pool like that. In fact, it was a miracle such a small creature had survived the deluge at all, thought Theo. He passed a saguaro and leaned close to inhale the unfamiliar smell of sodden plant flesh. It breathed back at him, with its warmed-up, earthy breath. It was as if everything had just been created afresh. As if he had woken up and found himself in the Book of Genesis. He was Adam, on the first morning, intro-ducing himself to his kingdom: *Good morning, saguaro, I'm Adam. My dear lizard, let me introduce you to Eve.*

Just then, something caught his eye. A flash of colour, the hard outline of a shape that wasn't normally there. He took a few steps to one side, peered through the mesquite branches and gave a little start, causing warm tea to slosh over his hand.

To his astonishment, a white van was sitting in the middle of the desert floor, roughly halfway between himself and the mountains. For a moment he stood still, then made as if to retreat inside his house, and then he told himself not to be so silly and decided to climb on to the rock to get a better look.

It was still very early, and his limbs were stiff from having spent the last two days inside, waiting for the rain to subside. Wobbling a little as he hauled himself up, he held on to his loose pyjama bottoms which were secured with a safety pin, the vanished end of the drawstring never having materialised, and ran one hand briefly over his naked chest. The sun pressed a warm, good morning kiss between his breasts. He tipped his weight from right to left in an effort to dodge a particularly tall saguaro on the other side of the fence. Yes – no doubt about it – there was a little white van with something written on the side. He was too far away to read the words, but there was a picture too, and if he wasn't hallucinating, he would swear it was an ice-cream cone with three scoops on top.

Theobald Moon ran his tongue quickly over his lips.

How very extraordinary: an ice-cream van pitching up in the middle of the desert. And so far from the main road, too. There was nobody in sight to whom it might belong. Perhaps it had run out of fuel and been abandoned, although surely its driver would have knocked on his door for help by now. His was certainly the nearest dwelling for a couple of miles around, although it was possible his house had been obscured from sight during the storm. Perhaps someone *had* come and knocked and he hadn't heard them through the noise of the rain.

He was about to scramble down again when he heard a shriek. A high-pitched female shriek. It echoed out around the valley, as sounds around here were inclined to do. Startled, he jerked his head backwards at the unfamiliar noise, like a jackrabbit. It was followed by silence, and then it came again, and this time it gave way to an uncontrollable fit of giggles. He could hear them quite plainly, even though the van was more than half a mile away. The giggles rose in pitch and turned into shrieks again, and at one point he thought the van lurched to one side as if kicked heavily from the inside.

Theo's belly gave a little heave.

He felt as if his kingdom had been invaded.

The problem with solitude, thought Theo as he passed his dirty dishes absentmindedly under the tap, failing to notice whether or not he was getting them clean before piling them on to the draining board, is that when you're alone, you get used to being alone. But as soon as the solitude is broken, even if only for a moment, you become lonely all over again.

As he washed, he stared out the window towards the small white van. Ever since it had appeared, crouched like a nesting hen on the valley floor with its tantalising image on the side, he had been unable to think about anything else. Its presence – and the presence of the people inside it – had disturbed his equilibrium. As he wandered amongst his plants with a hoe or a rake, halfheartedly attempting to clean up the debris from the storm, his eyes always found their way back to it, like two ball bearings trained by a magnet. When, at last, a figure emerged from inside, he drew himself up tall behind a saguaro, attempted to suck his enormous belly in, and peered around the edge.

What greeted his eyes was an entirely naked man. Theo pulled his neck in quickly, like a tortoise under threat. But his curiosity quickly got the better of him. When he looked again, he saw the tiny figure raise its arms above its head, stretch the muscles up one side of its body, and then the other, before breaking into a series of cartwheels. Startled, Theo watched as the naked frame spun, hand-hand-foot-foot, over and over. It made him dizzy to watch. It was Leonardo da Vinci's human wheel, perfect and beautiful, happening before his eyes.

Just then another figure appeared. He knew it was a woman because of the way she jumped from the back of the van – her arms rising untidily into the air, one leg reaching skittishly in front of the other. It was a joyful leap – a leap into the day, somehow expressing an implicit trust that the day would reach out and catch her. The childishness of the movement made him smile.

To his relief, this one was fully clothed. She was wearing pale green, perhaps a skirt and t-shirt. Once on the ground, she looked towards the cartwheeling man, but did not seem particularly interested. Instead she turned and walked purposefully away from the van, straight in the direction of Theo's house.

Theo felt like a coyote caught in a beam of light. He didn't know whether staying still was better than moving. He decided it was best to watch from inside. Sidling like a crab, he reached the safety of his steps and then, knowing that he was more likely to be seen as he climbed them, sauntered up as nonchalantly as he could.

He sat himself down at the kitchen window. The woman walked with her chin tilted down, fiddling with something on the back of her head. One hand reached forward to her mouth – collecting a clip, perhaps, or an elastic band, gripped between her teeth – and then returned to help the other, pulling back her hair from her face. When she'd finished, she gave her head a little shake, the sort of toss made by a horse irritated by its harness, except that by her movement she had somehow succeeded in shaking herself free. She stood still, then, put her hands on her hips and turned back towards the naked man. Looking at him, she had about her an air of intense satisfaction.

Theo swallowed hard, and took a gulp of his tea.

They would be gone by the following morning, he told himself. There was no way they would stay around. They did not have access to water, for a start, and if they were expecting to sell ice-creams out here, well, they were going to be hard pushed to find any customers.

But when, after forty-eight hours, the van had not moved an inch, Theobald's anxiety grew.

He had seen them several times by now. There were just the two of them – a man and a woman. He had even got to know the clothes that they wore – she, either a loose, pale dress or a pair of navy blue dungarees. He, khaki trousers and a black or a white t-shirt, some-times with a pattern on, or writing. More often than not he went bare-chested, and he regularly went bare-bottomed as well.

When he couldn't see them, he heard them. The clear peal of their voices travelled easily through the empty space, like tennis balls knocked into the air for him to catch. What language it was he had no idea. There was a strangeness to their vowel sounds that he didn't recognise. It was sweet and poetic, with a bell-like quality to it. Often there was laughter, the girlish, high-pitched squeal, the man's single, gleeful *'ha!'*. When the two sounds came together, it was almost too much for Theo to bear.

When Jersey came by in his truck for their fortnightly trip into Tucson, it was all they talked about. He'd noticed the newcomers too, of course, as he noticed any alteration to the landscape.

—Bin watching them from the road, admitted Jersey, un-ashamedly, a pair of binoculars round his neck. You can tell they've got the hots for each other. Sure as hell got a cute ass on her, anyways, he declared. Theo blushed furiously, and the ranch-hand immediately checked himself. Not that I'd know much about those sort of things, he muttered, and pushed the binoculars at Theo.

Theo wasn't sure he wanted to see what they looked like through the binoculars. He liked them as they were – too small to be quite real, more like a couple of plastic figurines that you might put on the top of a wedding cake than living, breathing people. They were, after all, on what he considered to be *his* territory and, as long as they were in miniature, he could carry on thinking of them as somehow belonging to him. Existing for his own entertainment. Squinting through one eye over the last few days, he had sometimes stretched out his arm and contained one of them between his finger and thumb, imagining how easy it would be to squash it, roll it into a ball, or send it sprawling to the ground with a flick.

Reluctantly, he brought the binoculars into focus on the figure of the woman.

—Seems to me she's got something of a stomach on her, too, he commented disapprovingly, to show that he was also capable of looking at a woman with a critical eye. Even as he said it he felt uncomfortable. Hiding his embarrassment by keeping the binoculars up close to his face, he watched her put her hands on her hips and arch backwards, the pale fabric of her dress pulling tight over her rounded belly. —Not that I'm one to talk, he added, with what he hoped was a self-mocking chuckle.

Jersey looked at him oddly, his head tipped to one side. He put his hand out to claim the binoculars back, as if Theo could not be trusted with them.

—You ain't seen a pregnant woman before, then, I take it, he said, and turned to walk over to his truck.

So far Theo had succeeded in avoiding almost all contact with other people in the desert, with the sole exception of Jersey. Occasionally, when out walking, he passed one of his distant neighbours on the tarmac road, and he gave them a nod which, he felt, was the mini-mum he could get away with. Most of the time he and they were safely hidden away down their long gravel drives, obscured by the billowy head of an aleppo pine or a dense oleander hedge. Con-fronting a crowd *en masse* in JCPenney or in the Tanque Verde garden centre, where everyone was simply a generalised blur, didn't really count. There, he found he could stay within the familiar confines of his own head, offering an occasional sprinkling of pleasantries – pleases and thank yous and Have a nice days – like a handful of birdseed tossed on to the lawn. Communication of that sort did not necessitate exposing his soul.

But he couldn't avoid the man and woman in the van. Not only were they physically *there* all the time, just across the valley floor and within his line of sight, but they continued to occupy a space in his imagination even when he wasn't looking at them. They were like a headache that followed him around wherever he went. He felt drawn to them in a way that he had never been drawn to anyone before. It wasn't that he was *attracted* to the woman. No; despite whatever womanly charms Jersey had identified in her, he found he didn't particularly prefer looking at her to looking at the man. To tell the truth, he didn't know which he liked looking at best. He liked them both, as a couple.

In fact, that was what fascinated him: their coupling. The way they watched each other, moved around each other. The way they played together, ate together, laughed together. It was their awareness of each other, the minuet that each of them danced as one half of a whole. Theo could not imagine living in such close proximity to another human being who wasn't his mother. Sometimes he caught them with their faces bent so close over an object one of them had found that their foreheads seemed to be touching. He could almost feel the tickle of the hair between them. Perhaps, he thought, they were whispering to one another in their strange, beautiful language. The sight was as touching as anything he had ever seen, and it filled his eyes with tears.

Seeing them kiss had the opposite effect completely. It had happened on several occasions. The man would come over to where the woman sat on a deckchair, squat on his heels and pull her towards him with one arm around her neck. Sometimes she seemed to resist, still intent on doing something else, but that only made him more determined. For some reason, the sight of their faces pressed together made Theo want to giggle out loud. Slightly embarrassed by his own reaction, he shook his head, as if he were actually laughing at a private joke that only half of him understood, and which was not worth the bother of explaining to the other half.

That evening, standing over the bathroom sink with a pair of nail scissors in his fingers, he looked at the soft pouchy *m* shape made by his lips in the mirror and realised that they had never kissed or been kissed like that. This suddenly struck him as a reason to feel sorry for himself. He poked the little scissors up his left nostril and chopped at the hairs inside. A little dusting fell on to the basin. He snipped gently at the right side too, creating a second little dusting of snuff on the damp enamel. Looking down at the twin circles he failed to remove the scissors in time and nicked the delicate skin on the inside of his nose. The tears were quick to prickle, the rims of his eyes reddening and beginning to brim. He sniffed hard, and swilled cold water quickly round the basin, avoiding the sight of his own eyes in the mirror.

His home began to feel different. Everything he saw became a jeering reminder to him of his solitude. His bedroom with the narrow bed, the empty spare bedroom across the hall, the jar on the bathroom sink with its single toothbrush, the kitchen with its half-sized pots and pans. Even the fact that the garbage man only bothered to come by once a week, instead of twice.

He could no longer escape the problem of eating alone by taking his dinner outside, because *they* were there to remind him – in case he had forgotten – that he was still alone when he was in his garden. How could he forget any more? His treasured sense of connected-ness to the desert – to the birds and the creatures and the cacti – was breaking down. They had come between him and his desert. No longer was it the laughter of the gila woodpecker he listened to; instead he heard their laughter, and it tormented him. It was laughter from which he was excluded.

At night Theo was haunted by images of entwined limbs, of the casual brush of hair against skin, of two bodies locked in a sweat-sealed embrace like twins in a womb. He found himself imagining how they would chatter to one another in the dark, telling each other their innermost thoughts, teasing each other for their silly habits, praising each other's cleverness, adoring each other's ways of looking, of smiling, of thinking. Feeling bereft and hollow, he curled his arms around his chest to give himself the sensation of being embraced. He drew his knees up as far as he could and made himself into a ball.

And sometimes it didn't stop there. In his head he saw the man roll on to the woman, and he in turn rolled on to his front and began to work himself slowly up and down against the mattress, his chin pushing against the pillow like a walrus manoeuvring up a beach. He slipped his hand beneath the waist of his pyjama bottoms, wrapped it around his swelling penis, closed his eyes and pretended he were sandwiched between them, locked into the strong clutch with which they held each other, intercepting the warm breath from their mouths, the wet lick of their tongues, the caress of hard nipples and soft breasts, one pair from above, one from below. He drove his body deep into the mattress, drilled hard with his fist, breathed as they breathed, moaned as they moaned, and when the wetness oozed at the tip of his fingers he imagined it was the wetness inside her. His hand working faster, he spilled himself with an anguished sob into the crotch of his pyjama bottoms and his head flopped down on to his pillow, his heart thundering painfully against his ribs, his squashed hand drying stiffly against his stomach.

All around him the silence of the desert panned out, still and complete.

One afternoon, as he sat on his rock and peered over the top of the largely unread page of his book, Theo saw the dark curly head of the man appear through the sliding window of the van. He called out, a sound like a long 'aaayyyy', tipping up into an 'aaahhhh'. She approached and stepped up on to a crate that had been positioned beneath the window. She lifted her face to meet his. They're going to kiss, thought Theo, his throat constricting. But they did not. Instead, there was a glint and sparkle of something metallic between them. She must have opened her mouth, for the shining object disappeared inside. They were both still for a while, and then she began to nod enthusiastically and lean towards him for more.

It was a decisive moment for Theo. His own mouth filling with saliva, he rubbed his sweaty palms against his thighs, and took himself off for a bath.

He wasn't used to getting ready to go out. He had never been invited to Jersey's home – he didn't even know where he lived – and Jersey only climbed the steps of Theo's when something needed fixing inside – a tap with a worn-out washer or a loose hinge on a cupboard door. It was an unspoken rule of their friendship that it be conducted in the open air. Sitting side by side in the truck was all right, because there was the road and the driving to think about, rather than the proximity of one another's bodies.

Theo padded through from the bathroom to the bedroom, leaving wet footprints in his wake. At least he didn't have to go through the trouble of deciding what to wear. His white ensemble had become a uniform now. Unhooking a clean shirt from the peg on the back of the door and retrieving a pair of crumpled trousers from under the bed, he dressed himself with a certain delicacy, even tenderness, as if he were doing up the buttons for somebody else. He smoothed down the sparse curly strands on the top of his head, oblivious to the fact that they sprang up again as soon as he took his hand away, and wrapped round the homemade white turban he had started to wear, taking care to tuck in his ears. He looked in the bathroom mirror to make sure he didn't have anything unpleasant in the corners of his eyes. A quick once-over with the toothbrush – never a favourite job – on with the Oxfords, and then he was ready to go.

On the way to K-Mart the other day, Jersey had said he thought the couple were from Eastern Europe. He had recognised a soft throatiness in the sounds that they made – a profusion of *shh* and *ch* and *ts* sounds. Theo had never heard Jersey speak about his origins, except to confirm that his surname was Polish. He had always seemed one hundred per cent American to Theo; to be someone who belonged. But it occurred to him now, for the first time, that the generosity he had shown towards Theo in the course of the last year was more typical of someone who was something of an outsider himself.

Perhaps the possibility of shared origins explained why the couple seemed to have aroused as much interest in Jersey as they had in Theo. He had clearly been thinking about them, suggesting to Theo that they might be political refugees or Jews or some such thing. Theo felt jealous of his interest. He felt as if he had a right to the couple that Jersey did not have. He had spotted them first. Somehow it felt of vital importance that he should be the one to meet them first, too. That way he could stake his claim. If he let Jersey get there before him, he might lose out.

And so it was that a freshly scrubbed and talcum-powdered Theo bravely descended the steps, crossed his little garden, and let the white gate swing shut behind him with a click. Introducing a defiance into his stride that he didn't actually feel, he began to march across the open valley floor. He would have preferred to have approached unseen, but he didn't have that option.

His route entailed negotiating a wide, rocky area that he had never crossed before. A wiry and very prickly long-stemmed cactus grew in abundance close to the ground, and tried to nip at his bare ankles as he made little jumps from rock to rock. Once he reached smoother territory he popped a gobstopper into his mouth as a sort of reward and made a mental note to look up the unfamiliar species in *Discover the Sonoran Desert* when he got home.

As he walked, a passage from *A Manual for Living Comfortably in the Cosmos* came into his head – the one about being connected to everything else. Before, of course, it had made him think of his relationship to the desert. Now it seemed to speak to him of his relationship with the man and the woman in the van. Despite not having met them, he felt he had a bond with them, and he wondered, a little plaintively, if they felt it too.

He looked up, and found he could now make out the words on the side of the van. 'Slowakian Ice-Cream' he read, over what was indeed a picture of a three-scoop cone. At least that was in English – near enough. Losing his footing slightly, he descended at a little run into the gully in which they were parked. Bang slap in the middle of an arroyo, they were, not far from a couple of canyon hackberrys, and for a moment he wondered if they had been washed down from the mountains by the flash floods the other night.

He was drawn up short by a small blackboard on an easel. Written in coloured chalk were the words:

Real Slowakian Ice-Cream!!!

Slivovica Kissiz
The Poppy Seed Kake of Mrs Ligocká
Midnite in the Dezert
Sunset over Choklet Mowntens

The words made Theo light-headed, as if he had spent too long in the sun. He reached for his flask of water and helped himself to a swig, knocking it back in a quick slug and opening his mouth to let out the air afterwards, as if it were something rather stronger.

There was no answer when he knocked on the side of the van. Theo walked around the vehicle and shielded his eyes to peer through the passenger window. Nothing except for an empty pickle jar on the seat. He tried the handle of the rear door, and when it twisted easily in his grasp, he allowed it to swing open. Before he knew what he was doing, he'd hauled himself up and promptly received a heavy wallop on the centre of his forehead.

Staggering and blinking in the semi-darkness, he reached out with his hand. It landed on a heavy copper saucepan that was dangling from the roof. He steadied it, and then steadied himself, and stooped to look around him. Gradually the shapes of the interior of the van began to reveal themselves to him. As they did, a volcano of saliva erupted in his mouth.

Lining the shelves were row upon row of little phials with pipette tops – vanilla essence, lime and cranberry cordials, apricot and elderflower nectars. There were screw-top jars of ginger in three different forms – fresh, candied and crystallised; packets of spices – nutmegs and cinnamon and vanilla pods; assorted jams and syrups; bags of nuts and packets of perfumed tea. The sight of so many deliciously sweet things made Theo feel suddenly weak. He blinked again, as if convinced it would all disappear. Not only, it seemed, was he linked to this young couple by Universal Energy, but also by what they liked to eat.

He raised a hand to his lips to catch the beginnings of a sly dribble. It had been a long time since he'd been in anyone's kitchen but his own, and he knew the contents of that inside out. This was all the more enthralling for being unexpected, with no one else around. *No one else around.* He had almost forgotten there was supposed to be anyone here in the first place. Presumably they had gone for a walk; they must have set off when he was busy doing his ablutions in the bathroom.

On the worktop were two mixing bowls covered with a single teacloth. Theo lifted the corner to peep underneath. His heart did a little skit to one side. One of the bowls had been used to mix something pale and creamy, and the remnants were still stuck to the sides. The other was full of a rich, dark chocolatey concoction with interesting looking lumps mixed in.

As a boy it had always been his job to lick out the mixing bowls. His mother would save them up for when he came home from school. There had been a lot of baking in their house in Bellissima Street. One or two cakes a week – a chocolate and a lemon, sometimes a banana, often a fruitcake – plus a batch of shortbread or jam tarts.

He picked up the bowl that was almost empty. First he dipped in a finger. A dabble of the pale, creamy mixture on the tip. To his surprise, a strong stab of alcohol hit the roof of his mouth – it was hot, like brandy – followed by an intense creaminess as rich as Cornish clotted cream. He wiped a clean rim around the edge of the bowl, and once he'd done that it seemed a bit silly not to do the job properly. He found a spoon – perhaps the very same one which he had seen disappear inside the woman's mouth that morning – and scraped the bowl out thoroughly. He smacked his lips. It was quite extraordinarily delicious. When every last bit was gone he washed the bowl up in the sink, pouring water from a plastic container. With a bit of luck they'd forget that they hadn't washed it up themselves.

The problem with licking out a bowl was that it was never quite enough. It tended only to make you hanker for more. Theo thought he'd have just a taste of the mixture in the second bowl. To his delight, it was very strong, dark chocolate – the kind he liked best. He managed to fish out a lump of something rather wonderful that crunched in his mouth – a piece of crystallised biscuit – and then he found another lump that was even better: a thick piece of candied orange peel that, when he bit into it, released a lovely sweet flood of nectar on to his tongue. The combination of the three flavours together was quite sublime.

Theo was enchanted. The first few spoonfuls were, without much hesitation, followed by more, and after a while he couldn't pile the spoon high enough. By the time he had got halfway to the bottom of the bowl he was barely giving himself time to swallow one mouthful before pushing in the next. What he was tasting was unlike anything that had passed his lips before. It was like something from another world.

At last, forced to pause for breath, he put down the spoon. A knot of terrible queasiness had formed in his belly. It was richer than he had realised – the chocolate was very intense – and now he was feeling unmistakably sick. With trembling fingers he washed the second empty bowl in the sink – more to give himself time to think than from any intrinsic sense of good manners – and laid it upturned on the draining board. A long, plaintive whine issued from the tunnels of his digestive system, and he looked down, half expecting to see a lump of crystallised biscuit attempting to negotiate a congested corner of his oesophagus, and finding instead only a series of brown dribbles running down the front of his shirt.

Wiping his hands on the teacloth, he scrambled out the back of the van and started to walk away as quickly as he could. He didn't dare look back.

13

—Don't make me laugh.

   —I wouldn't dream of it.

   —Then stop tickling.

   —This isn't tickling.

   —Ti*bor*!

   —What?

   —Tibor, that's tickling!

   —No it isn't. *This* is tickling.

Eva shrieked as Tibor renewed his attack. She kicked out and got him in the middle of the face.

   —Oh God.

   —It's all right, it's not broken, said Tibor, clutching his nose.

   —No, it's not that.

   —What then?

   —Oh God. Eva scrambled to her feet and clutched a blanket between her legs. I think I just wet myself.

   —You *what*?

   —I told you not to make me laugh first thing. It's all this weight on my bladder.

   —We'll have to get you some nappies, said Tibor, and pushed open the rear doors to let her out. He watched her wander a few feet from the van and squat to one side of a small bush, lifting the corners of the blanket she had wrapped around her on to her knees.

—You're looking.

—So?

When she'd finished, she draped the blanket over a few bushes to dry it out. Tibor noticed the Motel 6 logo stitched to a corner.

—What's wrong?

She returned his accusing stare, purposely misinterpreting it.

—I'll wash it later.

Tibor had tried the engine that morning but it had refused to turn over. He'd lifted the bonnet and peered inside, but apart from drying the spark plugs he couldn't think of anything else to do. Perhaps it just needed a day or two to dry out completely. The battery was low; they'd have to turn the fridge off before it ran right down. In the meantime, he wanted to make the most of a few stationary days.

He was starting to feel very at home in his new kitchen. Without looking, he could reach up to the shelves with one hand and have it land on whatever he wanted: a packet of nuts or a bottle of brandy, a phial of vanilla essence or a jar of poppy seeds. He had come to possess the tiny space like an artist who knows precisely the distance between his palette, his water jar and his canvas.

He lined up a motley collection of ingredients. A packet of Medjool dates they had bought at Mecca, on the edges of the Salton Sea, still in the brown paper bag which had hung around them as they grew; a kilo of oranges and another of shelled pistachios; a fresh coconut; a packet of cookies; several bars of chocolate which had no doubt been sequestered down Eva's dungarees before leaving the store; and a packet of Turkish Delight. She'd taken to her new vice with the same gusto she had brought to all her new roles – as lover, as mother-to-be, as immigrant to a new country. First it had been food – a frozen steak or a banana – things that she craved. Then it was clothes – a couple of pairs of socks, a t-shirt with *Have a Nice Day* printed on it. For Tibor she had stolen a pair of Levi jeans and a matching jacket. Other items – pots and pans to cook with, cutlery, a sepia print of Geronimo, chief of the Chiricahuas, which she hung on the wall – she'd found at garage sales. Tibor always pressed a few extra dollars into the hands of the people holding the sales as they left, just in case.

Whenever they stopped for more than one night, they brought their few possessions outside and arranged them around the van. A green-and-white striped canvas deckchair, a child's blackboard standing three feet off the ground, a hand-woven Navajo rug in muted reds and browns.

—We need a television set, Eva said, surveying the scene of domesticity.

—We do not.

—Yes we do, she insisted. Eighty per cent of Americans own a television set. I heard it on the radio.

As he began to chop the oranges – still undecided as to how he would use them – the smell of shoe polish reached him on the fresh morning air. Eva's own peculiar perfume. Through the small window he could see her perched on the front bar of the deckchair. She was surrounded by her collection of shoes, emptied from their boxes and spread out as if they too needed an airing after the rain. Something about the image made him feel content. It was a vision of normality. The thought surprised him a little – he hadn't realised that there was a 'normal' in their lives. He split a date down the seam with his thumbnail, flicked out the stone, and put it in his mouth. He loved to watch her when she didn't know he was there. She was working her way through the shoes, pushing her hand inside each as if it were a shoehorn, and bringing them up close to her face. Her inspections were of military standards. Sometimes she found a crease or a scratch, and a parallel crease would form on her own skin, right between the eyes. She licked a finger and rubbed at the leather, and the mark on the shoe and the mark on her face faded in tandem.

They had found their new van on a garage forecourt in Venice Beach. Its rounded roof and bonnet were caked in droppings from the seagulls that used it as a launching pad for raids on the open-air café next door. It was an old army vehicle which had at some point been converted into a travelling hot-dog stall. Ventilation grids had been cut into the rear and a small sliding window in the side. Across the back doors you could just make out the peeling remains of a crudely executed brown sausage drooping from its soft white bun, dribbling sauce. A couple of onion rings hovered overhead. On the side in faded, mustard-yellow lettering were the words 'Hungry-man's Hot Dogs – you won't find nothin' hotter'.

They had haggled over the price with a sheet of paper and a pen. Tibor wrote one figure, the garage salesman another, and then Eva joined in with a third, even lower than Tibor's original. The sales-man, his short, reddish beard gathered under his chin with an elastic band and a single black bead, scratched his head, quizzically, thinking he must be missing some invisible logic.

When they bought it, the inside of the van was encrusted with several years' worth of dirt. In the cupboards they found red plastic bottles in the shape of tomatoes, their nozzles congealed with long-dried-up ketchup. While Tibor looked under the bonnet, Eva dug a penknife into the thinning fabric of a tyre. She watched it deflate, then called the salesman over.

—Well, I hadn't noticed that flat. Guess you can have another twenty-five bucks off for that.

Tibor had looked at her wonderingly.

—How are we supposed to drive it away? he asked her loudly in Slovak.

—We get him to mend it for us and we pick it up this afternoon, she had replied, and turned a ravishing smile on the uncompre-hending mechanic.

The gardener at Motel 6 had loaned them his hosepipe and a couple of sponges to wash the van down. He seemed to speak no more English than Eva could and was used to communicating via a range of facial expressions. He and Tibor took off their shoes and rolled up the hems of their trousers. Eva watched how the water dripped from the bumper of the van, making it look like the white tasselled fringe of the three-piece suite everyone had on the Kúpel'ný ostrov estate. The gardener used his baseball cap to motion the action of painting, speeding up as he covered an entire wall of air. Then, nodding energetically in answer to his own suggestion, he disappeared and came back with an old washing-up bowl full of spray-paint cans. By the end of the afternoon, the van was resplendent with a giant ice-cream laden with one scoop each of chocolate, raspberry-ripple and vanilla.

Tibor looked down at the worktop. Half-eaten tins of sweetcorn, baked beans and tuna fish stood forlornly to one side with their lids jerked open, the forks sticking up like flags. They had got through a lot of supplies these last few days. Till now they had travelled almost at random, west out of California through the East Mojave Desert, passing the sand dunes of the Devil's Playground on their right, Providence Mountains on their left. In the valley between these high walls of rock, the air gathered the heat up in its arms, held it still and heavy like a precious infant during the hours from ten till three, then released it to the ground towards evening. They had stopped at little wooden shacks on the side of the road, the word 'Store' hashed with a thick paintbrush above the door, sometimes an old cow bell hanging from a rope outside. Nothing moved in these stores: the windows were covered with dense squares of chickenwire backed with paper, keeping out the air as well as the flies. Scantily clad women peered out from faded magazine pages beneath tins of peaches and peas, packets of blueberry cheesecake mix, instant mashed potatoes. Once a fat, black dog had lifted its head from its paws, made as if to bark, then changed its mind, letting its head drop down again in the heat, the large, apologetic whites pushing up the muscles of its eyebrows as it followed them around with its eyes.

In the Painted Desert the pink rock had spread out around them like a tablecloth. Sometimes it ruched up into rugged, low-slung mountains to one side, and in their baldness these mountain ranges appeared prehistoric, like vast, crouching lizards with shadows folded into the baggy skin of their flanks. Overhead hung small, flat-bottomed clouds, their bases dusted with the same pale pink as the rock, as if they had drifted down to rest on the surface when no one was looking and come away with a powdery tell-tale smudge. At dusk, just before sunset, the rock ignited, turning from dusky pink to an angry red. Six hundred feet above a hawk rode wheels of air.

The roads they travelled on linked one horizon to the other in long, straight ribbons of grey. This, Tibor told Eva, was the land-scape of the Wild West. The windscreen was large and deep and from their high seats they had a good view of everything. At the point where the tarmac met the sky, the heat caused the air to reverberate, as if the road was a jumping-off point, a diving board into the blue. For days at a time their van, crawling over the surface like a hard-backed albino beetle, had been the only thing in the landscape that moved.

They had skirted the city of Phoenix for a couple of weeks. Each time they returned from a trip into town, Eva whipped surprises from her sleeves or from behind the bib of her dungarees – exotic fruits which neither of them had tasted before, candies with un-familiar names, little bottles of liqueurs. Once the cupboards were full, they stacked packets of caster sugar and cornflour beneath the worktop, and used them as pillows at night.

For the first couple of months, the nights were much cooler than they had expected. They would park in a lay-by and sleep on the floor of the van, as they had done in Germany, squeezed this time between the kitchen fittings on one side – the little freezer, fridge and single electric ring with a water-boiler designed for heating frankfurters suspended above – and their own belongings on the other – the stack of shoe boxes, several cartons of ice-cream cones. One night she woke to find him holding down her arms – his turn to straddle her.

—Who's Pavel?

—*Pavel?*

—Yes. You called out his name.

—I did?

—Yes.

—Was I screaming?

—No, you were smiling. Who is he?

She laughed. —My God, I never knew he'd made that much of an impression. The little grease-block. Get off my arms.

—I'll kill the bastard.

She narrowed her eyes at him.

—Not a good joke, coming from you.

He stared at her, dumbly, then rolled off. When he spoke, the insistence in his voice surprised her.

—Who is he, anyway?

—Oh, he's just someone I used to flirt with at the factory. Or, to be fair, someone who used to flirt with me.

—Did you sleep with him?

—What sort of a question is that?

—A simple one.

—You think no one else ever noticed me before you came along? That I just hid myself away like some virginal princess, waiting for you?

—Yes.

She rolled away from him and looked at the white shoe boxes piled up beneath the sink.

—Well. So what if I did.

—So much the worse for the men of Slovakia.

—And what about you, hidden away in your chalet in the Tatras? I presume you weren't living the life of a monk.

—Well, there was a certain Anna.

She tried to sound unconcerned. —And who was Anna?

—A seventeen-year-old brunette from Košice.

—What happened?

He shrugged. —She was on the run too. She'd stabbed her stepfather with a penknife fourteen times.

—What a charmer.

—She had the most fantastic legs.

Still, sometimes, she watched him – not to discover him any more, but to enjoy her new-found knowledge of him. She knew his entire repertoire of night-time noises – the little mewls, the sighs, the snorts and growls, the little jolts of surprise when his body jerked in a spasm as he fell off the edge of a cliff in his dream. In the mornings he jumped out of bed, boasting that he'd hardly slept a wink.

—You're a liar, Tibor.

—I had to pee in the night. I couldn't get back to sleep.

—Oh yes you did.

And she'd tell him how he'd got up, suddenly, throwing the blankets off both of them, kicking open the rear doors noisily, flooding the van with the mottled grey light of the night, and how she'd heard him splash against the van itself, as if it didn't occur to him to direct it anywhere else than against a wall, and then he'd climbed back in and immediately fallen into a state of deep breathing beside her, and she'd felt the damp tip of his cock against her leg.

—That's not how I remember it, sulked Tibor.

The mornings, too, were cold to begin with. After the bedding was rolled away, they filled a washing-up bowl from a flagon of water and sponged themselves down. They washed as Tibor had washed in the Tatras, keeping their trousers on while they washed above the waist, and putting a jumper on to wash below. Sometimes Tibor stripped off all his clothes and dried himself by walking around on his hands. He made going upside down seem effortless – just a matter of placing his palms on the ground and presenting the soles of his feet to the sky, his legs flailing ungracefully to the sides like flowers too heavy for their stems. When he walked past the van like that, she'd reach out and grab his ankles and clasp them together with one hand, and the position made her think of her grandmother, carrying a chicken by its legs.

They stopped off in bars and found new beers to drink. Coors, Hamms, Löwenbräu. They ate at a diner called Mike & Ronda's where pictures of pink flamingos hung on turquoise walls and high plastic swivel stools laced the counter.

—Two times two plus two plus two, announced the waitress, slapping down plates of eggs, pancakes, sausages.

—You don't need to do that, said Eva, noticing the dollar bills that Tibor had tucked beneath his plate. There's a way out through the men's room at the back.

Tibor looked at the chopped orange peel. It was always the moment just before he began that was hardest; once he got going, everything fell into place. He knew he had a gift for it. It was an instinctive thing.

A shadow fell over his hands. —What is it?

—It isn't anything yet.

She ignored him, waiting expectantly. Tibor levered open a jar of maple syrup. He watched the pursing of her lips as she held it a while in her mouth.

—It's After the Storm, she said. After the Storm the Sun Comes out Again.

—No it's not, said Tibor. It's maple syrup. It says so on the can.

—Look. Can you do anything with this? It's from the giant cactus plants that are growing everywhere.

She held out a thick-skinned, oval-shaped fruit. It was overripe and half eaten by wasps or ants. Tibor sniffed it, suspiciously. It was sweet and pungent, a little alcoholic. He knocked it against the edge of the window to get any insects off, then cut a clean slice from its core, giving half to Eva.

—It's almost delicious, she said, slowly, and he nodded.

—It's a little like that water melon we had the other day. A cross between that and a fig.

—It makes me feel . . . I don't know . . .

—Horny? he suggested, his face lighting up.

—You think it's an aphrodisiac?

—Seems to be doing something to me.

—Me too.

—Give it here. I'll make an aphrodisiac ice-cream.

Tibor spread a map out on the ground in the shade of the van, a bottle of beer holding down each corner. The area was divided up into swathes of colour – green for the forested areas, yellow for the Indian reservations, orange for national monuments. In between were vast areas of white with few markings, straddled only by the spidery lines of roads like red veins across an eye.

Every time he looked at it, something responded deep in his gut. He had not seen many maps in his life. Czechoslovakia, Russia, Hungary. A small-scale map of the world. Detailed maps of other countries had been hard to come by at home. Now, with this American state spread out before him, he felt hungry for every inch of it, to cross from one corner to another, to know each part of it as well as he knew the back of his own hand. He translated the names that appealed to him most. *Big Bug Creek*, *Bumble Bee*, *Snowflake*, *the Chocolate Mountains*, *Window Rock*. His eyes lingered most over the white areas, where towns and villages were sparse. Undesignated spaces, they seemed to him, voids that most people just passed through, or around. Perhaps they drew him because they did not seem to have been claimed yet. He felt drawn to them with the pull of a magnet.

Eva picked up one of the corner bottles and rolled it across her forehead and around her neck. She stood behind Tibor as he crouched. His t-shirt was marked with sweat in the shape of a butterfly.

—Here, he said, his finger denting a new valley in the map.

She squatted behind him and rested her cheek against the dampness, the smell of him filling her nostrils. He still smelt of the spruce forests back home – of rain and earth, resin from the trees.

—But there's nothing there, she said. It's just a blank space.

—Exactly. That's where we are now.

—You need to take a shower, Tibor.

He climbed up her arm with his hands, as if it were a rope, until he had his nose deep in her armpit.

—And you don't?

She stood up, flung her arms to each side and fell on him in the shape of a star. This time he rolled over and caught her before she hit the ground.

Sometimes she sidled up to the side mirror, shimmying down until she could see her face.

She found a wariness there, as if she were greeting someone who might not be pleased to see her. She ran a finger over the pale freckles that had emerged on her cheek, then along the line of her upper lip. She had not used any make-up for weeks.

She had changed a lot in the last six months. When Tibor had met her, she had been trussed up in the unworldly winter garb of small-town Slovakia, her ankles thickened by bunched-up leg warmers, her hips invisible beneath the long, woollen skirts which billowed out like a bell from the waist, her breasts flattened beneath the tightly embroidered tunic tops that were the speciality of her bread-making grandmother. Now, she was like a forest thawing out. Layer by layer the clothing was coming off, revealing first her ankles and wrists, then her arms and legs. Her skin, once the colour of soft boiled potatoes, was taking on a burnished glow.

She tilted the mirror upwards and began to gather the hair at the nape of her neck, dipping her head as she scooped it into a high ponytail, pulling in even the fringe that she had hidden behind for so long. It was an action that had become a part of her morning ritual, this gathering of the hair back from her face, something Tibor came to see as a literal opening up of herself to whatever the day had in store. She took a clasp from between gripped teeth, fixed it into place with a click, and the newly clear face was locked in place. She shook what had once been a tightly-curled helmet but now swung in a loose, wavy pendulum, the bottom end just grazing the bump at the top of her spine. Like Tibor's hair, it had grown fast out here in the heat.

Tibor, approaching round the side of the van, looked up at her

216

sharply, as if struck by her beauty afresh. She smiled with pleasure at this, but even as she did so she was aware of a certain duplicity. She was not quite familiar with her new appearance yet herself.

In the late afternoon, she leant against the bonnet of the van, tilting her face to receive the yellowing sun, resting the phrase book against her breast as she continued from memory. *Would you like cake. Would you like sandwich. We haven't any coffee. Usually we take tea at four o'clock in the afternoon.* She closed her eyes and continued to mouth the words silently at the sun, as if she were whispering a prayer or an incantation.

He climbed behind her on to the sun-warmed bonnet and pulled her into the armchair of his legs and stomach. When she leant backwards, the shape of her womb revealed itself through the fabric of her dungarees. Tibor reached down and ran a large flat palm over her breasts to her belly, travelling the terrain, riding her bumps and hollows, ending up by wrapping his hand around the hummock of her crotch.

She still hadn't learnt to trust him completely. She had never forgotten his sudden departure from the forest and she was unhappy when she did not know where he was. At the exit to the supermarket in Phoenix she had shouted to him —*Where were you? You disappeared.* He had looked at her, amazed, and placed his hands either side of her face.

—I was getting you a present. Eva. Listen. I was getting you a present. She peered down the sleeve of his jumper. Not there. Higher. There was a bulge in his cheek, as if he had a boiled sweet inside. With her fingers she prised his lips apart and reached inside. It was a digital watch. She had never seen one before. She was silent, still recovering from the upset.

—Look, you press this and you can set a clockwatch, to time things.

She cheered up quickly then, like a child.

—What do I need to time?

—Your baby.

—My baby?

—You know, the contractions.

—That's your job. You keep it.

—What?

—You're the one who's got to deliver it.

Now she lifted his hand and took it with her through the side opening of her dungarees and underneath the elastic of her knickers.

—It's nice not to be moving on every day, she said. I'm tired. We need to find a place for the baby to be born.

—Yes, said Tibor. As soon as we find the right place, we'll stop.

Standing behind her on the second day of rain, he had slipped the straps of her dungarees off her shoulders and begun to undo the buttons at her waist. She ignored him, trying to spoon melted ice-cream into her mouth. Above them, the rain drummed down on the roof of the van. When her arms prickled up in goose bumps he ran his hands over them, smoothing them down. As he tried to pull the dungarees over her hips she carried on eating, until he pulled the chair from beneath her and she had to clutch at the bench to stop herself falling.

—Ti*bor*. Leave me alone.

—No. You're coming outside.

—It's raining.

—I know.

He moved to the front of her, yanked her dungarees down and lifted her t-shirt to her chin.

She flung the spoon down on the table.

—Jesus Christ.

She held her arms up above her head, as she used to do for her mother or her grandmother when she was tiny, while he took off her t-shirt and unhooked her bra. Only when her knickers were on the floor and it was time to step out of the legholes did she reluctantly lift her feet up, one at a time.

—That's better.

He unbolted the rear doors of the van, and pushed his shoulder against them. A rush of cold air and water greeted them. He took her hand and they jumped down with a shriek into the unknown river beneath. Immediately their bodies fell backwards, their feet slipping in soft mud. Holding on to her with one hand and the van with the other, Tibor hauled them both upright. They dug their fingers into the loose grit on the edge of the bank and, gasping for air, clambered out on to the flat.

—Tibor, this is mad. We're going to drown out here.

—Look! It's like being under a waterfall.

The rain hit them in fistfuls of little pellets, pummelling their shoulders and backs. Tibor tipped his face upwards, letting the water stream into his eyes and mouth. Around them the ground was alive with bouncing crystals.

He looked at Eva standing miserably beside him, at the water streaming down her in gullies, finding a network of streams down her back, over the jut of her buttocks. She was divided in two where she had caught the sun – her neck, the tops of her arms and her calves were tanned; the middle part of her, the pregnant part, was still pure white. Her belly was taut and hard, like a rock worn smooth in a river. It gleamed with the sheen of water running over it.

He presented her with a folded hand, the magician again. She softened a little, peeling back his fingers. Inside was a bar of soap.

—Our first shower since LA.

He held the soap out to the rain, then rubbed his hands round it, making a lather. He started with her shoulders, spreading the bubbles up her neck and down her arms. She stood still as a statue, not quite ready to forgive him completely, but beginning to enjoy it nevertheless, her arms outstretched when he got to her armpits, water dripping off the tips of her fingers. He lathered her back in gentle circles, holding out the soap for more water, rubbing it between his palms, then turning her round to do the other side.

When he came to her belly he sank down to his knees in the mud.

He rubbed it tenderly, round and round, as if he were polishing a lamp with a genie inside, encouraging it to emerge. He brought his tongue to her and tasted soap.

They lit a fire from bits of dry bush and cooked sausages on skewers. The darkness fell suddenly, marooning them on their flame-lit island. They could almost have been back in their forest, except that the noises were different: the occasional yelp of a wild dog instead of the cooing of pigeons.

—Tomorrow we'll go into Tucson and find a mechanic, declared Tibor, accepting defeat.

She said nothing, allowing her silence to emphasise the fact that this was what she had been suggesting all along.

When the sausages were cooked, they dipped the ends into a jar of mustard and ate them with slices of stale bread.

—What's that?

She pointed at something snagged in a bush on the perimeter of their island, a long, snaking strand that trembled in the air. Tibor hooked it with a stick. It was the brown ribbon of a cassette tape, unspooled, dragging its box after it like a discarded shell. He reeled the plastic holder in.

—'Whale Music,' he read, slowly, in English. 'Relaxation for the Mind, Body and Soul.'

—What's that mean?

Tibor shrugged. —Must be the name of an American band.

Eva had picked up a number of spoils from the storm – a collection of Coca-Cola cans with bullet holes in them, the bleached skeleton of a cactus plant, twisted and laced with its own natural holes, which she hung over the doors of the van, proclaiming that it would ward off evil spirits. Somehow she felt it was important to gather what the desert offered and bring it inside, make it a part of their lives. Most bizarrely of all, she had found a pair of very large underpants lodged in the fork of a cactus plant.

—Tibor, do you believe in fate?

—In what sense?

—Like, your life is in somebody else's hands.

—Oh yes. Mine's in yours, *zlatko.*

—But I mean more than that. Like, you think you choose things. But maybe they're choosing you. Maybe it's not up to us.

—Precisely.

In the flickering light, she saw the lines breaking open around his mouth. He was laughing at her. She persevered, anyway.

—A year ago, I'd never have thought . . . Her voice trailed off into nothing.

He reached out and took the sausage she was taking so long to eat.

—I couldn't imagine being here with anyone else, he said, simply.

He handed her a piece of bread in return.

The next morning, Tibor jumped into the back of the van and kicked the bedding aside irritably with his feet. He picked up a spoon from one of the bowls on the worktop, and let the mixture cascade down.

—This is a disaster. It's all a disaster.

—You're a chef. You would be melodramatic.

—Well, it is.

She followed him back outside, where he stood with his hands in his pockets, pushing a small pebble around with his toe.

—You should wear something on your feet. There are scorpions here.

—You're a shoe-maker. You would say that.

—Tibor, we just have to find a mechanic, get him out here, and we're on the road again.

—I thought you didn't want to move.

—I didn't say that. We can't stay here without power or water. How much water have we got left, anyway?

—About half a litre.

—Let's take it with us. We'll walk into the town. We can probably hitch a lift.

—There's a man out there.

—What?

—Over there, between the trees.

She came and stood beside him, following the direction of his gaze. It was hard to measure distances in the desert, but some way away, almost hidden by a dense clump of vegetation, a figure dressed entirely in white was crouched on all fours, like a dog. As they watched, he rose up slowly from the ground, bringing his head up last and stretching his arms to the sky until they bent him over backwards. Then he brought his palms together, level with his chest.

—Whatever is he doing? asked Tibor.

—Saying his prayers, I suppose. We need a pair of binoculars. As well as a television set.

14

Outside school the kids line up on the sidewalk, waiting to be matched to a car. One by one I watch them walk up to voluptuous Chevrolets and Sunbeams with long hoods and long trunks, all contained within a gleaming chrome bumper. Their mothers stretch their arms over the backs of the seats and open the doors without bothering to get out and the expensive smell of hot leather and perfume empties itself on to the street.

And then my father rattles up in his dented white Bug, revving the engine too hard before cutting it off with a painful jerk of the handbrake. I pretend I haven't heard him. I look down the street in the vain hope that a woman with a head of soft dark hair will wind down the window and call *Josephine!* in a breezy voice.

But I can't ignore him for long.

—Coo-eee! Over here, Sugar Pie!

Red-faced and puffing, my father clambers out on to the sidewalk and levers his seat forward. He ushers me in with a bow and a theatrical sweep of his arm.

Before we can leave, there's a whole routine to go through. He has to check all three mirrors, look to see that he's strapped himself in correctly, that the hazards work, the turn signals work, that his passenger is strapped in too. Gas, water, lights. Windows up, or down. Usually he forgets to turn the hazards off again before pulling out, which is probably just as well. I stare out the window, away from the other kids.

—Dad, can we get a move on? This is really embarrassing.

When we're finally on the main road he perches on the edge of his seat, as close to the steering wheel as his belly will allow him to get, and peers shortsightedly through the windshield. The rear end of the truck in front rises up like a brick wall, perilously close.

—Dad, you can pass, you know. That's what the other lanes are for.

—I'm quite happy in this lane, really, Honey Pie.

—Aren't you going to ask me how my day was?

—I was just thinking the very same thing, Sugar Pie. Holy Moses, what a day it has been. First I got back to find there was no running water. The tank's completely empty – I think there must be something wrong with the pump. As luck would have it, there are plenty of emergency flagons in the living room. I've already used what there was in the cistern so now you have to pour half a litre of water down it. Or go and do your business outside. And then, as if that wasn't enough for one day, the delivery man turned up saying there's been a commotion about the Banana Milkshake ice-cream. Someone found a peanut in it. That must have been your fault, Sugar, when you were throwing them at me the other day.

He turns to look at me, hoping for an apology. I don't give him one. There's an alarmed tooting from the car to our left and my father swerves back into his lane.

—Anyway, Sugar, I don't really mind because it gave me an idea. Tell me what you think of this.

He throws me an excited glance. He needs to make sure that I'm paying enough attention.

—Don't take your eyes off the road.

—Don't you want to hear my idea?

—Go on, then.

—Well, my idea is that we should make a peanut butter-flavoured ice-cream. He leaves a gap before delivering the punch line. With *real peanuts*. Real peanuts, Sugar Pie! What do you think of that?

—Aren't you going to turn off here?

He stamps on the brake and the clutch simultaneously, and I switch the gears just in time for us to get off the main road.

—Well?

I look at him and shrug.

—Yeah, it sounds OK, I guess.

When we finally pull up outside the house, he straightens his arms and legs and pushes his butt into the back of the seat as if he were slowing down from seven hundred miles an hour and has to withstand the rush of the runway. By the time he gets out, he's exhausted.

Inside, I make him a cup of tea with three sugars and plenty of milk.

In my bedroom I open my schoolbag and take out the envelope. *Mr Moon*, it says, in big, rounded letters. I stick my finger under the seal and slide it along.

The letter is typed on headed school paper and signed with a red marking pen.

Dear Mr Moon,

    I am writing with regard to your daughter, Josephine. Both myself and the principal, Mr Lord, feel that her level of achievement is still far below what it should be for a girl of her age. She was, of course, a late starter, but I fear her attitude is not what it should be. Last week she didn't turn up for any of her afternoon classes. She seems to be spending a lot of time with her friend Walter Lee, which may or may not have anything to do with this. We don't doubt that you are doing all you can to help and encourage her at home, but if you would like to come and discuss your daughter's special needs with us, we would be very pleased to welcome you to Santa Catalina.

    Sincerely,

      Margaret Bird,

        Teacher, Seventh Grade.

I put the letter back in its envelope and slip it between the mattress and the floor. *Special needs.* Whoever heard anything so ridiculous. I let myself flop back on to the mattress and look up at the ceiling. It's decorated with all the photographs we've taken over the years. There's the white Bug with its half-collapsed bumper posing in the foreground of all the places we've been to for picnics. There are various, unidentified sunsets – each one taken in the hope that it is more dramatic than the last. There's a picture of a rock at the bottom of an arroyo taken from such a long way off that you need to be told there's a tarantula crouching on top. There's one of my father sitting down to a forty-eight ounce steak at the kitchen table, holding up his knife and fork and sporting a Stetson. He said it was a private joke, something about an image he'd seen years ago in London. And there's a rare one of the two of us together, my father and I, me peeping out from behind the side of his leg, the saguaros standing behind us like two additional members of the family. Jersey's magnified finger runs across the top right-hand corner of the frame.

Dear Mrs Bird,

When we got your letter Josephine and I nearly fell over from laughing so much. In England, where as you know we come from, we call people like you interfering old cows. It is a term you Americans could well do with appropriating. I am perfectly happy with my daughter's progress, and suggest that if you are not, you should keep your opinions to yourself.

Yours,

Josephine's adoring and proud father.

P.S. Leave Walter out of this.

There are pictures of Cindy, too. In one of them she stands up close to the camera, long strands of blond hair blowing all over her face. Jersey's in the background, turning round to look. A wide, happy grin on his face.

I roll over, on to my side.

Dear Mrs Bird,

You really should think twice before writing letters like that. Josephine and I have been thoroughly entertaining ourselves with images of you succumbing to a variety of sticky endings. We particularly liked the idea of hanging you from the windmill and allowing our pet mountain lion, Max, to disembowel you as you bounced up and down. Another idea was to strap you to the roof for a week so that we could watch the vultures carrying you away, piece by piece. We even considered force-feeding you ice-cream, then freezing your vomit and serving it up for dessert. We both have very vivid imaginations, you see.

It occurs to me that you might sleep more soundly if you refrain from writing such letters in the future.

Sincerely, etc

In the bathroom I strip down to my bra and panties and soap my underarms. The razor slides firmly over the surface, slicing the tops off the little black hairs. My father has his things in the cabinet on the left side of the basin, and I have mine in the cabinet on the right, and if ever I put a used razor back in the wrong cabinet, he switches it across immediately. He's funny about things like that. I always have a look in his cabinet, just in case there's anything interesting that I can borrow, but there hardly ever is. It's all nasal sprays and calamine lotion and mouth ulcer ointment. Sometimes I take a couple of his Q-tips to clean out my ears.

The roll-on deodorant stings my armpits. I have to clamp my arms down and blink back the tears till it stops. Then I get out my lip-liner, prop one knee on the edge of the bath, and lean up close to the mirror. It's hard to get the line right, especially when the mirror steams up with your breath. Martha says you have to keep licking your lips to make them shiny in the middle, but I can never remember to do it.

I don't bother with mascara because it runs in the water. I do my hair, though, mussing it up with a bit of gel. Then I pull on my cut-off denim shorts and a t-shirt, balance on the edge of the bath and twist round to check the back view in the mirror.

My father's outside in the garden, watering his plants.

—Sugar?

—Umm.

—Where are you going?

—Out.

—Where to?

—Just out. You're not invited.

He puts the watering can down on the ground.

—I'd just like to know. I am responsible for you, after all.

—I'm quite capable of looking after myself.

—I know, Sugar Pie, but I worry—

—That's your problem.

He sighs, and wipes the back of his hand over his mouth.

—Will you be back for tea, then?

I shrug.

—Bring your friend, if you want, Sugar.

I don't know why he bothers to say that. He knows I won't.

—So long, Pop. Don't wait up.

I can feel his eyes on me, watching me go down the drive.

I run along the arroyo until I can see the peeling branches of the eucalypts and then I slow to a walk, because I don't want Walter to think I ran all the way there for him. Walter lives the other side of the tank, but he normally gets there first.

—Ah, what a rather fine day, what-ho!

He gives me his easy smile, his face spreading open like a book.

We shake hands and settle ourselves in the shade of the eucalyptus trees. Three branches laid along the ground form the walls of our camp; the side of the tank is the fourth. The corrugated iron is cool against our backs.

Walter takes two chocolate cupcakes from the pocket of his shorts and peels off the paper holders. They're warm and soft from having travelled next to his thigh.

—Bring anything to drink, old bean?

By the look of the two sticky, shining triangles at the corners of his mouth, Walter's already cleaned off the soda himself.

—I thought you were bringing everything.

—Damn and blast. I knew there was something. Fancy a spot of swimming later on?

—Spiffing idea.

—I say, it's terribly nice to see you, old thing.

—Absolutely ditto.

Sometimes the children from the reservation are there. They tuck themselves up into tight balls in mid-air and bomb each other out of the water. Occasionally one of the ranch-hands comes by and fires blanks into the air and they run off squealing and throwing fistfuls of stones behind them. The ranch-men never notice Walter and me, crouched down the side, eating our cake and burying dead bees and scorpions in the ground and marking their graves with twigs in the shape of a cross.

When everyone's gone, something shifts between Walter and me. We become a little shy of each other. Walter channels his nervousness into making grandiose plans for our lives.

—When we emigrate to England, he announces, we'll have ourselves a fine old pool. All to ourselves.

—What about the sea? Can't we swim in that?

Walter looks unsure. —Well yes, I suppose. Silly me, eh? Must be losing my nuts and bolts.

—But we could have one anyway. I want one like they have in Los Angeles. They have them there in different shapes.

—I say, do they really? What sort of shapes?

—Whatever shape you want.

When Walter watches you, his eyes don't stay still but flick from side to side, as if he can't decide which of your eyes to look at. In his left eye he has a little discoloured spot, just falling out of the iris, like the blood spot in the white of an egg. His parents have told him that England is full of mixed-race families, so we have bought a map and decided that Bexhill-on-Sea is the place to be. We'll get a bus to LA and then a boat, because we both want to see the Atlantic. According to my father, the sea collects treasures, like the desert, preserving them in brine like a can of tuna fish.

—Maybe we could go via Santa Barbara, says Walter.

—Who's she?

Walter sticks out two fingers and shoots a bird out of the branch above us. *Schtoof!* His wrist flicks up with the force of it and the bird hops graciously on to a neighbouring twig.

—Lordy, old bean, don't you know anything? Santa Barbara's a place.

—According to my dad, I tell Walter, to show him that I do in fact know something, we all began in the ocean. As slimy-crawly creatures on the ocean floor. Later we evolved into little fish with fins and then reptiles with tails.

Walter looks at me with his serious eyes, left to right, the little black spot tagging along behind, then all of a sudden his lips burst open like curtains hitching up at the theatre.

—Your dad's a nutter, he says delightedly.

I look at Walter's lips, wondering what would happen if I leaned across and kissed them.

—So's yours, I say instead.

—No he's not.

—He is so.

Walter's lips go slack.

—Let's get in the water.

Before he has time to respond I pull my t-shirt over my head. Walter goes very still. He stares at my loose-fitting bra.

—Haven't you got your swimsuit on?

—Couldn't be bothered. Anyway, haven't you heard of skinny dipping? It's what everyone does.

He fumbles at the fastening to his pants, clumsily, as I pull down my shorts and panties and roll them up in a ball.

—Come on.

I run round to the side of the tank, and climb up the ladder.

—Come on!

I dive in and it's suddenly quiet in the sun-warmed water, except for the sound of the blood pumping in my ears. I stretch my arms and spear a path for myself, pulling the water apart to let me through. The light coming through the eucalypts flickers on and off, and if you open your eyes, you can see little amoebas floating around in the murky grey.

When I bob up into light and sound again, there is Walter's smiling face sticking up at the other end. I somersault down and so does he and in the cloudy strangeness of the underwater world we find each other with our hands. The bubbles come out of his smiling mouth and surround our faces. I hold on to the jut of his hip, and he takes hold of my shoulder. We pull each other until our stomachs meet, our legs kicking softly underneath. In the buoyancy of the water, our oily skin touches then drifts then touches again. He sticks out his skinny barrel chest and rolls it against my titties, pushing me gently backwards. I can feel him tickling down there and I smuggle my hand down and catch it, and it's soft and buttery, squirmy as a fish in my fingers. I give it a squeeze. Walter lets out a watery yell and kicks out and shoots to the surface, all thrashing arms and legs. Anyone would have thought he'd been bitten by a shark. I follow but he thrusts me down by my shoulders, and for a moment I'm struggling amid the bubbles and the creatures in the darkness, and by the time I've surfaced and got the water out of my eyes and nose he's halfway across the tank.

Just before darkness, the dragonflies come. There's only one at first, its body flaring a brilliant, luminous blue. A cusp of low sunlight shines through its wings, showing up the intricate pattern of lines, the surrounding rim. Then, suddenly, there are dozens of them, hovering and darting and settling on the weed, then taking off and hovering again.

We haul ourselves on to the edge of the tank to watch them, the roughness of the cement scraping at our bare skin. We hug our knees to our chests so that we can ignore our nakedness.

—They're only alive for one day, I whisper to Walter. That's why they're in such a hurry.

Walter looks at me carefully, to see if I am telling the truth.

—Then I'm glad we're watching them. If I were only alive for one day, I'd want someone to watch.

We fall silent, both of us trying not to miss a single dragonfly.

—The thing is, Walter, I might not be able to go to England straight after we get out of High School.

—Why not?

The sun makes moving patterns on Walter's face, drying his shiny skin to a matt grey-brown.

—I might go and live with my mother in Las Vegas. She's a blackjack dealer there.

He eyes me carefully again, the uncertain little black spot moving from left to right.

—I thought you didn't have a mother.

—Of course I do. Everyone has a mother. I just didn't know where she was.

—Your dad would never let you.

—He doesn't need to know.

Walter picks a loose piece of cement from the wall of the tank and throws it into the water. There's a plop and a couple of dragonflies dart away.

—If you change your mind, you can still come to England with me.

—OK.

When it starts to get cold, we climb down and silently put on our clothes.

—You're lookin' mighty fine, Josephine, this morning, if I may say, says Jersey, meeting me at the mailbox and jumping down from his pickup. He rolls his shoulders back in their sockets to stretch his chest. I'm almost moved to ask you to join me in a quick two-step, though it ain't even nine o'clock.

He does a little kick to one side.

—I don't do the two-step, I mutter, scuffing my toe against the ground.

—Well what about the three-step or the four-step?

—I don't do any of that stuff any more. That's *hillbilly* stuff.

—*Hillbilly*, eh? That what you think it is?

I look to one side, avoiding his eyes.

—Well, I don't know, Josephine, where you got that highfalutin' notion, but dancin' is one of life's greatest pleasures, yes it is, and it's free to anyone with two legs and a beat in their heart. And there ain't nothin' wrong with that.

He does a little pirouette with his arms above his head.

—Jersey, are you drunk?

—No, missy, I'm just high on life. Yes, siree. You're not going to tell me that's hillbilly too, are you?

He comes to a standstill in front of me with his hands on his hips. I lean over and take the unlit cigarette from his mouth.

—You are drunk. I can smell it on your breath.

I put the cigarette back.

—Well if you say so. Jeezus, what is this, a quizitation from the Feds?

—An inquisition.

—A quizitation.

He has a go at lighting his cigarette.

—Do you want to come in for a cup of tea?

He flings his lighter on the ground, sticks his hands in the air, and takes a big step back.

—Now. Listen to me, young missy. You can accuse me of drinking beer before nine o'clock in the morning, and I can take it like a man, but ain't nobody going to accuse me of drinking tea at any hour of the day. That is something I would not do. Never have, never will. I swear on the sacred name of our Lord Cindy.

I look back at him, startled, and he holds my gaze, but it's clear he's a little surprised by it himself.

—She's not sacred.

—She is and I'll prove it.

He drops down on his knees. —Dearly beloved. You see? That's what she's called, too. We are gathered here today to beg for mercy. For we have sinned. As you well know.

He lets his head drop down on to his chest. The skin on the back of his neck is tanned a deep reddy brown.

—And even if you disapproved of our sins, which you made it very clear you did, then you might have the decency to drop us a line and tell us you've forgiven us. Because it was a very long time ago.

—Who's 'us', Jersey? I ask.

—Well, your father and me, of course.

His head drops down further, and for a moment I wonder if he's passed out. But then, suddenly, he gets up, dusts off his knees and gives me a sheepish smile.

—Did you give me back my lighter, young missy?

—It's on the ground. What did you do, Jersey, you and Dad, that made Cindy angry? What made her leave?

—We didn't make her leave. No one made her leave. She was so damned headstrong, she made these decisions for herself, if you remember.

—Then why didn't you go to Vegas with her?

—And what would have happened to you and your father if I had? You'd probably still be running around in diapers and your father would have got himself stuck down the bottom of that well by now. He throws his head back and laughs, pleased with this vision of Jersey-less chaos.

—Didn't you ever hear from her again, Jersey?

He doesn't answer right away. He reaches for his lighter and snaps it in the cup of his hand.

—Truth is, I ain't ever heard from her once, Josephine. And that's a fact. See this raw patch of skin here?

He shows me the side of his hand. I can't see anything wrong with it.

—Well, that's worn away by the number of times I've sat down to write to her. Too many times to count. A thousand times, most probably, to tell you the truth.

—And she didn't reply to any of your letters?

A crack opens up in Jersey's hardboiled face. He holds a lungful of smoke in his chest.

—Oh, she never got 'em. I didn't send 'em. She couldn't have got 'em if I never sent 'em, could she? Ha! Even I can work that out.

He staggers backwards, coughs, then looks distractedly at his truck.

—I bet it's very busy in Vegas, is all it is, he says quietly. I bet she's having a fine old time.

He looks back at me, square between the eyes.

—Missy, have I told you anything I shouldn't have?

—What?

—Have you been quizzing me, is all.

He comes up close and stares at me hard. —Huh?

I shrug. —No.

—Well don't. Thassall. Don't. Now, give me back my lighter.

—I don't have it. You have it.

He looks down at his hand. A soft breeze catches us both on the cheek and we look up, as if expecting to see it pass by.

—Real fine, you're looking, Miss Josie. Did anyone tell you that? He says it in a whisper, looking at me out of the corner of his eye. I give him a small, conciliatory smile. He returns it with a gaze of inebriated, doleful-eyed tenderness. And then he takes a long drag of his cigarette and throws his chin up as if he's a giraffe, looking out over the treetops.

—So, is your father up yet?

—What do *you* think?

—We'll soon see about that. How long d'you reckon it'll take if we start fryin' up some bacon?

He turns and strides purposefully down the drive, his left leg thrown out slightly to one side, as if by the bulge of the cigarette pack in his jean pocket – a bulge that's as much a part of the shape of his body as his arms and legs.

Sometimes, if I can't sleep at night, I go into the kitchen and pour myself some Kool-Aid and take it back to my room. I twist the rod of the blinds so that if there's any moon, it filters through the gaps. Then I take the shoes out of their boxes and line them up on the floor.

The white stilettos. The tall red boots. The gold sandals. There are fifteen pairs of shoes in all. Sometimes they make me smile – the styles are so overly fussy and old-fashioned.

In the soft grey whispery light, they seem to be waiting for something. They are like living, breathing presences, held in suspension by a spell. What they need is a foot – the warmth and solidity of a human foot, slipping easily into their open mouths, wiggling its toes. That's all it would take to bring them to life. They are dignified in their patience, standing motionless in the moonlight.

My feet are the same size as hers now. I can bring them to life myself when I choose to. One pair a year, regular as clockwork, they came to me, until I told him that they fit, and then he gave me the last few pairs that remained. Presumably, he thought I would make use of them. He no longer minds if I do. But I never take them out beyond my bedroom. If I did, I would replace the imprint of her that they still carry, and these imprints are the only visible proof of her that exists.

Some of them carry a stronger imprint than others. The walking boots are worn the most – scuffed along the edges, ground down at the heels – but there is no sign of her foot inside because she would have worn socks with them. The same goes for the red boots and the tassled ankle boots. With the canvas shoes, on the other hand, the markings are so smudged with sweat that they are too blurred and blackened to make out.

The shoes that have captured her best – as well as a sculptor, nearly – are the white stilettos and the green mock-crocodiles. If you pick up one of these and look inside, you can see her – the dark stain of the five toes, a perfect crescent in descending order of size, the pad of the ball, the circular sweep of the heel. The implied grace of the invisible arch.

They are ghostly imprints. Evidence that she stepped here once, and then was gone.

If you can imagine the arch, I tell myself, then surely you can imagine the rest of her. Work your way up – the ankles, the calves, the legs. Surely it is possible! But it doesn't work like that. I end up envisaging Cindy's long legs, or my own, and then I lose my fragile grasp of her.

No shoes have ever been scrutinised like these. I've extracted every last ounce of information from them that I can. That she liked to dress up, of course. That she was graceful and feminine, and at the same time adventurous and energetic. Her favourites were the gold sandals. I know that not because she wore them a lot, but because she didn't. Instead, she fingered them, turned them over, played with them until the glitter fell off, leaving bald patches. She didn't think much of the red shoes with the bow on the front. The leather at the back is hard and ungiving, as if she never wore them in. Perhaps they gave her blisters on her heel. Perhaps, like me, she thought the bow over the top.

Sometimes I'll finish my Kool-Aid and then take one of the shoes back to bed with me. Under the covers I crane my nose into every inch of it, attempting to disentangle the waft of the leather and the musty smell of the cupboard, and discover if there's anything left underneath – a vestige of the scent of her skin, perhaps, or the perfume that she wore.

Every year it gets harder and harder to tell if she's left her smell behind.

At recess Walter and I meet behind the cafeteria. It seems odd, somehow, to see him in long pants and a sweatshirt.

—Jeepers creepers, says Walter with a big smile. What-ho.

—Cut it out, Walter.

—What?

—The English shit. I don't want to do that any more.

The black moons in Walter's eyes drop down with disappointment. I sit on the step next to him.

—Listen. I want to go out on a date.

—What for?

—What do you mean, what for? A *date*. You know.

His eyes grow round and big again.

—Like, real dating?

—Yeah. Why not?

—Where do you want to go?

—I dunno. That's for you to decide.

Walter nods, slowly. He takes it all in, very seriously.

—The water tank?

—Don't be a jerk, Walter. Into town, like everyone else.

—Into Tucson?

—Yeah.

He looks at me and nods.

—OK, then.

—Saturday night?

—Yeah.

—Shake my hand, Walter.

He puts out his hand and I take it.

—What time will you pick me up? Six?

Walter nods. —OK.

—See you at six, then. Old chum.

When I get home my father's leaning over the well. He's trying to dribble oil into the hinge of the pump. He has taken his shirt off and hung it around his neck, and his back has turned lobster pink.

—Your back's burning.

He turns round and almost smashes his head on the gear stick.

—Sugar? What are you doing home so early?

He pulls the shirt from his neck and absentmindedly uses it as a cloth to wipe his hands, covering it in grease.

—I'm having a go at fixing the windmill, he says, before I have a chance to answer.

—So I see.

He wobbles a little, light-headed from the heat, and has to clutch the pump to steady himself.

—Dad? Do you know why Cindy and Jersey broke up?

My father's eyes come to rest on my forehead. He frowns.

—Sugar, what have you done to your hair?

—I back-combed it.

—Oh.

He wraps the shirt around his neck and holds on to each end.

—Don't avoid the question.

—What was it again?

—Cindy and Jersey. Why they broke up.

He turns his attention back to the pump.

—Why on earth are you worrying yourself about that? It was years ago.

—I don't know. It's just something Jersey said.

—Well, I don't know why you're asking me, Sugar Pie. It's Jersey's business. Ask him.

—He's never sober these days.

My father ignores this, and carries on with what he's doing.

I perch on the edge of the well, between him and the pump, forcing him to stop what he's doing.

—Did he have sex with someone else?

—*Really*, Sugar.

He blushes, visibly shocked. — *I* don't know—

—It's all right. I know about stuff like that. I know they had an argument, that night of my birthday. Don't you remember? That was the last time we saw her.

—Well, now, Jersey was very fond of Cindy. You know that. He wouldn't—

—Then it must have been something that we did.

—Us?

—Yes, you and me.

—Of course it wasn't. What could we possibly have done?

—I don't know, but whatever it was, Cindy was really mad about it.

My father looks down at his feet, shaking his head.

—I don't know where you get these ideas, Sugar, I really don't.

—What do you mean, these ideas?

He shakes his head, helplessly. —I don't know why you're bothering with it all, Sugar Pie. It was such a long time ago.

I stand up, a sudden anger rising in my throat. My cheeks flush pink, like his.

—That's the problem with you. It's always *I don't know what to say. I don't know what to think.* You think that gets you off the hook, don't you?

I stand and glare at him. He avoids my eyes, wiping each finger along its length with his shirt.

—There's no hook, Sugar.

—It's all this pretending. Pretending everything's all right, pretending nothing's happened. Pretending you don't know anything. I think you know exactly what happened but you don't want to tell me about it.

He looks at me, mournful as a cow. He pulls the corners of his mouth down and shrugs.

—I just – I don't—

—Oh, forget it.

I swipe at the air with my arm, as if it's the air that's the problem, and stalk back into the house. I close the door of my bedroom and throw myself down on my bed. Outside, I hear the pump handle falling down with a clank. Then the pad of his feet coming up the steps.

—Sugar Pie, can I come in?

—Get lost.

—Don't say that to me. I'm your father.

I jump up, pull the table out from the wall and ram it against the door. I throw the chair on top, and stand back.

—Sugar Pie, what's going on in there?

He turns the handle and hits the door against the table.

—Sugar? What's got into you? You've never been like this before. I'm coming in on the count of three. *One.*

I go and sit quietly on the edge of the bed, listening to the sound of his breathing, hard and fast.

—*Two.*

From my bedside table, I take out a bag of cotton balls, pull out a few tufts and stuff them between my toes. Then I get out a bottle of nail polish and start to paint my toes.

—*Three.* With a crash the table lurches on to its side and my father comes charging through, shoulder first. He shields his face with crossed hands, cowering behind them, as if expecting to be hit.

—Sugar?

He looks at me suspiciously. Then he takes hold of the door behind him, partly to steady himself, and partly so that he can beat a quick retreat, should that become necessary. His bare, sweaty chest is heaving with shallow breaths.

—Sugar, what are you doing?

I give him a withering look. It's a stupid question and doesn't deserve a reply. His eyes flicker nervously around the room.

—Well, if you want to talk—

—What's the point. You never know what to say.

—Well, I don't sometimes, Sugar Pie. I really don't.

—Then we won't talk, and I would like to be left in peace.

—All right, Sugar Pie, whatever you want. I really only want – well, whatever you want, you know.

I roll my eyes to the ceiling to show how tired of him I am.

Still he hesitates at the door.

—If I go for a walk, do you want to—

—*No.*

—Why not?

I put down the nail polish.

—Because I hate going for walks. I'm *bored* of your stupid walks. All there is to do here is go for walks.

—I don't know, Sugar Pie, I just thought—

—Well, believe me, I would rather *die* than spend as much time in this stupid place as you do.

—Sugar!

—What's so terrible about that? It's perfectly normal to get bored.

—But you've always found something—

—Well, I'm not a kid any more.

—Oh but you are, Sugar Pie. You're only thirteen – that's still a baby, really—

—Oh, fuck off.

We stare at each other. I've never said that to him before, and neither of us knows what we're supposed to do now. My father's lips are trembling.

—All right, he says suddenly. I'll go. If you don't want me to talk to you, I won't.

—Fine. Good riddance.

—To you too.

There's a moment's pause, and then he leaves the room.

15

From behind, Tibor smirked at the waddling walk Eva had developed. It was as if her belly were being pulled along by a rope, and the rest of her was simply trying to keep up. He reached forward and took hold of her two bags, so that her hands were free. She turned round briefly and smiled.

—Can't have a pregnant pack-horse.

—Listen. Can you hear that noise?

It reminded Eva of goat bells in her grandmother's village in the Tatras. It was muted, even a little eerie, with bells of different tones clashing and then coalescing, as if the notes were made of liquid. Now that they heard it properly, it occurred to both of them that they had heard it before, at night, without being fully conscious of it – a sound that carried on the breeze and which, in their sleep, they had probably mistaken for the breeze itself.

Approaching down the long, curving track, they saw that the area within the white fence was surprisingly large and immaculately kept. There were cacti of every imaginable shape and size – from tiny bulbous plants barely an inch across armed with fierce, needle-sharp prongs, to the giant cacti with limbs on either side – the classic cactus shape used in all the adverts for Western goods. Some of them grew in clusters close to the ground, sending up phallic, curved arms lined with golden spines and tipped with fruit; others were solitary, fat and barrel-shaped. There were a number of woody-trunked yuccas, with their lower leaves browning and dry, and, just the other side of the fence, a row of fine grey-green agave plants, their heart-shaped, juicy leaves outlined with a rim of violet, and long upright stems rising from the centre bearing the dried-out remains of that year's flowers.

The house itself had once been painted blue; now it was faded and peeled in places from the constant exposure to the sun. On each corner grew a willowy tree just topping the height of the roof and casting a circle of mottled shade.

When they reached the front door, they saw what was causing the music: a cluster of wooden windchimes hanging from the roof jut. Eva swung the central hammer briskly, but the sudden jangling disturbed the quiet of the garden so suddenly that she immediately pulled it tight, silencing them again. She looked at Tibor for support. Determined to affect confidence, Tibor knocked boldly on the door. No answer. He knocked again, more loudly.

—That's odd. He was certainly around half an hour ago.

They decided they might as well sit and wait. Tucking the bags of ice-cream cartons into the square of shade beneath the steps, Tibor sat on the bottom step. Eva went to look around the back of the house.

The vegetation was wilder here – she had to pick her way through clumps of grass with sharp, spear-like blades. To one side of the house was a well with a cement surround, shaded from the sun by a cluster of tall, thin whispering trees. A creaking windmill made occasional attempts to lift the pump, but the breeze was not strong enough today to push it round a full rotation. Circling round to the front again, she followed the meandering path through the orna-mental cactus garden. It had been lovingly, tenderly created. Here and there he had placed a small rock – a rounded piece of granite or a more irregular block of limestone. A layer of fine gravel in be-tween the plants was raked into wavy lines.

When she looked up again she saw a much larger rock, almost the height of their van, sitting at the far end of the garden. It was utterly incongruous; in fact, its size and density seemed somehow tactless in all this light and air. It was as if it had been placed there as a unit of measurement by which to get a bearing on the great void around it. She went up close and pressed her palms and cheek against it. It was cold, as she had hoped it would be, and rough, embedded with little crystals that glinted where the sun picked them out.

It was only when she took a step back that she noticed the top of the boulder was alive. Two rounded humps, the shape of a cello laid on its side, were heaving slowly up and down. After an especially tremulous upwards heave, the rock emitted a loud and congested snore.

—*Ahoj*, she called out, simply.

The humps faltered mid-swell.

—*Sme tu*, she found herself saying. *Prišli sme.*

We are here. We have arrived.

He was an enormous creature. Dressed entirely in white, he reminded her, for a fleeting moment, of an outsized, burly angel descending from the sky in a religious painting. As he detached himself from the rock and tumbled down, he brought with him a waft of sour sweat, yellowed and hardened into the creases of his clothes.

Involuntarily, she took a step back.

At first she thought there was something wrong with his face – that he had a disfiguring birthmark down one side. But then she realised that the skin was simply pitted and pockmarked where it had been pressed against its stony pillow, and that bits of loose grit were still embedded in the skin. The rims of his ears were burnt scarlet and his hair stuck up in tufts, like the crests of an exotic bird.

Before he spoke, he shifted something hard and round from one side of his mouth to the other. It bulged through the skin of his cheek and got in the way of his words.

—Ah! he said. The voice was unexpectedly high-pitched for a man. You must be my neighbours. How nice of you to come.

The round protrusion disappeared, then reappeared again on the other side.

—Theobald Moon, he announced, holding out a plump hand. Very pleased to meet you at last.

Eva smiled, and took his hand.

On entering the house they were greeted by such an overwhelming stench of disinfectant that their nostrils bristled. For a moment Eva had to steady herself against a wall. Oblivious, their lumbering neighbour padded through into the front room, sweeping them inwards with his arm. In this room the light fell in three stepping stones across the floor. It was cool in there, like a church.

—Please sit down, he said. I'm afraid all I can offer you is a cushion. I never got round to buying any chairs.

They hovered uncertainly while he busied himself in the kitchen: filling up a saucepan of water, then seeming to change his mind and pouring it down the sink. They could hear the opening and closing of cupboards, the crunch of glass against glass. They didn't speak to one another, knowing that the moment they did, their host would realise they didn't understand a word that he was saying.

—I get these sent over from England. He came in with a tray, indicating with his head a little plate of biscuits. There were three long glasses of iced tea. —By my Aunty Drew.

They smiled and nodded in agreement.

—I'm sorry, I – I only have cushions. Do you mind—?

They realised then that they were supposed to sit down on the floor. He waited while they made themselves comfortable and then leant down to their level with his tray. Eva looked closely at his eyes. They were the palest blue she had ever seen – delicate and watery and round, and looking out at the world with an expression so willing, so full of eagerness to please or to admit culpability for any offence going, that she felt moved to reach out and brush the grit from his plump cheek.

As if fearing precisely that, the large man retreated abruptly and shifted the tray across to Tibor. Silhouetted for a moment against the window, Eva saw the outline of his bulky frame beneath the baggy shirt, the folds of the stomach collapsing one on top of the other. The strange thing was that though he took up so much space in the room, almost filling the doorway when he passed through with his tray, his attitude was so tentative that he seemed to detract from his own presence, to be there but also to suggest that he was not. He was a mixture of weight and weightlessness. Of occupancy and void.

The tray now empty, their host chose a cushion for himself, and lowered himself carefully down. They watched in silence as he shifted his buttocks from side to side as if to spread them flat, and then proceeded to cross one bulky leg over the other, manoeuvring and wriggling until he had succeeded in pulling two bare feet up from out of the folds of white cotton, like pale vegetables plucked from the ground. He wedged each upturned foot on to the flank of the opposite knee. When at last he was finished he looked up, a little flushed from all the exertion. Tibor and Eva stared in amazement, both wondering if he'd ever be able to unknot himself again.

—Won't you have a chocolate digestive?

The sight of the biscuits reminded Tibor of why they had come in the first place and he leapt up, nearly upsetting the plate in the large man's hand.

—Excuse myself!

He came back in with the four carrier bags and took out one of the cartons. Peeling back the lid he held it out towards their host who, following the instructions of Tibor's eyes, the little nod that he gave, leant towards it, poked in his nose and sniffed.

—*Zmrzlina*, said Tibor.

The large man looked up slowly, wonderingly, his eyes grown wide and fearful as moons.

—*Kaput*, said Tibor, motioning with the carton, then running a finger horizontally across his throat.

Increasingly alarmed, their host's hands hovered close to the floor, as if in readiness to propel himself up.

—Need freedge, said Tibor. Freeze. He dumped the carton on the floor and grabbed the tops of his own arms and began to jiggle up and down. Eva started to laugh.

—*Rozumieš?* Freeeeze!

Slowly, the man's pink-cheeked face began to relax, the corners of his mouth pricking into a tentative smile as comprehension dawned.

—Ah, you need a freezer! he exclaimed. For your ice-cream! That's no problem at all. I've got one of those!

He insisted they stay for a meal, ushering them into his tiny kitchen, and laying down place-mats, a knife and fork and spoon for each. He looped a plastic-coated apron over his head and tied it behind him before fetching a loaf of bread from the fridge. Tibor watched with mounting disbelief as he poured half an inch of sunflower oil into a pan, dunked three thick slices of bread into a dish of beaten egg and lowered them one by one into the spitting fat. He added rashers of bacon to the pan and had to leap back to avoid being showered with oil as it fizzed and bounced like popcorn. He set the plates before his two guests heavily, squeezed himself into his own chair, and tucked a napkin into the neck of his shirt. Then he up-turned a bottle of brown sauce, gave it two hearty thwacks with the flat of his hand, and allowed a huge dollop to land on the top of his bread.

Eva raised her eyebrow at Tibor across the table.

Their large host ate quickly. He brought his chin down close to the plate, and only when he had mopped up every last greasy smear did he appear to remember they were there. Tibor, meanwhile, cut his portion up into small squares and arranged and rearranged them on his plate as if they were pieces in a jigsaw. As soon as he felt he could get away with it, he excused himself and went out on to the steps for a cigarette.

Left alone with the large man, Eva felt the atmosphere in the room heighten. There was no attempt at conversation, and however much she tried to search his face out, he was reluctant to meet her gaze.

Several times his meandering eyes came to rest on the bulge of her belly, and she found herself covering it with her hand, protectively.

—*Čakám dieťa*, she said, deciding that even speech he couldn't understand was better than none. *Je to moje prvé. Narodí sa o mesiac.*

He lifted his eyes briefly in acknowledgement, and she tried to coax him with a gentle smile, hoping to set him at ease. Instead he produced a loud burp from deep inside his chest and, bringing a curled fist to his mouth, he muttered an apology, pushed back his chair, and scrambled out the door. She heard the lock of the bathroom door slide to.

On the step, Eva helped herself to a drag of Tibor's cigarette.

—Helps my stomach, she murmured, before Tibor had a chance to object. All that grease.

—That was the most revolting meal I've ever tried to eat.

—But it was kind of him, all the same, said Eva. I was so hungry, I could have eaten anything. Who do you think he is?

Tibor shrugged. —I wonder if he'd let us have a bath here.

—Do you think he has hot water?

—Yes. And a proper toilet. I had a look.

Eva borrowed the cigarette again.

—I'd feel uneasy about it. He's so awkward.

—It would be good for you to have a hot bath. Ease the pains in your back.

Eva rested her chin on her knees. —I suppose it would.

There was a small cough behind them, and they turned to find their host hovering in the hallway. In one hand he wielded an ice-cream scoop.

—Pudding?

They packed the ice-cream cartons – twelve in all – into his freezer, displacing several boxes of frozen meat pies to fit them in. When they tried to stop him throwing the pies away, he became quite agitated. He piled them on to Tibor's arms and motioned for him to come round the back of his house, where he made a great show of dropping them one by one into the dustbin. When they were all gone he brushed his hands together with a look of immense satisfaction and all they could do was shrug in return.

He gave them four large flagons of water – enough to last them two or three days – a box of candles and, when he saw Eva eyeing it, the remainder of the loaf of bread. At the last minute, he went back to the kitchen and brought out a carton of milk and several jars of different coloured jams.

—Any time, he called out as they left. Bring as much as you like!

—*Prosím?*

—*Zmrzlina!* he shouted, picking up the Slovak word. More *zmrzlina!*

Tibor made a semi-circle of candles in jars on the ground. He sat behind her, taking her weight, his arms wrapped around her belly, a blanket around them both.

—It's like me. It never sleeps.

—Do you talk to it?

—Pleez, can I have tea/coffee/lunch/dinner/somebody *Česky* to talk to, Eva recited.

—That's not English. That's Slovish.

—You wouldn't understand, Frenchy.

Tibor put a cigarette in his mouth and leant sideways, taking his flame from one of the flickering candles.

—He told me there's a friend who drives him to the supermarket, said Tibor. We can go with them.

—I'd like to start collecting things for the baby.

—I'm running out of cigarettes.

—Thank God. I never liked those Sparta cigarettes. Start smoking Marlboros or Pall Malls.

—You're letting this country corrupt you.

He exhaled and Eva stared into the darkness.

—Look, said Tibor. His light's just come on. He's in his kitchen.

She twisted her head to look. She could just make out a dark silhouette moving slowly within the square of light.

For a moment, Tibor rested his cheek on her shoulder, his lips searching for naked skin amongst the folds of the blanket at her neck.

—Hah – I nearly forgot. Close your eyes.

—What? You haven't made anything for days.

—It's not what you think. Look.

From behind his back he brought out a cardboard container, just bigger than a soda can.

—I found it in the *Angličan*'s bin. Smell it. It's what passes for ice-cream round here.

—Eugh. That's nasty. So sweet!

She held it close to one of the candles.

—'Baskin Robbins', she read slowly. Is that what they call it?

The flame began to lick hungrily up one side of the container and she let it catch, dropping it on to the ground when it got too hot to hold.

—What are you trying to do, set fire to the entire desert? asked Tibor, taking off his shoe and batting the flames down.

She had found a wide-brimmed hat with a string that swung beneath her chin – a useful design, she told Tibor, for when she developed a double chin. Tibor had immediately picked at the greasy knot in an attempt to shorten it. That way, he said, she would have to limit herself to the one chin.

—It's a sombrero, she told him, snatching it back. It's supposed to be like that.

They used a length of wooden rib taken from the barrelled skeleton of a dead cactus to knock the fruit off. It was not the best time of year for harvesting – the fruit was mostly overripe and had already been scavenged by insects – but it came off easily. Twice, Tibor brushed too close to the giant plants and received a scratch that drew blood. By the time they had filled two bags, the smell of the sweet, fermenting flesh was so strong that they were attracting flies.

The Englishman didn't seem surprised to see them. Eva stepped forward cheerily, her pre-rehearsed line at the ready.

—Sir, we need use electric mixer!

She showed him her bag of rotting fruit and waited for him to click. It didn't take him long. His face lit up.

—A liquidiser! I have one! Do come in!

They all joined in with the chopping, removing the rotten bits, checking for insects. Tibor swore at the bluntness of the Englishman's knives; he tried several and gave up on them all, eventually leaving the other two to finish the job without him.

—*Zavolaj ma, keď skončíš*, he said, irritably, to Eva. Call me when you're done.

On his way out of the kitchen, he hesitated in the hallway. The door to the Englishman's room was slightly ajar. Looking through, he could see a high, single bed, rather like the cot bed he had slept on in the Tatras. He pushed the door further open with the flat of his hand, and his attention was caught by a silver frame propped up against a lamp beside the bed.

It was a colour photograph, bleached yellowy by the sun, showing a woman standing in a doorway, one hand on the door frame, the other clutching a round wicker basket. She was either on her way in or on her way out, and had been surprised by the photographer – half turning in response to a shout, one side of her face lost in a blur of movement.

She was in her late forties, Tibor guessed, or early fifties. She had the same large bones as the Englishman, the same bland face and rather bovine, wide-set eyes. Reams of bleached-blond hair were piled up above a broad expanse of forehead, and round her neck was a chunky ring of popper beads, half engulfed by flesh. She had a good neck, Tibor saw, despite the thickness of it – strong and sturdy, and the large beads offset it well. She was dressed in an apricot jacket and matching skirt, and from somewhere inside her open mouth came the glint of a gold tooth, picked up by the flash of the camera.

252

A handsome woman, all in all. Number 36, it said on the wall outside, and for a moment it seemed to Tibor that the number applied to her, rather than to the house in which she lived.

Then he saw, carved into the silver frame along the bottom, the words, 'Josephine Moon, 1914-1978'.

A sound from the kitchen made him jump – the whizz of the liquidiser being turned on. A shout and a laugh from Eva. Tibor put the frame down, guiltily, feeling as if he had seen something he shouldn't have. And yet he did not want to leave the room. Without knowing what he was looking for, he found himself scanning the walls, the floor, the bed. His eyes ran quickly along the bookshelf with its neatly ordered line of books, but the titles contained no words that he recognised. On the bedside table was a box of tissues with one or two half-used ones stuffed back into the top. A little avalanche of scrunched-up tissues spilled over the rim of the waste-paper basket in the corner. Clearly, this was a man who blew his nose a lot.

Tibor hitched up the bedspread and saw, bizarrely, that the bed legs were standing in little plastic beakers, half filled with water. A pair of house slippers – soft leather, with a plastic heel and sheep's wool lining – were tucked neatly underneath. They were the sort of slippers an old man would wear.

It struck Tibor how very alien this room was to him. The musty smell, the stillness, the sense of things not being moved about by different pairs of hands – there was a lifelessness in here that oppressed him. Spend too long in here and you would petrify. How far it was from the atmosphere of the home that he and Eva had made in their van. Being around Eva made him feel vividly alive – the ease of her laugh, the almost daily burgeoning of her size, the sweet smell of the almond oil that she used on her skin, the grace of her movements, the swing of her ponytail – it all came together to produce a vibrancy that lifted him out of himself whenever he saw her, or even thought of her, flooding every nerve in his body. Quite simply, he realised, he loved to be with her. She made him incredibly happy.

Yes, *happy*. The word came as a surprise to him, but it was the right one. Over the last few months, it had begun to seep inside him, and now he knew it was there, and he was living it, consciously.

With an awareness of it came a terrible fear of losing it. Filled with a sudden, searing love for her and for the precious life that was growing inside her, he left the bedroom quickly, closing the door behind him.

In the kitchen, a greenish juice spread over the worktop and ran in sticky dribbles down the cupboard doors. Thick peelings of the tough, knobbled skin lay in a heap on the table, crawling with the odd ant. The fruit that was to be used had been collected in a large bowl, and the Englishman was lifting messy handfuls of it into the liquidiser. When he turned it on, the green juice sprayed up between the clasp of his fingers.

—We're having fun, shouted Eva in Slovak over the noise. The *Angličan* and me.

She wiped a splash of juice from her cheek and licked it off her finger.

—It's definitely an aphrodisiac, she laughed. You should see the way he's been smiling at me.

—I think that's enough, said Tibor, picking up the bowl the Englishman was filling from the liquidiser.

—No! We can't stop now, Tibor. We're on a roll, aren't we, *Angličan*?

She flashed a smile at the Englishman. He offered a nervous one of his own, his glance darting anxiously between their faces.

—To tell the truth, I think this is the only fun he's had in ages, said Eva loudly as she wiped her face with the kitchen teacloth. He's probably suffering from constipation. That's what happens when you don't laugh enough, according to my father.

Tibor looked across to the Englishman, searching for a sign of understanding in the blank blue eyes.

—Yeah, he looks pretty constipated to me.

—What do you want us to do, head chef? Should we add the sugar now? He says we can use whatever we can find.

—You two go outside. I'll take over.

—I think he wants to watch you. He wants to learn how to do it.

Tibor looked at the Englishman. He looked back at Tibor expectantly, like a dog waiting to be fed. A splash of green juice was dribbling down his chin.

—I don't know what it is, but he's started to give me the creeps, said Tibor. You take him outside. I can't have him in here.

They bottle-necked in the doorway, Eva pausing on the top step, wondering if she should go back for her hat. She didn't realise he was standing so close behind her until she felt the hot breath on her neck, and then a slight pressure on her shoulder blade. Could he really have touched her? She turned round sharply, uncertainty clouding her eyes. His face was so close to hers that she could see the freckles on his skin, the buds of colour in his cheeks, a bubble of moisture gathering between his hesitant lips.

—Oh, sorry – I—

Between his finger and thumb he held up a single hair. It must have been stuck to her t-shirt, and he had plucked it off. It was an action that presumed an intimacy which they didn't have – she could see that he realised that now.

She smiled and a wave of relief washed over his face.

—*Tak dobre*, she said. It's all right. It's quite all right.

They walked down the garden in companionable silence. At the bottom, he showed her a hammock, hanging beneath a white sheet. Eva sat down in it, tapping her hand beside her to indicate he should join her. She felt a need to put him at his ease. As he lowered his heavy frame down, she noticed the two rings of sweat spreading outwards from beneath each armpit. The hammock rolled them together, pressing his damp flank against her thigh.

Acutely aware of their proximity, the Englishman curled his fists, placed them squarely on his knees, and fixed his eyes straight ahead.

Eva picked up a jagged piece of stone and made tally marks in the grit at their feet. After five, she drew a question mark, and pointed to the house.

He swivelled his head briefly, not quite far enough round to see her, and returned it to centre again, before holding up a single finger. One. He had been here one year, she understood. She noticed the deep red crease lines carved into the back of his neck, a freckle on the skin behind his ear, the curl of his hair making a clear space for it.

—Just over, in fact, he said. Last month I celebrated my first anniversary.

She nodded, pleased that they had managed to understand each other so far.

—Hippy birthday, she said suddenly – the phrase coming back to her from an English lesson at school – and she laughed. He smiled too, and as he did so, she saw a blush scrambling up his neck like a stain. To her surprise, it gave her a prickle of pleasure. He seemed to like her, and want to please her. She leant forward and laid her finger on a scab on the back of his hand, asking the question with her eyebrows.

She had barely touched him but he retracted his hand as if it had been scalded, cupping it protectively in the paw of the other one. The blush in his face intensified.

—The saguaro, he mumbled and nodded towards the tallest of his two chief cacti.

—How you say? Suwarro?

—Yes.

—Ah. Suwarro. Tibor, he make *zmrzlina* with suwarro. Suwarro ice-cream.

—Yes, exactly. He paused. Well done.

He swivelled towards her again, briefly, and his glance rested on her belly. He pointed down at the tally marks. —How long to go?

She held out nine fingers, then folded them one by one, until just her forefinger remained standing.

His lips twitched a little, then opened up.

—How exciting, he said, his eyes gleaming. Really, I am so excited about it.

This was a good sign. Becoming bold, she took his hand firmly – the one with the scab – and laid it on her belly. He looked at her fearfully, but didn't withdraw it this time. He seemed afraid to apply any pressure, so she squeezed it down with her own. After a few moments there was a movement inside, the child's head rising up as if to receive the double-handed blessing on its crown. The Englishman's jaw dropped open and he looked at her, astonished. She saw the Adam's apple in his throat move slowly up and down.

—*Moje dieťatko!* she said. My baby.

She laughed, lightly. But the Englishman didn't join in. When she looked more closely, she saw that he had tears in his eyes.

—You're jealous, she said to Tibor. He lay with his head resting lightly on her belly, waiting for the little muted kicks and fist-thuds which he loved to feel against his face. He still found it hard to believe there was a baby in there, a child that would one day run around and scream and laugh and talk to him. He fantasised frequently about this. The sound of its voice – *Oci! Oci!* – its sense of humour, the way she or he would look up at him with big brown eyes. He would teach it to do handstands and cartwheels.

—I'm not jealous. I just don't like the way he stands in the corridor and doesn't step aside to let you pass.

—He's just awkward. He doesn't know what to do.

—He wants to feel you press up against him.

He caressed her mound with his palm, tapped it gently.

—Do you have any idea what it is?

—I'm hoping it's a baby.

—Pedant. A boy or a girl.

She shrugged.

—No names, then?

He didn't dare admit to it, but in his head he had compiled two lists already – one of boys' names, one of girls'. Every day he went through them, crossing off one, adding another.

—You're not naming it, she said, as if reading his mind. You lack poetry, Tibor. It'll end up with a name like Lemonade Fizz.

He had suspected this was coming.

—OK. But do I get to say yes or no to whatever you decide?

—Tibor, your beard is scratching me. You need to shave.

—The *Angličan*, he said suddenly, turning to face her. His voice was animated. He doesn't have any beard to speak of. I don't think he even shaves. Have you noticed?

She sighed. —No, I hadn't noticed that.

—He's not such a fine figure of a man as me.

She rolled over on to her side, forcing him off.

—Had you noticed that? he insisted.

She laughed at his childishness. —Yes, Tibor, I had noticed that.

—*Tak dobre*, he said, quietly. All right.

He got up and took a towel and a razor and filled a small basin with water. At the door of the van he hesitated, his fingers on the handle. There was something else he wanted to say, but he didn't know how to say it. He wanted to suggest they abandon the van and move on. To New Mexico, or back to California. It wasn't too late. He wanted to say that he would get work in a restaurant, making real food – not just ice-cream. Perhaps they'd live by the sea. She always talked about how she wanted to learn to swim. And then, once the baby was born—

His internal voice trailed off and he stared at the basin of water, oddly, as if he were searching for his reflection. Why did it seem like an admission of failure? They had never planned to be here, and yet to leave now felt like giving up. His mouth was stretched flat, the brackets deep on either side.

And then, once the baby was born—

But it was as if his imagination had driven down a cul-de-sac. No words or images came to mind after that. He stood there for a long time, staring at the water, the unfinished sentence hanging in his head.

Behind him, he heard her breathing deepen into sleep.

When Eva woke up, she found herself alone. Wet with her own sweat, and irritated that she had fallen asleep during the day, she rolled the bedding into a corner and slid open the side window to get some air. A yellowy light burst in like a length of thick rope being pulled and twisted through the window, dense with particles of dust disturbed from the blankets. She shielded her eyes with one hand. There was a note on the worktop, written in Tibor's untidy scrawl.

—*Zlatko*. Gone shopping with the *Angličan*. Will buy food for a feast tonight. We'll show him how it's done. Love, Tibor.

She read the note again, looking for something in it to lift her spirits. But still she felt irritable, even heavy-hearted. She poured herself a glass of milk from a warm carton the Englishman had given them, picked up her sombrero and went outside.

Sitting on the deckchair, she looked across at the uneven line of mountains on the horizon, sticking up like hardened, yellow toenails on the ends of a giant pair of feet. She must ask Theo how far away they were. He must know. He saw them every day, after all.

Every single day.

For a fleeting moment, she thought she understood what it must be like for the Englishman to live out here by himself. The utter quiet, the stillness, all this space. Sitting here now, for instance, felt very different without having Tibor a few feet away, knocking around in the kitchen. It gave her a heightened awareness of herself, a sensitivity to the thoughts inside her own head, the mechanics of her own body. She took a gulp of milk, and listened to the sound of her throat clutching around the swallow. Inside her, she felt the baby shift, turning in its warm sac of fluid. She had had no idea it would move about as much as this, always wriggling and punching at her, as if unable to get comfortable. It would have its father's restlessness, this child.

The heat was intense and there was no movement in the air today. The milk was making her feel a little nauseous, despite her thirst.

Perhaps it had gone sour already. She tipped the hat forward so that it shaded her entire face, but she could still feel the rays burning through the straw weave. She flapped the neck of her dress to create a ripple of breeze for her body. Her old needlework skills had come in handy the last couple of months. She had released the seams on the sides of all her dresses. Even the dungarees still fitted. She'd just moved the buttons a couple of inches back.

A knot of tiny flies clustered a few inches away from her face. She swiped at them, but they reformed their little tangle instantly. In the opposite direction to the Englishman's house she could just make out the line of the main road. The night the rain started, Tibor had turned off on what had turned out to be a dried-up river-bed, strewn with stones. The mistake could have been disastrous; once the river had filled, it had swept past them with great force. But they had been lucky; the van had held up. She scanned the road for a sign of a vehicle. A cloud of dust, perhaps, billowing into the air like a message from an Indian camp fire. For a moment she felt very ancient, a woman waiting at the homestead for the menfolk to return. Distracted by a tickle of sweat working its way down the ladder of her spine, she heaved herself up again. It was too hot to be outside.

No doubt her irritability was heightened by the fact that they had been stuck in one place all this time. Over the weeks she'd become used to the daily change of scene. Even the preparations for departure – hooking the wire meshes across the front of the shelves to stop the pots and jars falling off, securing the contents of the fridge, packing their few possessions back into the van – were enjoyable. She loved the constant feeling of renewal as they started up the engine at the beginning of another day, another set of roads. They took a quick look at the map and then set off, the air pouring through the open windows, both of them charged with a renewed sense of freedom. The landscape was brought to life as they moved through it.

It felt hotter in the van than outside it. Listlessly, she used the hem of her dress to wipe her face. Her belly was pulling at the base of her spine, and it was an effort to be on her legs. She hoisted a flagon of water to her lips. The water dribbled around the sides of her mouth, spilling on to her dress. It was too warm to refresh her. What she needed was a couple of hours in the Englishman's hammock, just until the sun was lower in the sky. Perhaps she would walk over there and, if the house was locked, she would wait in the hammock until they got back. If it was open, she'd be able to get some ice-cubes out the freezer and make herself something cool to drink. Tibor would be pleased to find her there when he got back.

She picked up the flagon of water, tied a cardigan around her waist for when it got cooler, and headed off towards the white fence posts.

16

Walter's father is a well-built man. He walks towards our house with a purposeful swing to his hips, like he's got some serious business to sort out with us. My father looks up with a spoonful of peas and gravy halfway to his mouth and for a moment doesn't know what to do, whether it's better to put them in quick, just in case he doesn't get the chance later, or return them to his plate.

—Oh, I forgot to tell you. I've got a date.

He's still not speaking to me, but he shoots me a look of alarm.

—Not with him. That's his dad.

He looks unconvinced.

—Look, Walter's sitting there in the car, right?

Walter's dad spots us from the garden and brings his swaggering stride to a halt with a little jump. He raises a flat palm in greeting. My father puts the peas in and gets up, reaching for a large checked napkin to wipe his chin. A ball of damp tissue makes a bulge in the sleeve of his shirt.

—Dad, sit down. You don't need to meet him.

He pauses, the napkin pressed against his lips.

—Will you leave the door open? Or should I take a key?

He nods his head. Then shakes it.

—I take it that means you'll leave it open.

He sneaks a quick look at the half-eaten food on my plate.

—Help yourself, I say, and grab my bag.

—Anyone know where we're going? 'Cause as much as I like my new job as chauf*feur* – Walter's dad accents the end of the word in a way that makes me look up – I don't like clients who can't make up their minds, and so far this one ain't doin' too well.

He glances in the mirror at Walter, and then across at me, his eyebrows raised. When he takes in my bare legs, sticking out from under the short red skirt, there's a gleam of amusement in his eyes.

I cross my legs and look out the side window.

—To Century Park, chirrups Walter from the back seat. I can see him in the side mirror, strapped in. He looks very small, with his concave chest and his pants bunching up around his waist.

—Did you hear that, Josephine? 'To Century Park!' he commands, with great authority! Man, will that boy go far.

Walter does his utmost to avoid my eyes in the mirror. His dad chuckles and shakes his head from side to side.

From the high road, the city of Tucson spreads out beneath us like a shimmering lake, hemmed in by dark mountains on all sides. Some of the lights have spilled over on to the lower slopes of the foothills, as if they have been splashed there. Lights travel around the grid of roads in red and white pairs; people on the west side wanting to be on the east, people on the east wanting to be on the west. Motel signs blink on and off and a monstrous cut-out of a bull rises up against a strip of pale sky on the horizon.

It all looks pretty to me, although my father has done his best to instil a fear of it in me. He doesn't approve of the frenzy of the town, he says. The hurried lives, the people without any time. Besides, Jersey has told him stories that he listens to with bulging eyes, believing every word. There are gangs of car thieves who lie in wait beneath the chassis of your car, he says, ready to slice the tendons on the backs of your ankles when you go to unlock the door. Muggers who come at you with outstretched arms and a shout of recognition, moving in to kiss you on the cheek, a long-lost Aunty Drew, only to nuzzle your neck with the cold butt of a gun. Lots of people carry guns down there, my father whispers to me, his eyes wide with fright. They strap them to their calves, beneath their trouser legs. Never trust someone with a padded calf, he says.

When we get out, Walter's dad motions to me with a private jerk of his head.

—Go easy on him, Josephine.

I have one leg in the car and one leg out. Quickly, I yank down my skirt as best I can.

—Sir?

—Girls grow up a bit quicker than boys, that's all.

I dangle my bag in front of my legs instead.

—Goodnight, sir.

—See you later, kids.

In the movie theatre we buy a popcorn and two large Cokes and Walter heads for the back row, without me having to suggest it. When we get there, it's already taken up with a line of boys from Santa Catalina High. They're boisterous and noisy, leaning over each other to talk. We shuffle into the row in front and the boys behind clock us in an instant, nudging each other and whispering. Walter looks longingly at the empty seats further away.

—I don't think I can see from here, he says.

—It'll be all right. I'll tell you what's happening.

I stick the straw in my Coke, pull my hair out from under my jacket and give it a toss. I'm so aware of the boys behind me that I only half watch the movie. Walter's hand goes up and down rhythmically to the popcorn.

I hardly notice it at first. A delicate swishing of my hair with a finger. I don't dare to move a muscle. After a while the finger grazes the back of my neck, and begins to stroke up and down, very gently. I glance across at Walter, but he hasn't noticed anything. When the action reaches its climax, the finger stays still, and then afterwards it goes to work again. I try to untangle the voices behind me, to work out which one belongs to the finger.

By the time the movie's over I'm so nervous I have no strength in my legs. Walter jumps up quickly and immediately looks for the exit. I pull him back by his shirt.

—Wait for me.

—I need to pee. Desperate. Meet you outside in a jiffy.

He pushes ahead of the thickening crowd. The boys from behind jostle me amongst them, and a hand brushes my butt. It's him again: he's behind me, lifting up my hair and bending his face to my neck. There's a line of fur over the top of his lip.

—Where are you going now, sweetheart?

I shrug my shoulders, still not daring to turn around.

—Wanna come to Tovi's?

—OK.

—Better get rid of that boyfriend of yours.

Walter is waiting obediently outside. He doesn't have a jacket, and he's got goose-bumpy arms from the cold.

—I'm going to Tovi's.

Walter's eyes flit from side to side, chasing the little black speck.

—Who with?

I point towards two cars filling up with the boys from Santa Catalina High.

—What about my dad?

—Tell him I met a friend.

Walter looks half relieved, half not. He nods his head.

I get into the car with the boys from Santa Catalina High. Turning round, I watch the slight figure of Walter receding out the back.

There are six boys in the car and me. They're quieter now than they were in the movie theatre. I'm not sure which one was the guy who invited me along – they all look the same in their white t-shirts and black leather jackets. Some of them grin at me, but most of them don't. No one asks me my name. They pass a bottle and cigarettes between them. Sometimes they stop, and someone gets out and someone else gets in.

For an hour we drive up and down the arteries of Tucson, the windows steamed up from all the bodies. I'm sitting half on someone's legs and half off, and my skirt keeps riding up. When we take a sharp corner on to Camino Seco, I lose my balance and lurch towards the window. A pair of hands hauls me back.

—Hey, don't you like me any more?

It's the guy who touched me in the theatre.

—You're not holding on tight enough, Jay.

We take another corner and this time I clutch at the lapel of Jay's jacket behind me. He twists his face around to meet mine and before I know what's happening he pushes his tongue in my mouth. It's cold and it tastes of hot dog and onions and mustard. He moves it around for a while until I pull back.

—You're a cool customer.

—Here, Jay, give her some of this.

He offers me the bottle but I shake my head, so he swigs at it himself. Afterwards he wipes his mouth with the back of his hand and gives me a grin.

At the lights they wind down the windows and shout to the people in the next car. There's a lot of laughter and someone throws an empty bottle which smashes against the passenger door. Then both cars drive off, the tyres screeching on the asphalt, but nobody says anything about it. The car pulls over and parks. We all get out except one guy who's sitting with his cheek squashed flat against the window and his eyes closed. He looks very pale.

—Should I wake him?

—Leave him alone, sweetheart. He's no use to anyone now.

There's a line of men sitting on high stools at the bar. They turn to look as we traipse through. There are ten of us, maybe more, and they don't look pleased to see us. When they're done with their shots they nod at a woman leaning against the far wall, and she comes over slowly and fills the glasses up, pouring from a bottle with a metal spout on the top. Then she goes back to leaning against the wall, as if that were the main reason she was here, to prop up the wall, and filling up glasses is just something she does in between.

I have my arm around Jay's waist and he has his arm around me. We're going right through to the back of the room where the pool tables are.

—Hey, I play pool, I tell him.

—You're not goin' anywhere, pussycat.

As he says it he fiddles with the band of my skirt and slides his hand down. He finds his way beneath my panties. His hand is cold around my butt. He goes right into the crack and rubs hard.

—Ooh, girl, he says into my ear, tickling me with his tongue. Ooh, girl, do you know how good that feels?

The boys spread out and pick up their cues around the four or five tables. The clunk of the balls rolling through the chute makes me think of Cindy. She and Jersey taught me to play pool. *Let's us girls take on the boy*, Cindy had said, and showed me what to do. It was a Saturday afternoon, and we played until it was time to go home for tea. I'd like to tell Jay about this, but he doesn't ask me anything. He just rubs his hand deeper into my crack and then he takes me to a table in the corner and heaves me on to it by wrapping his hand around my butt.

—Ooh, girl, he says.

I let myself fall back on to the table. Around my head are empty bottles and an ashtray filled with cigarette ends. I can hear the snap of the balls, and imagine the triangle splaying out. His rubs up and down beneath my panties. I wish we were playing pool instead of doing this. I wish someone would come over and tap him on the shoulder and say, Jay, why don't you guys join in. But no one pays any attention to us, or if they do I can't tell. My mouth is dry and I wonder if can ask Jay for a drink. I'll have a Coke, I practise saying, in my head. But he takes hold of my chin and bears down on me with his hot-dog breath, and this time his tongue is strong and sour and

267

muscular, working itself round mine. He rubs his fingers hard between my legs and then he pokes them up inside me and the surprise of it makes me gasp and he grins at me, his tongue sticking out. *You like that, don't you, pussycat*, he says, and then he digs the heel of one hand into my chest and levers himself on to me, and he pulls at the flies of his jeans. *You're really hot, you know that?* he says, and he yanks my panties to one side and his flies tear at the skin of my thighs and he shoves his dick inside me and I suck my breath in because it's hard and dry and I wonder if I will ever breathe out again. *Come on, little girl, get moving, you can let me in deeper than that*, he says, and he shoves it in so hard that the pain is like knives inside. *Harrumph*, he goes, his mouth twisting to one side, shoving and shoving, and the table bangs against the wall and the bottles fall around me like bowling pins, and my mouth is in the ashtray and my eyes don't know where to look. *Harrumph!* he goes and the table bangs again, *harrumph, harrumph, harrumph!* and he's pressing so hard on my ribs I wonder if they will crack and he'll fall right through and then he's *Oo-ooh, girl, ooh-ooh-ooh girl can you believe* and his chin sticks out and his eyes bulge like a fish's that's about to die, and he collapses on top of me, his hair in my mouth, his mouth on my neck and there he lies, a dead weight, and I cannot move beneath him. I think how strange I must look to the others, with my legs dangling off the edge of the table, and I wonder, did they see all that, were they watching, did everybody see, all the men lined up by the bar, were they turning their heads to watch, and the woman leaning against the wall with her arms folded, was she watching too? And are they laughing or are they quiet, because the *te dum* of the blood in my brain and the *te dum* of the table against my ear is too loud in my head to hear.

17

Something woke him in the early hours. Automatically, he tensed and relaxed the muscles around his bladder, but he could detect no tell-tale ache.

He got up anyway, pawing the darkness for his white towelling dressing gown. It didn't seem to be in its usual place on the back of the door. That disappointed him. It had been a Christmas present from his mother ten years ago, and he was as attached to it as if it were a cat. He concentrated instead on his feet, which were finding their way into his slippers, the toes nosing in then crunching and releasing down to the ends.

Opening the door, a cold draft tumbled in on him. The front door was open and there, on the step, was his dressing gown, hovering just above ground level, like a ghost.

—*Prosím*. Where Tibor?

—Come inside, he said gently.

It wasn't completely dark; there was a half-moon in the sky, cut perfectly straight down the middle as if with a wire on a cheeseboard. Just beyond the perimeter of the fence Theo noticed the black silhouetted stalks of the agave flowers, standing very still, as if he'd caught them having a game of musical statues. The stalks had shot up as high as fifteen feet in the spring, but turned woody and brown almost immediately, spending more time as effigies of themselves than they had spent alive.

Gently, he put his hands on her shoulders. She didn't try and shake him off. He turned her round so that she pointed back indoors. All he could think of was that the bottom edge of the dressing gown was trailing and that it was going to catch on the wooden step if he didn't do something about it. He manoeuvred himself behind her and scooped it up with one hand. Then he followed her inside, holding the hem like a pageboy holding a train.

That afternoon there had been three of them in the front seat of the truck. Jersey had dressed for the occasion in a cream cowhide Stetson with a handwoven Tohono O'Odham braid around the rim. He had a good, broad chest, the ranch-hand, and he could cut quite a dashing figure in a clean pair of jeans and a crisp white t-shirt, as he did today. Theo had felt a little piqued at being upstaged so markedly, and had taken his place in the truck in mawkish silence, making no effort to help the conversation.

As it turned out, he hadn't needed to. Jersey had kept up a running commentary on the landmarks that they passed in his loud, even-toned voice, and Tibor, relaxed and excitable between them, responded by exclaiming loudly in Slovak, though it was impossible to tell whether the two sets of remarks bore any relation to each other.

—That there in the distance is the peak of Mount Lemmon, where folks goes skiing in winter, though me personally I never seen the point – the point of skiing, that is, not the point of the mountain, which I've seen plenty of times. This here's the post office run by Miss Betty Morgan since the beginning of time. They say she's a hundred and ten or thereabouts. Jeezus peezus, would you believe it? That there's the asshole got his hands on my .357! We had a bet 'bout young Sheila Stanton's vital statistics three years back at the Hoof 'n' Horn and I ain't found a way of getting it back off of him yet bar going in to Sheila with a tape-measure and asking if she'd oblige.

Theo had sat quietly, rolling his gobstopper around his mouth, learning more about Jersey's life in this one journey than he had in the course of the previous year.

They had dispersed as usual, arranging to meet in the parking lot in half an hour. Theo had headed for the meat counter, Tibor for the fresh fruit and vegetables. Jersey poked his face into Theo's bags as he lifted them on to the back of the truck.

—See you got yourself some hot-dog materials, he said, approvingly. Now will you be boiling or grilling, do you think? Never been sure in my mind which is the best way to proceed.

Jersey lit a cigarette and they were leaning against the dirty chassis of the pickup when they saw the two security guards in uniform marching across the lot. Between them was a figure with an unruly mop of black hair, twisting his neck round towards them. It took them a few seconds to register that it was Tibor.

—Well, I'll be damned—

—Holy Moses.

Theo made as if to run towards them, but Jersey put a restraining hand on his arm.

—I wouldn't do that.

—What d'you mean?

—You don't want to get messed up with it. If he's done something wrong, and you're with him, then you've done something wrong too. That's the way it works out here.

—But what could he possibly have done?

Jersey rubbed his chin.

—Don't move, all right?

Leaving Theo with the truck, he walked nonchalantly back into the store, pausing only to tread on his discarded cigarette butt. Theo watched him exchange a few words with the woman at the cigarette counter. He came out and jumped straight behind the wheel.

—Caught him putting a six-inch blade inside his shirt, he said as he put his foot down on the accelerator. Taken him off to the county jail for questioning. Reckon we had a close shave, you and me.

*

—Go, she said to him, at her bedroom door. He put his hands up, protesting innocence. Of course he would go. He had no intention of following her inside.

—No. She shook her head violently and flung her hand above her head. *Chod'!* Go, Tibor!

She meant him to leave the house. To go and find her husband and bring him back. He glanced at his watch: it was four o'clock in the morning. It was cold out there, and dark.

He gave her a theatrical shrug, his eyebrows rising up with his shoulders.

—What can I do?

The look she turned on him was so icy that he found himself taking a step backwards. Nodding quickly, he reached inside the coat cupboard and grabbed his anorak.

—All right. I'll go. Right away.

He pulled on his thick socks and boots and zipped the anorak up over the top of his pyjamas. The problem with anoraks was that they were never long enough; they only ever covered half your bottom, or half your stomach, and if you pulled them down over one, they lurched up over the other. In the kitchen he filled his water flask from the tap and hung it round his neck, satchel-style.

He shut the door behind him, feeling odd to be leaving his home with someone else inside it. But he had no intention of going anywhere. What did she expect him to do – wake up a neighbour at this hour? And then what? Even if he did go to the police station and find Tibor, he wasn't going to bail him out. The man was clearly dangerous – most probably a lunatic – and Theo didn't want him back in the house. Eva needed protecting from him too, although she did not know it yet.

Besides, it was a rule of the desert. He'd read it in his book: *Never go out in the desert alone at night.* You can't see where you're walking, and you could easily lose your way, or step on something you shouldn't. Besides, the temperature plummets at night, and the chances are you'll be under-dressed. She'd be in a sorry state if something happened to him as well. She'd have no one to look after her then.

There was an eerie silence in the garden. The birds weren't up yet, and most of the night-time prowlers had found their dinners and gone to sleep with full stomachs. The crunch of his boots on the gravel seemed unreasonably loud. He didn't know what to expect of the desert at this hour. Perhaps there would be a whole new set of creatures that he had never encountered before. He narrowed his eyes and tried to pierce through the mealy gloom, scanning it for the whites of eyes, or claws, or teeth.

He shone his torch on to the granite boulder, and it glinted back at him.

It wouldn't be long before the first shards of sun would spread over the valley from the east. He hadn't seen the sun rise out here before. It would be an opportunity to greet the dawn. To do some Sun Salutes at the correct hour. Pulling the anorak forward so that it covered his stomach and left his more insulated buttocks exposed, Theo sat on the top of the boulder, wrapped his arms round his legs, and rested his chin on his knees.

This time it was spider-legs of light flickering over his face that woke him. In the distance, he heard the sound of a lawn mower starting up. Gingerly opening one eye at a time, Theo discovered it was broad daylight. Dawn had been and gone – some time ago, by the looks of things. Damn and blast.

He had lost all feeling in his buttocks. Testing his muscles and joints gingerly, he unwedged his feet and gently lowered himself to the ground. What he needed was a nice hot bath.

As soon as he went in the house he realised the door to the spare room was open. His heart lurched in his chest as he took in the empty mattress, the rumpled sheets stripped back on both sides. Had she set off into the desert herself? She must be mad, in her condition. And then, from behind the bathroom door, he heard the sound of running water. For a moment he wondered if she had read his thoughts, and was preparing a bath for him. He was filled with a rush of tenderness for her, mingled with relief. But then he heard a strangely lilting wail filter through the sound of water, the occasional harsh corner of her language.

—*Už je to tu!*

He tapped, gently. There was no answer, just a faint whimpering, more like the whimper of a small dog than a woman.

—*Ach bože! O môj bože! O môj bôže!*

Theobald opened the door. Eva was standing in the bath, naked, her thighs and legs streaked with pink. As he watched, she bent from the waist and fiddled with the taps, trying to splash cold water between her legs. Theo's eyes went straight to the belly – so big and firm and round. When she had let him touch it in the hammock, he had expected it to have some give, like a balloon. But it had been hard as rock. He saw now how the belly button was stretched into an oval. A dark line ran beneath it to her groin, like the stain beneath the porthole of a ship.

—Eva.

Her face was wet, and strands of hair were stuck across her cheeks. As she turned to him she drew the back of her hand across her open mouth. The muscles on her face were quivering, as if she were sprinting towards him very fast.

—It's all right. It's only me.

He held his arms out to her. For a moment she stared at him as if she did not know him, but then, gulping on her tears, she allowed herself to be helped over the rim of the tub. Theo's heart thudded in his chest as her fingers sunk into the palm of his hand. He wrapped her in a towel, and gave the sides of her arms a quick rub.

He guided her into the bedroom and laid her down. Immediately she thrust her pelvis upwards, her face contorting in pain. The towel fell away and he stared at the hair at her crotch, matted with blood-stained water. I should get my special flannel, he thought.

—*Tibor.*

It was plaintive, pleading, the last *r* rolling deliciously even in her agonised state.

—There, there. He'll be here soon. Any minute now, you'll see.

He bit his lip at the sound of his own words. Eva let out a little cry as another contraction took hold and Theo looked about him in desperation, not wanting to look at her, but not knowing where else to look. He ended up by grabbing an empty tea cup from the floor and rushing out with it to the kitchen. When he reached the sink he stood still, momentarily frozen by the sudden drama, the intimacy, of what was happening.

Come on, Theobald, he said to himself. *You have to be up to this.*

He wiped his palms down the front of his thighs, filled a glass of water – a rather random attempt to be constructive – and went back to her room.

At lunch time he heated up a tin of chicken soup. She ate it propped up in bed, wearing his dressing gown. The initial contractions seemed to have died down, and she was relatively calm. He found he couldn't sit with her for more than a few minutes at a time – he ran out of places to look – and so he busied himself with household chores. He sloshed a generous amount of bleach into the washing-up bowl, filled it with warm water, and delved in with his plastic gloves. At least he could get the place free of germs.

By mid-afternoon the sounds emanating from the bedroom were considerably more alarming. Her groans were deep, guttural, wrenched out from the bottom of her throat. He had been present, some months ago, at the shooting of a cow that had been bitten by a rattlesnake, one side of its face puffed up like a pillow and completely engulfing its eye. It lay on its flank with its legs sticking out rod-straight, as if rigor mortis had taken advantage of the cow's immobility to set in early. As Jersey rested the cold steel of a barrel against its temple, the cow had sensed its fate and emitted a deep and, he had thought at the time, strangely human groan of anguish.

Remembering the cow, he thought of Eva and, hearing Eva now, he thought of the cow.

—Tibor?

The air was stuffy in her room, tinged with the salty smell of the chicken soup. Ready for bed in his pyjamas, he padded softly over to the window and levered it open.

—No, it's not Tibor. It's me. Theo.

—*Kde je Tibor?*

Theo motioned with his arm towards the front door.

Her expression seemed to suggest that it was he who was the cause of her pain. All traces of the kindness she had shown him in the hammock were gone.

—*Opustil ma?*

She stared at him, seemingly terrified.

—*Opustil ma!*

Theo shrugged and smiled nervously. A lopsided, slack-lipped smile. He didn't know what to do with his hands. He wanted to crouch down beside her, perhaps to stroke back the few damp hairs that were sticking to her forehead, but he didn't dare. He wanted to tell her he would be with her, that he would not leave her, not ever.

—*Musíš ho nájsť a priviesť späť! Potrebujem ho!*

Her tone was hard and fierce, and it frightened Theo. Coming up on to her elbows, she levered herself upright and swung her naked legs out on to the floor beside him. Theo stepped backwards, making space for her as she tried to find a grip on the wall. For a moment she looked up at him with an expression of exasperation and immense fatigue, the hair still stuck in childish wisps to her face, and then with a huge effort she hauled herself up and staggered past him through the doorway.

—Where do you think you're going? You're not going anywhere.

It was something his mother would have said. He had never heard himself use words like that before. Emboldened, he swung round into the hallway, ready to grab her and restrain her. But he didn't have to. She lurched with the effort of pulling the front door open, nearly losing her balance, then teetered on the top step. Her gaze travelled out to the horizon, the distance seeming to have taken her by surprise. It was as if she had suddenly found herself on a cliff-edge. She scanned slowly from one side to the other.

He held back, knowing that she would see the impossibility for herself. Sure enough, as he watched, she sat down on the step abruptly and let her head fall into her hands. It was only after a few seconds that he realised her shoulders were shaking.

He came in with his hardback notebook, bound with string. He had moved on to his second notebook now, and hadn't looked back at the stories in this one for several weeks. Perching on the edge of her bed, his blunt, tubular fingers could make no headway on the knot.

—*Daj mi to.*

He handed it to her and she picked between the braids with the nails of her finger and thumb. Theo had never seen such fine fingers and perfect nails – each crescent of white strong and tapered. The admiration shone in his eyes. To his delight, she gave him a little self-congratulatory smile as she handed the notebooks back.

He doubted she would understand a word of what he read. What little English she possessed had gone out the window today. But there was a lot one could glean from the rhythm. Fairytales the world over began and ended in the same way, reached the same climaxes at roughly the same points in the story. Everyone understood the rise and fall of a fairytale.

Hearing himself utter the first words was like listening to a stranger read. It was so long since he had read aloud, and he was shy of the sound of his own voice. He coughed several times, clearing away the uneasy croak. Sometimes he faltered over his own hand-writing – the pencil lead was too thick in places. But gradually he got into the swing of it, even allowing himself to get involved in the stories themselves. They were his own idiosyncratic versions, littered with modern, real-life props – cars and aeroplanes, gangsters and fistfights, Mars Bars and Sainsbury's supermarkets. The more he read, the more he found they were rather good.

Every once in a while he dared to let his eyes leave the page and flick up to her face. Sometimes he found her eyes on his, full and attentive. Sometimes she was gazing wistfully through the half-closed blinds, her expression misted up.

It was a moment of calm amidst all the commotion. She seemed grateful for it – the chance to rest, to recoup some energy. After twenty minutes or so she touched him on the knee and he understood that she had had enough. It was time for her to sleep. A touch and a look – that was all it needed. They had that connection now. He closed the notebook between the fold of one hand, as they used to do it on *Jackanory*, and gave her a little nod. They didn't need any words. It was a special moment, and when he got up and left her, pulling the door to but not closing it completely – for he wanted to be able to hear her when she called for him – he felt the hairs prickle on the back of his neck.

In the middle of the night he brought her ice-cream. His freezer was packed to the hilt with cartons, all neatly labelled and arranged in piles. Some of the names were smudged where melted ice had caused the ink to run. He had got Tibor to write down a list of ingredients for each flavour, although he had refused to specify quantities – he was the sort of person who did these things by eye. With the help of Eva's phrasebook, they translated the list into English.

He picked out a carton of the saguaro fruit batch and dusted off the ice. *All the Stars in the Universe*. She had named it in her strange language, and then, word by word, translated it for his benefit. He had been unable to hide the look of admiration in his eyes, for he could not have dreamt up a more beautiful name himself. And then Tibor broke the spell, jerking his thumb towards Eva, his black eyes shining. —Poet, he declared triumphantly to Theo, his grin uncontrollably wide. He was making fun of her, of her imagination. Disgusted, all Theo could manage was a nod.

She opened her eyes and let out a moan, turning her mouth away.

—Eat some. It'll give you some energy.

He tried to spoon it into the dryness of her mouth but she flung her face over the edge of the mattress.

—*Nie.*

—Go on, Eva. There's a good girl. Open wide.

He nosed the spoon at the corners of her mouth.

But she refused to eat. Instead, slowly, she began to speak. To his surprise, it was in English.

—Tibor, he go home. Slovakia. He leaved me.

Something in her eyes had hardened during the night, giving them a strength they had not had before. Until now, she had been the sort of girl his mother would have described, a little dismissively, as pretty, Theo thought. *A pretty little thing.* But tonight, those green eyes that looked at him so penetratingly from under the fine eyebrows were devastatingly beautiful. They were deep-set and filled with light. He took her hand and interlocked his fingers with hers, squeezing them gently.

—OK. Whatever you say.

She shut her eyes abruptly. With her lips she mouthed the only word she'd understood: OK. Theo noticed a couple of tears slide out from beneath her closed lids.

By five in the morning, twenty-four hours after her waters had broken, the contractions became regular and frequent. Innocent though he was in the area of female anatomy, Theo had a fair idea that this meant it was going to happen any moment now. He collected clean towels from the bathroom cupboard and put a saucepan of water on to boil, without knowing quite what he would use it for. With trembling hands he searched the kitchen cupboards and drawers for things which might be useful: a fresh pair of plastic gloves, some clothes pegs, a rubber band, a bottle of bleach and a rather blunt carving knife.

When she saw him enter the room with this fearsome collection of tools, a look of dread passed over Eva's face. Theo didn't notice. Emboldened by the drama of the situation, as well as the fact that Eva seemed to be in too much pain to be fully aware of what he did – let alone in a position to object – he knelt beside her and, before he knew it, he'd reached down and wiped that hair off her forehead at last. A little tickle of pleasure travelled from his fingers down to his groin. The simple action of stroking triggered a memory in him – perhaps of his mother doing it to him, or him doing it to his mother in her last days.

She closed her eyes. The sweat was gathering quickly on her face. Soaking his face flannel in a bowl of cold water and ice-cubes, he pressed it to her forehead, her cheeks, her eyes with their stained, dark rings. He went down her neck, towards the tops of her swollen breasts, heaving beneath the sheet. He stopped himself there.

When she next opened her eyes, they were fearful and confused. He could sense her resistance to the increasing pain – as if she wanted to say, Stop, let's do this another time. Theo wondered if it was like being in a plane when it's picking up speed for take-off, all resistance useless in the face of the unstoppable momentum.

Each time a contraction came juddering through her, she screamed and grabbed his hand, wrenching his fingers backwards to the wrist, and shouted Tibor's name.

He peeled down the sheet, exposing the solid belly, the thighs, all the way down her legs to her feet. The little blue rounds of his eyes travelled, unblinking, over the hills and valleys of her body, eyeing it as if it were the surface of the moon. She was extraordinary to him – not just her enormous belly, but the soft white flesh of her thighs, the underarm hair that he caught a glimpse of from time to time, even the delicate feet, with their even line of toes. When she arched her back, he held on hard to her feet. It seemed to help her manage her pain. She tried various positions to ease the pressure on her spine: sometimes she rolled on to her side, sometimes she went on all fours and he saw her breasts dangling beneath her like udders. He pressed the cool flannel to her tail bone, watching the sweat gather in the crease of her buttocks. He moved around her, administering to whichever part of her body he deemed appropriate, becoming more and more bold in deciding which parts he could touch.

When it happened, it was sudden. She lay on her back with her knees out to the sides, and suddenly it was there in the yawning hole of her, a dark, hard oval appearing through the stretched red vulva. A spurt of thick, dark blood slapped against her thighs as the skin ripped apart. Eva gave an unearthly wail of disbelief. Theo thought of the time Tibor would have touched her in that delicate place, put his fingers or his face to the soft velvet of it, treated it so gently. She battled for breath, taking little gasps at the top of her lungs. He squeezed her hand tightly.

—Big breath, Eva. Big breath.

He tried to show her that he was breathing with her, but her eyes were tightly shut and she was screaming with every exhalation. Just in time, Theo reached out and caught the mucus-covered head as it flopped into the palm of his hand, face down. He cradled it awkwardly, feeling the outline of a tiny nose with his fingers. One of its hands had come out too, tucked up around its ear. To his surprise, there was a luxurious layer of fine, moist hair – black, and sticking up in difficult tufts, a little like his own. Theo felt light in the head, and for a moment he thought he was going to faint. The scene around him suddenly seemed unreal, looming up at him in lurid colours and incredible shapes – the baby's dark head, Eva's red mouth, the splattering of blood on the white sheets.

Blinking back the stars, he stared at the bruised and bleeding flesh through which the baby was now fast emerging. The tear stretched wider to make way for the shoulders, and then the body slithered through in a flood of dark blood and milky fluid and suddenly there it was, a baby in his hands. He turned it over and for a fleeting moment he was the nine-year-old boy attending a first-aid seminar at Boy Scouts when they blew into the rubbery mouth of a dummy and some of the boys said *Did you French kiss her?* and he laughed though he didn't know what they meant.

He drew the tiny body towards him and held it up with trembling hands. There it was! A little girl. She was slippery as a seal, the bulging lids of her tightly shut eyes blue and puffy, as if the ink of the irises had leaked. Baggy, runkled-up skin gathered at the wrists and ankles, as if she was dressed already in an oversized skin-coloured jumpsuit. There was a little red mouth clamped shut. A network of turquoise veins like underground streams just visible through the hair. She gave off a smell of stale, yellowed milk.

—*Moje dieťatko?*

He had almost forgotten she was there. He glanced down at the exhausted figure of the woman, her belly still strangely inflated, her body gleaming with sweat. But the baby was silent – it hadn't yet drawn breath – and he knew he had to see to that first. It was relying on him to bring it to life, this baby – to open its eyes, its mouth, its lungs. He started to pull it away, before he realised that it was still attached to her, like a kite.

From some distant, rarely visited corner of his mind – perhaps the memory of a book he had read, or a film he had seen – the notion came to him to clamp the cord with the clothes pegs. He stuck one at each end and watched as it turned gradually from pink to white. He put the baby down on the bed and, with the knife, sawed the cord through as close to the stomach as he could get. Nervous of cutting the baby itself, he lowered his mouth to the last thin thread and bit through it, as if it were a string of sausages. Almost immediately a bubble formed between the baby's lips, and it took in its first complicated breath, letting it out again as an outraged cry.

—*Dajte mi moje dieťa!*

But still he didn't hand it over. Drawing it to his chest, he ran with it to the bathroom, and put his hand under the tap until it felt luke-warm. He could hold the entire creature in the cup of his hand. Its arms and legs curled upwards and wavered, uncertainly, as if baffled by this strange, non-fluid environment.

He missed the moment when it opened its eyes. One minute they were closed and the next, after he'd wiped the mucus off with his flannel, there it was, staring sternly up at him – or not so much *at* him as *through* him, and with a shock he saw that the eyes were not the watery, glassy blue of his own, as he had somehow expected, but a rich velvety blue, like the sky at night. *What are you looking at?* he asked it, softly, his voice cracking through from a whisper. And then, as if noticing him for the first time, the baby pulled in its gaze and seemed to focus on Theo himself. Theo stared into the tiny eyes and the baby stared back at him so intently, so gravely, so studiously, that Theo burst into tears.

Because there, in those serious eyes, was everything that he yearned for – the secrets of life, of death, of eternity, of the universe itself. This baby, Theo realised, blinking through his tears, might be a tiny, defenceless creature, utterly reliant on him for its immediate survival here on Earth, but it had not come out of a void. It had come knowing everything. It had come full to the brim with a knowledge of the ways of the universe more profound and wise than he could ever hope to attain.

As if taking its cue from Theo, the baby opened its mouth wide and started to scream.

—It's a girl, choked Theo, coming back into the bedroom. I think she's hungry.

Eva opened her eyes and looked at him blankly, all fear and confusion drained from her face. Her wide mouth seemed broken and flayed. She made as if to speak, tensing her throat, but no sound came, just a dry cracking of the tongue. Theo rested the tiny creature between her breasts and it lay there, maggot-like. Eva did nothing to help it; she did not seem to have the strength to lift her own arms. Gently, Theo nudged one of the breasts towards the baby's face, guiding the nipple to its mouth. As soon as it brushed her lips, she opened wide, taking in a big mouthful of flesh, and started to suck.

—That's it, my little princess! That's it!

Clutching the breast in his own damp hand, and cupping the child with the other, Theo helped her feed. The bulging eyes were closed shut, the creases on the lids rippling with the movement from beneath. When she stopped sucking he lifted the tiny creature up and cradled her to his own chest, allowing the few drops of milk on her chin to soak into his shirt. Pulling the soft cream blanket he had brought over from his own bed, he tenderly wrapped it around the tiny body and rocked it gently, gazing at her restful face. The next time she opened her eyes, Theo dipped his little finger into the melted remains of the saguaro ice-cream and offered it to the tiny mouth. She let him in, and immediately began to suck with surprising force, as if she had been practising the action for weeks inside the womb. *It's me she's sucking*, thought Theo. *My finger, my body, my energy. The Universal Life Force, coming through me.* He dipped his finger into the ice-cream again and this time the baby greeted it with an eager, open mouth. When Theo took his finger away, she cried out for more.

While Eva slept, he covered her with a sheet. He didn't want to look at the sticky pool of dark blood that was spreading out, around her thighs. When the baby cried, he lifted the sheet down just far enough to give her a breast to suck; otherwise he left the woman in peace, and kept the baby with him, close to his chest, so that she could hear the beating of his heart. He had read that a baby needs to hear the sound of a heartbeat after the trauma of leaving the womb.

There was enough clean sheet on the far side of the bed for the baby and him to sleep on. He lay on his side with his back to Eva and looked down at the soft, downy head with its turquoise veins tucked against his naked chest. *What a marvel! A complete marvel!* The words spun nonsensically in his head and he could not step out of them. *Marvel, marvel, marvel.* With a finger he prodded at its tiny, curled fist, willing it to open up and take hold of him.

Softly he began to sing: *There were three in the bed and the little one said—*

He stopped. The little one. He rolled over and shook Eva gently by the shoulder.

—What's her name? he hissed.

She didn't move at first. Then, with a terrible effort, she lifted the dark lids of her eyes. Inside, Theo could see the slow, green irises moving across like boats beating through a troubled, grey sea.

—Tibor, she croaked. The accent on the second syllable.

—Nonsense! cried Theo. It's a girl. We can't call her Tibor!

—Tibor. Tibor.

It was a whisper, and yet she said it like a command, an instruction for him to enter the room. Theo felt exasperated, as if he were speaking to a child that refused to listen. He felt angry with her, careless. Why did she keep having to think about that rascal? There were more important things going on now.

—He's not coming, he whispered irritably. You're wasting your time asking for him.

He rolled away from her and snuggled up to the baby, unable to take his eyes off her. She was such a wonder, this baby that he had delivered himself. He wanted to stare at her all day long. But if his eyelids dropped, it didn't matter. When he woke, she would still be there, his little girl, lying beside him with her tightly curled fists and tightly curled toes.

He was woken by the smell of urine. It was different to his own: a sweeter, less toxic variety. Almost immediately there came a startling, high-pitched scream.

That'll be my new human alarm clock, he thought.

He opened his eyes and was confronted with a toothless black hole so wide he wondered if the child had grown in the night. He watched for a moment as the scream turned into a yawn, wide and unselfconscious. He breathed in, enjoying the comfort of the smell, and then became aware of a seeping wetness against the wall of his arm.

—Sssh, you'll wake Mummy.

He scooped her skull up in his left hand and tucked his right one underneath her bottom. The action still felt odd, but he was getting used to the weight of it, which parts he had to support. The contraption he'd wrapped round as a nappy in the night – a square of torn sheet with a slab of cotton wool inside – hadn't been quite as watertight as he'd hoped. It occurred to him that he might adapt a drawer from the kitchen as a makeshift cradle. The baby would be snug as a bug in that, and it would mean he wouldn't have to change his own sheets whenever it wet the bed.

With a shock, he realised his pyjama bottoms were stained with blood. It was dried and brown. There was a lot of blood, he realised now, spreading all over the mattress. It had probably penetrated right through. He glanced at the motionless shape beneath the sheets. For a moment he hovered over it, undecided. Then he pulled the blanket up over an exposed shoulder and left the room.

He took the baby outside. It was a beautiful afternoon. The air tasted very clean after the stale atmosphere of the bedroom. He stepped lightly down the steps, jigging the baby against his shoulder, drawing the air into his lungs. It was wonderfully cleansing for the nasal passages. Sharp enough to cut. The sun seemed to have mellowed after the heat of the last few days, too. The worst of the summer was surely over. Now it was rolling towards autumn.

Here it was: his desert. Behaving just as usual, as if nothing had changed. Typical! The sun with its artificially innocent look, like an English gentleman at a tea party pretending not to notice that he'd farted. He chuckled to himself. But someone *has* farted, he felt like exclaiming, loudly, holding the baby up as evidence. Look! Incredible things have been happening during the night!

But he did not care about the desert's indifference. He was aware instead of a feeling of liberation, as if the dramatic events of the night had given him the green light to behave in a way that, up till now, he wouldn't have expected of himself. It had made him bold. He had delivered a baby with his own two hands. No mean feat for a single man of thirty-five. He had a sudden, ludicrous vision of himself getting down on the ground and writhing along on his stomach, propelled by a swinging movement in his buttocks. Ever since he'd come to the desert, he'd had this idea that it would be interesting to see what the world looked liked from the point of view of a snake. The very idea had embarrassed him. Yet today he could imagine himself doing it. He could do anything now that he had a baby.

What moved him most was that the desert was *his* again. I've missed you, he felt like whispering to it, although when it came to the crunch he was a little too shy to say it out loud. It was as if they'd been physically apart, he and the desert, these last few weeks, but they were back together again now. Reunited.

But he did not allow himself to feel sentimental about it for long. There were more pressing concerns today. All the paraphernalia he'd have to buy – the bottles, the milk, the nappies. A little bib for it to be sick on. A big tub of Nivea to stop it getting nappy rash. He knew enough about babies to know about nappy rash.

The baby's wail, temporarily reduced to a miserable whimper, had reached full blast again. It resounded loudly around the basin of his valley, as if introducing itself.

—Come on, he said, cradling her in the crook of his arm. We'll go inside and fix you up some breakfast.

By evening, the house was smelling bad. He kept the door of the spare bedroom firmly closed, but he had a problem with the bathroom too, as he'd been shoving the dirty cotton wool pads into the pedal bin and now it was starting to overflow. It occurred to him that as soon as he'd got her potty trained, he'd be able to start using her pee for javelina deterrent.

Laying the blanket-wrapped baby in the sink, he tore off a heavy-duty bin liner from the roll, and emptied the bathroom bin. He separated the top of the bag into two parts and tied them together in a knot. If it had been orange, the package would have looked like one of those space hoppers the kids in the garden next door used to play with in Clapham. He dragged it down the steps and round to the back of the house. For once the bins had been left undisturbed by the coyotes. Perhaps they'd been aware of the drama going on inside the house and decided to leave him alone.

He squashed it down as far as it would go. It would be another week until the bins were collected, and there would be a lot more to go in there over the course of the next few days. Standing up, he suddenly felt very tired. He hadn't had a lot of sleep in the last twenty-four hours. At some point, he realised, he'd have to try and get some uninterrupted kip.

—Mr Moon?

He looked up. A man dressed in a tight grey shirt and trousers was standing a few feet away. He had a gun in a holster attached to his belt. While the Officer spoke, all Theo saw was the gun.

—Truly sorry to disturb you, Mr Moon. How's it going, here?

—Yes, Officer. Absolutely fine, thank you. Is there anything—?

—Just two minutes of your time, no more than that. We've been holding a man charged with theft and possession of a dangerous weapon since the day before yesterday. Just been transferred to the County Sheriff's office downtown. Illegal immigrant, overstayed his welcome. We'll be holding him till he goes before the judge and then he'll be deported if we don't find someone to vouch for him. See, we asked him if there was anyone we could contact, and he keeps on about an Englishman. Englishman this, Englishman that. Sheriff thought of you, that's all. Just a notion, and Sheriff likes to go on his notions.

The Officer held out an open passport. Theo stepped closer. The photograph showed a man with a short crew cut, a firm mouth, a square jaw.

Didier Jacob, he read. *Né 1954 La Rochelle, France. Nommée de spouse, Ernestína.*

—Ever come across that name before?

Theo shook his head. —No, sir, I can't say I have.

The Officer turned to look around him, shielding his eyes from the sun.

—Well, nice yard you have here. My wife would be greatly impressed by your cacti collection out the front. Sorry to trouble you, Mr Moon. Have a nice day.

He turned round and headed back round the side of the house, but stopped halfway.

—There's one more thing, Mr Moon.

Theo looked up.

—There's a van parked in the middle of an arroyo about half a mile from here. Sheriff noticed it a few days back, when he was driving past. Any ideas where it came from? It looks to me like it's just been dumped.

—That there van is mine, Officer. It was Jersey, coming round the side of the house.

He touched the brim of his Stetson and stepped forward, into the sun.

—I found it in a junk sale up Sabino Canyon way, he continued, helping himself to a cigarette. Fifty dollars is all they wanted for it an' I couldn't let a deal like that pass up. I have a knack for finding old cars.

—What are you going to do with it? asked the Officer.

—I ain't rightly decided yet, laughed Jersey. I got a mind to make something of it, though. Maybe get Mr Moon here started in business. It's about time we found him an honest livelihood.

Amazed, Theo said nothing.

The Officer was laughing, shaking his head.

—Well, looks like you've got yourself a mighty good friend, here, Mr Moon.

He looked at Theo, his eyebrows raised.

—Yes, Theo managed. It does.

—Well, so long, folks. If you want any help with getting that van back on the road, I suggest you give Hank Dower a call. He's on Wilmot, the right side of town for getting here. Have it started in no time at all.

They followed him round to the driveway, and he gave them a

small wave as he got into the car. He reversed around Jersey's truck, the tyres picking up pieces of gravel as they rolled over. When he reached the junction with the road, he hesitated for a second or two, then drove off to the right.

Just then, from inside the house, came the sound of a baby crying.

—I'm coming, Sugar Pie, Theo called softly, swallowing down the lump that had formed in his throat. He threw a quick glance at Jersey's startled face, then carried on up the steps. Don't you worry. Daddy's here.

18

When I was little, my father used to dress me in my best clothes every fourth Sunday, hoist me on to his shoulders and march me purposefully to the end of the drive. He wrapped his fingers firmly around my ankles while I counted the freckles on the top of his head.

As we let the garden gate click shut behind us, the desert welcomed us into its broad expanse, bubbling and simmering at the edges like an omelette in a pan. Red-tipped ocotillo wavered between the gnarled and twisted junipers and a scattering of yellow flowers flecked the ground. Sometimes, if it had rained in the night, there'd be the sharp, spicy scent of creosote on the air and a herring-bone pattern of clouds overhead, like a giant fish leaping through the sky.

If we'd timed it right, we only had to wait a few minutes before we saw the glint and sparkle of a windshield like a giant jewel catching in the sun. A few seconds later we'd see the van itself, careering and lurching over the potholes and ruts in a spinning ball of brown dust. We watched its approach with baited breath, afraid that if we spoke too early it might turn out to be a mirage, or a figment of our imaginations. But as soon as we could make out the triple-scoop ice-cream cone on the side we knew it was for real, and my father would tilt his body forwards and brace his hands against his knees, while I slid down the smooth broadness of his back as efficiently as a fireman down a pole.

The delivery man always greeted us with a formal nod of his head: *Mess Josephine, Mess Moon*. Coughing from the dust, I hauled myself up on to the high, hard seat and shuffled along beside him, my bare legs sticking to the hot black plastic. The delivery man smelled of engine oil and the chewing tobacco that he kept tucked in the pouch of skin in front of his lower teeth, making his bottom lip protrude. He was an old man, and I liked to stare at him. His fingers stuck out in awkward directions from the swollen joints and his face was lined with a thousand criss-crossed wrinkles, as if he had a hairnet over his face.

As soon as we were all safely aboard, he turned the van round and headed back the way he had come, driving straight into the ball of raised dust that still hovered behind him, uncertainly, like a dismissed escort. He drove with one arm straight on the wheel, the other hanging out the window, fingers raking the heat. He always had the radio on although we were too far away from anywhere to pick up any stations well, but sometimes, through the crackles and whines, would come the clear, winnowing strains of a cottony-voiced cowgirl singing the blues, and the delivery man would turn the volume up high and we'd all join in, the delivery man drumming his fingers on the chassis of the van, my father emitting a thin, off-key wail, and me singing at the tops of my lungs to drown out everything else.

Miss Gail's Ice-Cream Parlour is a flat-roofed adobe building on Gates Pass Road, five miles from the edge of town. When I was little I thought of Miss Gail as a beautiful spider in a web. She catches her customers in the middle of the morning as they head out to the National Monument, the cars swerving suddenly off the road so that it's a wonder there are not more head-on collisions at that spot, and then catches them again in the afternoon as they drive back. In between, she steps off the platforms of her feathery mules, wanders out to her back yard, and sinks her bright-nailed feet in a bowl of cold water as she yaks away to the humming-birds she keeps in a cage.

Most of Miss Gail's customers are local but some come from far and wide – as far as Utah and Colorado and California. She treats them all as if she had known them since they were babies, showering them with fuss as they take a seat at her high, glass-topped bar.

—Well, darlin' boy, you look seriously parched an' about to die. Can I recommend a scoop of Peppermint Toothpaste Refresher to get you going with perhaps some Oreo Pie to fill you up and a Bitter Lemon Virginia to round it off?

But the biggest fuss of all was saved for my father and me. The VIP Sundaes she called us. When we walked in, she dropped whatever it was she was doing, and flapped her chubby fingers around her head.

—Jimmy darlin'! I see you brought me my Sunday treat! Well if that ain't the sweetest sight in the whole wide world, the two of you together, then I am my father's whore.

She plumped her enormous bosoms down on the bar and unstuck her thick scarlet lips. We knew the names of the ice-creams by heart, of course, and so did she, but she always gave us a menu each as we caught up on the latest news. My father would ask whether requests for Rhubarb 'n' Custard were picking up yet, and Miss Gail would ask when the trial batch of English Toffee Apple would be ready for delivery, and all the while she'd be counting off the names of her customers with her fingers and who'd had what, and how many times, and where they were from, and who had died and who had been born, and when she hoped to see them again, her lips sticking and unsticking as she spoke with the glue of her scarlet lipstick, till eventually my father would emit an enormous yawn and his heavy-lidded eyes would come to rest on the deep, shadowy crevice between her breasts.

—Well, now, you'll be gettin' hungry with all this talk. I'll get you your usual selection – a scoop of each and a little bit extra thrown in.

We watched her wide hips roll from side to side like the hull of a boat as she arranged the assorted scoops on a large round plate, making it into a sort of dance with the plate held high, and when she put it down between us, we dug straight in, my father at nine o'clock and me at three, rotating the plate as we went, taking care not to take more than our fair share of each flavour. Every now and then my father would cast a quick glance around the plate to keep an eye on the proceedings.

—I guess there'll be a rush after church, Miss Gail would muse, looking at the clock, and tapping her nails on the counter, and watching with an affectionate smile as we savoured each and every mouthful, but after a while she gave up trying to draw us into a conversation and left us to our ice-cream in peace, wandering back out to her humming-birds in the yard.

I could sit here wishing it had stayed that way for ever, but wishing won't change anything. I sit on my bed and watch the quality of light shift as the sun rises behind the house. Soft, fleecy shafts filter through the slats in the blind and lay themselves in stripes at my feet. I am shivering with cold, but I won't move until the dawn unfolds completely, bringing with it the safety of the day.

There is a trick to making things not matter. Anything which anybody says or does can be tucked away at the back of your mind, and you can go on as if it had never happened at all. That way you can arrange the world the way you want it, just as my father does.

Somehow, it's easier when you live in the desert. With the sun shining down and everything stark and shorn in the blistering light, you can convince yourself of anything. That people exist, or that they don't. That my mother is alive, or that she's dead. It doesn't really matter either way. It doesn't matter what people say about my father. It doesn't matter whether my mother will ever come back for me, calling me by the name that only she knows. It doesn't matter if someone wants to love me, or just to fuck me on a table in a bar. It makes no difference, when you're faced with the brutal, bare facts of blunt-edged stones and frazzled bushes and razor-sharp light all around you. In the desert it's clear that nothing matters in the overall scheme of things, and that makes everything OK.

At least, that's what my father would say.

Sometimes I catch a glimpse of my mother. I see her through an open window, the playful breeze plucking at strands of her soft hair, then letting them go again. She is stirring something in a saucepan with a spoon, the motion of the spoon mirroring the circular contentedness of her thoughts. A man wearing glasses comes through a doorway holding a newspaper, brushes against her as he goes by, and she turns briefly to watch him with a little smile playing on her lips, the spoon slowing almost to a halt. And then the lights turn green and we drive on.

I see her in line for the bus, at the check-out, at the swimming pool on a Saturday morning surrounded by a bunch of clamouring kids. Once I saw her sipping a margarita on the terrace at Hotel Congress, a briny line of salt on her lip. She was elegant in wide silk trousers and a Panama hat. She looked up and caught my eye, a question surfacing in her dark, mysterious eyes. *Excuse me, do we know one another?* For a moment there's a fleeting recognition, for I look just like she did as a young girl – the same dark brown eyes, the unusually wide mouth, the skinny legs. She looks at me fondly, her gaze dipping to the layer of puppy fat beneath my chin, remembering. She even puts her hand to her own neck, which has thinned as she's aged, pillared with tendons that reach up as slenderly as a vaulted ceiling.

—Sugar, what are you staring at?

I move on, and put the picture behind me. Just as my father would do.

When there are things I want to forget, I lie on my back on the boulder at the bottom of our garden, my arms spread out to the sides like I'm a sacrifice from the Bible. All I can see are the acres and acres of blue stretched taut overhead like a canvas pulled out to dry. It is so big. So blue. From this position I can't even see the horizon, let alone the top of a saguaro or the roof of our house. I am a part of the rock. I mould to its dips and curves. I have been here as long as the rock, which is almost as long as the Earth itself. Like the rock, I am neither alive nor dead. I lose all sense of my body, of where I am in relation to everything else. For all I know, the Earth could be tipping me up at an angle as it rolls over for the night.

And sometimes I wish it would. It would never be easier than this. The Earth just tipping me up like the back of a dump-truck and letting me slide off into the blue. I would take my place in the cosmos as silently and effortlessly as a body bag slipping into the sea.

But I don't want to live like that. I don't want to forget, or to be forgotten.

I don't want to grow up to be like him.

At eight o'clock he opens his door and pads across the hallway. Through the thin partition wall I can hear him pissing in the toilet bowl, the drumming of water on water that always goes on for longer than you expect. There are pauses in between the last few dribbles, and at the end there's an up-turn in tone like a question mark.

Are you there, Jelly-O? it seems to whisper. *Are you still my own little girl?*

Instead of flushing, he places the lid back down. He still hasn't got the pump working.

I stand up unsteadily. Folded in a small pile in the corner are my clothes from last night. I don't remember folding them; I don't even remember taking them off.

In the mirror I look at my chest. There's a bruise opening out on my skin like a greenish flower, directly above the place where my heart is. I could decide that it doesn't matter. In a few days it will be gone, after all, and in the meantime nobody will see it. I could lie on the top of the boulder and offer it up to the sky, and the sky will absorb it like a droplet of moisture held up on a fingertip. *Zap!* – and it never happened at all.

I pull on a pair of jeans and a t-shirt, and open my bedroom door.

The house is a dump. The bath is full of containers, waiting for Jersey to collect and refill. We're supposed to be pissing in containers, too, but my father always forgets. There's a nasty smell wafting up through the plughole in the sink and the bath, as if there's something rotten beneath the floor. I step over piles of dirty laundry that have been left in the hallway, the underarms of the shirt sleeves stiff with dried sweat, a confused scattering of pale pink underpants amongst them. He must have put my red skirt into his wash one time.

He's on his way back from checking the mail when I come out of the bathroom. He doesn't look at me, just carries on pottering about, bleary eyed and with crusty patches of pink camomile lotion on the rims of his ears. He lays the table with a fork and a spoon on one side, a bottle of maple syrup making a sticky ring on the oilskin cloth. He doesn't lay any cutlery on my side – that's his way of telling me he hasn't forgiven me yet.

When I sit down he turns his attention to a pack of powdered pancake mix on the bench.

—No feet on the table, Sugar. Not while we're eating.

I drop them down to the floor.

—Anything in the mail?

—There's a letter from a solicitor, about Aunty Drew's estate.

He takes an envelope out of his dressing gown pocket and tosses it behind him on to the table.

—I thought she might leave us something, but it's all going to the Cat Protection League.

I turn to look out the window. As I watch, a cactus wren with something in its beak lands on the edge of a scabby hole in the tallest saguaro, and then disappears inside.

—About last night.

I tilt my head to one side. For a split second, it occurs to me that he knows, and the thought turns my stomach cold. But he can't, of course. There's no telephone here, and he won't have been out of the house. He takes a big breath, as if he's been rehearsing this little speech for some time. When it arrives, it comes out in a rush, his voice clipped and unnaturally high.

—I've decided that I'm not letting you go out again unless you promise to be back by eleven. It's not fair. I couldn't sleep—

297

I turn back to the window. The cactus wren flies off again, beak empty. She'll be back in a while with another insect or two. Behind me, I hear my father putting down a carton of milk with a sigh. He has another go.

—It's all very well you saying that you're old enough to look after yourself, Sugar – because I know that's what you're thinking – but you don't understand what it's like—

—Neither do you, Dad.

—Beg pardon?

He swings round, and his eyes scramble over my face, searching for something familiar to latch on to. To anchor him. He is a big man, and he needs a heavy anchor. For a second I look up and our gazes lock. A look of bewilderment passes across his face, slowly, like a long-winged bird. It's as if he doesn't recognise me. I have short, tousled hair where once it was long and smoothly brushed and pulled into shiny braids, eyes that are smudged with last night's make-up, nails that are bitten down to the quick. I am wearing jeans and a t-shirt where once I wore brightly coloured smocks with iron-on patches on the front. But it's the voice that really does it – the unfamiliar accent that sends him clawing in vain for proof that we really belong to one another. He is an English man. I am an American girl. When – and how – did this happen?

By the time he turns back to the counter, his eyes are filmy and moist. He picks up the bowl of pancake batter and swills it around between his hands.

—Honey Pie. Please.

His voice is reduced to a tragic whisper. It almost makes me want to laugh.

—There's cochineal scale on the prickly pears! my father cries out, to anyone who might be listening. I look up from where I'm reading on the steps. He's standing among the cacti, waving his empty watering can around. What they need is a good strong jet of water on them. Otherwise they'll be dead by the end of the week. All of them! Just take a look.

He swipes, irritably, at a fly buzzing too close to his mouth.

—And that's not all. He comes over towards me. Did you see that spider in the bath? A big brown one. I don't know what it is. I suggest we stay out of the bathroom completely till Jersey comes.

—Of course, we can't do anything without *Jersey*.

—Look at you, Sugar, with your hair sticking up all over the place. I don't know why you can't brush it. It's a wonder you can read with all that in your eyes.

—And I don't know why you can't drive into town and get someone else to come and mend the pump.

—Damn these flies! The thing is, I haven't had a bath all week and they can smell you, and the more you sweat, the more they smell you, and it just gets worse and worse.

He drops the watering can and swipes again at the little scribble of flies around his face, accidentally batting one into his mouth. He spits quickly, and wipes his tongue against his hand. There's a tremor in his cheek.

I put my book down. With a sigh I reach out and put a hand on his rounded shoulder. It heaves, damply, under my palm. His eyes crease up and his mouth pulls into the thin edge of a wail.

—I don't—

—For God's sake, Dad. Get a grip.

He sniffs and nods.

—You're right. It's just that everything—

—I know. Just don't get in a stew. There's no point. Things'll sort themselves out in the end.

—Will they, though, Sugar? Will they?

To my relief there's a crunch of tyres on gravel and we both look up to see the familiar shape of Jersey's truck coming down the drive. He starts speaking before he's even got out.

—Shit man, you wouldn't believe the stench of this place. I smelled you from half a mile downwind. What have you been doing?

—Only the usual, mutters my father, defensively.

—Something rotten in the pipes? Or down the well? Overflowing septic tank?

—Shouldn't wonder.

—It's not the septic tank, I say. Somebody came and emptied it the other week. You can smell it in the bathroom, coming up through the gaps in the floor.

—Then something must have found a way in underneath.

He cocks his shoulders, one up, one down.

—You two all right?

He looks from my father to me and back again.

—We're fine, I say. It's just that everything's going wrong. We need a plumber, a mechanic and a carpenter to dismantle the skirting.

—Don't need a carpenter to do that.

My father is looking at Jersey very oddly. There's a crease across his forehead and a look of paranoia in his eyes.

—What?

I look at Jersey, but he's seen the expression on my father's face and is trying to ignore him. He shoves his hands down his tight front pockets and winces at the corners of his clear blue eyes.

Nervously, I start to laugh.

—*What?* What is it, you two?

My father bobs his head, wiping at a line of sweat popping on his top lip.

—It's not what you're thinking, says Jersey quietly. Not after all these years. It ain't possible.

There's a pitiful, pleading look in my father's eyes.

—No, he says.

—What is it? What are you talking about?

They say nothing, just avoid looking at each other's eyes.

—Jesus, you guys.

The only sound is the buzz of the flies hovering around our faces.

—Well, while you guys stand there like a couple of deaf mute idiots, I'm going to get started on the skirting myself. Any idea where we should start? I guess we have to look for a place where there's a crack.

—Don't do that, Sugar.

—Why not?

—Leave it to me, Josephine. Me and your father.

Jersey's voice is quiet but firm.

—I'm more use to you than *him*.

—No. This is a man's job—

—Jersey! I'm laughing out loud now. Don't give me *that*.

—Sugar, he's right. Leave it to us.

I put my hands in the air, submitting.

—All right. Whatever you say. Jesus.

I go back to sitting on the step.

Jersey drives off and comes back within the hour with a bunch of tools. I watch them critically as they hack at the skirting – or at least Jersey does, and my father hovers anxiously to one side, clearly thinking the house is going to collapse. Every now and then he carries off a jagged piece of wood with nails sticking out of it and starts to create a pile on the gravel at the top of the drive.

I go inside and fix them something to drink, bringing out three sodas on a tray, the ice-cubes clinking in the tops of the glasses. There's a scoopful of plain vanilla in the top of each one.

—Isn't that enough? I'm sure I could crawl through there.

The smell is worse now that there's a hole opened up.

—Just a little bit more, and I'll make it through too, says Jersey.

—Why don't you let me do it? I'm kind of curious to see under there.

—Because there may be snakes, snaps my father. He's still fretful and close to tears.

—And anyway, Miss Josie, whatever it is we find ain't going to be too pleasant. Jeezus peezus, this stink is bad.

—Suit yourselves.

—Why don't you leave us to it, missy. It ain't going to be pleasant, like I say.

—But I want to see it.

—Then go inside and get me a flashlight.

Jersey rips off the last plank with his hands. He hands it to my father, who grips it tightly, staring at the growing hole. Jersey bends down on his hands and knees, pokes his face inside, and turns it sharply to one side in disgust.

—*Jeez*us.

He crawls in with the flashlight. I try to peer in after him, but my father pulls me out of the way.

—Don't look, he says, the wide-eyed paranoia still etched on his face.

—I didn't *see* anything.

We stand in sullen silence, until there's a muffled shout from Jersey.

—Here she is!

My father drops the plank and the exposed nail stabs at his toe. He cries out and clutches his foot. A moment later, Jersey's butt appears with its familiar cigarette-pack bulge. He works his way out butt-first, dragging something behind him by a leg. The putrid stink is overwhelming, but we all take a look. It's a young coyote, its belly ripped open and where its innards should be is a pulsating creamy mound. It has empty sockets instead of eyes and green foam around its mouth. At the same moment, we all realise that its belly is heaving with maggots.

I walk quickly down the arroyo, the smell of the dead coyote thick in my nostrils and on my tongue. The retch brought up nothing but bile, but in my mind it was maggots and green foam. I clamp a hand over my mouth and keep running from it, my vision blurring with tears. The sun finds an exposed ring of skin at the neck of my t-shirt.

The water level in the tank is high but covered in a dark green film of weed. I dunk my head in anyway, feeling the oiliness of the weed give way around my face. It smells pretty bad here too – turgid and brackish – but just to be wet is a relief. I come up for breath, slimy strands dangling over my face, then plunge my face down again. When I've had enough I wipe the weed off me, climb down and keep walking, not towards the ranch house or back home but out to the west, in the direction of the mountains.

After half an hour a small bluff rises up. I climb over the rough scree, using my hands, covering myself in pink dust. When I get to the top, the plain sweeps out before me, and cutting through it is the ribbon of Interstate 10, heading out towards Cochise and Wilcox and beyond that all the way to Las Cruces.

It's untidy, scrubby country. Makeshift shacks heave themselves out of the desert floor at seemingly random intervals. They have a blurred, unsettled look, as if from having always been glimpsed from the windows of moving cars. Scattered around each one in a circle, as if flung by some centrifugal force, are a selection of discarded belongings – the wire-sprung skeletons of an old armchair, an up-right cooker, a sewing machine, an empty cage for canaries hanging from a tree – the debris of lives lived lazily and far from towns. The junk peters out at a certain radius from each house. All of it is tended to by the sun, picked clean and preserved from rust by its careful, tinder-dry fingers.

Apart from the cars I am the only thing that moves. Half running, half skidding, I slide down the loose scree, a tail of red dust rising up in my wake. I run towards the highway – towards the noise and smell of the traffic that carries heavily on the air, pooling in a metallic sweetness at the back of my tongue. I have an urgent need for motion. For the speed and the flurry of it. I go quickly over the uneven ground with its hillocks of twisted creosote, my ankles twisting and righting themselves without strain. The closer I get to the highway, the thinner the vegetation gets, and the faster I can go. I run right up to the edge of the asphalt and stop just short on the gritty shoulder.

There are two lanes going in each direction, and the cars and the lorries go past in a chaotic flash of colour and movement and thundering wheels. It's the sense of other lives I like – all the people heading towards other places. One day soon I will wave one of them down and go wherever it takes me.

A truck bears down on me with its gleaming paintwork and brilliant chrome, threatening to engulf me with its monstrous weight. At the last minute I catch the eye of the driver inside, sitting up high in his cab in a soiled t-shirt and a wide, rough-shaven face, the look of surprise and panic peaking in his eyes in the second before he passes. I take a step closer and wait for another. It's a blue one this time, with a teddybear attached to the grill. I catch sight of the driver stretched back in his seat with his hands behind his head, steering the wheel with his toes. The pocket of air bursts in my face as it rams past, klaxon blaring, slapping dust into my eyes, whipping the breath from my lungs.

I look out for our house from the bluffs. Instead of the little white fence or the blue walls, all I can see is a swollen white mass of cumulus, like an isolated cloud that has lost its way. It confuses me. I head directly towards it, skirting the water tank.

It's better not to walk fast when you're thirsty, even if it takes you longer to get there. Rushing makes it worse. The sweat running down my legs compacts the dust and turns it to a pink sludge. It dries on me tightly as I walk.

By the time I reach the gate, the smoke has thickened and blackened, filling up the driveway and the garden. I cover my mouth with my hand and run blindly into the thick of it. Ashes rain down on me, tingling my skin.

—*Dad?*

There's a flare of orange, a splintering of wood. I run towards it. For a moment the smoke clears and in the gap I see Jersey's face. It pulls me up short. He is staring at the fire, his expression serious and drawn. In his hand he holds a saguaro rib, and he uses it to hook something and push it deep into the centre of the fire. He is mesmerised by the fire. There is a movement about his lips, as if he is muttering like a shaman, communing with the flames. Every now and then he turns his face to one side, wipes his eyes, and takes in a lungful of air.

I step around the side of the fire, out of the wind, so that the smoke is no longer blowing in my face. I can see the bonfire now, see the long planks cracking as the flames eat through. In amongst them, I can make out the hard cover of a book, its pages eaten away. There's the remains of a length of green and white striped canvas that I don't recognise, fluttering up like the wing of a trapped creature. As I watch, Jersey steps forward and beats it back down with his stick. As he does so, he disturbs a small hard object, and it rolls to the ground. It takes me a few moments to work out what it is. And then I rush forward, reaching out with both my hands, and the heat is nothing as I plunge into the flames.

—*No!*

The scream is so full of anguish that I don't recognise myself. I am in the fire, reaching in among the wooden planks for the flash of a buckle, a strip of red leather, a tapering fine white heel. As I delve for them, the planks give way beneath me, and my treasures fall deeper into the fire. Behind me I hear Jersey shouting.

—*No!*

He grabs at my arm, but I knock him out the way. He comes back again, clutching me around my waist. I try to fight him off, but my feet lose touch with the ground. There, beneath me, a tongue of flame curls around a gold strap. I snatch at it, swinging it clear as my body is hurled through the air. My chin is the first thing to hit the ground, and then he is dragging me just as he did the coyote, my stomach scraping against the grit as he hauls me away from the heat. I am hysterical now.

—*My shoes! Why are you burning my shoes!*

He slaps at me with his hands.

—That was a real silly thing to do, missy! Damned silly.

I roll free of his hitting hands and scramble to my feet, backing away.

—I have half a mind to throw you back in there, while I'm at it, he shouts, furious. What the hell's got into you? You'll drive your father to distraction by the time you're done. It ain't respectful, Josephine. If it weren't for your father and me, you wouldn't be here today. Do you realise that?

He makes a dive for me, but I scramble out the way and run towards the house, still choking from the smoke. The soles of my feet have gone numb. Ahead of me, I can make out the steps, the blue of the door. I stumble into the kitchen, gasping for breath. There is my father, sitting quietly on a chair. His face is streaked too, meandering tear-tracks through the soot. Behind him on the kitchen counter are piles of dirty dishes waiting to be washed.

—My Sugar.

I collapse against his knees, gulping for air. I have lost the feeling in my fingers, but in my hand I have something that seems to weigh a hundred tons. I heave it up on to the table and as the heel hits the surface, a little shower of gold falls off.

My father stares at it wretchedly, his shoulders slumped.

Very slowly, he turns to look at me, where I cling tightly to his knees. Tentatively, he reaches out towards my face and carefully draws the hair away from my eyes with two slow movements of his finger. When I don't pull away, he licks his thumb and rubs at the blood on the tip of my chin.

—Dad?

He stops. He lets his hand drop to his lap. He knows the time has come.

—All right, Sugar Pie. All right.

He smooths down the creases in his trousers. Then he clears his throat and begins.

ACKNOWLEDGEMENTS

I am indebted to the Harold Hyam Wingate Foundation, whose generous scholarship in 1994 first took me to Arizona; to Charlie, who lent me his car; to Buzz at the University of Arizona, who let me stay in the poets' cottage (even though I wasn't a poet); to Lucia, who lent me her house; to Billy Sol Estes, who showed me his garden; to Teresa Griffiths, my fellow cowgirl; to George Brookbank and his book *Desert Landscaping*, for information about gardening in the desert; and to Vic and George Willits, who took me in and made me cornbread.

To my students of 1991 in Partizánske, Slovakia; and to Slavka Poláková and Alžbeta Valachová, for their help with translation.

I am also indebted to Curtis Brown Literary Agency for their scholarship to the University of East Anglia; to my teachers there, Malcolm Bradbury, Rose Tremain and Terence Blacker, and to my fellow creative writing students of 1993–4; to Derek Johns, Tracy Chevalier and Bonnie Powell for reading the manuscript along the way; to Colin Wakelin for giving me a timely kick; to my brilliant editor, Katie Owen; to Molly Boren for her invaluable help with Americanisms; and to my inspired and inspiring agent, Clare Alexander.

Finally, to Will Noel, who was there from the beginning; Heather Millar, Ella Berthoud and David Zilkha for making me laugh at critical moments; Alex Finer, Rosie Atkins and Andrew Hirsch at John Brown Publishing for their support; and Anand Tucker, for sitting in the mythical armchair in my head as I wrote. My biggest thanks of all go to my parents, for taking me back long after they thought I'd left home, and never once doubting that it would be worth it in the end.